THE
FRENCH
PRIZE

＊

THE FRENCH PRIZE

JAMES L. NELSON

＊

THOMAS DUNNE BOOKS
ST. MARTIN'S PRESS
New York

THOMAS DUNNE BOOKS.
An imprint of St. Martin's Press.

THE FRENCH PRIZE. Copyright © 2015 by James L. Nelson. All rights reserved. Printed in the United States of America. For information, address St. Martin's Press, 175 Fifth Avenue, New York, N.Y. 10010.

www.thomasdunnebooks.com
www.stmartins.com

Map by Cameron MacLeod Jones

The Library of Congress Cataloging-in-Publication Data
is available upon request.

ISBN 978-1-250-04661-1 (hardcover)
ISBN 978-1-4668-4702-6 (e-book)

St. Martin's Press books may be purchased for educational, business, or promotional use. For information on bulk purchases, please contact the Macmillan Corporate and Premium Sales Department at 1-800-221-7945, extension 5442, or write to specialmarkets@macmillan.com.

First Edition: July 2015

10 9 8 7 6 5 4 3 2 1

To Nathaniel James Nelson,

my son of whom I am so proud.

I pass the literary torch to you.

Acknowledgments

As with any literary endeavor, there are many people to thank, some who might not even be aware that their support has been a critical part of the writing process, a very complicated and all-consuming process, indeed. Long overdue thanks to Joe Donovick for all his help and support over the years (and for teaching my kids to shoot safely!) and to Dan Lessard and his family, old friends who have so often and so generously allowed me to crash at their home when research has called me south. Thanks to all the people at Maine Maritime Museum with whom I had the great privilege to work these past seven years, in particular Jason Morin, Amy Lent, Kurt Spiridakis, Barry Craig, Matt Williams, Christine Titcomb, Joy Wiley, Rebecca Roche, Janice Kauer, Nathan Lipfert, Chris Hall, Teresa Gandler, Kelly Page, Sue Steer, and all the gift shop folks; Kathy Perkins, Sandy Lederman, Liz von Huene, Gay Lauderback, Cynthia Dolloff, and Chrystine Cromwell, who so kindly push tourists in the direction of my books. You have not seen the last of me. Thanks to all the good people at St. Martin's Press, including Melanie Fried and in particular Peter Joseph, with whom it is an honor and a privilege to be working again. Thanks to Peter Rindlisbacher, kindred spirit, for all your effort in making the cover art perfect (and for all you've done for the world of maritime art in general). Thanks, as ever, to Nat Sobel, Adia Wright, and all the people at Sobel Weber.

And thanks, and love always, to Lisa.

ARMED MERCHANT SHIP *ABIGAIL*

1. Jibboom
2. Bowsprit
3. Jib
4. Fore Topmast Staysail
5. Fore Staysail
6. Foresail or Fore Course
7. Fore Topsail
8. Fore Topgallant Sail
9. Fore Topmast Studdingsail
10. Mainsail or Main Course
11. Main Topsail
12. Main Topgallant Sail
13. Mizzen Topsail

14. Mizzen Topgallant Sail
15. Spanker
16. Fore Mast or Fore Lower Mast
17. Foretop
18. Fore Topmast
19. Fore Topgallant Mast
20. Main Mast or Main Lower Mast
21. Maintop
22. Main Topmast
23. Main Topgallant Mast
24. Spanker Gaff
25. Spanker Boom

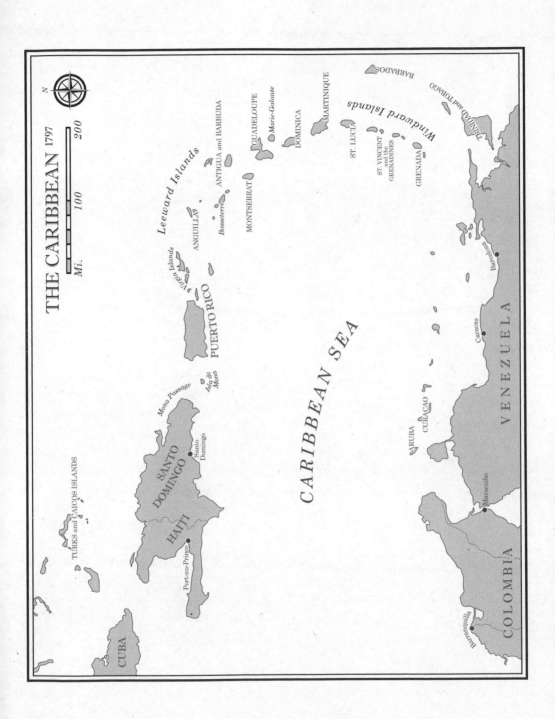

THE CARIBBEAN 1797

N

Mi. 100 200

TURKS and CAICOS ISLANDS

CUBA

SANTO DOMINGO

HAITI

Port-au-Prince

Santo Domingo

Mona Passage

Isla de Mona

PUERTO RICO

Virgin Islands

ANGUILLA

Leeward Islands

Basseterre

ANTIGUA and BARBUDA

MONTSERRAT

GUADELOUPE

Marie-Galante

DOMINICA

MARTINIQUE

ST. LUCIA

ST. VINCENT and the GRENADINES

Windward Islands

GRENADA

BARBADOS

TRINIDAD and TOBAGO

CARIBBEAN SEA

ARUBA

CURAÇAO

Barcelona

Caracas

VENEZUELA

Maracaibo

Barranquilla

COLOMBIA

THE FRENCH PRIZE

1

Before Jack Biddlecomb came fully awake, before he had even opened his eyes or moved at all, he knew two things. One was that he had taken a severe beating. The other was that he had reason to be enormously pleased. He could not recall in either case exactly why that was.

As to the beating, he recognized the signs right off. His body felt stiff and cramped, and he knew, even without experimentation, that certain movements would cause considerable pain. He could feel areas of bruised flesh in the usual places: gut, jaw, the side of his head. He could taste a faint trace of coppery blood in his mouth.

Tavern brawl . . . he thought, to the extent that he was able to formulate any coherent thought. His condition had the earmarks of a shoreside rough-and-tumble, one that he had lost, apparently, and lost decisively. If that was not the case, if he had won, he hated to think of the condition in which his opponent must find himself that morning.

He tried to recall, but was not yet awake enough, or, indeed, sober enough, to bring up the details of the night's adventures. He wondered if the sheriff would be coming for him. He wondered if he was, at that moment, in a jail cell. That possibility made him even less eager to open his eyes.

Jack was only nineteen, but he had spent years enough in the rugged world of a merchant ship's forecastle to know well the results of a beating in a tavern. He had given and taken beatings in New York, Philadelphia, and Savannah, in Nassau and Kingston and Barbados, and once even in London. It was a self-imposed exile from the civilized world ashore in which he had spent his younger years, an exile from the officer's quarters aft that many considered his birthright. It left him with skills, knowledge, and sundry scars that were foreign to the coach-and-four set from which he had sprung.

And then he recalled the source of his pleasure, and with that he realized where he was, or at least where he should be. He gave an experimental kick with his right leg. The action caused considerable pain in his knee, but his shoe (he was still dressed to his shoes, he realized) connected with a wooden leeboard, which told him he was in the berth of the master's cabin of the 220-ton, full-rigged merchant vessel *Abigail*, which was his command. His first command. At nineteen years of age.

He tried to open his eyes, but that effort met with less success than the exploration with his foot. He left eye was sealed shut. Why, he did not know. Dried blood or excessive swelling was usually the culprit, but he had seen others. Happily, his right eye opened and seemed to function tolerably well. Just as fortunate, lying on his left side as he was, that eye was at a higher elevation and thus allowed him to see over the leeboard.

He guessed it to be late morning, judging by the light coming in though the stern windows, but what really caught his attention were the stockings. Reddish brown, homespun, pulled over a set of beefy calves. The cuffs of brown breeches were buckled around the upper edge of those stockings. Jack did not recognize either stocking or cuffs, or the man who occupied the clothing, though he was seated in a chair not far beyond where Jack lay. He could, he understood, turn his head a bit and see who it was, but the effort seemed too much to contemplate.

Jack Biddlecomb had difficulty controlling his impulses. It was not as if he did not understand the relationship between cause and effect, as if he could not anticipate that action *A*, becoming drunk and loud in a shorefront tavern, say, might lead to reaction *B,* a sound thrashing, and that *A+B* might well equal *C*, which was waking in his present state.

He had known men enough, foremast jacks in the main, who could not seem to grasp this. Men who could, at a glance, comprehend the enormously complex interaction of wind and sail, the tension applied to rigging, the stress on spars, how minor alterations in any one of those might affect the whole, and yet could not seem to grasp that telling some drunken packet rat he met in a tavern that his mother was a sodding whore might lead to a certain and predictable response from the packet rat and his shipmates.

Jack was not like that. He understood those things. He was educated. But he just could not seem to control himself.

He closed his eye against the light and the unfathomable mystery of who was seated by his berth. He had confirmed that he was indeed in the *Abigail*'s master's cabin, and that was enough for now. But then the voice came, just as he was happily slipping back down into sleep, and pulled him grudgingly to the surface again.

"Ah, Captain Biddlecomb," the voice said. "You are awake."

The title "Captain" was delivered without the least hint of irony, which was a good thing, as it would have gone badly for the gentleman in the homespun socks if he had said it otherwise. Or at least it would have gone badly if Jack had been able to move with any kind of force or speed. Which he could not.

He opened his eye again and this time managed to swivel his head enough that he could see the rest of the man with the stockings. Square-jawed, rather ugly, arms that stretched the fabric of his well-worn coat. *Sailor,* Jack thought. *Or was . . . boatswain or carpenter, perhaps . . .*

With more than a little effort, Jack tenderly sat up and swung his legs over the edge of the berth. His ribs and his knee were the worst of it. He reached up and touched the eye that would not open and was relieved to find that it was just dried blood, not some horrible swelling, that had sealed it shut. He rubbed the lashes, felt the dried blood flake away, and blinked the eye open.

The man in the stockings made no move to help. That was just as well, too. It would not have been well received.

"Did I win?" Jack asked at length.

"Pardon?"

"The fight. Tavern fight, correct? Wait, don't tell me . . . I recall it now. The Blue Goose, am I right?"

"You are right, Captain."

"Did I win?"

"Not you. 'We.' By 'we' I mean you and your companions. Not me. And yes, unlikely as it might seem, you won. Or were winning. Afore I dragged you out of there. Three steps ahead of the sheriff."

"Bolingbroke? Was Bolingbroke there?" Over the years, when fate had tossed Jack and Jonah Bolingbroke together in the same forecastle, or the same tavern, a brawl was often enough the end result.

"Bolingbroke?" the man said. "Don't know. Don't believe I know the gentleman."

"'Gentleman'? No, I reckon you don't know him."

Jack Biddlecomb took a moment to look around the cabin. The deckhead and the ceiling planking were fresh painted and brilliant white in the morning sun. The light reflecting off the water of the Delaware River below the counter made bright, dancing patterns on the overhead. He could see ships through the aft windows, ships at anchor, ships tied to the quays. He could see the river's far shore. It was mid-April and the snow was gone but the grass and leaves had not yet appeared, giving the place an unkempt look despite the sunshine.

The brilliant light seemed to accentuate the emptiness of the cabin. Jack had been master for all of two days, and in that time the vessel had remained tied to the wooden dock jutting out from the Philadelphia waterfront. Before coming alongside the dock they had been anchored in the river, swinging back and forth at the whim of the current. The day before that, they had worked their way up the river at the head of the flood tide, two weeks out of Saint Lucia with a holdful of molasses.

When at last the worm-riddled snow that had occupied their present berth finished off-loading its cargo and warped into the stream, they had hauled anchor and hove the *Abigail* from warping post to warping post until she was safe alongside. Captain Peter Asquith, now the ship's former master, had stood silent and slightly bored on the quarterdeck as Jack Biddlecomb, former first mate, directed the evolution with a firm and competent hand.

They had not been alongside two hours before William Dailey came aboard. Dailey, whom Biddlecomb had always reckoned looked more like a weasel than any man he had ever seen, was agent to Robert Oxnard, merchant of Philadelphia and owner of the *Abigail*, among other vessels. Many other vessels. Dailey and Asquith had disappeared into the cool of the master's cabin while Jack, sweltering in the abnormally warm spring day, continued to oversee the swaying up of cargo.

Jack, it was true, was not exerting himself like the sailors and longshoremen knocking the wedges free from the battens, heaving the grating off the hatches, attaching the barrel slings in the dust-choked hold, or swaying away at the stay tackle and heaving the barrels up into the sun. But neither was he stripped to the waist, barefooted, bareheaded, or with a rag bound around his sweating brow as they were. He wore breeches and stockings and shoes. Hat on his head, coat on his back. He had spent time enough as one of them, one of the foremast hands, and he did not miss it, generally. Now he was a mate, *the* mate, and he knew his place.

Twenty minutes later, Asquith appeared on the quarterdeck. He took a moment to run a critical eye over the men's efforts, the smooth transition of molasses barrels up from the hold at the end of the stay tackle, a momentary pause as they hung over the gaping hatch, then out and over the dock as the tackles at the yardarms were swayed away. Neat, seamanlike, utterly routine. He seemed satisfied. He made no comment.

"Mr. Biddlecomb, would you come below, please?" Asquith said at last. Biddlecomb turned the supervision of the work over to the second mate and followed Asquith below and into the master's day cabin. It was a generous space, as far as small merchant ships' cabins went, and nicely fitted out. A raised doghouse on the deck above gave more than adequate headroom, and a skylight on top of that provided an abundance of light. A scuttle in the doghouse allowed for a private ladder to the quarterdeck.

There were curtains, lovingly sewn by Mrs. Asquith, hanging along the stern windows. Most of the deck space was taken up by a richly varnished mahogany table that Jack had helped wrestle aboard in Nassau. On the larboard side was an oak sideboard crafted by one of the better Philadelphia furniture makers and discreetly lashed to ringbolts in the ceiling planking. Sitting on its polished surface was a crystal decanter and glasses, once again in place now that *Abigail*, tied to the wharf, was a reliably stable platform.

Asquith gestured toward a chair and Biddlecomb sat and was grateful to do so. He reckoned this meant he was not in any trouble, and in truth he genuinely could not imagine why he would be. That in itself was unusual. Generally there was something.

But no, he had not had the chance to go ashore yet, and that was where the trouble usually started. They had been at sea for weeks, and it was rare that any fault could be found with his behavior at sea, unless it was his penchant for driving the ship harder than most masters wished it to be driven.

"Jack, you recall that Mr. Oxnard has a new ship? We saw her tied up at Southwark as we came up river."

"Yes, with the lowers just in and the pretty sheer. Three hundred and fifty ton, I would reckon."

"Three hundred and seventy-five, actually," Asquith said. "And Mr. Dailey here informs me I am to have command of her."

Jack smiled a smile of genuine delight. Asquith could be fussy and old-womanish on occasion, but Jack genuinely liked and respected the man, and in the year and a half he had served as Asquith's chief mate he felt that he had learned a considerable amount.

"Congratulations, sir!" Jack said and extended a hand, which Asquith took. "It could go to no more deserving a man!"

"Well thank you, Jack," Asquith said, with a sincere gratitude and a touch of embarrassment. "But there's more news. You, my boy, are to have command of this ship."

Jack did not smile at that, did not respond at all. He was as stunned as if he had been hit with a handspike upside his head. He had always hoped for a command, indeed had expected it if he managed to live even a few more years, which was sometimes in doubt, but he did not expect such a thing yet. Not at nineteen. And suddenly the swaggering confidence for which he was so often and so justly criticized utterly deserted him.

"Oh, sir . . ." was all he managed.

"I wish I could take all the credit for this step, and to be sure I've put in a good word when I could, but Mr. Dailey here tells me that Mr. Oxnard has had his eye on you for some time. I should think that business west of Montserrat sealed the deal for Oxnard."

That business west of Montserrat . . . That allusion should have pleased Jack, but in fact it only annoyed him.

"Oxnard doesn't want to risk losing you to some other merchant, you see," Asquith was saying.

Jack nodded as if he did see, which he did not.

"Now look here, Jack," Asquith went on in his avuncular way, "you can be a hothead and you can be impetuous, we know that. You'll have to grow up a bit. You're not before the mast anymore, and you're not a mate. You are in command now, and that will require you to act as a master should act."

"Yes, sir," Jack said.

Dailey spoke next, for the first time since Jack had stepped into the master's cabin. "You know your way around the docks and the counting houses, we have no concerns there. Captain Asquith has attested to your thoroughness with the manifests, bills of lading, that sort of thing."

"Yes, sir," Jack said.

He had, in fairness, always been meticulous about paperwork, keeping records in order, accounting for every penny. He hated it more than a fog-bound lee shore or an Italian opera, but he understood that care in that department would play a bigger role in his eventual rise to command than seamanship or navigation ever would. Because the men who owned the ships cared more about the paperwork and the pennies than they did about anything else.

"I've never said this before, Jack," Asquith was speaking again, "but you have a way about you when it comes to ships and the sea. I was just telling Mr. Dailey how you talked me into making more northing from Saint Lucia and how we found that westerly flow. It's like you can smell wind, and can find a knot of speed in a ship that no one else would have guessed was there."

"Thank you, sir." It had been a guess, taking that northerly route, based on the rise of the glass and the set of the clouds on the horizon, but he had guessed right. It had shaved days off their passage and given him a nice patina of brilliance.

"You just grow up a little, take your responsibilities seriously," Asquith said with a conclusive tone. Jack braced for what he knew would come next. He literally clenched his fists and clamped his jaw shut, as if expecting a punch in the gut. Asquith continued. "Then one day you will be as fine a mariner and an officer as your father."

Jack grinned a weak grin and nodded his head. He resolved that he would indeed take his responsibilities seriously. Not so he could live up to his father's reputation. That did not seem possible or even desirable. Captain Isaac Biddlecomb, wealthy merchant captain, leading light of that much-lauded generation that had won the War for American Independence a decade and a half before. Captain Biddlecomb, who had known President John Adams when he was Continental Congressman John Adams, and George Washington back when there was still a real possibility the man might be hanged by the British for treason. Captain Biddlecomb, who the year before, in the election of 1796, had garnered the new title of Representative Biddlecomb, congressman from the state of Rhode Island and Providence Plantations.

No, he would not be living up to his father's reputation anytime soon.

He had resolved, rather, to become a sober and responsible adult because he was no longer a boy and no longer a foremast hand, he was now the master of a vessel, a full-rigged blue-water merchantman of 220 tons burthen. That resolution had lasted just as long as it took for word of his new command to spread along the waterfront, for his numerous friends among the Philadelphia carrying trade to descend on the *Abigail* and insist that they celebrate his new status with a flowing bowl.

Which led him to where he was that morning, sitting on the edge of the master's berth in the *Abigail*'s great cabin, head pounding, body aching, regarding a big man in reddish-brown stockings whom he did not know.

The big man looked around the cabin, as if trying to see what Jack was seeing. "Not much in the way of furniture, is there?" he observed.

"Captain Asquith took his belongings. I have not had a moment to outfit it," Jack explained, and then, the absurdity of the situation dawning on him, said, "By the way, who in all hell are you?"

"A friend. Friend of a friend, really. He asked me to keep a weather eye on you."

'Weather eye,' Biddlecomb thought. *Sailor.* But he did not need the jargon to tell him that. This fellow had the inimitable look that marked the true deepwater man.

"My father?" Jack said. "My father sent you?" Even as he said it he knew it was a bad guess. His father was not the sort to think of sending a man to drag Jack out of a tavern brawl.

The man in the stockings shook his head.

"Uncle Ezra," Jack said with certainty, and at that the man nodded. Ezra

Rumstick, his father's closest friend, former chief mate, former first officer, former captain of several of the ships in the Stanton and Biddlecomb fleet. Not really Jack's uncle in a family sense, but in terms of their relationship, every bit the part. Rumstick was, strictly speaking, Jack's godfather, but Rumstick's religious leanings were like that of most mariners, that is, he did not lean too far toward the religious side of things, at least not until the wind reached a steady fifty knots or better with sens cresting at twenty feet, and the godfather designation was generally used only when one or the other of them found it convenient.

Rumstick had come up the hard way, a berth in a forecastle and two fists to defend his place, and he was most certainly the sort to make sure Jack would be pulled out of any trouble.

The man in the reddish-brown stockings leaned back in his chair, causing it to creak in an alarming way. "I weren't there when the fight begun, so I don't know what started it," he said. "You and your mates made a goodly show, I can tell you, and you was outnumbered."

"A tread on me coat and all hands in?" Jack said.

"Very like," the man said. "And Captain Rumstick, he says to remind you you was to dine with your parents today and he would take it as a personal favor if you was to not look like an absolute pile of shit when you arrived."

Jack nodded. "Very well, I'll take that under advisement."

"Good," the man said and stood. "You're alive and not in jail and you've been reminded, so I reckon I've done my duty. Good day, Captain." He gave a tip of his hat and was gone, leaving Jack alone with his thoughts, his pounding head, and his empty cabin.

2

A ship's mast may be called a mast, but it is, in fact, made up of several masts. Thus a mainmast might be, as a whole, a mainmast, but in its component parts it is a main lower mast, a main topmast, and a main topgallant mast. These sections overlap where they are mounted one upon the other in a carefully balanced system of perfectly fit parts.

Each of the masts is supported by its attendant shrouds: lower shrouds, topmast shrouds, topgallant shrouds. Those and the backstays keep the masts from falling forward, while the forestays keep them from falling aft. All of those parts pull in opposing directions, holding the others in check, a balance of tension. All of those parts get worn with use until they fit easily into their familiar places, and resist any change, reject any effort to make them assume a different position.

And so it was with Jack Biddlecomb and his family. And so it would still be, Jack knew, as he sailed through the open door of the Biddlecomb home and hugged his mother where she stood just inside. She and the house were of a piece: elegant, tasteful, ageless. In the foyer behind her, portraits hung on the flawless white walls and oak stairs bordered by a mahogany handrail ran up to the second floor. A chandelier, one of several in the house, hung above their heads. Around the edge of the intricately woven carpets, oak flooring peeked out that was polished until it looked like it was under a sheet of glass.

The house itself was a three-story brick affair on Second Street, just to the south of Market, an easy stroll from the dock where *Abigail* was tied up, a great blessing to Jack in his present condition. As much as Virginia

Biddlecomb had made the home their own in the short time they had occupied it, it was not, in fact, their own, but rather one they had rented. In the
volatile world of United States politics in the 1790s, with the great stabilizing
presence of President George Washington yielding to the Adams administration and the full flourishing of party politics, one did not buy in Philadelphia. If your business in that city was government, you rented. If your
business involved intriguing against one faction or another, however, you
might reasonably hope for more permanence.

"Jack, dear, you are looking well," Virginia said, a thing she would have
said no matter how he looked. She proffered a cheek for a kiss, then drew
away, quickly and discreetly looking him up and down. He had done his
best to clean up in the time he had, a cold water wash, a shave, a clean suit
of clothes, fresh stock, but he still looked like something that had been
sloshing around for some time in the bilge. He knew it and he was sure
his mother, for all her graciousness, did, too.

His father was standing right behind his mother, very erect, dressed with
precision, ship-shape and Bristol-fashion, as the sailors would say. Jack would
not say that, however, because he feared a mention of Bristol would lead to
the story of how his father rescued Uncle Ezra from Bristol Harbor in
England itself. *Bristol? I recall some excitement there! Must have been the year
'75 . . . no . . . '76. Was it? Virginia, do you recall?*

Jack kept his mouth shut.

"Jack, my boy!" Isaac stuck out his hand, and his look was genuine pleasure as they shook. Jack was pleased to feel the strength in his father's grip,
though the hard calloused palms he recalled from years past were gone,
and the dark, nearly black hair—the hair that Jack had inherited—was
shot through with gray. "We heard the good news. Word on the waterfront, you well know how that goes. Congratulations."

"Thank you, sir," Jack said. Again, his ears were alert to any false note,
any tone of irony or disapproval, and again he heard none. But their visit
had just begun. There was time enough, yet.

The sound of activity in the foyer had drawn the other Biddlecombs like
moths to the flame. Elizabeth Biddlecomb swept in, sixteen years old,
favoring her mother in coloring: the deep chestnut hair, the striking beauty,

the quick wit. Jack had watched the girl fade away, the young woman take her place. Now he snatched up her hand and gave it a kiss. *"Enchanté, chérie,"* he said.

She withdrew her hand and gave him a light slap on the face. "You take liberties, sir," she said, "and you know we have no use for Frenchmen in this house."

Virginia's eyebrows went up, a warning like a round shot across the bows. Politics would not be entertained at a family gathering, not even when all parties generally agreed with one another, which, incredibly, they did. Or, more to the point, Jack did not care enough about politics to argue with his father, which could be said of few other things.

"Wasn't there another child?" Jack said, and even before the words were out the shout of, "Jack!" came bounding down the stairs, eleven-year-old Nathaniel Biddlecomb right behind. He stopped a few feet in front of his brother and bowed with all the faux seriousness he could muster.

"Arise, Sir Nathaniel," Jack said.

Nathaniel straightened. He was happy, very happy, to see his older brother, and that in turn made Jack profoundly happy as well.

"Lord, you look a fright," Nathaniel said, eyeing Jack up and down, less discreetly than their mother had done. "Whatever happened to you?"

"Come, let us off to the dining room," Virginia said, gesturing the way down the hall. "Maurice will be furious if the soup is allowed to cool."

"Pirates," Jack said.

"Pirates?" Nathaniel asked.

"Swarms of them. Coming through the Mona Passage, three leagues east of Hispaniola. You should have seen them, boarding us starboard and larboard, cutlasses in their teeth." Virginia gestured for them to move along, and they obeyed.

"You can't hold a cutlass in your teeth, they're too heavy," Nathaniel pointed out.

"Not if you are as big as these devilish pirates were."

"Well, you look as if you've been beaten with a handspike. Why didn't the pirates toss you overboard? I take it you lost."

"Lost?" said Jack with mock outrage. "Never in life. You should have seen what the pirates looked like when I was done with them."

They took their familiar places around the dining room table, Isaac at one end, Virginia at the other, Jack amidships with Elizabeth and Nathaniel on the other side. Maurice brought the soup, which was still blessedly hot.

"Good to see you, sir," he said, placing a bowl in front of Jack. "We'll have two Captain Biddlecombs now." Maurice was a black man with a fringe of white hair and sixty years or more of adventurous living, by Jack's guess. He was a former ship's cook whom Isaac had hired when he was still going to sea, a ship's cook who, Isaac discovered to his surprise, could in fact cook and cook well, given the chance. When Isaac had come ashore, Maurice had come with him, and he had been with the family ever since.

"Thank you, Maurice." Jack gestured toward the soup. "I have missed this, let me tell you."

"It don't got to be all salt horse and burgoo at sea, but you won't find no one willing to cook who's willing to learn."

"I know that, Maurice," Jack said. "That's why I plan to ship you as cook on my next voyage."

"Ha!" Maurice said, distributing bowls to the younger Biddlecombs. "Ain't gonna catch me on no ship. Them days is over."

"Then it's the press gang for you."

"As long as I got a skillet in one hand and a butcher knife in the other, ain't no press gang gonna take me," Maurice said, making his way back to the kitchen.

"Maurice would do considerably better at avoiding the press gang than I ever did," Isaac observed, but no one pressed him for more because they knew the story well.

Dinner progressed from soup to an excellent crown roast of lamb, with the conversation moving along its well-plotted course. "Tell us more about these pirates," Isaac said. "You do look as if you have taken a beating."

Jack was thankfully in mid-chew, which gave him a moment to assess the situation. He heard the note this time, the subtle melody of disapproval. The pirate story was for Nathaniel's benefit; his father would not buy it and was not meant to. After a lifetime at sea Isaac Biddlecomb would have a better idea of what the truth of the matter might be, and he certainly would be of the opinion that tavern brawls were not the sort of thing in which men of Jack's station indulged.

The bruising was apparently more visible in the well-lit dining room than the small mirror in his cabin had led him to believe.

"Very well, you've found me out," he said after swallowing. "No pirates, I fear, Nathaniel. We got into a bit of nasty weather off Hatteras and I took a flier across the cabin. Very lubberly, I'm embarrassed to say."

Isaac grunted. He was not buying that one either, and Jack understood that he could certainly recognize the difference between a collision with a hanging knee and a beating from a fight. But for the sake of family unity, perhaps, or to shield Nathaniel from the truth about his prodigal brother, he said, "Well, the most experienced of us will do something lubberly on occasion. I know that for a fact." There was an awkward silence, and then Isaac added, "But see here, pray tell us more about your step to the quarterdeck. First smart thing Oxnard's done, to my knowledge."

Were the table not populated exclusively by Biddlecombs who were generally of a like mind, such a statement would not have been allowed under Virginia's strict embargo of political discourse at dinner. Oxnard was a well-known and vocal Republican of the most vicious stripe, close associate of Benjamin Franklin Bache, who published the *Philadelphia Aurora*, the paper that dubbed recently inaugurated President John Adams, "His Rotundity."

Isaac Biddlecomb was of the Federalist faction. Like Adams. In truth, he was like Adams in many ways; a New Englander, strong advocate of American commerce, proponent of a strong United States Navy and damn the cost, suspicious of the excesses of revolutionary France. That Isaac should be a great supporter of the nascent United States Navy was hardly a surprise—it was as a naval officer that he had won considerable fame, not to mention a fortune in prize money, during the War for Independency.

But Isaac's opinions, like Adams's, were not reactionary or ill-considered. Men like Bache and Oxnard might well portray all Federalists as monarchists, men as eager to crawl into bed with the king of England as they were to go to war with revolutionary France, but there was more subtlety in the positions held by the thoughtful men of that faction. Just as not all Republicans were mad radicals screaming *Liberté, Égalité, Fraternité, ou la Mort* in the streets, though many Federalists did not appreciate the nuance.

"Thank you, sir," Jack said, "I'm not sure exactly what induced Mr. Oxnard to do something of which you approve." Virginia's eyebrows went up again, and Jack, trained from birth to react to that gesture, altered course. But it was too late.

"First thing, indeed," Isaac said. "And it makes me wonder . . ."

Jack turned back to his dinner, cutting a piece of lamb as he grit his teeth and considered whether or not he could unclench his jaw enough to chew. *Damn the old man*, he thought.

Of course the Great Man would imply that his son's step to the quarterdeck must somehow be about himself. Jack felt like a rope stretched so hard it creaked under the strain, and his father's words like a sharp knife. Just the merest touch and the rope would burst apart. The snapback could injure or kill anything it hit.

But in truth, Oxnard's politics made Jack's promotion all the sweeter. There was no possibility that Oxnard had given him the command just to get in the good graces of Representative Isaac Biddlecomb, war hero, because that would never happen in any circumstance, and Oxnard did not want it. Jack's step up was therefore untainted by any suggestion of favoritism.

That's what galls him so, Jack thought.

What's more, despite his father's apparently genuine pleasure at his advancement, Jack knew that it truly galled him that his son was working for the noxious Robert Oxnard. And that was another source of secret delight.

"Captain Asquith put in a good word for me, I believe," Jack said when he again trusted himself to speak. "And I think I've been in Mr. Oxnard's service long enough that he's formed some favorable opinion."

"No doubt," Isaac said. "And I have no doubt that that business west of Montserrat played its part in his decision."

"I've heard that from other quarters. A bit too much made of it, I think."

"I think not," Isaac said. "You saved Oxnard a fortune. And it's an admirable thing that Asquith gave you the credit when it was due you. Not all masters would have done so."

"He's a good man," Jack agreed. "A good seaman," which in his estimation was the highest compliment he could give.

"In any event, that business west of Montserrat . . ." Isaac went on. "There'll be more of that, mark my words. The French are stepping up their harassment of American shipping, the privateers will be swarming like maggots."

Elizabeth made a squealing sound to register her disgust.

"Isaac," Virginia warned, but in this case it was the imagery, not the politics, that offended her. Isaac muttered some sort of apology. When Virginia spoke, men obeyed. Jack had been aware of this ever since he was old enough to observe and understand this phenomenon. His mother was a beauty, gracious, witty, able to put anyone at their ease. Every man quickly became Virginia Biddlecomb's slave, and Isaac and Jack were no exceptions.

"Why should the French be stepping this up?" Jack came to his father's aid not out of empathy but because this was a subject in which he had a genuine interest. "I had thought things were getting better, that the Directory or whatever the Frenchies call their government was looking for some sort of reconciliation."

"Not a bit of it," Isaac said. He had put down his knife and fork, which told Jack he was about to set all sail, rhetorically speaking. "It's chaos over in France, as many of us knew it would be. The French are utterly unable to govern themselves. Heads are rolling through the streets like an apple cart's been upset."

Elizabeth made her squealing sound again, this time adding, "Father!" But Isaac was well under way now.

"They pretend these fellows are privateers. They probably have some sort of paper, I shouldn't wonder, though whoever signed it is likely off to the guillotine before the ships could raise our coast. The point is, these so-called privateers are no better than pirates. They can make a fortune raiding our commerce. The French government, such that it is, won't stop 'em and we can't because we don't have a navy, do you see?

"So now we've elected a president who can see the truth of the matter, who isn't wearing a tricolor cockade and shouting *Liberté, Égalité* and all that, like our Mr. Jefferson is. Which is good for us, but the French don't like it, so you can count on their redoubling their depredations, the dogs. They're right off our coast, you know. French privateers sailing free as you please within sight of our very coast, and not a damn thing we can do about it."

"Speaking of a navy," Jack said, wishing to change the course of the conversation, but not so radically that his father would notice, "did I see the *United States* planked up and near ready to go down the ways?"

"Yes, yes," Isaac said with enthusiasm, his mounting irritation with the French blown clean away. "Beautiful, isn't she? Humphries is building her, as you know. He built the frigate I commanded in the War, the *Falmouth*, built her pretty much where the *United States* sits now."

"I recall," said Jack, stabbing a substantial piece of meat with his fork and swaying it aloft.

"A month or so, Humphries tells me, and she'll be going down the ways."

Jack, his mouth now full of lamb, nodded. *United States* was one of six frigates that had been authorized in March of 1794, more than three years prior, back when it was the Algerians who were causing so much trouble for the American carrying trade. Now, with that crisis past and the Algerians having been bought off for nearly a million dollars and, most humiliating of all, the gift of a thirty-two-gun frigate thrown into the bargain, only three of the six were slated for actual completion. Happily, *United States* was one.

Jack swallowed. "She looks just the thing," he said. "And if Humphries has drawn her and built her she'll be a good sea boat, I'll warrant."

"She has diagonal bracing, do you see?" Isaac said, holding up crossed arms by way of demonstration. "Diagonal, running fore and aft from the midships and drifted into each frame. It'll keep her from hogging, despite the fine entry she has, and the weight of the guns."

Jack nodded. "Isaac, dear," Virginia interrupted, "this is all terribly boring."

Jack looked at his siblings. Elizabeth, he could see, was indeed bored and doing nothing to disguise the fact. Nate was enjoying it because it was manly talk and seafaring talk, even though he probably did not understand it, at least not entirely. As for himself, he was finally finding the conversation stimulating, but his mother had spoken and that was an end to it.

They moved on to more mundane topics, more mundane, at least, to Jack: talk of Philadelphia society, gossip about the other members of Congress, news of old friends from back home in Rhode Island. Jack discovered that President Adams had called a special session of Congress to consider the French problem. Isaac expressed amazement that he could have not known that. Jack pointed out that just a week before he had been crossing the Tropic of Cancer in a full topsail breeze.

The meal passed in a more or less amiable manner. Despite Jack's flashes of anger it was better than it had been in years past, when such an evening might have ended with shouting and slamming doors and his mother fleeing the room in disgust. But now he did not seem to feel that passion, and his father seemed less likely to provoke.

Jack understood he was no longer a boy. He was master of a vessel now. *I have my responsibilities*, he thought, *I am a responsible man now.* That seemed to better explain his changed attitude, but then a twinge of pain in his ribs brought back memories of the night before, or what he could remember of it, and made him question just how responsible he really was.

Maybe it's the old man who's growing up, he thought. *Maybe it's his attitude that's changed.*

The shadows were long in the streets, the evening chill settling in on the city when Jack said his good-byes, kissed his mother, shook his father's hand, teased his sister one last time, and assured his brother he could come by the ship when they were taking on cargo. He stepped through the door, down the four steps to the street, and nearly collided with the man hovering there, waiting.

"Good evening," Jack said by way of inquiry, but this fellow did not look to be having a good evening.

"Good evening, *Captain*," he said, and there, for the first time, the word was used with a mocking, ironic tone. Jack's reaction was instant: the flush of rage, the balled fists, but the man did not seem to notice, or care.

"I'm here at the behest of Mr. Jonah Bolingbroke," he said. He spoke like a man struggling to talk above his station, the words stilted, the accent wrong. Normally, Jack would have found this amusing, but he was too angry now.

"Mr. Bolingbroke takes exception to your conduct last night, and demands satisfaction of you on the morrow. There's an empty lot on Second Street in the Southwark—"

"I know it."

"Sunrise. Tomorrow," the man said.

Biddlecomb searched his memory, trying to recall what obligations he had for the morrow. Cargo was coming aboard, but he would not be needed for that until sometime later.

"Very well, then," Jack said, then thought better of that arrangement. "No, hold a moment, I'll never find a second would agree to sunrise. Pray, make it eight o'clock. There's no one in the Southwark will care either way."

Bolingbroke's second seemed a bit taken aback by this arrangement, but he nodded and said, "Very well then, *Captain*, eight o'clock."

He turned on his heel and marched off, not so much appearing in a hurry as appearing to want to seem as if he was in a hurry. Jack watched him go and thought, *I reckon I have time enough to kill Bolingbroke in the morning and then get on with my business.*

This was all very surprising. Over the years he had beaten Bolingbroke senseless and Bolingbroke had beaten him senseless but neither had taken offense enough to demand satisfaction. Jack wondered what might have changed. Could Bolingbroke have been pushed to this by Jack's elevation to command? Could he not stand the adulation that had come Jack's way after that business west of Montserrat? That had been a close-run thing. And now, nearly a year later, he might die as a result of it.

"That would be ironic," Jack said out loud. Jack Biddlecomb hated irony.

3

That business west of Montserrat. It was nearly a year gone and Jack was only now realizing that it had made a pretty big splash among the mariners of Philadelphia. Why, he could only imagine. Perhaps because it was one of the Americans' few unqualified wins, after so many merchant ships of United States registry, hundreds, in fact, had been picked off like birds in a tree by French privateers.

They had cleared out of Barbados two days before, well laden with sugar and molasses, which was pretty much all they shipped from the West Indies because they were just about the only things the West Indies produced that were of any value. *Abigail* caught a nice slant of wind that drove her along to the east of the Leeward Islands as they shaped a course to catch the prevailing southeasterlies and the Gulf Stream north.

The morning watch belonged to Jack Biddlecomb. It was ten minutes shy of eight bells, 3:50 A.M., when he came up on deck to relieve the second mate, Oliver Tucker, standing the night watch. From the stuffy confines of the after cabins Jack stepped through the scuttle and onto the quarterdeck, into the embrace of the reliable trade winds off their starboard quarter.

The stars were formed up in their brilliant cascade overhead, a great sparkling dome unbroken by moon or cloud, but Jack's eyes went to the sails, always right to the sails, every time he set foot on deck. He looked aloft, past the crossjack yard to the mainsail, the main topsail and the main topgallant. The canvas was barely visible in the sweep of stars, but there was light enough that he could see their set, and he saw that it was good. There was about eight knots of breeze and Jack's instinct told him it was building, but for now he was comfortable with the sail they were carrying. Tucker, he knew, would be thinking about stowing the topgallants, but Jack was willing to hang on to them for a while longer.

He stepped clear of the scuttle and moved quietly down to the leeward side of the quarterdeck. This was a moment he loved: when he was on deck, lost in the dark, his watch not yet begun, no one even aware that he was topside. He could stand still and let the beauty of the ship and the sea and the night envelop him. He could feel the warm, regular breeze on his face, and the long, steady roll of the ship underfoot. He could hear the sound of the water rushing down along the hull and gurgling under the counter as *Abigail*'s bluff bows parted the seas and the sails above drove her hundreds of tons of bulk along its steady track.

He took a deep breath. This was the reward, the moment of rest as the sun was setting, the warm fire at journey's end, the cool dip in the pond when a long summer's day of labor was over. This was the prize won by hours and days of standing the deck through blowing wind and freezing rain and seas piling up like mountains to windward. This was the compensation for standing watch upon watch in bitter weather, struggling with torn sails, shattered spars, rigging snapped like cotton thread, for bearing the responsibility of driving a ship through reefs and bars and shoals, through waters swarming with pirates and privateers and customs agents and tight-fisted merchants. This was why he went to sea.

This, and because he was not sure he was capable of doing anything else.

Jack saw a seaman heading aft to turn the glass and ring out eight bells, so he pushed himself off the rail and sought out Oliver Tucker on the windward side. Tucker was bigger all around than Jack, who stood five foot eleven and had his father's muscular build. Tucker was toying with six feet, was inches wider than Jack, and ten years his senior, but he lacked Jack's time on blue water.

Tucker had spent most of his career in coasting vessels, or fishing for cod on the banks, and had only recently taken to the deepwater carrying trade. That was why, despite the difference in age, he was second mate and Jack first. And that seemed to be fine with Tucker, who was competent but unimaginative and largely devoid of ambition. He said little and seemed quite content with his place in the world and in the hierarchy of the ship.

"Evening, Jack," Tucker said on seeing the mate's approach.

"Evening, Oliver. Fine night."

"Fine indeed," Oliver agreed, then went about the formalities of turning over the watch. "Course is northwest, and Montserrat bearing west south-west and about ten leagues distant. Not much else to report, we haven't touched a rope since I came on deck. Wind does seem to be building. I was thinking of handing the topgallants, but reckoned I'd wait for the change of watch."

Jack nodded. *Abigail*, like most merchantmen, carried a bare minimum of crew, because Oxnard, like most merchants, was too mean to pay for more hands than were absolutely necessary, and generally less than that. There were ten men in the forecastle, five for each watch, along with a cook, steward, two mates, and Asquith, making a total of fifteen souls aboard, excluding the two cats, who displayed even less evidence of having souls than did the cook.

Any task of notable difficulty, such as winning the anchor or reefing topsails, required all hands, but stowing topgallants did not rise to that level. In truth, Jack knew, Tucker was under orders not to make any sail changes without waking the captain, and he did not want to wake the captain, so he had waited for Jack to make his appearance.

"We'll probably need to hand them soon," Jack agreed, "but I reckon I'll hang on to them a bit longer."

"You'll hang on to them till they blow out of their boltropes," Tucker said, and in the dark Jack smiled.

"I might yet, but only if I can figure a way for you to take the blame."

They said their good nights. Tucker and his men headed for the scuttles and their watch below, Jack's went to their various stations: helm and forward lookout, the rest milling about amidships, waiting for orders. There was a good chance that the four tricks at the helm, requiring slight turns of the big wheel one way then the other, would be the most taxing part of the watch.

Had it been daylight, Jack would have set the men to a half-dozen different tasks; tarring down the standing rigging, slushing the topmasts, end for ending the running rigging, mending sail, polishing brass, making up sword mats, and refreshing the chaffing gear; but as it was dark, and because he knew the men would work like dogs when called upon to do so, he let them stand easy. Or sit, as the case may be. Such was watch standing in the Caribbean.

Asquith had the reputation of being a fair captain, and Biddlecomb a hard driver, a mate not shy about carrying sail, a man who knew his business but not one who sought authority through fear and brutality, as some did. The profit on that was that they had their pick of the seamen along the waterfront. *Abigail* had a small crew, but a good crew, and when it came to seamen, quality counted for considerably more than quantity.

Jack took his place by the weather rail, looked down the length of the ship at the water rolling and curling off her rounded side, flashing with light as the phosphorus was churned up in her passing and stretching away in a long wake astern. He walked over and glanced at the compass, illuminated by a candle in the binnacle box. Northwest. John Burgess, the seaman at the helm, was holding her so steadily on course the compass card looked as if it was stuck in place.

"How does she feel, Burgess?"

"Feels well, sir. Helm answers right and proper."

Jack nodded. He paced. He ran his eyes over the sails, and the time rolled past like the dark water moving under their keel.

The first hints of dawn were starting to show themselves when Noah Maguire, once just another Irishman from Cork, now an able-bodied seaman from Philadelphia, a good man at sea but a fearsome drunk ashore, came ambling aft, turned the glass, took up the bell rope, and rang out four bells.

"Maguire," Jack called. "First light soon. Take this glass and up aloft with you."

Maguire responded with an "Aye," took the telescope that Jack offered, and disappeared up the main shrouds. This was a precaution that his father had often told him about, how in the naval service in times of war they would have a lookout aloft at first light, to minimize the chance that the dawn might reveal some unhappy surprise, such as a powerful enemy in the offing. Indeed, according to his father the entire ship would go to quarters at dawn, just to be ready.

Jack would not go that far. And of course there was no such thing as "quarters" in the merchant service, and since no merchantman carried any sort of weapons with which they might reasonably defend themselves, such a precaution would be pointless in the extreme. But in waters infested with French privateers, having a man aloft at dawn seemed a reasonable precaution.

It was not long after Maguire had disappeared aloft that the first gray light began to spread along the deck. The masts, hatches, the fife rails and pumps, and forward, the windlass and the heel of the bowsprit slowly revealed themselves in the gathering dawn. The sky to the east took on a pinkish hue. Just forward of the mainmast *Abigail* sported a galley, housed in a deckhouse about the size of a generous privy, and now the first puffs of black smoke began chuffing from the galley's stovepipe and whisking away forward and downwind.

It was no more than ten minutes after that, with the sun finally breaking the rim of the horizon, that Maguire sang out from aloft.

"On deck! Sail, ho! Two points off the larboard bow and all but hull down! Can't make out more than that, Mr. Mate!"

"That's well!" Biddlecomb called back. "Keep your eye on it, sing out when you can see more!"

Sail . . . Jack swallowed down a rising panic, chided himself for a coward. *You're in the West Indies, you damned fool!* he thought. *Of course there's a sail, there are more damned sails here than the damned bloody sail loft in the Royal Dockyard in damned Portsmouth!*

And, inevitably, there was the image of his father, standing unmoved amid the flying metal, the hero of the War for Independency who most certainly did not urinate in his breeches at the sight of a strange sail on the horizon.

"Oh, damn it all!" Jack said, which earned him a "Pardon, sir?" from the seaman on the helm.

"Nothing, Lacey, it's nothing."

Six bells and Jack was about to call up to Maguire to ask if he could see anything more, an undignified display of impatience and he knew it, when the captain appeared on the deck. He was still dressed in his nightshirt, as was his custom in the warmer latitudes. "Jack, did I hear something about a strange sail?"

"Two points off the larboard bow, sir, and all but hull down. That's from Maguire aloft, sir, don't know if we can see it from here."

Asquith raised the telescope he had brought from his cabin and swept the horizon. "Yes, there's the buggerer," he muttered. "Tops'ls, that's all I can see," he added, then he looked aloft. The rising wind was making his thin, white hair stream out to leeward. "Still carrying the t'gan'sls, Mr. Biddlecomb?"

"I was just about to order them handed, sir," he said, which was not strictly the truth. Actually, it was not the truth in any sense. But, motivated by Asquith's pointed hint, he called an order forward that sent men running to the foremast, casting off the topgallant halyard, hauling away clewlines and buntlines to bring the yard down to the cap.

Make us less visible from a distance, in any event, he thought.

"Deck, there!" Maguire called down. "She's hull up now, schooner or brigantine, I'll warrant!"

Jack could take it no more. "By your leave, sir, I'd like to go aloft and have a look."

"Of course, Mr. Biddlecomb, of course," Asquith said. Jack took off his hat, a moderately high-crowned, round-brimmed affair, and stuffed it between the binnacle box and the aft skylight, shed his coat, and swung himself up into the main shrouds. Climbing aloft, up the hundred or so feet of a swaying, plunging mainmast, over the futtock shrouds that ran at a sharp angle from the shrouds to the edge of the maintop, up and over and up the topmast shrouds, it warranted no more consideration than climbing a set of stairs and, young and fit as he was, took only a bit more effort.

He reached the topmast crosstrees and continued up the topgallant shrouds. Had the topgallant sail still been set, he would have had to climb all the way to the masthead to see over it. But by his orders (and he could feel that the wind had indeed built considerably, and knew he should have taken in the topgallant sail an hour before) the yard had just been lowered, the sail clewed up. Jack could feel the vibration in the mast as somewhere below him two hands were climbing aloft to stow it.

Five feet up the topgallant shrouds Jack swung inboard and stepped onto the mast cap. Maguire, perched in the ratlines to leeward, handed him the telescope and pointed toward the western horizon. Biddlecomb could see the sails now, whitish gray with a geometric appearance that showed they were not clouds but rather something made by the hands of man, barely visible against the dawn sky. Fifteen miles or so of rolling, deep blue water separated the two vessels.

Jack wrapped an arm around the topgallant mast. The tallow slush applied to the wood to ease the topgallant yard's travel was sticky and black and fouled his linen shirt, but there was nothing for it. He held the telescope to his eye, swept the horizon until the sails came into view. He twisted the tube, bringing them into focus.

"Hmmm . . ." he said. *Schooner or brigantine . . .* Maguire was right about that. He could make out no details, just the general profile of the distant vessel, but he had seen ships enough that he could tell a great deal from what to a landsman would be just an innocuous shape on the horizon. And he did not like what he saw. There was a pronounced rake to the masts, and the sails had a towering quality, suggesting a lofty ship. A ship built for speed. Such as a privateer might be.

On the other hand, she seemed to be under easy sail and making toward the northward, not on a course to intercept. Jack lowered the glass. "Has she altered course at all, or made any sail change?" he asked.

"Not what I've seen, sir," Maguire said. John Burgess and an ordinary named Ratford came swarming up over the crosstrees and out along the topgallant yard, gathering up great armfuls of the beating canvas and bundling it up on the yard.

"Hmmm . . ." Jack said. He raised the glass again. The sails had a pink hue, shading by the rising of the sun.

He hasn't seen us yet, the blind buggerer . . . Jack thought. From the schooner's perspective *Abigail* would be right in the sun and the blazing dawn light was hiding them.

We'd better turn and run like the devil was on our arse, he thought. It was not his decision, of course, but he reckoned that Asquith would do as he suggested. Not that it was quite as simple as that. This brigantine son of a whore was downwind of them, which meant the only way to run was a beat to windward. Any other point of sail would put the two ships on headings that would eventually intersect. But from the lean, weatherly look of the stranger, there was no chance that the tubby old *Abigail* would ever outrun them on a taut bowline.

Still, if they were to haul their wind now, run off to weather while the sun was in the stranger's eyes, they might put enough distance between them that the privateer, if such he was, would never close it. They might be gone over the horizon before the Frenchie even knew they were there.

"Oh, he's seen us now," Maguire said. Jack put the glass back to his eye. He could see the distant ship was altering course, turning toward them, and he saw the gray patch of sail grow taller as they set more canvas.

Damn . . . Jack wanted nothing more than to curse out loud, but he knew better than to let his building panic show in front of Maguire or any of the men. Still, he could not help thinking about what a French privateer could mean. Rotting in a prison while some wild-eyed radicals decided the fate of the ship, cargo, and crew. Fever, dysentery, starvation. The guillotine, perhaps. With everything blowing to hell in France, that possibility did not seem too farfetched. Jack swallowed hard.

And then he had an idea.

4

Jack handed the glass to Maguire, grabbed a windward backstay, and slid down to the deck. The captain had gone below, and Jack was morally certain he was seated in his day cabin with a cup of tea and two slices of toast with butter and jam. It was his custom every morning, and Asquith was not the sort who liked to vary his routine, no matter what was happening beyond the confines of the ship.

Jack ran his eyes over the sails, nodded to Lacey at the helm. "Steady as she goes."

"Steady as she goes, aye."

Jack disappeared down the scuttle, down to the little space set aside for navigation, just forward of the bulkhead that separated the master's cabin from the rest of the lower deck. Spread out on the small table was the chart of that corner of the ocean, and spread across the chart, the smooth arc of pencil marks, tiny dark points representing *Abigail*'s real progress along her watery track.

They had been dead reckoning through the night, making calculations of the ship's position based on her speed, course, the leeway she made, and any currents setting through. Which meant her current position was a guess. A highly educated guess, to be sure, but a guess just the same. With the coming of daylight, however, Jack would be able to take bearings on Montserrat and Antigua to the east and more perfectly establish exactly where they were.

He traced his finger along the chart. Northwest of their fix, north of their intended track, he saw the faint circle he had drawn on their voyage outward bound, two weeks before. The single word he had written in pencil. *Bank.*

"Jack, what's acting?" Asquith came out of his cabin. He had pulled on breeches and stuffed his nightshirt into them. He was still wiping his mouth with a linen napkin.

"Schooner or brigantine, sir, and a lofty one by the looks. She altered course in our direction when she saw us, which don't look good."

"No . . . no it does not," Asquith agreed, though he did not seem terribly concerned. Jack figured the old man was either too cool to show any worry, or getting too infirm to recognize the danger. In the way of first mates, Jack reckoned it was the latter.

"So, here's what I was thinking, sir," Jack went on, speaking slowly. "We won't outrun him on any point of sail. But see here . . ." He pointed to the pencil line representing the bank. "You recall this, from when last we passed this way?"

"Yes, I recall," Asquith said. It was a sandbar, reaching up from the bottom to just a few feet below the surface of the sea, shifting and unmarked on any chart, one of the great hazards of navigation in that part of the world. It was invisible from deck level, and Burgess just happened to have spotted it while aloft seizing new ratlines on the larboard topgallant shrouds.

"Well, sir," Jack continued, "my thought was, if we set our course thus . . ." He traced a line on the chart with his finger that moved from the *Abigail's* current position to a spot just to leeward of the bank. "We could haul our wind and scrape past this bank, still on a starboard tack. This other fellow would make to overhaul us thus . . ." Jack now traced out the most reasonable course for the stranger to take, if he was indeed trying to intercept *Abigail.* "But if we make him fall off more trying to intercept us, he'll never weather the bank. Either he would tack and tack again, which surely would give us time enough to sail away, or, with any luck, he would not know the bank was there and run aground."

Asquith looked at the chart and said nothing.

"Do you understand, sir?" Jack asked.

"Of course I understand, I've not gone soft in the head quite yet, you know," Asquith snapped. "This is all very well, but it means maintaining

our present course for an hour or more, which means he gets damned close
to us before we haul our wind."

"Yes, sir, that's right, but there's nothing for it. If we make a simple footrace of it, we lose. If we can hang him up on this sandbank, we might get
away yet. If not, it hardly matters if we are taken within the hour or four
hours from now."

That was the simple fact of the matter. It was geometry really, nothing
more. The ships were sailing straight lines, the sides of a triangle that must
meet at a fixed point. The direction of the wind, the direction in which the
ships could sail in relation to that wind, the location of the submerged sandbank, they were all factors in the geometric puzzle, nerves and seamanship
the human aspects of the equation.

Asquith sighed. "You make a point, Jack, you make a point. If we do
nothing, we are taken, and it hardly matters how soon. Very well, we shall
try this trick of yours." He sounded resigned and not particularly hopeful.
"It will be Mr. Tucker's watch soon, but I'll ask you to keep the deck," he
added. "I don't think Mr. Tucker will object to having this cup taken from
his hands."

"No, sir," Jack agreed. He bent over the chart, marked his course, walked
the line to the compass rose with the parallel rule. By the time he looked
up, Asquith was already gone, up the ladder to the quarterdeck. Jack followed behind.

The sun was well up now, the sky a cloudless blue, the distant sail considerably less distant and clearly steering to intercept them. Maguire had
replaced Lacey at the helm, and Jack gave the order, "Make your course
west northwest, one half west."

There was just the slightest catch in Maguire's response as he repeated
the order back, an order that would turn *Abigail*'s bow more toward the
strange sail on the horizon rather than away from it, probably not the helm
command Maguire was anticipating, or hoping for. His eyes shifted from
sails to compass as he made the subtle adjustment of the helm. Jack called
for sail trimmers to brace the yards around ever so slightly.

"Mr. Biddlecomb," said Asquith, who had taken a place by the weather
rail, "let's call up all hands, set up some temporary backstays, and get the
t'gan'sls back on her."

"Yes, sir, of course," Jack said, giving himself a mental kick for not having thought of that himself. He turned on his heel, called for all hands, called for light hawsers to be run aloft to the topgallant mastheads and set up well taut. With the temporary backstays taking the strain, the light poles would bear the topgallant sails in winds that would otherwise threaten to snap them off. Or so Jack hoped. Even with the backstays, he knew, they would be pushing their luck.

It was here that the ship's good reputation, and the concomitant ability to ship good men, paid dividends, as on fore-, main-, and mizzenmasts the hands swarmed aloft, sending the hawsers up on a girtline, bending them on, setting them up, with never an order given by Jack or the captain. Half an hour later, the topgallant sails, which an hour before had been stowed, were set again and straining in the twenty knots of wind blowing over the starboard quarter. *Abigail* heeled further over, her plunging and yawing more pronounced under the lofty canvas, but her speed was a good two knots greater.

Jack looked across the impossibly blue water of the Caribbean. He could now see the brigantine clearly from the deck, hull up, driving hard on a starboard tack, as close hauled as she would lay. She was straining her very fabric to get at *Abigail*, a fat, lumbering merchantman, irresistible prey, and *Abigail* in turn was running for all she was worth. But not running away. And not running toward the Frenchman, either, but rather sailing for a point just beyond her bow.

What must they think we're about? Jack wondered. Assuming this privateer had not guessed what Jack had in mind, then *Abigail*'s actions would make no sense at all. Set topgallants in that wind, just so the two ships might converge even quicker? Jack hoped that his actions would sow confusion, and perhaps even suspicion or fear, in their frog-eating hearts.

"Deck, there!" Lacey called from aloft. "She's showing colors, sir, looks like the Stars and Stripes!"

Jack put his glass to his eye. A spot of color was visible at the stranger's gaff, and though it was not discernible in any great detail, Jack was all but certain it was the flag of the United States: fifteen stripes, a blue canton with fifteen white stars.

"I think not, Monsieur Jean Crapeau," Biddlecomb muttered to himself, his eye still to the glass. He swept the horizon to the northward, hoping to see some sign of the bank, breakers, some indication on the sea's surface of where the treacherous sand might lie. But he could see nothing, so he lowered the glass and focused on the set of *Abigail*'s sails, the trim of the yards, the curve of the long wake astern.

For twenty minutes the ships continued to converge, the details of the brigantine becoming more visible; the steeve of her bowsprit, the rake of her masts, the flash of water kicked up under her bow, the grayish-white mass of sails resolving into their individual components. They were close enough that Jack did not need a glass to see the Stars and Stripes come down, the Tricolor of France go up in its place, a switch that surprised no one.

The sails, Jack noted, were more white than he might expect, the square sails lacking the ubiquitous black streak down the center where they had rubbed against the dirty slush of the masts. He hoped this meant the ship was new to the Caribbean, that her master did not know about the dangerous sands lurking beneath the surface to the north. It could well mean that. Or it could mean that he had been so long in those seas he needed a new suit of sails.

Either way, this was going to be a close run thing, and it depended entirely on Jack's being able to swing *Abigail* away from the privateer before the two vessels were so close that the Frenchie's guns could do real damage, at just that point on the ocean where *Abigail* would be able to weather the sandbank and the Frenchman would not. He looked aloft. He looked at the ship closing with them. He looked at the horizon to the north, and he did not know what to do.

To time this right, he had to be aloft, where he could see the sandbank, but he did not want to leave the deck, and he did not really trust anyone to handle the ship the way he wanted it handled. But he could not be in both places.

"Captain," he said, deciding in that moment, "I am going to the mainmast head to keep an eye out for that bank."

"Very well," Asquith said.

Jack hesitated, unsure how to say the next thing, which was not at all a proper thing to say to one's captain, but Asquith spared him the awkward moment. "Sing out when we should haul our wind," he said, "and I'll set her full and by."

"Very good, sir, thank you," Jack said, stuffed his hat in its familiar place in front of the binnacle, and raced aloft once more. The topgallant sails were set again, so Jack continued up the topgallant shrouds until he was able to throw a leg over the narrow yard, his heel resting on the stiff canvas that bulged with a bellyful of wind. He settled there and ran his eyes around the scene above and below.

The sky was a great dome, stretching horizon to horizon. Off to the east was the green and rugged hump of land that was Montserrat, and to the north, Antigua. He looked down to the deck below. From that perspective it always seemed impossible to him that the ship was able to remain upright; seen from aloft it appeared too top-heavy, as if it should roll over under the weight of the masts and yards.

Jack turned his eyes to the more pressing business for which he had made the long climb to the masthead. There, off to leeward and off the larboard bow, the French privateer was plunging along, bow rising and coming down in a welter of spray as it met each sea in succession. If they maintained this heading for another forty-five minutes, the Frenchman and *Abigail* would literally run into one another.

Off to the north he could see it now, the bank, a yellowish tan stretch of sand just below the surface, a great, sleeping beast ready to wake and snatch the keels of unwary ships. The endless waves swept over it, throwing up breakers that in calmer air would have been as easy to read as a tavern sign, but with the whitecaps kicked up by the building wind and flashing across the surface of the ocean, they were not so obvious.

Do you see that, Jean Crapeau? Jack wondered. The Frenchmen would only see it if they had a man aloft and he was keeping a bright lookout. Jack calculated the speed, the wind direction, the relative bearing of the eastern end of the sandbar. Another five minutes on this course and then they would swing around to starboard, bear up, full and by, and scrape past the sand with the Frenchie too far downwind to weather it.

He looked back at the Frenchman, saw a jet of gray explode from the bow, which he took to be spray kicked up by the hull, and then two seconds later came the muffled thump of the gunfire, the scream of flying metal, and a ragged hole appeared in the fore topgallant sail, forty feet ahead and a little below where he stood.

"Damn my eyes!" Jack shouted with surprise because he knew no one could hear him. He felt something in his bowels loosen up. He had been ready for the possibility of a few long shots from the Frenchman, but he had not thought they would get so close that their shot would be up among the topgallant gear.

His eyes were still on the hole in the fore topgallant sail when the sound of the gun and the scream of the roundshot embraced him once again and then the whipping sound of the foretopsail brace parting. The fore topsail slewed around a bit, but it was mostly held in place by the fore yard and the fore topgallant. He looked down to the deck, mouth open to shout orders, but he could see figures already heaving spare cordage up from the boatswain's locker to reeve off a new brace.

"Mr. Biddlecomb!" Asquith's voice came up clear and strong from the quarterdeck. "Now would be a fine time to haul our wind!"

Jack looked out toward the bank, and every bit of him, down to his kidneys and liver, wanted to turn the ship at that instant and run for safety. But it was not time.

"Five minutes more, sir!" he shouted down, and that was greeted by silence at first, and then Asquith called up, saying, "Five minutes and not a second more, Mr. Biddlecomb!"

It's not some favor you're doing me, Jack thought peevishly, but that thought was cut short by another shot, the ball making its noisy passage between fore- and mainmast but striking nothing. Jack's father had described often enough the weird buzzing scream made by passing roundshot, and as a young boy Jack had always tried to imagine what it must sound like. He had often enough, in the younger days, pictured himself standing as brave and unmoving as his father on a quarterdeck with the iron flying freely. But those fantasies had fled long ago, and here was the reality at last, no longer welcome or looked for.

Come along, come along . . . Jack thought, wishing another half a knot from the *Abigail* so that she might reach that spot where he calculated that she must turn, and he could go back to the deck, the blessed deck.

Another shot, so close Jack could feel the wind of its passing. The temporary backstay set up on the main topgallant parted, giving the mast a hard jerk like it was trying to fling him off, and the long rope fell down, down, doing a weird spiraling dance as it collapsed. Had it been the weather backstay, then the topgallant mast, the sail, the yard, and Jack Biddlecomb would have followed the cordage in its plunge to the deck, but as it was the leeward stay, the mast remained thankfully intact.

Jack thought he might puke. He had never feared the height or the motion, but he had never been at risk of being shot out of the rigging, either. *The dogs are aiming for the masts!* he realized. But of course they would. They would have no interest in sinking a valuable merchantman. Bring down a topmast, bring her to, sail her to France, that was the plan.

Oh, Dear Lord! Jack thought. So distracted was he by the near miss he forgot to keep a weather eye on the sandbank.

"Mr. Biddlecomb!" Asquith's voice rose again from below.

"Now sir, now!" Jack shouted. "Haul your wind, sir, close hauled!" He reached out and grabbed an intact backstay with an unseemly degree of relief at the prospect of gaining the deck. He swung over and wrapped his legs around the thick line even as *Abigail* began to swing onto her new heading, close hauled, as nearly into the wind as she could sail. Legs wrapped around the backstay, feet controlling the rate of descent, Jack slid down the long, tarred line until he reached the level of the rail, then swung down to the quarterdeck, ten feet from the helm.

The Frenchman fired again and a spray of wood exploded from the mainmast fifteen feet above the deck. "Ever been under fire, Mr. Biddlecomb?" Asquith asked in the same tone he might use if he were asking after Jack's family.

"No, sir. You?"

"Privateering, in the war. By God, this is making me quite nostalgic."

"Yes, sir." Jack braced for the inevitable comment about his father, the amount of gunfire the Great Man had endured, but Asquith seemed too wrapped up in his own memories to think along those lines, so Jack walked down the canted deck to the leeward rail. He looked forward, down the length of the ship and the tumble of white water running down her side. Spread out ahead he could see the chop where the seas were breaking

over the sandbank, hardly distinguishable from the whitecaps curling
around them, and disappearing from sight around the turn of the bow.
Jack wondered if he had misjudged. Perhaps they would not weather the
bank at all.

He pushed off the rail and hurried forward, past the main hatch, the foremast, the windlass, and up into the bow. The spritsail, with its larboard
yardarm cocked high, blocked the crucial view of the breakers so he ran
out along the bowsprit, grabbed the forestay, and held fast as the ship rose,
plunged, and twisted underfoot.

Damn it all . . . The breakers stretched across the horizon to a point all
but directly in the ship's path. If they could not sail higher on the wind, or
if they made too much leeway, they would run their bow right into the sand,
and there they would sit, waiting for the Frenchman to tow them off.

He climbed inboard, hurried aft, calling as he went, "Hands to the braces,
let's brace her up, sharp as can be!" The men, who by now had guessed at
Jack's plan, moved fast, taking up the lee braces, ready to haul with a will,
while the cook and steward lent a hand slacking away on the weather side.

Jack gained the quarterdeck and took the weather main brace off the
heavy cleat, shouting, "Haul of all!" All along the lee side the hands sweated
the braces, hauling, grunting, pulling inch by painful inch as they hauled
the yards farther around. Jack shook a few feet of slack into the main brace
and then grabbed the wheel from Maguire.

"Bear a hand to leeward, there," he ordered, then slowly, slowly, turned
the helm to weather and watched as the bow swung more and more up into
the wind. "Well the braces, belay!" Jack called. Foot by foot the ship turned,
and then the edges of the square sails began to shudder and curl, a warning that he was too close to the wind.

"Hands on the weather bowlines!" he shouted. "Haul, you sons of bitches,
haul with a will!" Eager hands cast off bowlines, hauled away, drawing
the edges of the sails tight again. And that was it, *Abigail* was as close to the
wind as she would lie. They would make it or they would not, but there
was nothing more he could do.

The Frenchman fired again, the ball passing over the quarterdeck,
slicing one of the main shrouds in two, but Jack hardly registered the shot.
He could hear the strain in the rigging, the sharp creaking of the hull

pushed right to her limits. The breakers stretched away from the larboard bow, a great long line of roiling water.

Once again Jack heard the dull thud of the French bow chasers, the scream of the ball, and a sharp crack as the new main topgallant backstay was parted by the shot. The line whipped off to leeward, a wild black snake, and high above, the telltale cracking of the mast. Jack looked up in time to see the topgallant sail collapse in a heap, a great tangle of broken wreckage a hundred feet above the deck.

Abigail's bow fell off and he turned the wheel to weather, saw the leeches of the sails flog, turned half a spoke to leeward. He felt like his guts had folded over. He braced for the impact on the sandbank. The deck jumped below his feet, the ship shuddered, the masts swayed as the keel struck, and a great scraping sound reverberated through the very fabric of the vessel.

And then just as suddenly, they were past. Jack could see the yellow sand feet below the surface, he could feel *Abigail's* speed building again as they passed over the bank and kept on going. And even as he was watching with delight as the sandbank slipped astern, he saw the French privateer strike. She was under a full press of canvas, in twenty-four knots of wind, making all the speed she would ever make, and then she stopped, her bow buried in the sand, her masts whipping forward, hanging for a delicious second, then coming down like trees with their trunks cut through.

After that narrow and, as Jack was willing to admit to himself, very providential escape, even the foremast jacks, the most taciturn of men and the least likely to ever dole out praise, had to admit it was a neat bit of seamanship. When they landed in Philadelphia some weeks later, tales of Jack's cunning and ship handling, augmented as sailors will, spread like yellow fever along the waterfront and then through the city.

For days Jack enjoyed the adulation. And then someone remarked how like the incident was to the time his father, Isaac Biddlecomb, had tricked the British man-of-war *Swan* onto Narragansett Bay's Halfway Rock. That theme was taken up in the local press, *Son of the Great War Hero Takes After Father, Apple Does Not Fall Far from the Tree*, et cetera, et cetera, and the whole thing turned to ashes in Jack's mouth.

5

The second morning that he woke in the master's cabin of the *Abigail* merchantman Jack Biddlecomb was in considerably better shape than he had been the first, but he was still not exactly fresh as a new day in springtime. He felt stiff and achy and decidedly unrested. In the fitful dream he had been enduring in his last minutes of sleep, the ship had gone up against the rocks and was pounding itself to bits. When he woke enough to be convinced he was indeed awake he realized that someone was stamping rhythmically on the deck above his head.

It was still dark and Jack had the sense that something very important was lurking just beyond his memory. The stomping continued and he shouted, "Belay that!" and happily it stopped, and behind it came the voice of his particular friend Gilbert Stiles calling down through the skylight.

"Jack? I say, Jack, there, are you awake, old man?"

Ah, yes, Stiles, Jack thought. He had hunted him down last night after meeting that unpleasant fellow outside his parents' house. He had thought to look for Stiles at the Blue Goose, but then reckoned he and Stiles might not be much welcome there, after having apparently inflicted considerable damage to that establishment. Instead, he sought him out at the Fraunces, where he correctly guessed Gilbert had found a new home.

After formally requesting that Stiles stand as second for him, he had accepted the invitation to a drink, which soon became more drinks than he had quite intended. He had stopped, however, before he became insensible, and secretly congratulated himself on his newfound maturity. Now, thanks to that relative abstinence, the thought of fighting Bolingbroke to the death that morning was not entirely out of the question.

"Come below, Gilbert, and stop the damned stamping!" he called, and he sat up in his bunk as he heard Stiles blunder around the narrow passage beyond the master's cabin, then open the door and step in. He was barely visible in the weak light. Jack glanced at the aft windows and saw it was just coming on sunrise and he was grateful for his own forethought that had led him to insist on a later meeting.

"Well, Jack, I didn't care to go stumbling about the ship, not knowing at all who might be below stairs," he said.

"So instead you stomp on the deck like some madman? The rats in the hold will be sending me a round-robin in protest of your noise, I shouldn't wonder."

"You should be more grateful, Jack. By the looks of it you would have slept right through your engagement if I had not woke in time to fetch you."

Jack assessed Stiles's condition and decided, far from waking in time, his second had never actually gone to bed. He and Stiles were the same age and had been friends for four years, since Jack began shipping out of Philadelphia. Stiles was not a mariner, but had worked for various merchants and was now one of several bright young men who handled the books for Robert Oxnard, which afforded Jack a view of the carrying trade he could not get from the quarterdeck. Stiles was good-looking and fashionable in a faux macaroni sort of way, his clothes and his lifestyle always outstripping his income.

Jack clambered out of his bed, washed his face, combed his hair, changed his shirt, pulled stockings, breeches, and shoes on, tied a stock around his neck, buckled his sword belt around his waist, slipped into coat and hat, and led Stiles topside into the cool of the predawn hours of spring.

They crossed the gangplank to the wharf and then headed off into the city, making their way through still-slumbering streets to the General Washington Tavern, which served a tolerable breakfast. Stiles pointed out that, as Jack's second, he could not allow him to kill Bolingbroke on an empty stomach, nor could he himself bear witness to it with never a cup of coffee in him. Stiles felt sure that he had read somewhere that protocol dictated the combatant should pay for his second's breakfast.

Meal finished, they emerged onto busier streets and walked south toward Southwark, past the boardinghouses and taverns and shops that catered to

the lower sort. "This is all a terrible bother," Stiles said as they reached
Second Street and made their way toward the meeting place, which was
not so much agreed upon as assigned by Bolingbroke. "We have the flour
arriving today, you know, and you'll need to get it stowed down ahead of
the barrel hoops."

"Yes, I know," Jack said. "And yes, this business is a terrible bother. I don't
know why Bolingbroke should suddenly feel the need to stick a sword in
me, but there you have it. I'll try to be quick about it."

They could see the others already in the empty lot, standing amid the
forlorn clumps of weeds; Jonah Bolingbroke and the unpleasant fellow who
had accosted Jack outside his parents' home, and another fellow in homespun, a wooden box in his hands, whom Jack did not recognize. He and
Stiles cut across the lot to join them.

"Bolingbroke," Jack said. "You are looking well."

"You made it," Bolingbroke said, taking an ostentatious glance at his
watch. "I had thought you might not," but Jack could hear that his heart
was not in the gibe. He looked a bit pale, and Jack wondered if he might be
afraid.

"Never in life would I miss a chance to run a sword through you," Jack
assured him, "nor would I be so impolite as to refuse your invitation to
do so."

"Sword?" Bolingbroke said. Jack was looking up into Bolingbroke's eyes,
which reminded him again of how big the fellow was, a bit over six feet and
with a physique earned by spending ten of the twenty years he had been
alive at hard labor, mostly, but not entirely, on shipboard. Being a seaman
and having the name Jonah was an awkward combination, and Biddlecomb
wondered if that was in part why Bolingbroke's attitude and general demeanor developed as it had.

The man in homespun stepped up and opened the wooden box as if
offering Jack a cigar. "Pistols, sir; a matched set, but you may take your choice."

"Pistols?" Jack said. "Now, do you see, Jonah, this is exactly why people
dislike you so."

"What?" Bolingbroke protested. "It's a perfectly honorable weapon."

"But why do you get to pick, is my question. First you dictate where we're to meet and now you presume to choose the weapons as well? What if I want to fight with swords, what then?"

Bolingbroke looked confused. "Someone has to choose," he offered.

"Well certainly, it's just that you assume the choice is yours. Isn't there some protocol for this? Stiles, how is this sort of thing supposed to work?"

"Well, I'm sure I don't know," Gilbert protested, "but I had thought it was the aggrieved party who gets to choose."

"Well, there, you see," Jack said. "And I am the aggrieved party."

"You?" Bolingbroke said. "Of course, you *would* think you are the aggrieved party, you arrogant son of a bitch. Always think everyone should be tugging their bloody forelocks to you, Your Highness Biddlecomb."

Jack shook his head, a gesture more of pity than disagreement. "Jonah, Jonah," he began, but the rumble of a coach and the clap of four sets of hooves in the quiet morning interrupted the thought. The sound of a wagon, heavy laden with barrels, drawn by some unhappy draft animal, was common enough in Southwark, but the sharper, sophisticated clatter of a coach-and-four, especially at that hour, made all heads turn.

Horses and carriage came into sight as they passed the battered clapboard house on the corner and emerged into the open space created by the vacant lot; a fine matched team pulling a black-lacquered coach with a coat of arms on the door. "Oh, damn," Stiles said out loud.

The driver reined the horses to a stop and the door flew open and Robert Oxnard leapt out, a large and frenetic man, more energetic than his frame would suggest. He walked quickly across the lot, tall polished black boots parting the high weeds like a ship buffeting its way through brash ice. "What, ho?" he called when he was still some yards away from the duelists. "What's all this? Come, come, we have no time for such nonsense."

He stepped up to the group of them like a father who has caught his boys in some mischief of no great consequence. "Stiles? Do you not have a place of employment?"

"Yes sir, Mr. Oxnard. As of yesterday, I did."

"Well, I suggest you get yourself off to it, if you wish for that advantageous arrangement to continue. Mr. Bolingbroke, I have no doubt you have more pressing matters to attend to."

"Yes, sir," Bolingbroke said. Bolingbroke was filling a second mate's berth aboard a merchantman of 350 tons, and though the ship was owned by one of Oxnard's rivals, Oxnard was still a man to be obeyed, because Oxnard could easily end the career of any man in the carrying trade if he so chose.

Having given his suggestions for how the others might more profitably spend their morning, Oxnard put a big arm around Jack's shoulders and half guided, half pulled him across the lot toward the carriage. There was never a question of whether Jack wished to go with him, because it never occurred to Oxnard that anyone might have designs that were in conflict with his, and if it ever did occur to him, he would not care.

"We must get us down to the *Abigail*, Jack," Oxnard said as they walked. "You sail for Barbados by week's end, you have a considerable amount of work yet to do. Also, I have a surprise for you. Flour is coming aboard today as well, though that don't answer for a surprise. No, this is much better, as you'll see!" The merchant kept up his running monologue the full length of the empty lot, then opened the door of the carriage for Jack. As Jack settled into the soft leather seat he glanced back the way he had come. The others were heading off in their various directions; Stiles back toward the waterfront, setting a course no doubt for the offices of Oxnard and Company, Limited, Merchants, housed on Chestnut Street. Bolingbroke and the unpleasant fellow were ambling off toward the Southwark docks, and the one in homespun was walking west. Oxnard was still talking.

"The flour, when you get to Barbados, Jack, the flour will be at a premium. I hear from a ship just returned . . ." But by then Jack had again stopped listening, and was simply making grunting sounds of comprehension and nodding his head as if it was some sort of mechanical device designed to move at regular intervals.

What on earth just happened here? Jack wondered. This whole issue of Bolingbroke challenging him to an affair of honor, of all things, was odd enough, but Oxnard's arrival made the whole situation positively otherworldly.

Oxnard's carriage had the finest suspension that could be had in North America, but even that was not proof against Philadelphia's rutted and cobbled streets, and the jouncing and shuddering prevented Jack from concentrating on much of anything until they drew to a stop on the wharf to which

Abigail was tied. The sun was not two hours up, but the waterfront was already a bustle, carts and drays rolling past, mates shouting orders, the squeal of tackles as cargo came aboard, carpenters pounding, hacking, sawing, seamen scrambling aloft to cast off sails and let them dry to a bowline.

Jack stepped from the carriage and replaced his hat. His eyes turned first to his ship, as they always did, and he could not fail to notice the considerable activity on deck, activity that had sprung up in his absence and through no orders of his own.

Abigail, like many moderately sized merchant vessels, never had any bulwarks, just a waist-high, stanchion-mounted rail running the perimeter of the deck and terminating just forward of the foremast. But this, apparently, would no longer be the case. A stack of yellow lumber lay on the wharf, giving off its pleasing smell of fresh-cut wood. A swarm of carpenters were at work on the deck, and already the first planks of the new, solid bulwark were being fitted in place.

Oliver Tucker stood in the waist, directing a gang of men fussing over the fall of a heavy yard tackle. Jack's eye followed the run of the line from waist to yardarm and then down to the dock until he came to its end, a squat, overbuilt cart, in the back of which rested the long, black barrel of a cannon. *And thus the need for the bulwarks,* Jack thought, with the unhappy dawning of comprehension.

"Come here, Jack, come here!" Oxnard said with enthusiasm, once again guiding Jack along with an arm over the shoulders. They crossed the rough boards of the wharf and stopped on either side of the cart. A gang of men from the *Abigail* was positioning the lower end of the winding tackle, a massive six-part tackle slung under the maintop that would bear the bulk of the cannon's weight in hoisting it aboard.

"Well, Jack, what do you think?" Oxnard asked, slapping the black iron.

"Of what, sir?"

"The cannon, Jack, the cannon! What do you think?"

"It's a great beastly thing, to be sure."

" 'Beastly'! That's good!" Oxnard barked. "It a regular animal! It's a six pounder, Jack, a six pounder!"

Jack nodded. "A six pounder, yes, sir." He looked at the gun, trying but failing to conjure up enthusiasm enough to match Oxnard's. "Am I to take it somewhere?" he asked, but he already knew the answer. The planks of the new bulwark, straight, fresh, and sturdy, pretty much gave the game away.

"No, no!" Oxnard said. "We are arming the *Abigail*, do you see? You'll have six all told, three to a broadside. I plan on doing the same to all my ships. Damned dangerous out there, you know. That business west of Montserrat, damned fine seamanship, but you can't hope to have a sandbar there whenever you need one. We need to prepare, because the French are swarming like flies to . . . honey."

Biddlecomb regarded the gun for a long moment and tried to think of something to say. As far as engaging in a sea fight with the *Abigail,* he felt about that the same way he might feel if Oxnard had asked him to compose a symphony; he was not necessarily against the idea, but he had no notion of how to go about it. He knew he must communicate this fact, but he also knew what Oxnard's nonsensical reply would be, so he braced himself for it as if preparing to take a blow he could not avoid, and said, "I appreciate the idea, to be sure, but I don't know the use of these guns, and neither do the crew."

"What? The son of Isaac Biddlecomb can't fire a cannon? Nothing to it! Can you fire a musket?"

"Yes, certainly."

"Well, this is just like a musket, but a damned sight bigger. And of course it has a vent and not a flintlock. And you must swab it out before reloading. In any event, you'll be taking a passenger with you, a particular friend of mine named Charles Frost, who is quite familiar with such things, and he can certainly help you drill the men."

"Yes, sir."

In truth, Jack knew more about great guns than he was letting on. He could hardly not, being, as he was so often reminded, the son of Isaac Biddlecomb, and as a boy desperately eager to learn of such things. He knew, for instance, that a six pounder would generally enjoy a gun crew of at least five men, which meant *Abigail* could man exactly three guns at a time if no one was needed for anything else, such as steering or bracing the yards. He knew that these monstrous things weighed about a ton and a half apiece and putting six of them aft would do terrible things to the trim of his lovely ship. He knew that the men would whine endlessly if, along with their regular duties, he made them drill at the guns, though that complaint might be mitigated if they were allowed to actually fire them.

In any event, Jack recognized immediately the enormous irritation that these great guns would cause, from ruining the trim of his vessel and consuming yards of deck space, to having his men maintain the guns and drill with the guns and move the damned guns, taking aboard and stowing powder and shot. It all meant a vast headache he did not need, particularly when he considered how wildly unlikely it was that they would actually have to fight someone.

"Well, Jack, what do you think?" Oxnard asked, his voice fairly brimming with excitement.

"I think it's a fine idea, sir," Jack said. There was nothing else he *could* say, and luckily, before Oxnard could plumb the depths of Jack's sincerity more deeply, a dray drawn by two oxen and stacked high with barrels came rolling up with a noise that did not allow for any subtlety of conversation.

"This will be your flour, Jack," Oxnard said, giving Jack a pat on the shoulder. "I'll leave you to it, then."

"Very well, sir," Jack said. He wondered, as Oxnard climbed back into his carriage, what odd turn would come his way next. He did not have to wait too terribly long to find out.

6

Upon his promotion to command, Jack asked Oliver Tucker to stay on and step up to chief mate, pending Oxnard's approval. In truth, Oxnard was easier to convince than Tucker was. Oxnard greeted the request with a wave of the hand, saying, "Of course, of course, Jack, pick any officers you wish, just so long as you understand, what with the insurance rates and such, I'm forced to reduce everyone's pay by a dollar a month. God's truth, I still don't know how I'm to stay in business. Say, that new cordage you ordered, is that entirely necessary? Sure you can get one more voyage from your running gear, not reeve off all new, what say you? Not the Royal yacht, you know."

In the end, and with considerable difficulty, Jack convinced Oxnard to keep wages as they were. Tucker, not certain he wanted the responsibility of chief mate, was just as hard a sell. But he and Jack had made three voyages together, and each felt he had the measure of the other. Tucker knew Jack for a fair man and not some noodle or Tartar who would expect too much and then scream like a lunatic when he did not get it, so he acquiesced.

And Jack in turn wanted Tucker because he knew him to be a decent seaman and a diligent and hard worker, and because Tucker was too unsure of himself to try and take advantage of Jack's youth and lack of command experience to undermine him in any way.

So, as Oxnard's carriage rolled away, Captain Jack Biddlecomb and Chief Mate Oliver Tucker met on the quarterdeck. Jack stood silent as Tucker called the order, "Heave away the windlass!" and the dozen men who stood with hands resting on the windlass's handspikes hove down on them, winding the creaking, popping, protesting fall of the yard tackle around the drum and causing the great mass of black iron to climb higher and higher above the wharf. There were faces at the windlass bars Jack did not recognize, and he guessed Oxnard had sent more men to help with this work. He wondered if Oxnard had been angry at his not being aboard that morning, and it occurred to him for the first time to wonder how Oxnard knew where to find him.

A quick movement aft caught his eye and pulled his attention from the delicate task of getting the cannon aboard. He looked toward the taffrail and there saw his brother, Nathaniel, fairly dancing with the excitement of it all, and he felt a flush of guilt at having completely forgotten inviting the young man down to take part in the getting in of cargo. But here was the perfect opportunity to make up for that negligence, and to play the part of decent big brother and undiminished hero, all at the same time.

"Nathaniel, come here," Jack waved him over and Nathaniel crossed the deck as swiftly as his adolescent sense of dignity would allow. When his brother was at his side, Jack said in a voice that could be heard fore and aft, "I think this task needs your firm hand on it, Nathaniel. Mr. Tucker?"

"Sir?" Tucker replied.

"Might young Master Biddlecomb here take over this job for you?"

Tucker grinned. The men at the windlass and the winding tackle grinned. "Tricky job, sir," Tucker replied. "I think we do indeed need Master Biddlecomb's particular skills here."

"You heard the man," Jack said to his brother. "Pray give your orders to see the cannon in its carriage."

Nathaniel's face was a mix of awe, fear, and exhilaration. He looked over at the gun, ran his eyes up the rigging. The cannon, a ton and a half of iron, was dangling from the yard tackle made fast to the yardarm directly above it. The upper end of the winding tackle was affixed under the maintop, and the lower end also attached to the cannon. The trick was to lift the gun straight up with the yard tackle, then haul it inboard with the winding tackle, and then ease them both so the gun came down on the point of the deck where it needed to come down.

Nathaniel considered the inverted triangle made by the yard, the yard tackle, and the winding tackle, the gun hanging from its lower corner. He considered the angle of the yard, the height the gun would need to clear the bulwark, and the distance it might be pulled inboard with the winding tackle. Jack could all but hear the calculations going on in his head. His brother was seeing the complex interplay of angles and tensions and weights not through any formal mathematical process but through pure instinct, in a manner that made Jack very proud in a paternal sort of way.

"Go ahead," Jack prompted.

"Heave away the windlass!" Nathaniel shouted, his high voice even higher with the excitement of it all. The men at the windlass began heaving at the handspikes once more. The fall of the tackle groaned under the weight, the cannon rose higher and higher, and the yard dipped and pulled against the rolling tackles set up to counteract the weight. And just as Jack was about to whisper a hint to his brother, Nathaniel called, "Well, the windlass!" in a voice now straining to find a deeper pitch.

Nathaniel took another look aloft and traced the lines with his eyes. "On the winding tackle, heave away, smartly now!" he called. He was not so much giving orders as imitating orders he had heard given many times, like a student painter who learns by copying the works of the masters. The men at the fall of the winding tackle hauled away with the coordinated ease of men who had hauled a thousand lines, and the great black gun swung in over the bulwark and hung above the deck and the waiting gun carriage.

"Well the winding tackle! Belay that! Let's check away that yard tackle, smartly, smartly!" The yard tackle was eased away, the winding tackle took up the strain, the gun swung inboard, and Nathaniel called, "Ease away the winding tackle!" The cannon came gently down and inboard, down and inboard until it hovered a few feet above the gun carriage. It was a neat bit of work, and while those able men of the *Abigail*'s crew might have easily done it even if Nathaniel had not issued a single order, Jack supposed that Nathaniel did not realize as much, or, if he did, the thrill of being able to oversee such an operation quite trumped any suspicion that his oversight was not entirely necessary.

"Ease away, ease away," Nathaniel called, and the cannon came down more, and just before Jack ordered them to do so, Maguire and Lacey leapt forward and adjusted the position of the gun carriage directly under the gun. The massive iron tube eased down those last few inches, the carriage groaned under the weight, and the yard tackle and winding tackle went slack as if they were settling down by a fire after a long day's work.

Jack looked at his brother and smiled. "Well done, young sir, well done," he said, and Nathaniel gave a half smile and a nod of the head, as if to suggest that there was no need to compliment him on so routine a bit of shipboard business. Tucker came aft and echoed Jack's words of praise and Nathaniel looked embarrassed.

"What think you of these, Mr. Tucker?" Jack asked, nodding toward the gun that a dozen seamen were now manhandling out of the way so the next could be brought aboard.

"Well, I'm not so sure, Captain," Tucker said, hesitant to give his opinion when he did know where Jack stood on the issue.

"I'm not sure, either," Jack said. "Not sure at all." Though in truth he was sure, quite sure, that he did not want them aboard. He did not, however, wish to impose his bad attitude on his mate, so instead he steered the conversation toward how and where the flour would be stowed down and the water brought on, the thousand details that were the purview of master and mate, and all the while, like a quintet playing softly at a grand dinner, the carpenters sawed and filed and drilled and hammered at the bulwarks, fashioning the gaping gunports from which the new arms would leer at any wanton Frenchman who came within their arc of fire.

Jack turned to Nathaniel. "When you at last rise to command of your own vessel, brother," he explained, "you will find that such amusements as hoisting cannons aboard are no longer yours, and your life is reduced to bills of lading and crew manifests and chandlers' bills and such drudgery as to make you yearn for labor in the salt mines. So with that, I will leave you in the good hands of Mr. Tucker while I retire to my cabin and my papers."

That very afternoon, on the day that Jack Biddlecomb missed his chance to dispatch Jonah Bolingbroke in accordance with the *code duello*, Captain Ezra Rumstick found himself seated in the parlor, which served as his office, in the set of rooms he rented on Third Street. He was slouched in a black-lacquered Windsor chair, feet splayed out in front of him. The chair looked to any observer as if it might collapse under Rumstick's considerable mass; his height was above six feet, and his weight was approaching seventeen stone, greater than it had ever been in his more active years, though, despite being in his fifth decade of life and having long since given up manual labor, the bulk of it was still muscle, and that which was not he carried well.

Like Rumstick, the chair was well made and not about to come apart. It was the work of John Townsend of Newport, one of a set of chairs and matching table that Rumstick had ordered in the years following the War for Independency, after his long association with his particular friend Isaac Biddlecomb had left him wealthy enough to afford such things. Both the chair and his friendship with Isaac had stood many a test and both were found to be durable, able to stand the strains, the bumping and scraping and occasional abuse that went with simple existence.

The chair, and Rumstick, were turned away from the desk. Across the room, sitting more erect than Rumstick in a chair that was sister to Ezra's, was Jeremiah Tillinghast, still wearing the reddish-brown homespun stockings that had greeted Jack on his first full day in command of the *Abigail*. Tillinghast was talking, Rumstick was listening.

"I could never discover the place they agreed to meet, you see, so I hove to by Oxnard's wharf and kept a weather eye on *Abigail*. I'll warrant I was coming to think Jack would take a pass on the whole affair, but at length his friend Stiles comes along, and off they go."

"To meet Bolingbroke?" Rumstick asked.

"To have their breakfast, if you can credit it."

Rumstick shook his head. "These young men today," he said. "Even an affair of honor won't get them out of bed before the sun."

"They're the future of our country, Captain," Tillinghast said.

"You put me in the dumps when you remind me of that. But pray, go on."

"Once they've had done with their breakfast they're off to the Southwark, and I'm in their wake, but well astern, so they never see me. They meet Bolingbroke at that empty lot on Second, you know the one?"

"I do."

"There's some business about weapons, I think. I was in an alley where I could see, but too far away to hear. In any event, they was talking about something, talking being what these young fellows do best. I was watching them all the while, and had they chosen pistols I was ready to step forward. Swords, I would have let Jack have a few passes, let him run free, as it were, unless he looked to be standing into danger. But before they even settled on weapons, up pulls Oxnard in that new coach-and-four of his, steps right up and orders everyone gone, like they was foremast hands and he the admiral. He takes Jack off in his coach, and that's an end to it."

Ezra frowned and stared at the pattern in the carpet. "It's passing strange," he said at last. "Jack and Bolingbroke have mixed it up over and again through the years, but I would not have credited Bolingbroke with being the kind would look for an affair of honor. A cove like that has damned little honor to defend."

At that, Tillinghast just shrugged.

"So now that you know what Bolingbroke looks like, tell me, was he at the tavern you dragged Jack out of?"

Tillinghast shook his head. "I was too far to get a good look this morning, and things was a bit confused the other night, so I can't say for certain."

Rumstick nodded. He could just picture Tillinghast and a few of his mates tearing up the Blue Goose and dragging Jack and Stiles and the rest of those young bucks out of there. Tillinghast exuded power, in the way he sat, in the way the cloth of his coat was stretched tight over the muscles in his arms. He was a tough son of a bitch, and Rumstick was one to know, because he had known plenty of tough sons of bitches in his near forty years at sea. He had seen men sit silent and unmoving as ship's carpenters used pliers to pull rotten teeth from their mouths. He had seen men spend hours aloft, bare-handed, pounding the ice out of the double-aught canvas of frozen topsails just to make the cloth pliable enough to reef. He had seen men with dreadful wounds keep on fighting as they slipped in their own blood. He had seen men with mortal wounds refuse to leave their stations, unwilling even in the face of death to abandon their shipmates.

Ezra had sailed with Tillinghast and he knew he was that kind of tough. His age was harder to figure. Rumstick guessed it was a little less than his own, late forties, perhaps, but with these seamen, with their lean, hard bodies and weathered faces, it was a tricky thing to gauge.

Rumstick continued to ponder the mystery of it all. With everything that had passed between Bolingbroke and Jack Biddlecomb, why would Bolingbroke call him out now, of all times? And for so minor an affront as a tavern brawl? "It don't answer," he said at length. "Bolingbroke just ain't a dueling sort of cove."

Not that any of this was any of Rumstick's affair. He had no official business in Philadelphia, or anywhere, for that matter. At the end of the war he had continued on with Stanton and Biddlecomb, Merchants, taking command of a series of ships on a series of voyages to the West Indies and beyond. But for Ezra, who had been part of that group of upstart Rhode Islanders who had begun fighting the Revolution before most others even knew there was a war, the merchant service was pretty small beer. After ten years of near constant armed conflict he found he could not muster much enthusiasm for haggling with merchants over bills of lading.

The monotony of the carrying trade pushed him from the sea, and the fact that a new nation was being built on the foundation he had fought so hard to lay kept him ashore. The War for Independency had left the former colonies a smoldering ruin, and now architects of every stripe were struggling to design what new edifice would be built in its place. After all the suffering that he had endured, witnessed, and doled out over the years of fighting, he could not spend his days worrying about the price of molasses in Barbados and take no part in this creation.

Lofty debate over the philosophy of governance was not for Ezra Rumstick and his ilk, and he knew it. The clever coves, the Adamses and the Madisons and the Jeffersons and Hamiltons, and, on another level, the Biddlecombs and the Stantons, were the ones who would build it up, who would make their long-winded arguments based on Cicero or whatever ancient worthy they were citing that week. They were the ones who would shape the United States to be the very thing for which so many had shed so much blood.

Creating a government was a messy thing, that was one of those truths Rumstick had discovered, to his surprise. Questions of how much power a federal government would wield in relation to the states, whether the Federalists wished for an American monarchy or the Democratic-Republicans following in Jefferson's wake would bring the nation down in chaos were not topics for effeminate debate in some salon, but issues that would genuinely determine what sort of a nation rose from the ashes.

There was a place for Ezra Rumstick, and it was not arguing in the fancy halls where the tables were covered in green baize and laid with silver writing sets. And just as he was coming to understand that, the French burst into a revolution of their own, to the near universal delight of all Americans, their former *compagnon d'armes*. Rumstick, like most *citoyens* of the United States, had cheered them on at first, seeing, correctly, that the French Revolution was a continuation of the spirit born in America.

But soon the glorious revolution in France devolved into a bloody, chaotic affair, and Rumstick, like many of his countrymen, felt his enthusiasm turn to wariness and disgust. His support for the revolutionaries of France fell by degrees with each head that dropped into a wicker basket.

Could the heads start rolling down Market Street in Philadelphia? To most it seemed impossible, but Ezra Rumstick had seen quite a bit of the true nature of men, even Americans, and he was not so sure. There had already been rioting a'plenty in America, with Jefferson and his followers standing in unwavering support of the Frenchies no matter how deplorable and bloody their behavior. So when his particular friend Isaac Biddlecomb was elected to the House of Representatives as a delegate from Rhode Island and Providence Plantations, Ezra understood where his place would be. On the streets. In the alleys. In the shadows. Making certain that the heads did not roll.

Keeping young Jack Biddlecomb alive and out of prison had become something of a sideline to his main concern.

"I don't care for this, Tillinghast, I tell you, I don't," Ezra said at last. "This business with Oxnard's promoting Jack never did smell right. And now you throw Bolingbroke into the pot."

"Jack's a damnably fine seaman," Tillinghast said. "Oxnard promotes him, he gets a good shipmaster, and gets to stick Isaac Biddlecomb's nose in it. And some of that will splash onto Adams as well."

"I know," Ezra said. "But it still don't smell right. I think we better have a word with Master Bolingbroke."

Tillinghast smiled and stood. "Aye, aye, Captain," he said, then turned and was gone. Bolingbroke, of course, would not come willingly. That was what accounted for Tillinghast's smile, and his genuine enthusiasm for the task.

7

It had, in fact, been two years since Jack Biddlecomb and Jonah Bolingbroke trod the same deck, and bunked in the same forecastle, and gone at one another with fists and knives. Jack had not been a mate then. He had not even been Jack Biddlecomb then, and that was where the trouble had started, that time, at least.

Jack had abandoned the name Jack Biddlecomb in Buenos Aires at the same time he had abandoned the leaking, half-rotten, hogging old bucket known as the *Queen of the Sea*, aboard which he had shipped in Charleston. He had not been overly optimistic about the *Queeny*, as she was known to those aboard her, based on the sight of her alone, the sagging and crooked ratlines, the white patches on her standing rigging where the cordage had been imperfectly tarred, like exposed bone on some sun-rotten corpse, the strands of oakum hanging like seaweed from her deck seams that all but assured a leaky, miserable time below.

He was less enthusiastic still after meeting the mate, an inarticulate brute with one good eye and one wandering eye, neither of which would meet Jack's when they spoke, so that Jack was not entirely certain which eye was which. The master was half drunk when they met and soon after achieved full drunkenness, and in their brief months together never seemed to be in any other state.

But Jack needed to get out of town quickly following an unfortunate misunderstanding at a local brothel, and since *Queeny* was hove short in the stream and ready to make sail, and for some reason in desperate need of hands, he signed aboard, able-bodied.

All of the shortcomings of the *Queen of the Sea* Jack might have overlooked, most of them being not particularly unusual for the carrying trade, including the near constant pumping he soon found was required to keep her afloat. And to be sure, she was blessedly free of rats, though that could have been construed as a bad sign. But two things pushed him beyond his endurance.

One was the captain's insistence, after they sailed, that he did not warrant the rating of able-bodied, or the concomitant pay, and so rerated him as ordinary. Such a thing was unusual to the point of being unheard of, and would have infuriated Jack in any case, he having by then sailed for more than a year with the rating of able-bodied. But when it became clear to him that he was by far the most active and skilled, if youngest, man in a forecastle full of broken drunks and skulkers and sea lawyers, it became more than he could tolerate.

And just as he was making his displeasure known to the master, the old man saw far enough through a rent in the fog of rum to say, "Biddlecomb, is it? Unusual name. You must be relative to Isaac Biddlecomb, what made such a name for himself in the war. So what in hell are you doing in the fo'c'sle, eh, boy?"

And that was that. From then on there was nothing that Jack could do that would not be referred back to his lineage. "Do you see how he spilled slush on the deck!" one might say, "the son of Isaac Biddlecomb!" (they having guessed at his relationship to the Great Man). "See what the son of Isaac Biddlecomb reckons passes for a proper long splice!" This, like the pumping and the water dripping from the deckhead, had long been one of the regular plagues of his seagoing career, but of all of them, this, he was finding, was the one he could not with equanimity endure.

So, once the *Queen of the Sea* dropped her best bower in the harbor at Buenos Aires, and all was snugged down and the sun set and the anchor watch passed out drunk in the longboat on the main hatch, Jack lowered his dunnage and then himself into the captain's gig floating alongside and pulled for shore. Abandoning the *Queeny* meant abandoning the meager pay that was due him, and since the misunderstanding in Charleston had left him without a sou, he knew he was in for a bit of a lean time until he could find another berth. But this was not the first time he had taken French leave of a ship he had signed aboard. Indeed his very first voyage had ended that way.

And lean it was, for the few days he spent haunting the waterfront of that South American town, looking out for the main chance and keeping a weather eye cocked for any from the *Queen of the Sea* who might be looking out for him.

He was in a tavern off an alley that shared a wall with a chandler, hoping that someone would abandon a meal with a tolerable amount of food still on the plate, when he fell in with two Yankee sailors off a Boston ship called the *Hancock* lying at anchor out in the roads.

"The old *Hardcock*'s in want of hands," one of the sailors said, sniggering at this, the apogee of the seaman's sly, droll humor, though Jack could not imagine that he had made that witticism up on the spot, or, indeed, at all.

"Is that true?" he asked. "Or do you practice on me?"

"No, it's God's truth," the other said. "We had one hand in the larboard watch break his leg and another got athwart the mate's hawse and run once he got the chance. The old man hates your dagos and Frenchmen, and would soon shoot an Englishman as let him slush the t'gallant masts, so an American is always welcome, especially a fellow knows a head from a halyard, which you look to be. What's your name?"

"Tobias Harwood," Jack said, extending his hand, "from Philadelphia."

The sailors, who were fully empathetic with the suffering of their brother mariner, ordered up breakfast for Tobias, and he in turn helped them load the boatswain's stores they had been sent ashore to purchase, first into the rented cart and, after a bone-jarring ride to the stone steps by the quay, into the ship's boat floating there. They rowed Jack out to the *Hancock* and introduced him to the mate. By that time Jack had entirely forgotten the name he had made up, but happily the older of the foremast jacks, whose name was Israel Ferguson, had not, and when he presented Tobias Harwood to the first officer, Jack took special care to commit it to memory.

At that point Jack would have signed aboard any bucket short of a slaver or a pirate, but as luck would have it the *Hancock* was a well-run ship, with as happy a forecastle as any Jack had known. He signed on the books as

Tobias Harwood, able-bodied, and made the passage to Kingston and then on to Tobago, from whence they caught the westerlies to Lisbon and then back on a more southerly route to the West Indies. Jack did his share of the work, more than his share, and his good humor, his willingness, his hard-earned skill, and natural ability made him popular with his shipmates.

He was no cock of the forecastle, did not act the strutting, self-appointed master of that domain. He may have had an intemperate streak as wide as Narragansett Bay, which showed itself to ill effect whenever he had a run ashore, but he also had a native humility that prevented him from lording it over others and made him popular among his fellows, popular at first in the manner of a well-liked younger brother and then, as he became more of an integral part of the machine that was the ship's company, popular as a valued and reliable foremast hand.

Tobias né Jack had been eight months aboard *Hancock* when Bolingbroke came aboard. The merchantman was anchored in the wide stretch of blue-green sea between Nassau and Hog Island that passed for the chief harbor of New Providence Island, and waiting only for their water to get under way, when a bumboat hove alongside and the new hand came up the pilot ladder, sea chest balanced with practiced ease on his shoulder. Bolingbroke.

Jack was up aloft patching broken service on the main topmast shrouds when he saw the man, and his heart sank. It had been two years since their paths had crossed, and Jack had thought himself rid of the son of a bitch, but here he was. He cursed his luck, but he knew that the world of the deep-water sailors was not so large. Such an unwelcome reunion as this was far from unlikely.

Their last parting had not been amicable, not amicable at all, and now the chance for revenge was served up to Bolingbroke like a two-penny or-dinary. Once Bolingbroke had had his laugh at the Tobias Harwood cha-rade, and revealed that Jack had signed on under a false name, Jack figured he would be quickly signed off again and left on the beach, most likely with his pay forfeited. Ship's masters did not care for subterfuge of any sort.

It was not until near suppertime, with the sun dropping toward the western horizon, that Jack at last climbed down from aloft to face the in-evitable. The foremast hands, finished with their day's work, were gath-ered in the forecastle, sitting sprawled on their sea-chest seats, stretched out in bunks, or at the table that ran down the center of the space. Bolingbroke was there, at the table, already making himself quite at home when Jack climbed through the hatch and down the ladder to the cramped, smoky, wedge-shaped cabin in the *Hancock*'s bows.

"Tobias," said Israel Ferguson. "New hand, here for the starboard watch. Jonah Bolingbroke. Jonah, this here's Tobias Harwood."

Bolingbroke turned with a look that suggested not the least interest in meeting another human being, but when his eyes lit on Jack's face, and a veritable Saint Elmo's fire of recognition and comprehension flashed over his features, a smile appeared and he extended a hand. Jack reckoned then that the cat was out of the bag, but Bolingbroke, he would soon realize, was far too skilled in the ways of torment to let so precious an opportunity go at the first blush.

"Harwood, is it?" he said, the smile now in full bloom. "Tobias? Your servant, sir."

"Bolingbroke," Jack managed to mutter as he shook the proffered hand.

"Say, Tobias," Bolingbroke continued, unable to wait for the fun to begin. "Which berth is yours, then?"

"Lower one, starboard side, forward there," Jack mumbled and the smile on Bolingbroke's face just grew wider.

"Here's the thing, Tobias," Bolingbroke went on. "The only berth left for me is the uppermost, aft there, and it won't answer, what with the draft from the hatch above and the people going in and out and whatnot. Not to mention the awkwardness of having to climb into an upper bunk. I would reckon it a friendly gesture to a new shipmate was you to let me have your berth, and you take the one aft."

Jack's berth was in fact a prime piece of forecastle real estate, one he had coveted since coming aboard. With each berth that came vacant as one hand or another left the ship, Jack had methodically improved his sleeping situation, until at last he had landed in that one, as far from the drafts and the noise as one could get in the forecastle. And so it was to the muted surprise of his shipmates that he agreed to Bolingbroke's request without so much as a word of protest.

If *Hancock* had been bound for some port in the United States, an easy run before the trade winds and the prevailing southwesterlies, with a convenient lift from the Gulf Stream, Jack might have been able to endure the brief tyranny of Jonah Bolingbroke. But instead, *Hancock* would be setting sail in the other direction, off to the Azores and then to Lisbon again before returning to Philadelphia, five months at least even if they were blessed with quick passages. Jack was all at sea as to what to do, whether to jump ship in Nassau or endure the torment Bolingbroke would dole out.

He was still pondering the dilemma by the time they had brought their water aboard, won their anchor, and stood out of Nassau harbor, and so the decision was made for him.

Bolingbroke, of course, did not relent, and he had a genius for pushing Jack right to the edge and no further. They were fortunately on different watches, Bolingbroke in the starboard watch and Jack of the larbowlines, so with their four-hours-on, four-off watch keeping at sea they were not so often in one another's company. But they were thrust together often enough that Bolingbroke could have his fun. Thus, on a particularly cold, wet, blowing night somewhere just past thirty-two degrees west longitude Jack found himself standing watch and watch, taking the place of Jonah Bolingbroke, who remained snug in his prime berth. Or Jack might find himself having to surrender to Bolingbroke his share of a plum duff, or patch a rent in his trousers, or put an edge on his knife.

To the rest of the "Hardcocks" it was a mystery why young Tobias, perfectly able to care for himself, would tolerate such treatment. But in the ways of sailormen they minded their own business and contented themselves to look on with curiosity. Israel Ferguson alone made discreet inquiry into Jack's behavior, and that went only as far as asking Jack if he and Bolingbroke had known one another before, to which Jack gave a vague and unhelpful answer.

The *Hancock* was at anchor in the harbor of Funchal, on the island of Madeira, when Bolingbroke finally managed to push Jack beyond the edge. It was not a stop they had planned, but on leaving Lisbon the second mate, a Boston buck named Timothy Noddle, had come down with a fever, and the old man decided to put in to Madeira so the man might get proper care.

That was what he said, in any event, though Jack was morally certain that he just wanted Noddle off the ship before the fever could spread. Jack liked Noddle quite a bit, reckoned him a friend, and so stepped up to be part of the boat crew that pulled him ashore and found the quarantine hospital at which to deposit him. There was nothing more he could do, and when he bid Noddle good-bye, he was not pleased about it. They would not wait on him, of course, but set sail on the next tide, and Noddle would have the devil of a time getting back to the United States.

And so Jack was in a particularly ill humor when he returned to the *Hancock*, climbed the pilot ladder, and helped sway the boat back aboard. He climbed sullenly through the hatch and down the ladder to the forecastle, nearly blind in the dim light after the brilliance of the island sun. He could see the shapes of men in the gloom, the hands stood down to an anchor watch. It would be dinner soon, and the men of both watches were crowding below, enjoying a few free minutes out of the officers' sight.

"Say, Tobias, there you are," Bolingbroke's voice came from somewhere forward. "I've a thought to take a run ashore if the old man gives us leave, but I'll need my shoes shined up and I would be eternally grateful was you to do that."

Jack looked in the direction of the voice. His eyes were adjusting to the half-light and he could see Bolingbroke sitting at the forward end of the table, leaning with elbows back and grinning that grin of his, and Jack realized then he was more sick of this torment than he was afraid of being put on shore. Let the old man set him on the beach, he and Noddle would make their way home together.

"Very well," Jack said. "I'll clean them up. Give them here."

Bolingbroke snatched the shoes from the bench beside him and tossed them to Jack. "Shine 'em up good, boy, the way the ladies like 'em."

"Special shine for you, Bolingbroke," he said. He put the shoes on the deck. Bolingbroke was looking away, confident that Jack would do his bidding. Jack unbuckled his belt, unbuttoned his trousers. His eyes were now adjusted enough that he could direct a steady stream of urine into Bolingbroke's shoes.

Even as Jack felt relief come over him, relief on many levels, he sensed a tension ripple through the forecastle, like the cold downdraft that presages a squall. He looked up just as Bolingbroke sensed it as well. Bolingbroke jerked his head in Jack's direction, and Jack had the great satisfaction of seeing Bolingbroke's shocked expression, his horrified expression at Jack's defiance. But the look was gone as quickly as it had come, and Bolingbroke was the picture of composure as he slowly rose from the bench and stepped aft. Jack quickly rebuttoned and rebuckled.

Jonah Bolingbroke was a big son of a bitch, with four inches and fifty pounds on Jack, but Jack no longer cared about that any more than he cared about being set ashore, or much of anything at that point.

What's more, it had been two years since they last met, two years during which Jack had been hauling lines, sweating lines, fisting canvas, wrestling with recalcitrant ships' wheels, coiling cables, leaning into capstan bars, or heaving at the handspikes of windlasses, two years of shoreside brawls, many a jolly good rough-and-tumble'o. He was not the boy he had been and he was not intimidated and he did not hesitate at all to step forward, cock his arm, and drive his fist into Bolingbroke's jaw so fast that Bolingbroke did not even have time to replace his cocksure look with one of surprise.

Jonah stumbled back, his hands to his face, and Jack tried to ignore the pain that exploded in his knuckles. A knot of their shipmates caught Bolingbroke before he hit the deck and set him on his feet. His hands came down and balled into fists. There was blood in the wake of Jack's punch, a split lip it looked like. "You son of a whore, Biddlecomb, I'll do you for that!" Bolingbroke said, more of a growl than an articulate sentence, and with that he bounded across the deck, straight at Jack.

His right hand swung around in an arc, making for the side of Jack's head. Jack lifted his arm to block the punch and realized his mistake even as he saw Jonah's powerful left come up from below and connect with his stomach, blowing the wind out of him and doubling him up. But Jack knew by instinct that the knee was coming next, so he twisted to the side and when Bolingbroke made his move, his knee found only air. That threw his balance off and Jack straightened enough that he could give Bolingbroke a left to the stomach and a right to the side of the head that sent him sprawling back but did no worse, since Jack, understanding that his fist would explode in pain with the blow, had pulled the punch.

Bolingbroke was more mad than hurt, and he was very, very mad. His hand went around behind him and when it returned it was clutching his sheath knife, the blade glowing dull and menacing in the gloom. Jack reached around and pulled his knife as well, and then strong arms grabbed him and held him immobile and he saw others grab Bolingbroke. "None of that, none of that," Ferguson said, and the knives were wrenched from the combatants' hands and they were shoved toward one another again, encouraged by their mates to beat each other half to death, but not to finish the job with blades.

Jonah swung, an ugly roundhouse, and Jack leaned back, felt the air of the blow on his face like the concussion of a cannon blast. He stepped in and landed a quick jab with the right, another with the left. Bolingbroke stumbled back again and then there was a loud knock on the hatch combing overhead and the voice of the first mate called down, "Holloa, the fo'c'sle!"

With that hail Biddlecomb and Bolingbroke dropped their fists and melted back among the men milling about, and the rest took on attitudes of nonchalance that were ludicrously insincere. The mate's shoes, stockings, breeches, and then the rest appeared as he came down the ladder. He stopped when his head was below the level of the deck, turned and looked around. He was no fool, and he had been to sea long enough to know that something was acting here, but in accordance with the hierarchy of the merchant trade he would let the forecastle sort out the forecastle's problems, as long as it did not interfere with the efficient and, more to the point, profitable running of the ship.

"Harwood, where the devil are you?" the mate snapped.

"Here, sir," Jack said, trying not to sound like a man in the middle of a fistfight.

"Get your dunnage and get aft. We have to leave Noddle ashore, so the old man's moved Dailey into his berth and he wants you to ship as third." He took one last glaring look around, and having said what he had to say, he was up the ladder and gone.

And that was an end to it. Because as pathetic a creature as a third mate might be, he was a mate nonetheless, and no one in the forecastle, particularly not as ill-considered a whore's whelp as Jonah Bolingbroke, would voluntarily get athwart his hawse. He would not cross him even after Jack, his sea bag over his shoulder, heading up the ladder on his way aft, pointed to the half-filled shoes on deck and said, "Bolingbroke, that's disgusting. Get that cleaned up and be quick about it."

So their enmity, by no means ended, was tabled until they reached

Boston, their next port of call, and Bolingbroke was paid off and disappeared in the mysterious and debauched way of sailors ashore. And Jack went on hating him, despite the fact that everything that Jack Biddlecomb was, everything he had thus far accomplished, he owed to Jonah Bolingbroke.

With his move aft, Jack was no longer Harwood but rather Mr. Harwood, and once he had left the *Hancock* in Philadelphia and shipped aboard another as second he became Mr. Biddlecomb, which he remained until the blessed moment when he became Captain Biddlecomb. And, as Captain Biddlecomb, Jack spent much of his time below, laboring over bills of lading, and bills of health and general clearances and clearing manifests and invoices, lists of passengers, lists of crew, lists of sea stores. He discovered that the life of ease he had always imagined his former captain Mr. Asquith enjoyed was not so easy at all, that it was, in fact, more drudgery and paper than he had quite realized. That, despite the fact that Jack had always had a hand in keeping the ship's books and accounts in order.

His days were spent pen in hand, or arguing with chandlers and sailmakers and riggers and ship's carpenters and, more obsequiously, with Robert Oxnard, as well as Oxnard's agent, William Dailey. Dailey, in particular, seemed to have an endless assortment of papers for him to consider, and on the worst of their meetings Jack found himself signing forms for this or that without even understanding in any meaningful way what it was he was signing.

In the evening, when the ship's carpenters and the riggers and the longshoremen were done with their labors, and there was no one left aboard in need of supervision, Jack and Stiles and a gaggle of sundry young gentlemen took their pleasure in Philadelphia, the greatest city in the burgeoning United States of America. Like a pack of feral dogs they roamed the taverns, pursuing women and the endless amusements that only a thriving port city could offer.

Philadelphia, capital of the United States, was no creaky, arthritic, staid farm community with its entrenched and homogeneous population, a churchgoing, disapproving community always keeping a weather eye out for impropriety, and quashing the first hint of it. This was a seaport, its life-blood flowed from the Atlantic, up the Delaware Bay to the wharves and anchorages on the Delaware River, and when it was spent it flowed out again. And carried on that stream the goods and the people of the Atlantic world, sailors with no communal ties who sated long-pent desires, always with the knowledge that, no matter how debauched they became, no matter how quickly they ran through three, four, or six months' wages, their hard-won abilities to hand, reef, and steer would provide for them both their passport and their breakfast.

It was midmorning, a week and a half after his aborted duel with Boling-broke, Jack having given up waiting for an invitation to continue the affair, that he returned after a particularly grueling and vexing time at Oxnard's to the wharf where *Abigail* remained tied, fore and aft. Jack had managed to infuriate Oxnard by returning to the chandler an entire delivery of salt pork, ten barrels of it, meant to feed the *Abigail*'s men. His reason for re-turning it, a reason by Oxnard's lights entirely inadequate, had to do with its being rancid beyond what even a foremast hand could be expected to eat. Jack suspected that some teamster along the way had emptied out most of the brine to lighten the barrels and make them easier to transport.

"Now see here, Jack, your foremast hand don't need fancy cooking, none of your French cuisine with sauces and such. Just give them their salt pork and dried peas and a run ashore and they're merry as grigs," Oxnard had explained. But Jack had served his time in the forecastle, had eaten his share of rancid beef purchased, as this no doubt had been, at a greatly reduced price, or taken off the chandler's hands in exchange for some other consid-eration. For his men, Jack would have none of it.

In the end he won that fight, but it meant Oxnard had little appetite for the next request. "And, pray, sir, don't forget that I will need that *rôle d'équipage*," Jack reminded him.

The *rôle d'équipage*. It was an innocuous document by any standard— a list of the ship's crew—but thanks to a decree by the *Directoire* it had become very crucial indeed. Since 1778, when France had first joined the Americans in their fight against the British, the French had required

American ships to show a passport, no more, to prove their nationality. But now the *Directoire*, furious at the new American treaty with England, was requiring a *rôle d'équipage* as well. Any ship boarded by a French privateer that could not produce one was considered a fair prize. It was retaliation and a chance for plunder, no more, but when one ship was armed with heavy cannon and the other was not, all the treaties in the world counted for little.

This was not a situation in which Jack wished to find himself, his own newly installed great guns notwithstanding. But for all the importance that the *rôle d'équipage* carried, Oxnard gave Jack's request a wave of the hand and a "Yes, yes, of course," by way of dismissal.

And that in turn put Jack in a foul mood, which he nursed and stoked on the way back to the *Abigail*'s berth. He paused on the wharf and ran his eyes over the ship tied there. The bulwarks were done now, the paint fresh; black from the rail down to the gunnel, which was a brilliant red, then the chief of the hull oiled down to the lower wale, which was black like the bulwarks. The gunports were neatly cut, three per side, and the great guns came poking out like some hibernating beasts testing the air for spring.

It was all excellently well done, shipshape and Bristol fashion, and normally Jack would have looked on it with the same appreciation with which he might run his eye over the fine lines of a young woman in a silk dress. But the presence of the guns, thrust upon him, still grated and made his mood fouler still.

With those irritants already gnawing at him, Jack Biddlecomb was not in an ideal temper for the surprise of finding, on entering his cabin, a young gentleman sitting at his table, scratching away with a pen at some correspondence, a small stack of papers to one side, a glass of wine at hand, a cigar smoldering in a saucer that belonged to a tea set his mother had sent aboard.

"What, ho?" Jack asked, too surprised to come up with more.

The young man looked up. A smooth, close-shaven face, good skin, very pale. Hair the color of wet sand. He looked to be about Jack's age, perhaps a year or two older. The shirt and stock visible around the periphery of his silk jacket were white beyond anything Jack could hope to achieve with his own shirts. Indeed, they made the fresh paint of the great cabin seem yellowed in contrast.

"Oh, yes," the young man said, showing none of the surprise that Jack was exhibiting. "My chest and bags are on the deck above. Pray, fetch them down here directly." He lifted the cigar, put it between his lips, and read-dressed himself to his writing.

"And you would be . . . ?" Jack queried.

The young man looked up again, and now there was the slightest crease of irritation on his brow. "William Wentworth, Esquire. Of the Boston Went-worths."

"The Boston Wentworths? Indeed?" Jack had no notion of who the Boston Wentworths were.

"Indeed, yes. You'll find the name on my chest. Which, you may recall, I requested that you bring down directly."

Jack took a step into the cabin. Wentworth leaned back in his chair, re-garding him with curiosity and vague amusement. "And why," Jack asked, "would you expect me to fetch your dunnage?"

Wentworth took a pull on his cigar and exhaled a column of smoke like a blast from a cannon's muzzle. His amusement at Jack's effrontery made his lips twist up at the corners. "Well, that is what you hardy tarpaulins do, is it not? Fetch one's 'dunnage'?"

Jack took another step and sat on the edge of his berth. Wentworth's eyes followed him, though his body moved hardly at all. "Fetching dunnage is indeed what we hardy tarpaulins do," Jack agreed. "Doling out sound thrashings to those who annoy us is another, so one must take care in our company."

Wentworth laughed out loud. He plucked the cigar from his mouth and tapped the ash into the tea saucer. "Oh, my dear man, I suggest you not try that, out of consideration for your own health. Now, Ned Buntline or what-ever your name might be, off with you and fetch my dunnage, as I asked." Once again he turned to his writing. He managed to scratch out a few more words in what Jack saw was an astoundingly neat copperplate before look-ing up again, the amusement quite gone from his face.

"I say, are you still here, Ned?"

"That's Captain Ned. Captain Jack, actually."

Wentworth leaned back again, but his look of mild irritation did not al-ter. "Captain Jack. Captain of . . . ?"

Jack held up his hands to indicate their surroundings. "All that you behold before you," he said.

"Really?" Wentworth said. "Captain of this ship? You are not the gnarled old sea dog I had envisioned. Forgive me. I am terribly disappointed."

"I quite understand," said Jack, who was also disappointed, having hoped to give greater discomfort to this loathsome intruder. "I fear you will be more disappointed still, Master Wentworth, when I tell you that you are in my cabin and I must ask you to leave it at once."

At that Wentworth smiled again and looked around with an expression approaching surprise. "This? The master's cabin? Surely not."

"Indeed it is. The cabins for passengers, if such you are, and I dare say it is looking less and less likely, but if such you are, those cabins open onto the alleyway outside my door."

"You know," Wentworth said, tapping more ash into the saucer, "I did look into those rooms, but I took them to be pantries or closets or such. Though now that you mention it, each did seem to sport a singular manner of shelving which might be construed as a sort of bed."

"We hardy tarpaulins call them 'berths' but yes, that is the very thing."

Wentworth shook his head at the wonder of it. "And here I had been congratulating myself on doing the decent thing and taking the most unaccommodating space for myself, thinking sure there must be finer cabins elsewhere aboard for the master—yourself, apparently—and Mr. Frost."

Jack had heard the name Frost recently but he could not recall where, and at the moment he did not care. His patience with this banter was at an end, so he said, "And why, pray, might you be looking for a cabin aboard my ship at all?"

By way of answer, Wentworth dug through the small pile of papers on Jack's table, extracted one, and handed it to him. Jack recognized immediately the flowing hand and ostentatious signature of Robert Oxnard, Esquire, and he read:

Dear Captain Biddlecomb,
This note shall be presented to you by Mr. William Wentworth, Esquire, of Boston, whom you will kindly provide passage to Barbados on your upcoming passage thence, and in addition . . .

The note went on to address such issues as cabin stores (Wentworth would provide his own), manner in which Wentworth was to be treated (decently), and sundry other concerns. By the end of the first paragraph Jack had read enough to know he was stuck with Wentworth, and between the great guns and this young scion of the Boston Wentworths he wondered what Oxnard might foist on him next. He handed the note back to Wentworth and shouted up through the skylight, "Maguire! What, ho, there, Maguire!"

A moment later the big seaman stood crowding the great cabin door. "Maguire, pray fetch down Mr. Wentworth's dunnage. Let him take out what he'll need for the voyage, then see the rest stowed down in the orlop. Mr. Wentworth may have his choice of any of the cabins forward."

"Cabins, sir?" Maguire asked.

"Yes. In the alleyway outside there. You know, the ones designed for the convenience of the gentry."

8

With the myriad of considerations and annoyances great and small that were part of preparing the *Abigail* for sea, Jack Biddlecomb entirely forgot Wentworth's allusion to a Mr. Frost who would apparently be requiring a cabin, and a good one at that. And Jack continued to not recall the gentleman for the next five days, until the moment he laid eyes on him, on the very morning of the day they were slated to sail.

They had worked like demons, he and Tucker and the men. The flour and sundry cargo, indigo, salt cod, barrel hoops, casks of nails, had been stowed down; the guns lashed tight in place; powder, shot, and other gunner's stores (*God help us!* Jack had thought as they came aboard) stowed down as well, with rammers, worms, sponges, and the like mounted in a rack built special on the mizzenmast to house them.

New hands had been hired to replace those who did not wish to ship out again, or those whom Jack did not wish to ship again, or who were unlikely to be sober or freed from jail by sailing time. Others who had signed papers and taken an advance were dragged from taverns and brothels and deposited in *Abigail*'s forecastle. For that task, Jack asked for and gratefully accepted the help of his Uncle Ezra, whose connections and influence on the Philadelphia waterfront made the task infinitely simpler.

Decent food and drink for the men, decent by shipboard standards, in any event, had been bullied out of the chandlers, a new fore topsail had been cajoled out of Oxnard and bent on under the supervision of John Burgess, whom Biddlecomb had named boatswain. Hatches secured and battened

down, masts slushed, hawsers to the wharf singled up, at last all was in readiness, with the tide set to begin ebbing a little after noon and the wind, which
was a fairly steady eight knots out of the northeast, enough to give *Abigail*
sufficient steerage as she drifted on the river, though Jack could have wished
for more.

Jack and Oliver Tucker were aft discussing tiller ropes and the longevity
they might reasonably expect from those currently rove when they heard
the distinctive approach of a coach-and-four, and they looked up at the
sound. An elegant carriage, not Oxnard's, but one they did not recognize,
drew to a stop just abeam of *Abigail*'s berth.

"Is Mr. Wentworth aboard?" Jack asked, he having blessedly forgotten
all about the man.

"No, sir," Tucker said. "I haven't seen him this week past. In truth, I've
never seen him at all."

"Well, let us hope for his sake this is him. We'll warp out into the stream
in an hour whether he's aboard or no." Jack noticed with some dismay that
there was a considerable quantity of luggage lashed to the roof, and the
coachman and liverymen scrambled up aloft to unlash it and hand it down
just as the door swung open and Wentworth stepped nimbly to the cobble-
stones.

Fore and aft he looked every bit the young dandy, from the shoes, black
and shiny as hot pitch, which made the silver buckles stand out in sharp relief, to the tall beaver hat he settled so carefully on his coiffed head. He
paused to take in his surroundings with the detached, slightly ironic, slightly
amused disdain that Jack, in the short time he had known the man, had
already come to recognize and loathe.

"Is that our Mr. Wentworth?" Tucker asked.

"Indeed it is."

Tucker gave a low whistle. "Now, ain't he the full-rigged macaroni?"

Before Jack could give his entire agreement, another figure stepped
around from the far side of the carriage. He seemed to be Wentworth's
opposite in every way, save for his clothes, which were at least as fine, if not
so showy. This other fellow was a big man, and seemed to take up more
space than even that which his large frame occupied. He was older than

Wentworth, in his forties, Jack guessed. There was something embracing and open about him, a genuine smile on his face, a look that took in every-thing—the quay, the ship, the street—with interest and enthusiasm.

"Oh, damn my eyes," Jack said, remembering.

"What, sir?"

"This must be Mr. Frost. I put him completely out of my mind. He was to have a cabin aboard, by Oxnard's express orders."

"Oh, that," Tucker said. "Mr. Oxnard sent a man a few days ago, when you was ashore, and let us know. Forgive me, I quite forgot to tell you, but I had the carpenter knock out a bulkhead betwixt two cabins, made one big one, and Mr. Frost is to be there, larboard side, and Mr. Wentworth is in the cabin to starboard."

Relief like a warm bath engulfed Jack, and he said, "Oliver, you have saved my bacon. I shall grant you whatever you might wish. You have but to name it."

"I guess I would be grateful was my salary to be doubled."

"No, I fear that will never happen."

"Oh. Well, you could—"

"No, sorry, you get only the one request. Come, let us meet our guests." Jack led the way ashore, over the gangplank and the cobbles to where the two men were waiting for the last of their luggage to come down from the roof of the carriage.

"Ah, Captain Biddlecomb," Wentworth said in a tone of obligatory civil-ity, with a touch of resentment at having to be civil at all. "May I present to you Mr. Charles Frost?"

Biddlecomb extended a hand and Frost took it in both of his and gave a warm shake in reply. He smiled and said, "Captain Biddlecomb! An honor! My friend Oxnard was to alert you to my coming, I hope that was arranged?"

"Yes, sir, indeed," Jack said. "My chief mate, Mr. Tucker . . ." Jack paused and indicated Tucker, and Frost shook the mate's hand as well, "has been the soul of diligence in getting things in order for you."

"Not put you too far out of your way, I hope!" Frost cried, and Tucker assured him it was no bother.

"I was starting to fear you both would be left on the beach," Jack went on. "We are set to warp off the dock in an hour, and . . . well . . . time and tide and all that. Waits on no man."

"Indeed," Wentworth said. "Pray forgive me, I have no doubt the accommodations on the boat are charming in the extreme, but I thought it best to take rooms at the City until the time of our departure."

"I quite understand," Jack said. "We tarpaulins are under way with our labors quite early of a morning, and if you was aboard we would either have to wake you or have all hands go a'tiptoe, and neither would answer. I'm sure the City Tavern was more accommodating."

"It was dreadful," Wentworth said, looking about as if he was bored by the conversation. "It made me long for a monk's cell. Or my cabin aboard your boat, even."

"It must have been hellish, indeed," Jack said. Insulting Wentworth, he could see, was like stabbing a crystal ball; no matter how sharp the point or direct the blow it always seemed to glance off.

And then Frost stepped in, all smiles and *bonhomie* and an expansive cheerfulness that seemed to draw everything around into its vortex. "Mr. Wentworth, I fear these gentlemen have too much to do to be chatting with landlubbers the likes of us! We've a whole voyage to make acquaintances, and I for one am looking very much forward to it! Let us get to sea!" He put an arm around Jack's shoulders, and the other arm around Wentworth's and turned them both and directed them toward the ship. Neither one resisted or even questioned him. Such was the force of Charles Frost's personality.

Another twenty minutes were consumed with getting the dunnage aboard, which was mostly Frost's, though some of it Wentworth's, he apparently having not brought everything on his first visit to the ship. Burgess took charge of the boat crew and ran the warps, fore and aft, out to the warping posts, and Tucker sent men aloft to loosen off topsails.

Oxnard and Dailey made their appearance dockside to issue last-minute instructions, to see all was well, and to wish them safe voyage. Jack had made his farewells to his family the night before, a scene that was all but routine by now, but Ezra Rumstick brought his brother, Nathaniel, down to the quay and they bid their farewells, then stood back to watch the evolution of warping the ship out into the stream.

Frost and Wentworth, having seen their belongings stowed down, took a spot on the quarterdeck from which to watch their departure from the city. Jack ignored them, and ignored how shabby his working coat, shirt, and shoes looked in comparison to what those gentlemen wore. *Well, idle gentlemen will wear what they will*, he thought with a disdain he did not actually feel.

"Ready, fore and aft, sir," Tucker called from his position on the larboard cathead.

"Very well . . ." Jack ran his eyes over the loosened sails, the warps run out at oblique angles to the warping posts. If the wind had been hard against them, or the tide setting strong, they would have run the warps to the windlass, but in the present conditions, four men on each hawser, walking away with the line, would be enough to move them into the stream.

"Take up the breast and quarter fasts, ease away head and stern fasts, take up on the larboard warps, walk away with them, now!" Jack shouted and the lines run out to the dock were eased, those run out to the warping posts hauled upon, and the *Abigail* eased out into the Delaware River.

"'Vast, there, the *Abigail,* 'vast, you great buggering boatload of . . . buggering . . ." a voice came ringing down the road, loud, insistent, and slurred and all heads turned in surprise. Noah Maguire came staggering toward them, his walk more like a long, protracted fall, though the man stayed miraculously upright as he approached. His breeches were torn, his shirt stained with what was most likely vomit, one shoe was gone. "'Vast there, my darling Biddlecomb, you can't sail the barky without ol' Mr. Maguire aboard!" He stopped at the edge of the quay, swayed a bit, then collapsed in a heap.

Jack turned an angry eye toward the mate. "Mr. Tucker, I thought Maguire was secured in the fo'c'sle!"

"He was sleeping it off last I saw," Tucker protested. "He must have snuck ashore again."

"Oh, damn my eyes, what a bother," Jack said. They were too far from the dock for the gangplank to reach, and with the wind holding them off they would have to run the fasts to the windlass to haul the ship back alongside.

"I'll whip him aboard, sir," Tucker said, guilty over his failure at keeping Maguire contained. He stepped forward and shed his coat, then called up to Lacey in the maintop, who was standing by to overhaul buntlines, to lower down the whip. Lacey cast off the whip, a single line rove through a block at the yardarm, and lowered it to the deck. *Abigail* was still close enough to shore that the far end of her main yard overhung the dock, so Tucker made one end of the whip fast to a belaying pin and with the other end swung monkeylike over the gap between ship and land, coming down right beside Maguire's motionless form.

Tucker worked the end of the whip under Maguire's body, which was enough to rouse him, cursing and bellowing, as Tucker made the line secure under his arms and shouted "Haul away the teagueline!"

The men at the inboard end pulled with a will, jerking the spewing, cussing Irishman aloft. Tucker grabbed Maguire's belt, pulled him farther from the ship, then let him go with a shove. Maguire's thrashing and kicking disrupted the perfect arc of his swing across the open water, and once he had cleared the bulwark the men on the whip let go the line and the big Irishman came crashing down just outboard of the main hatch. They untied the whip and swung it back for Tucker as Maguire pulled himself to his feet.

Maguire's wild, drunken eyes searched the deck until they met Biddlecomb's. The men were having a jolly good laugh at Maguire's expense, and he was not too drunk to know it. He took a lurching step aft, his hands balled up into massive fists.

"Maguire!" Jack shouted. "Lay below and sleep it off, you great Irish son of a whore!"

"Ah, Biddlecomb, you little rum bastard, I'll do for you!" He charged aft, Jack expecting him to go down with each step, but he didn't. Maguire was accustomed to keeping his feet on a moving surface, be it a rolling ship's deck or a swaying tavern floor, and he made it clean aft without faltering. He paused a few feet in front of Biddlecomb, cocked his fist and swung, a potentially devastating blow. Maguire was likely the strongest man aboard, far stronger than Jack, to be sure, but he was an awkward hand at a fight, even when sober, relying not on any technique but rather on strength and an extraordinary ability to endure pain.

Jack tilted back as the fist came around. He felt the swish of air as it

passed, and with it the smell of Maguire's body and clothing, which almost
did what Maguire's fist could not, that is, knock him down. But instead,
Jack stepped up and delivered a hard uppercut to Maguire's stomach, which
doubled him over, then another to his face, which snapped him up again
and tossed him back, so he landed with an impact that could be felt underfoot. He lay on his back, groaned, and then was silent.

"Could we get some hands here to secure this drunken pile of horse shit
in the fo'c'sle?" Jack called. "And see he stays secured, this time?" As Maguire
was dragged unceremoniously across the deck, Jack called for the men to
once again ease away the starboard hawsers, take up the larboard, and the
Abigail resumed her slow, sideways motion out into the river.

"Forgive that nonsense, gentlemen." Jack turned to Wentworth and Frost
with his apology. "Maguire's a good hand at sea, but the very devil when
he gets ashore."

"Indeed," Wentworth said, and there was a glint of genuine amusement
in his eye. "But, forgive me, surely fisticuffs is . . . below the station of a ship's
master?"

Jack laughed at that. "This is not the Royal Navy, Mr. Wentworth, and
it ain't an East Indiaman. Just a reasonably honest American merchantman.
If a thing needs doing, and I am the best man to do it, then it is not below
my station."

"How very republican of you," Wentworth observed.

"Well, I say that was very manly done," Frost said, with his big smile.
"Will you punish the man? What will be his sentence?"

"Flog him, perhaps?" Wentworth asked. "A dozen lashes at the grating,
is that how you tarpaulins do it?"

"I repeat, sir, this is not the Royal Navy. I have no authority to flog anyone. I could dock his pay, I reckon, but I wouldn't bother. It would only make
him sullen and I'd get less work from him. Forward, there, haul away
smartly!" That last he shouted to the hands at the forward warp, then turned
back to his passengers. "Besides, punishing Maguire for being an ugly
drunkard would be akin to punishing a wolf for killing a deer. It's just who
he is, and punishment won't change it."

"My, what a liberal fellow you are!" Wentworth said.

"And how might you have handled such a situation?" Jack asked.

"I don't know," Wentworth said, and he seemed to genuinely consider the question. "I'm sure I don't know. Not fisticuffs. I suppose I would have shot him."

"Shot him? Indeed?" Jack asked. "Do you always stand ready to shoot a man?"

"One likes to be prepared," Wentworth said.

Before Jack could make reply he heard Tucker sing out, "That's well the larboard warps!" and he saw that it was time to shift the lines to the next posts, thus ending their discussion. The warps were moved farther out into the river and the *Abigail* hauled bodily up toward them, but they had not half cleared the distance when Jack saw that he could brace the topsail yards hard up on a starboard tack and clear the warping post with ease. He ordered the sails sheeted home and hands to the halyards and a moment later the topsail yards began their jerky travel up the well-greased masts.

The breeze found the canvas, made it ripple and snap, and then filled it and held it in that long, gentle, elegant curve that a well-set topsail makes, a shape so fine and perfect that to the sailor's eye there is that same allure that a shapely female form might spark. *Abigail* heeled a little to larboard. "Ease your helm a bit," Jack said to the man at the wheel, a new hand but one who seemed to know his business.

The bow swung a bit to the left, the bowsprit sweeping past the distant shore like an accusing finger. With a series of even jerks the fore staysail crawled up the stay and spread to the wind. The water made a gurgling sound down the length of the hull. They were under way and making way, a fair breeze and an ebbing tide, headed for the sea. They were free of the land. And Jack was in command. And Jack was supremely happy.

9

Rumstick wanted to speak to Bolingbroke before Jack sailed. Jeremiah Tillinghast was well aware of that. Rumstick had a notion that something was amiss, and he had a nose for such things. If something was acting, if forces unknown to Jack Biddlecomb were working in the shadows, then Rumstick wanted it known and fixed before Jack went to sea. It was Tillinghast's job to bring Bolingbroke to Rumstick before the *Abigail* cast off. He almost made it.

He found Bolingbroke in a nasty excuse for a tavern on the Southwark waterfront two days after the aborted duel, still telling the story of how Jack Biddlecomb had backed out of an affair of honor. "Seen me with pistol in hand," Bolingbroke concluded, "and the sorry sod turns and runs. Just runs. Might have pissed himself, I couldn't tell."

"Just shoot the bastard," one of Bolingbroke's companions suggested, "just shoot him right in the back as he run. That's how I would have played it." This fellow, Tillinghast could see, was a little unclear on the "honor" part of "an affair of honor."

Bolingbroke's fellows, these hangers-on, were the problem. Bolingbroke seemed to have money, more than Tillinghast would have thought him good for, and that meant he had friends aplenty eager to hear his tales as long as he kept the flowing bowl flowing. Tillinghast could certainly have rounded up enough companions of his own to soundly thrash the lot of them in a brawl; he did not think Bolingbroke's friends would be too eager to risk serious injury in his defense; but the business had to be conducted more subtly than that.

If Bolingbroke was part of some bigger affair, then taking him up in a messy way might send ripples of alarm through whatever faction was behind it. Bolingbroke had to be plucked like a tick from a dog's neck. Ideally, he would be cowering before Rumstick and eagerly spewing information before his absence was even noticed.

Tillinghast followed him back to the rooming house that served as his temporary residence, but there was no opportunity to grab him unobserved. He returned the next day to speak with the particularly unhelpful keeper of the rooming house, who, after a silver dollar, hard money, had rendered him a bit more loquacious, would say only that Bolingbroke had cleared out that morning, having taken a berth on a ship just then loading for Jamaica.

It was a matter of half a day's inquiry to find the ship that Bolingbroke had signed aboard, but that information did Tillinghast little good. If plucking him out of a tavern or a rooming house was a tricky business, then extracting him from amid a ship's company was all but impossible.

That left Tillinghast with the singular option of waiting to catch Bolingbroke by himself, which he did at last when Bolingbroke made a somewhat furtive exit from the ship. It was just shy of midnight, eight days after the meeting with Jack, when Bolingbroke came slinking down the gangplank. And Tillinghast, happily, was as he often was: lurking in the shadows, watching.

He followed Bolingbroke down Second Street to Southwark, then up South Street and a left onto Fourth, the neighborhoods becoming more notorious by degrees. They had gone another two blocks before Tillinghast guessed at his destination, and when Bolingbroke turned into a narrow alley strewn with broken barrels and half-stove packing crates and sundry garbage, Tillinghast saw he was right.

Three granite steps leading to a single door in the back of one of the brick row houses, a lantern burning feebly above it, marked the unlikely entrance to one of the city's more well-respected brothels. A knock, a few hushed words through a half-open door, and Bolingbroke was inside.

I'd reckon this establishment a bit rich for that son of a bitch's blood, Tillinghast thought. Tillinghast knew the place by reputation only, but the reputation had always been that it was no half-dime-a-throw sort of house.

The creature seems to have money to toss about . . .

Tillinghast found a dark place not too far from the door from where he could watch and still remain unseen in the shadows. From there he saw one man make his sheepish entrance into the building, and two leave. Neither was Bolingbroke, but one Tillinghast recognized as a member of Congress. *And these damnable Republican dogs say our tax dollars are not well spent,* Tillinghast thought as the man stumbled off into the dark.

It was not above forty-five minutes later that Bolingbroke appeared, stepping slowly, reluctantly from the door. He looked up and down the alley with a wariness that made Tillinghast wonder if he realized he was being watched. It was pointless to try and sneak up on him, so Tillinghast took the other tack, stumbling out of the shadows, weaving toward the brothel door, the least suspicious of approaches.

They passed one another just ten feet from the door, and as they did, Tillinghast straightened, turned, and said, calm and sober, "Bolingbroke? A word, if I may?"

Bolingbroke stopped and turned. His eyes were wide, his face more panic-stricken than Tillinghast would have thought was quite appropriate for the pacific tone he was taking with the man. He shook his head, took a step back toward the wall that formed the east side of the alley. "No, no . . ." he said. He turned, his back hunched, his hands resting on the edge of the remnants of a wooden crate.

"See here," Tillinghast began, but Bolingbroke straightened and turned in one motion, the crate in his hands, and smashed it into Tillinghast's shoulders and head. Tillinghast felt a laceration open up on his cheek as he stumbled back, a minor wound compared to the humiliation he felt at allowing this little puke to fool him in that way.

He heard Bolingbroke's feet taking off down the alley. He tossed off the broken slats of the crate and ran after him, wondering if he had any chance against the younger man in a flat-out footrace. But again Bolingbroke did what Tillinghast did not expect, and rather than head for the end of the alley he bounded back up the brothel steps and through the door, Tillinghast right behind.

Bolingbroke was halfway down the hall by the time the startled doorman, some great heap of muscle in an ill-fitting suit, had taken two steps in his direction. He succeeded in blurting out, "Here, now—" before Tilling-hast charged in behind him and rammed him in the small of the back. Till-inghast heard the man grunt and had a glimpse of him lifting from his feet and coming down on some silly little table against the wall, which he turned into kindling on his way to the floor. Then Tillinghast was past, his eyes on Bolingbroke's blue jacket, which had ducked into the sitting room on the side and was just then leaping a sofa between two startled young women and their even more startled uncles.

Tillinghast followed right behind, putting a foot on the sofa, launching himself over the back. He had a glimpse of young women lounging about the room, men of various ages with stocks undone and legs splayed in casual repose jerking upright in surprise, a cloud of smoke hanging low, the sharp smell of liquor and perfume. And then he was following Bolingbroke out the back door of the room. He had no more than a glimpse of Bolingbroke's white duck trousers as the man disappeared through another door at the far end of the hall.

What he might find on the other side of that door Tillinghast did not like to think on, but he thundered down the hall and swung himself through the door and found it was a set of stairs leading to an uninviting cellar be-low. He took the stairs two at a time, landed on the dirt floor at the bottom. There were lanterns hanging from low floor joists casting a weak light around the place. Tillinghast looked right and left. Bolingbroke was not to be seen. He stepped cautiously off to his left, around a pile of what he guessed was old furniture with a tarp draped over it. He could feel cool, fresh air wafting through the musty space. He came around the tarp-covered pile. A door hung open, and through it Tillinghast could see the steps that led up to the street level.

"Of course there's a bloody back way out of a place like this!" he said out loud, disgusted by the great chain of blunders he had committed that night. *Damn Bolingbroke*, he thought, *of course he would know where the back way is!*

He heard footfalls on the steps behind him, and had no doubt it was the doorman, having recovered his breath and coming for his pound of flesh. Tillinghast sighed and headed for the door in Bolingbroke's wake.

The tide carried the *Abigail* swiftly down the Delaware River, but the breeze pushed her more swiftly still, so rather than simply drifting down to the bay, they enjoyed the benefit of steerage. That made the passage less stressful than it might otherwise have been, because having control, however illusionary it might be, was always more comforting than simply being swept along. Jack kept the quarterdeck, conning the vessel as needed, though the way was clear and the shipping not too numerous and for the most part he was not much needed at all.

He looked out over the shoreline, the stands of trees and the rolling fields turning an early-spring green. Windmill Island, League Island, Mud Island with Fort Mifflin and the new construction there. He could not pass that way without thinking of the brutal weeks of fighting that his father and Uncle Ezra and the others, the sailors of the ridiculous Mosquito Fleet of 1777, had endured in their vain attempt to keep the mighty Royal Navy at bay. It was heroic, almost beyond description, night after night in their little ships taking on the massive men-of-war. In the end it had been for naught, though it was heroic nonetheless.

But that generation, those who had won independency, were not lacking for admirers and hagiographers, and Jack did not much feel the need to add his hosannas to the rest. His father knew how he felt. Or he should, in any event. That was enough.

"A propitious start to the voyage, Captain, wouldn't you say?" Charles Frost called, emerging from the after scuttle onto the quarterdeck and pulling Jack from his reverie.

"All's well that begins well," Jack said. "No, forgive me, that's not how it goes at all. In any event, yes, a fine start, and we'll carry this tide for the next five or six hours, I should think. Your quarters, you find them accommodating?"

"Goodness, yes!" Frost said with enthusiasm. "The good Mr. Tucker has seen to doubling the space. I've made many a sea voyage, Captain, and I can tell you I have never had so commodious a cabin in so small a vessel. Beg your pardon, of course, I mean no disrespect to your command, sir."

"Nor did I take it as such," Jack assured him. "*Abigail* is of no great size, I'll warrant, but she's a fine sea boat."

"She is that," Frost said, and then, in a different tone, went on. "Mr. Wentworth, I'm afraid, was a bit put out that my cabin was rendered so spacious and his was not."

"Well, we can only make so many changes, you know. Who knows how many cabins we shall need for the voyage back?" Jack, of course, had had nothing to do with altering Frost's accommodations, though he was sorry he had not thought of it first, so he could at least give himself credit for Wentworth's discomfort.

As Jack had predicted, they did carry the tide for another five hours, but as the ebbing current began to grow weak with age they found the wind began to fail as well. Jack could see that they would soon be swept back up the bay just as they had been swept down, so he worked the ship over to Deep Water Point on the western shore and came to anchor with the best bower in four fathoms of water.

He felt keenly an obligation to invite Frost and Wentworth to the cabin for dinner, at least once at the start of the voyage. It was one of those duties owed by a ship's master to his passengers when the passengers were of the better sort. It was also true that Frost was a particular friend of Oxnard's, so it would do Jack no harm to get in his good graces. On the other hand, he felt oppressed by the many things still to be done, and did not feel he had the hours to devote to being a proper host.

What's more, it seemed a bit silly, dinner at sea, when they were in fact at anchor within ten leagues of where they had started, at a place where a man with a good arm might actually throw a biscuit onto the shore. And truly he did not really want to dine with them and play the smiling, gracious host, not for Wentworth's pleasure, in particular, so he made his excuses and bought himself an extra day.

The sun rose the following morning on a hazy sky and a wind fair for clearing Cape Henlopen, so they weighed even before the turn of the tide. With topsails, topgallants, and the foresail set they were able to stem the current with ease, and when at last the tide began to ebb they found themselves within a mile of the Capes. From there it was a matter of less than an hour's time before the waters emptying from the Delaware Bay swept them the balance of the way to sea, with Cape May passing down their larboard side, and, much nearer still, Cape Henlopen to starboard.

An hour after clearing the Capes, Jack found himself standing by the middle gun on the weather side, one foot on the gun carriage, his admittedly new favorite spot from which to look over the set of the sails. He was wrestling with a moral dilemma, but it was not much of a contest, since the easy way out, which he would have preferred, stood on very shaky legs. He gave a barely audible sigh, spun around, and approached Frost and Wentworth, who were standing by the leeward quarter and watching the shoreline disappear in their wake.

"Gentlemen," he said, "I would be honored if you would dine with me today in the cabin, four bells in the afternoon watch? Two o'clock," he added.

"Delighted, Captain Biddlecomb, delighted!" Frost said. "Wentworth, what say you?"

Wentworth gave a small nod of his head in Jack's direction. "I should be honored, Captain," he said. "But let me check my calendar. Oh, no, it appears I am quite free these next six weeks or more."

"Very well, then," Jack said, annoyed by Wentworth's tone of *noblesse oblige*, such condescension being the master's prerogative, not his passengers', but he said only, "It will be my pleasure to see you at table."

It would have been a nightmare, in fact, hosting the gentlemen passengers in the cabin if Jack had been left to his own devices. He had put no thought into cabin stores and would have contented himself with the same salt pork and salt beef and dried peas and ship's biscuits and such that were served out in the forecastle.

Had he considered the possibility of having to entertain, he would have thought vaguely that something could be done to dress up the seamen's rations into a meal acceptable to a more discerning palate, and would have thought no more about it. That is, until confronted with the horrible reality that nothing could be done to render a seaman's fare edible to any but a seaman.

Such a transubstantiation certainly could not have been performed by the ship's cook, a former seaman of indeterminate but advanced age named Israel Walcott, a man whose chief qualifications for the job of cook were that he was willing to do it, he could boil water, he had been taught how to make a plum duff, and he was too lame to do anything else.

Nor would his steward have been of any help, a young man named Barnabus Simon foisted on Jack by Robert Oxnard for reasons Jack did not quite understand, but which had nothing to do with Jack's convenience or comfort. In their short time together Jack had formed the impression that Simon was lazy, incompetent, ignorant of his duties, sullen, and dishonest. Once they had cleared land and the inevitable dinner with the passengers was behind him, Jack was determined to send him packing to the forecastle.

It was Jack's mother, Virginia Biddlecomb, who had seen to it that dinner would not be an utter humiliation. Unbidden, she had sent aboard cabin stores consisting of cured and fresh beef, hams, vegetables, chickens in portable coops, a goodly supply of wine, brandy, and port, cheeses of various descriptions, real bread as opposed to ship's biscuit, along with well-fruited spice breads, dried fruit, butter, jam, and even some dishes prepared by Maurice the day before sailing and packed to travel.

Each of those dishes was made in quantities to feed upward of half a dozen men, as if Virginia had anticipated this very situation, which, in fact, she had. She had never asked for Jack's input or permission, because she knew he would have had nothing of value to add, would have dismissed the very notion and then deeply regretted it later.

At noon, after Jack had fixed their position, triangulating off the Capes, he commenced to badgering Simon to prepare the meal and set the cabin in order to receive guests. One of Maurice's dinners, an asparagus soup and rabbit fricassee, was heated in the galley on deck, and since Simon was not to be trusted with such a task it was done under the watchful eye of Lucas Harwar, whom Jack had shipped as second mate.

And so, after considerable effort and forethought by a number of people, none of them Jack Biddlecomb, a respectable meal was laid by the time a seaman on deck rang out four bells, the last note just dying away when Frost knocked on the cabin door.

"Come, come, welcome," Jack said with all the graciousness he could muster as he led his guests around the narrow confines of the cabin and seated them at the table. "Simon! Some wine, here, Simon!" he called and soon the steward appeared with a bottle, from which he filled each glass with all the grace of a gin-house keeper filling glasses for his drunk-for-a-penny customers.

Despite the want of good service, dinner passed tolerably well, Frost doing more than his part to uphold the conversation and keep it on course, straight and true. Wentworth dipped heavily into the wine, and in truth Jack had the impression he had been doing so even before arriving for dinner, making free with his own private stores, which rendered the generally taciturn young man more taciturn still. But since he was unlikely to have anything to say that Jack cared to hear, it was not a problem.

"So, pray, what brings you gentlemen to Barbados?" Jack asked as Frost served out the last of the rabbit. "Mr. Oxnard never indicated you would be returning in this ship, so I assume you are bound for an extended stay?"

Wentworth made a sort of noncommittal face and poured the remains of the wine into his glass. Frost looked up from his task. "Business, this and that. Some work for the government. I have any number of friends in the administration. I help out where I can, on an informal basis, you know. But still, the less said . . ."

"Oh, of course," Jack said, embarrassed to have appeared to be prying. Then Simon stepped up and took the empty serving dish, sloshing juice on the tablecloth, and Jack was for once happy for the distraction.

The meal had been cleared, only a single plate and one wineglass dropped and broken, cheese and port were laid out, and cigars fired up when Frost asked, "What of your man, Captain, the big Irish fellow? Maguire? Is he up and about?"

"Oh, certainly, a good night's sleep on a soft deck and he's right as rain. I believe he's standing his trick at the helm as we speak," Jack said. The skylight was partially open and Jack had been keeping tabs on what was taking place topside, sometimes without even realizing he was doing so.

"No punishment?" Frost asked. "No consequences for his actions?"

Jack shrugged and took a puff of his cigar. "No," he said. "It would be pointless, as I said at the time. If he were a poor seaman I would leave him on the beach, but since he's a most excellent hand once he's beyond the reach of liquor, I am willing to forgive his foolishness."

"Foolishness, indeed?" Wentworth asked. "And what if he had struck you? What if his fist had connected, had knocked you to the floor in front of your men?"

"I don't know," Jack said, and he genuinely did not, as he had never thought on that. "It's never happened. A man must be pretty well in his cups to swing at a ship's master in that way, and thus their punches are generally pretty easy to avoid."

Wentworth made a grunting sound and took another puff on his cigar, then removed it from his lips and regarded it. "It's all so wonderfully in keeping with this spirit of republicanism that seems to run amuck these days," he said.

"Now, Mr. Wentworth," said Frost, and Jack could hear just a hint of alarm as the conversation wandered into the shoals of politics, "Captain Biddlecomb has his ways, you know, which come from being at sea many a year."

"No, truly," Wentworth said, looking up from his cigar. "Was it not the worthy Sir Francis Drake who said, 'I must have the gentleman to haul with the mariner, and the mariner with the gentleman'? Such a good republican spirit that reigns here at sea."

"Don't believe it, sir," said Jack. "On a small ship such as this, the master must wade in more than aboard some grander vessel, but don't mistake this for any sort of democracy. When we are at sea, this is as great a tyranny as you will find in the Christian world, and I am the absolute tyrant."

"Ha! A benevolent monarch, I have no doubt!" Frost said.

"Well I am pleased to hear it," Wentworth said dryly. "With all these French notions spreading like a pox across the country, one never knows. Hah! French pox, there it is." He waved Simon over, who was lurking by the forward bulkhead, and signaled for his glass to be refilled.

"A ship cannot be run in that manner, Mr. Wentworth," Jack said. "There needs a chain of command that is not questioned."

"Nor can a country be run in that manner," Wentworth replied, after taking a healthy sip of the port. "There is a class of men who are born to lead, and a class who are born to follow. And yet here we are, with the middling sort snatching at the reins of power, every self-important shopkeeper, every blade who farms a few pathetic acres thinking himself worthy to be a senator."

"Now, sir," said Frost, "surely the War for Independency was not fought so we might replace one aristocracy for another?"

Wentworth shifted his gaze toward Frost with a look that Jack thought was part suspicion and part—a large part—intoxication. "The War for Independency? Made officers of men quite unworthy of the rank, and now those officers would put themselves over the rest of us. I wish to God they had all gone back to the plow, as Washington did. Most I wish would have stayed there. That rascal Jefferson would do well to keep to his farm, spouting off about the injustice of slavery as his darkies tend the fields."

Jack, like his father, was no fan of Jefferson, and when he thought on it, which was not often, he tended to lean toward the Federalist camp, with its belief in the strength of the new federal government and a strong navy. So, apparently, did Wentworth. Where Frost stood, Jack could not tell. He seemed most concerned that a battle between political factions not break out in the great cabin.

Having spent half his life on shipboard, Jack understood hierarchy as mankind's central organizing principle. But a growing number of Americans loathed the Federalists, and suspected them of trying to create a British-style aristocracy in America. Jack and Wentworth were ostensibly on the same side of this political divide, but listening to Wentworth reminded Jack of why it was so easy to despise the Federalist faction. Even he was ready to take offense.

"Men unworthy of the rank of officer?" Jack said. "Would you put my father in that company?"

"Your father?" Wentworth said. "You have a father? You didn't seem the type."

"You don't know who my father is?"

"No, should I?" Wentworth asked. "I believe you said you were from Rhode Island."

"His father—" Frost began but Jack cut him off.

"He was an officer in the war. Naval officer. One of your middling sorts, elevated well beyond his natural station."

Wentworth lifted his glass. "I congratulate you and your family then, sir, and I am delighted to find you so elevated. *Liberté, Égalité,* and all that."

"Pray, sir," Frost said to Jack with a tone that suggested a desire to change the subject, "but why do you look at the barometer so? Forgive me, but I could not fail to notice you stealing glances in its direction. I would be sorry if we were such dull company as to make it so fascinating. I dare say, if you were looking at the clock the same way I should be worried."

Jack smiled. He was not aware that he had been glancing at the barometer, any more than he was aware of monitoring the goings-on on deck. It was a lovely mahogany instrument crafted by the renowned Jesse Ramsden of London, its long cylindrical body gimbal-mounted and swaying with the roll of the ship. It had been a present from his father, given to him just a few days before he sailed. Its polished beauty alone might have been enough to attract his attention, but it was in fact the fall of the glass, not the aesthetic quality of the instrument, that had gained his notice.

"Forgive me," Jack said. "The conversation has been delightful in the extreme, but there is nothing that can command a shipmaster's undivided attention, save for his ship. And I'm afraid my eye has been drawn to the steady fall of the glass this hour or more."

"Falling quickly, is it?" Wentworth asked. "I once knew what that meant. 'When the glass goes high . . .' No. What is it you tarpaulins say, now?"

" 'When the glass goes high, let your sails fly, when the glass goes low, you're in for a blow.' I believe that is the bit of doggerel you are searching for."

"Ah, yes!" Wentworth said. "What poetic blades you are! And the glass goes low, you say? Is it falling fast?"

"The glass is indeed getting lower," Jack confirmed, "but not at any great rate, which is more worrisome. You see, when the glass falls quickly, it means you will see a violent storm, but one that will soon pass by. But when it falls slow, as it is doing now, it means we may be in for a nasty time of it, a storm of some duration."

"Well, then, we must see all is secured in our cabins, what, Mr. Wentworth?" Frost said.

"I shouldn't think that will be much of a problem for me. I didn't find room for above half a dozen items in my closet. My cabin, I mean. A long and nasty storm, you say, Captain?"

"It seems likely. But do not fear, Mr. Wentworth, *Abigail* is a sound ship."

At that Wentworth smiled, as genuine a smile as Biddlecomb had ever seen on the man. "Oh, I am not afraid, sir," he assured Jack. "I think I would take the thrill of a near drowning over the slow death of a monotonous ocean voyage. Perhaps even an actual drowning would be preferable." He signaled for Simon to refill his glass, and Jack wondered that anyone could be so bored after being under way for just a bit more than two days. If Wentworth did not find the foul weather sufficiently thrilling, would he throw himself overboard before they even raised Barbados? Jack knew that he could do no more than hope.

10

Dinner over, William Wentworth made his awkward way around the table in the ridiculously small, cramped great cabin, thanking Biddlecomb with all the enthusiasm he could muster for that tedious affair, which was not much.

He wondered vaguely where the dinner had come from. A rabbit fricassee and asparagus soup that was really quite good, certainly beyond the abilities of anyone he had observed aboard that wretched boat. Well beyond the abilities of those who could only facetiously be called the cook and steward. If Wentworth had been able to bring his own wine, and dine alone, he might have actually enjoyed it.

Having spent an hour and a half in the cabin, nearly choking on the smoke produced by Biddlecomb's noxious seagoing cigars, he felt the need for a turn on deck and some fresh air before he could return to the cramped but blessed privacy of his cell. He made his way down the alleyway onto which the great cabin opened, the walls of which formed the inboard side of his and Frost's cabins, then up the companionway and through the hatch to the weather deck.

He was not steady on his feet, and moved from handhold to handhold to avoid taking an ignominious tumble. He had consumed quite a bit of wine, a bottle cumulatively during dinner and the better part of a bottle in his cabin beforehand, fortifying himself for that ordeal. But still he had to guess that this was not all the doing of the alcohol, that surely the motion of the ship had changed, and not for the better.

When he emerged on deck he found that the milky white sky of the morning hours had been replaced with something altogether more threat-ening. The sun was lost behind a thick cover of clouds, a variegated blan-ket that was gray in places and in others closer to black. The sea was gray as well, a dull pewter stretching off in every direction, the mounting chop crested with whitecaps that roiled and flashed clear to the horizon. When Wentworth had last been on deck the Capes were just astern of them, but now land was nowhere to be seen. It was a bit unsettling.

Having been born and raised in Boston, to a father who owned a fleet of merchantmen, William was familiar with shipping, or at least that part that involved the ship being tied to the dock and discharging a cargo. He had never actually been to sea, save for a few short coasting voyages. Never be-yond the sight of land. Other than knowing what ships looked like and a smattering of nomenclature (which he didn't really care to know, since a familiarity with words like "yardarm" and "windlass" had such a trades-man quality about it) he knew nothing of the ways of the sea. That put him at a terrific disadvantage on shipboard, and William Wentworth did not generally enter into situations in which he was at a disadvantage.

Despite his studied indifference to the ways of the sea, however, he found himself irresistibly curious about the goings-on on deck. The ship was tilted to one side, and the high side, the windward side, what the tarpau-lins called the "weather side," seemed to offer a better vantage, so he walked up to that side and grabbed on to a thick black rope, ignoring the tar that would invariably get on his hand, and looked aloft.

There were two men near the top of the foremast and two near the top of the mainmast and on each the yardarms were all askew, as if something had gone very wrong with them.

No, not the yardarms, that's not the word . . . Wentworth thought. He had been corrected once in that regard. These were the yards. The yardarms were a part of the yards, the very ends, he seemed to recall. Those were the topgallant yards on which they were working.

The *Abigail* bucked and plunged and rolled in the mounting seas and the tall masts described wild circles against the gray sky but the men aloft seemed to work as if they were standing on the ground. Wentworth had seen countless men working aloft but always at anchor, or tied to a wharf.

It had not occurred to him how very much more difficult it would be to do that work when the ship was rolling so. If he had thought about it he would have realized that such was obviously the case, but he had never thought about it.

The men aloft were moving fast. The yards rose and tilted until they were nearly vertical, and then together, like a choreographed dance, they were lowered away toward the deck. The main topgallant yard reached the deck first, by a matter of seconds, and a few of the tarpaulins grabbed it in their arms and eased it down the rest of the way. They let out a cheer as they did, and William realized they had been engaged in some sort of competition, foremast against mainmast, to see which could get their yard down to the deck the quickest.

Why should they go to all this effort to take the yards down, he wondered, *when one assumes they will just have to put them back up again?*

As the fresh air and the bracing wind and the occasional shower of spray cleared his head he realized that there was considerably more activity on deck and in the rigging than he had initially thought. Men were aloft with great tendrils of fuzzy rope, like enormous caterpillars, and they seemed to be wrapping them around various thicker ropes. Others were hovering around the anchors forward, though what they might be doing, William could not imagine. *Surely the water is too deep for their use*, he thought.

He looked aft. Captain Biddlecomb was there, conferring with the mate, a man named Tucker, he recalled. Then Tucker nodded his head and stepped off forward, leaving Biddlecomb alone by the helm, hands clasped behind his back, eyes aloft. He had none of the supercilious look of a self-important mechanic that William had come to associate with Biddlecomb. The fellow styled himself captain though he was certainly younger even than Wentworth's two and twenty years. He was the sort who might ape the conventions of a formal dinner with no real understanding of how such a thing was to be executed. Now, that facile look, that pretentious quality, was gone, and in its place was a look of command, and William found it intriguing.

Despite himself he let go of the rope and stumbled his way aft. The cannons, he noticed, had been quite thoroughly lashed in place. Whereas before they had simply been run out with the block and tackle attached to their sides hauled taut and made fast, now the breechings were also hauled taut and seized, and various other ropes wrapped about and secured to the eyebolts in the bulwark.

Better those should stay where they are, he thought, touching his hand to the cold, wet iron of one of the barrels as he passed. Biddlecomb pulled his eyes from the rigging for a mere second as Wentworth approached, enough to give a nod of the head and the greeting, "Mr. Wentworth," before looking aloft again.

"So, Captain, pray, is this your storm?" Wentworth asked, speaking loud over the wind.

Biddlecomb gave him a curious look, a hint of smile playing on his lips. "This? The storm? No, sir, nothing of the kind. If a storm were one's wedding night, this would be but the first kiss."

"Indeed," Wentworth said, refusing to give Biddlecomb the satisfaction of appearing shocked at so bawdy a metaphor. He had been a perfect ass to Biddlecomb, of course, which he did not necessarily regret. He considered himself under no obligation to be kind to those below his station, and only for reasons of duty, self-interest, and social obligation was he polite to those few at or above his station. But such a policy had its inconveniences, like now, when he was looking for answers and found Biddlecomb disinclined to converse with him.

"But tell me," Wentworth persisted, "why are those men taking the yards down? Don't you need them up to safely navigate the storm?"

Biddlecomb again turned his eyes to Wentworth. "Have you never been to sea, Mr. Wentworth?" he asked.

"No, indeed, I have not, not beyond sight of land at any rate," Wentworth said, surprising himself with his candor even as the words were leaving his lips. This curiosity about something as base as the seaman's trade was unseemly, but he was not able to help himself, like a glutton at table.

"Well, here's how the matter lies," Biddlecomb said, his patronizing tone so subtle it might have been missed if Wentworth had not been looking out so keenly for it. "A ship is a carefully balanced thing, the weight of her top-hamper, that is, her masts, rigging, sails, and such, the pressure of the wind on her sails, acting against the weight of her hull. In moderate weather, that balance is just right with the t'gallant gear in place, but as the wind builds we must strike it all to deck or we will be . . . one might say top-heavy, for want of a better term."

Wentworth followed Biddlecomb's eyes aloft and saw that now the men on the fore and main were lowering those upper masts down as well. "And the next level of masts, will those also be taken down?"

"Tops'l yards and topmasts? No, indeed. The tops'ls are our most important sails, we shall keep those for as long as we are able, though you can see they're reefed as deep as can be. Again, the balance is the critical thing here. If we reduce the weight aloft too greatly, well, then, rather than enjoy a nice, slow roll, the ship will roll very quickly. In that case she might roll so quick she'll roll the masts right out of her."

"I see . . ." said William, and though he had in fact only understood a fraction of what Biddlecomb said, he was not about to ask for clarification.

"But never you fear, Mr. Wentworth," Biddlecomb continued, "we jolly tars have it well in hand, and there is little chance that the gentleman will have to haul with the mariner."

With that not so subtle dismissal, and not wishing to expose himself to the possibility of insult he could not ignore, William Wentworth nodded his thanks for the information and resumed his place at the weather side. The ship seemed abnormally crowded, and he realized that rather than allow half the crew to loiter in the forecastle as was the usual custom, Biddlecomb must have ordered all the hands to work on the deck. This seemed to William a reasonable enough arrangement and he wondered that it was not more generally the case.

After some time of watching the activity aloft and alow, William found that the motion of the ship, the heavy meal, and the wine were all conspiring to make him drowsy, so he quit the deck and made his way back to his cabin. The tiny space galled him, and he was quite certain that Biddlecomb had purposely doubled the size of Frost's cabin, and not his, for just that reason. He could not, of course, complain about it, as that would make him sound too petulant by half, so he resolved to endure it until such time as he could exact some revenge.

In this case, however, he was too tired to be much upset with his sleeping arrangement, so he flopped down in his coffinlike bed and closed his eyes and soon he was quite dead to the world.

He woke some time later to a heavy thud and a trembling that jarred him awake, as if God himself had rapped on the outside of the hull. He lay quiet, eyes open, though he could see nothing, the darkness having set in. He thought at first there was something wrong with his head, or perhaps the effect of the liquor had somehow multiplied as he slept, because everything seemed to be moving, rising up and swooping down and tossing side to side. He could hear creaking such as he had not noticed earlier in the voyage and again and again the smacking on the hull, sounding for all the world as if something had collided with the ship.

As William shook off sleep he realized that the storm had intensified, and what he was feeling and hearing was the ship working in the mounting seas and wind. He braced himself against the sides of his bed and in doing so realized that the criblike nature of the thing, which he had considered absurd at first glance, actually made some sense.

This is absolute madness, he thought. From the sound of it, it seemed impossible that the ship was not being torn apart by the seas. He was not afraid, of course. William Wentworth was genuinely a stranger to fear. His wealth and standing were such that he had always been sheltered from the common anxieties of life, never wanting for the basics, or the luxuries, either. He was naturally strong and athletic, which had always given him a dominance in any sort of physical endeavor. He was an expert with pistol and sword, and so those few times when his behavior had been so inexcusable as to result in an affair of honor, concern over the outcome had never given him pause. Nor had he ever been scratched by blade or ball.

And so, lying in his dark cell, listening to the fearsome pounding that the cockleshell of a ship was receiving, holding on with hands and feet to keep from being tossed to the floor, he felt a thrill, a firing of all his nerves that he rarely experienced in the well-ordered, luxurious, tailored life of breeding that was the birthright of any Wentworth of the Boston Wentworths. He would not call it fear, but it was a near relative of that emotion. And he liked it.

Moving carefully with the roll of the ship, he swung his legs over the edge of the bed, held himself in place as the ship rolled to starboard, then let the momentum of the roll to larboard pitch him out. He found a handhold on the cabin bulkhead and steadied himself, let his legs get the feel for the motion of the ship.

Sea legs, that's what the tarpaulins call it, he thought. *I must get my sea legs.*

The Wentworths' family butler, who had packed William's numerous trunks, had had the good sense to include an oilskin jacket, and William had had the good sense to take it from the trunk before it and the rest were stowed below. He felt along the cabin wall until his hand fell on the slick surface of the garment. He lifted it off the hook, felt for the cabin door, and stepped out into the alleyway.

It was not so dark there. A lantern hung at the far end, where the alley opened onto the main deck, a wildly swinging tin lantern, a metal cylinder perforated with holes that gave off the feeblest of light, but after the blackness of the cabin it seemed quite bright indeed.

William stopped below the lantern and sorted out his oilskin and shrugged it on, no easy task with the motion of the ship threatening to toss him to the deck, and forcing him to grab for a handhold every few seconds. Once the coat was on and buttoned he staggered forward, grabbing at the ladder that led up through the scuttle just as the *Abigail* took a sickening roll to leeward.

He steadied himself and looked up, and for his effort received a great bucketful of water in the face, such a cascade down the scuttle that he might have thought someone had flung it on him purposely, except that it was a greater deluge than any one bucket could hold. He spit and shook his head and thought how comic that must have appeared, his taking that water in the face, and how very many people would have delighted to see him so incommoded, Jack Biddlecomb foremost among them.

Wentworth wiped his eyes, grabbed hold of either side of the ladder, and climbed slowly up through the small open scuttle and onto the weather deck. And there he found, to his genuine astonishment, that what he had thought was a wild scene down below was cigars and brandy in the parlor compared to the world topside.

11

The air was filled with water, driving sideways, and Wentworth would have been soaked instantly if he had not been soaked already. He blinked and squinted. He could not tell if it was rain or spray or both. What rigging he could see was either bar taut or whipping wildly in the wind. The ship took a hard roll to leeward and William staggered and felt himself going down. He flung out his arms, flailing for support. His hands fell on a rope, waist high and hove so tight that were it not for the coarse feel of the fibers he might have mistaken it for an iron rail.

Now that's damned convenient, he thought as he clung to the rope, holding himself upright on the slick deck as the ship rose and plunged. He could not recall the rope's being there before. He wondered what purpose it served.

Out of the dark a shape materialized, a man moving aft, his hand on the rope William gripped. A big man. The Irishman Biddlecomb had knocked senseless, he realized.

"Beg pardon, sir," the man said, loud, his voice a deep growl, the words respectful but the tone pure irritation. He stepped around William and continued aft. William realized then that the rope was there for just the thing he was using it for, as a handhold for moving fore and aft.

Well, I guess even the tarpaulins don't have their sea legs about them all the time, he thought, and the thought made him feel a bit better about his own failures in that regard, the stumbling and the water in the face.

After even the feeble light of the hold, it took his eyes a moment to adjust to the alien world on deck, but slowly it all seemed to resolve itself out of the dark, worse even than he had thought. The great, black, curling waves came rolling up out of the night, rolling up under the *Abigail*'s starboard bow, lifting the ship up, up, as if she might be tossed aside, then moving under her and sending her bow down in a sickening, twisting motion into the trough.

And then the blunt, unyielding bow would strike the sea, the ship and ocean slamming into one another like some ancient contestants for this patch of watery territory. The ship would shudder to the deepest places of her oak-and-yellow-pine being, and then shoulder the sea aside, sending a great spray of salt water high in the air and dipping the rail under until the seas ran inches deep down the deck, breaking around the legs of the men working there, breaking against the great guns fixed by their lashings, like surf against outcroppings of rock on some jagged coast.

Wentworth stared. He could not pull his eyes away. The sight was magnificent, frightening and awe-inspiring, wonderful and sickening all at once. He had never seen anything like it, or felt the wild surge of power the great seas bore on their backs. He smiled, got a mouthful of water, half rain, half spray, and spit it out on the deck, aware that that was probably the first time he had ever spit in public, even if no one was paying attention.

He turned and looked aft. There was the faintest of lights there, and William guessed that the fellow steering the ship needed illumination of some sort by which to see the compass. Two fellows, actually, the wheel was double-manned now. He could just make out the shape of Jack Biddlecomb, perhaps twenty-five feet away, standing pretty much where he had been standing when William had last been on deck.

Has he left that spot at all? William thought. Jack was now wearing an oilskin coat and a hat, and William wondered if he had gone below stairs to fetch them or if he had that horrible little weasel of a steward bring them on deck. He could make out something odd about the rigging on the mizzenmast, but it took a minute of squinting and blinking before he realized that they had tied a cloth of some description to the heavier ropes, and that must be providing some degree of shelter to Biddlecomb and the helmsmen.

For the second time that day Wentworth's curiosity overwhelmed his natural inclination to avoid the likes of Biddlecomb, or to give Biddlecomb the satisfaction of showing himself to be ignorant on any subject. Hands on the taut rope, he made his way aft, pausing as the ship rolled hard to windward, threatening to pull his grip free, then tumbling along as the ship plunged down again.

It took what seemed an inordinately long time to cover the twenty-five feet back to the helm, but he was rewarded with a look of surprise on Biddlecomb's face when the captain realized who it was moving aft. Wentworth stepped into the lee of the canvas lashed to the rigging and suddenly the noise and the flying water diminished by half.

"Captain!" Wentworth shouted. "It would appear you have your storm now!"

"A damp evening, Mr. Wentworth, to be sure!" Biddlecomb shouted back.

"Have you . . ." Wentworth began, paused to spit out a mouthful of water, began again. "Have you ever seen a storm so fierce as this?" he shouted.

Once again Biddlecomb gave him that curious look, the look of vague amusement, and Wentworth felt himself flush with irritation and annoyance for allowing Biddlecomb the upper hand. "We're still carrying fore and main tops'ls!" Biddlecomb shouted, as if that was some sort of an explanation. "This is far from what I would call a terrific storm. But if it is any comfort to you, it promises to get tolerably worse in the next few hours. We shall be handing the fore tops'l directly."

"Handing?" Wentworth shouted.

"Furling! Tying it up to the yard!"

Wentworth looked up, toward the foremast, but the sail was lost in the night. He could see someone coming aft along the lifeline and he thought it to be Mr. Tucker, the mate. Wentworth staggered as the *Abigail* took a particularly ugly roll, released the lifeline, and leapt for the weather shrouds, taking a firm grip on the heavy, tarred, unyielding rope as Tucker came aft. Biddlecomb was shouting to Tucker, though no more than a few feet separated the men, and Wentworth heard him say, "Let's hand the fore tops'l, Mr. Tucker, and we'll see how long she'll bear that forc's'l!"

"Hand the fore tops'l, aye, sir!" Tucker shouted and headed back the way he had come.

It was clear to Wentworth even from the few words they had thus far exchanged that Biddlecomb was in no mood for conversation, which Wentworth could understand, even if he didn't care. "Captain!" he shouted.

"Surely you don't mean the men will climb up there?" He pointed in the general direction of the fore topmast.

"I do. I know of no other way to hand a sail."

"That's madness!" Wentworth shouted. He had never really thought about what the tarpaulins would do in a truly biblical storm, because he never put much thought into what the lower sort did, as long as they continued to do it. Had he thought about it he would have guessed they would all huddle below and drink themselves to insensibility until either the storm passed or they all drowned. But apparently not.

"Will you go up there?" Wentworth shouted.

"That is no longer my place, Mr. Wentworth!" Biddlecomb replied, also shouting above the shriek of the wind, awkward conditions for discourse. "I am one of your middling sort who now thinks himself a gentleman, and as such I will not haul with the mariner!"

Wentworth opened his mouth to protest but Biddlecomb cut him off. "See here, Wentworth, I have no time for this! It would be better was you to go below, but if you will not, pray understand that if you're hurt, at best we can stuff you down the hatch. If you go overboard we can do nothing at all. Now, please forgive my discourtesy!" With that he turned and worked his way a few feet aft to where the helmsmen wrestled with the wheel and, leaning close to the binnacle, studied the set of the compass.

As a matter of reflex Wentworth ran those words over in his mind to determine if they called for his demanding satisfaction. They were dismissive, to be sure, but were they insulting? And if they were, could Wentworth forgive them, based on the fact that Biddlecomb's ship was clearly falling apart around him, and he was no doubt extremely frightened. Generally, Wentworth did not feel extenuating circumstances should excuse another's behavior.

The ship rolled again, a deep, stomach-turning, twisting roll that set the masts to swaying and the rigging slatting and banging, and Wentworth recalled that Biddlecomb had claimed the men would actually be induced to climb up into the rigging and *hand* the fore topsail, those drunken, miserable insubordinate malingerers risking their necks to save a bit of Oxnard's canvas. Wentworth thought it very unlikely.

He waited until the ship hit the trough and the seas cascaded down the deck, and as she rolled back, as she came onto an even keel for a second or two, ready to crest the next roller, Wentworth launched himself from the mizzen shrouds and grabbed up the lifeline and staggered forward. When the *Abigail*'s men refused to obey orders and knocked Tucker on the head and retreated below, Wentworth wanted the satisfaction of seeing it all.

He moved forward. The storm, he realized, was indeed growing worse. The note that the wind made as it tore through the rigging was pitched higher, the motion of the ship more pronounced. As the next roller came up under her and her bow rose to meet it, it hung there for a long and uncertain moment, as if ship and sea were pausing to decide if this should be an end to it. And then the bow plunged down again, the angle more pronounced, the impact with the sea making the vessel shudder in a way she had not done before.

Once again the seas came over the bow, not inches deep this time but feet deep, a great Red Sea on the charioteers arrayed around the deck, and even Wentworth, standing amidships, found himself buried up to his knees. His shoes, stockings, and breeches were soaked through, and though his oilskin had been doing a noble job of keeping the water at bay, it, too, was losing the battle, the cold rain and spray working its way down his collar, soaking his coat, waistcoat, and shirt.

The foremast hands were standing in clusters, a cluster to larboard, a cluster to starboard, a group at the base of the mast. The water rushed along the deck and the men at the larboard rail were waist deep in it as the new bulwarks held the boarding seas in like a cistern before they could gush through the open gunports. The men were hauling on the rigging, pulling, swaying, staggering from the impact of the water. Wentworth looked aloft and he thought he could see the sail being hauled up like a curtain to the yard, but it was so dark it would have been hard to see even if the flying water was not blinding him.

Whatever ropes the men were hauling, they apparently had hauled enough. They made them fast and then began working their way up to the weather side, moving slowly and deliberately from one handhold to another, seemingly oblivious to the seas crashing around their legs and sometimes swirling up to their waists.

If that sail is hauled up, I'm sure there'll be no need for them to climb up there, Wentworth thought, but even as he considered it, the first of the men grabbed hold of the weather shrouds, climbed up on the pin rail, up onto the bulwark, then stepped onto the ratlines and made his labored way aloft.

My dear Lord . . . Wentworth thought as he watched another and another of the men make the same tricky move from deck to shrouds. He had seen them do this before, when the weather was fair, and they all but ran as they headed aloft, but this was something very different. Each step was a labored motion, and when the ship rolled to weather and threatened to fling them off the ropes and into the black cauldron they clung tight and did not move, and when the ship rolled the other way and pressed them into the shrouds they scrambled up, one, two, three ratlines, using the slingshot motion of the ship to ease their way. And so they went, nearly all the hands, by Wentworth's count, up aloft to battle with the fore topsail, which he could hear flogging and slamming in a most discomforting manner.

But to Wentworth, it was all discomforting. Any reasonable man, of course, would have been discomforted by the fact that the ship was caught in an epic storm, laid nearly on her beam ends with every massive wave, shipping tons of water that ran like a swollen river down her deck and threatened to carry all away before it. But none of those things bothered him, not really. He was bothered by the sight of the men climbing aloft, and the thought that he himself might not have the nerve to do it.

Nonsense . . . he told himself. If it was his business to climb up into the rigging then he would climb up into the rigging. If he remained on deck it was simply because he was born to a higher station, and a man of his position and native ability did not debase himself with brute labor.

An excuse, a weak excuse . . . he chided himself. Of course he could climb up there with them, the damned bloody tarpaulins—there most assuredly was nothing they could do that he could not.

Biddlecomb is not climbing aloft . . . he reminded himself. *Even he feels it's below his station.* But Biddlecomb's words had suggested that he had, in the past, gone aloft in such a storm. Wentworth loosened his grip on the lifeline, took a step toward the shrouds, then stepped back again and renewed his hold on the rope.

No. He would not.

But not for want of courage. He was satisfied that it was not fear that kept him on deck. Rather, it was the absolute certainty that once he was up aloft he would have no notion of what to do, a humiliating circumstance. He could face the possibility of an ugly death, but embarrassment was more than he was willing to risk.

Soon the men climbing aloft disappeared into the darkness and Wentworth turned and made his way aft once more. The wind was like a solid thing that pushed him sideways, hard against the lifeline as he struggled along. What little regularity there had been in the ship's motion seemed gone now, and she rolled and bucked and heeled with no method to the madness. The great seas lifted her bow and tossed her aside and she lay down on her leeward side, the water boiling up through the gunports, the masts groaning even over the cumulative noises of ship and storm.

Wentworth was thrown against the lifeline as the ship rolled farther than she had rolled yet. He hung there and they paused, man and ship, and Wentworth wondered if she would come up again, or if she would lie there on her beam ends until another sea rolled her over completely. But then, with a slow and deliberate motion, a fighter knocked down but unwilling to stay down, *Abigail* shook off the tons of seawater on her deck and slowly stood again, ready for the next.

William had nearly reached the mizzenmast before he could make out Biddlecomb standing where he had left him, one hand on the lifeline, unmoving, and Wentworth resisted a natural tendency to find something comforting in the captain's stolid aura of command. Wentworth paused, not sure of where he should go. He could not stand the thought of going below with all this happening on deck, but he did not think he was particularly welcome on the quarterdeck. Wentworth, however, did not much care where he was welcome and where not, so he made his way further aft and resumed his place at the mizzen shrouds, sheltered by the cloth lashed there.

Biddlecomb did not move, only glanced over at him, then turned and shouted something to the helmsmen, but the words were whipped away from Wentworth's ears by the banshee wind. They stood there, Wentworth and Biddlecomb, unmoving save for the constant effort required just to keep their feet. The ship rose and the men at the helm turned the wheel hard, eased it, turned it the other way. The bow plunged down again, scooping the seas and sending them cascading down the deck until, to Wentworth's astonishment, there was never a plank to be seen, the entire deck was submerged, masts and fife rails rising up as if from the bottom of the sea.

Incredible . . .

Abigail rolled and the water broke against the bulwark and jetted out the gunports around the muzzles of the guns and everything groaned and clattered and roared and screamed. Then the ship rolled again, rolled hard as a big comber came up under her bow, rolled far over on her beam ends so Wentworth was sure the main yardarm had gone in the water. She hung there, then rolled back, and as she did another wave broke over her weather bow and a great surge of black water came tearing down the length of the deck. Wentworth twined an arm through the mizzen shrouds and grabbed hold with both hands. He heard Biddlecomb shout a warning to the helmsmen.

The boarding sea smashed against the mainmast, against the mizzen, buried the fife rail in tumbling foam, hit the guns with a terrific force, burying them, too, rolling over them, sinking Biddlecomb and the helmsmen up to their waists, Wentworth on the weather side up to his knees. The *Abigail* staggered like she had taken a blow to the head, righted herself in a groggy roll, shed the seas from her decks with a waterfall sound.

Wentworth let out his breath, which he realized he had been holding. Biddlecomb was shouting to the helmsmen. The ship began to rise again on the next wave and suddenly Wentworth caught a motion to leeward, like some great animal waking up. Biddlecomb saw it too, looked over quick, and above the wind Wentworth heard him shout, "Oh, damn my eyes!" as they both realized in that instant that the aftermost gun had broken clean out of its lashings.

12

A *loose cannon* . . . William had heard that expression often enough, had used it himself. It meant someone who was unpredictable, a danger. But he had no idea of the real implications of the term. Until now.

The water poured off *Abigail*'s deck as the bow climbed on the next roller, and the gun, which certainly weighed above a ton and was mounted on wheels, began to careen aft, rolling downhill, as it were. Biddlecomb allowed himself a second or two at most to evaluate the situation, then he ducked under the lifeline and stumbled toward the gun, slipping, falling, pulling himself up.

Stupid bastard, what does he hope to achieve? Wentworth thought but he, too, was moving in that instant. He let go of the shroud and the ship rolled and he felt his feet come out from under him as he went down, slamming shoulder-first into the deck. He tried to push himself up but the motion of the ship held him flat. He had a sudden vision of being run over by the cannon, but remembered that the skylight and the raised overhead of the great cabin were between him and it.

He put his hands against the wet deck planks and pushed and then the boarding sea rolled over him, swirling him away, tumbling him like a toy boat in a stream. His mouth was full of salt water and his legs and arms flailed for something to grab. He slammed into some unyielding thing, felt the sharp pain in his side from the impact, but he grabbed it and held on as the water drained away. Some sort of low wooden device with a heavy rope wrapped around it. He felt a hand on his collar and before he quite knew what was happening he was lifted to his feet. He grabbed hold of the bulwark and the helmsman who had picked him up said, "Keep a weather eye out for them boarding seas!"

He nodded and looked toward the leeward side. Biddlecomb was splayed out over the skylight and the big gun was rolling forward. It slammed into one of its mates and staggered to a stop and Biddlecomb pushed off and went after it.

Wentworth's head cleared and he waited until the ship was more upright, then raced forward, grabbing the lifeline and ducking under it. The bow rose and the gun began careening back again and he jumped up on the raised cabin top as Biddlecomb leapt onto one of the stationary guns and the great iron brute rolled past, knocking the wheel off another gun carriage and slewing sideways.

Wentworth's hand fell on the rail around the mizzenmast. There were coils of rope there that seemed to be serving no purpose so he snatched one up and found the bitter end. He was no mariner, no jolly jack-tar, but he had considerable experience with horses, some of them quite wild. He leapt as the gun slammed to a stop, took several turns of the rope around the muzzle, and held tight.

"Belay that! Belay it!" Biddlecomb shouted but Wentworth could only shake his head to indicate that he did not understand. Then the bow plunged down again and the gun rolled away and the rope tore through Wentworth's hands, which were naturally soft and made softer still by the constant soaking of the past hours. He shouted with pain and let go and the gun slammed forward again, smashing into the middle gun and threatening to tear that one free as well.

Where in all hell is everyone? Wentworth wondered. *Why are we bloody all alone?* And then he realized that the rest must still be aloft, and the helmsmen unable to let go of the wheel. There was no one else.

He picked up the rope again, ignoring the burning agony of his palms. "If it rolls away it'll smash through the side!" he shouted to Biddlecomb.

"Damn the side, let it go!" Biddlecomb shouted back. "We must stop it from—"

He managed to say no more than that. The ship hit the trough and twisted and rolled and the seas came crashing aft and Wentworth and Biddlecomb could do no more than hang on to keep from being swept away. Then the bow began to rise and the gun began to roll aft, smashing into the raised hatch, bouncing off, moving faster as the deck slanted steeper and steeper. Biddlecomb leapt forward and looped a rope around the gun's cascabel and Wentworth got his rope around the muzzle again, and he saw that rather than hold the rope, Biddlecomb twisted it around a substantial-looking wooden beam, letting the wood take the strain, not his hands.

"Belay your line! Tie it off!" Biddlecomb shouted and Wentworth looked desperately around for something to tie it to. The line on the cascabel came taut, the great gun tipped and pivoted on the steep wet deck. Wentworth tried to hold his line but even if his hands had not been flayed he would not have been able to do so, and he let it go before it did further damage to his flesh.

The gun twisted on the line Biddlecomb was tending, the barrel cleared the raised overhead, spinning under its own weight. In the binnacle light Wentworth could just make out the looks of terror on the faces of the helmsmen and then they released the wheel and leapt clear, larboard and starboard, as the cannon swung around and smashed into the wheel, two tons of gun and carriage hitting the fragile steering gear and smashing it to kindling.

"Damn it!" Biddlecomb shouted and he dropped the line and ran aft. "Grab up the relieving tackle!" he screamed as loud as he was able, and he could just be heard above the wind. Wentworth looked around. He did not know what relieving tackle was. And then he realized Biddlecomb was calling to the helmsmen, not him.

Abigail fell off the wave and her bow came down and the gun staggered and swayed and lifted on its two left wheels. It hung there for an awful moment and then toppled over, hitting the deck with an impact that Wentworth could feel in his shoes, even with all the other shuddering and banging of the ship in the seaway. With palpable maliciousness the gun began to slide forward, swinging around as if reaching out for Wentworth's legs. He glanced up but Biddlecomb was yelling at the helmsmen and pointing forward and paying not the least attention to the gun.

Wentworth leapt up as the ship rolled under him and he came down on the cabin top. The rope he had made fast to the muzzle was still there, and as the barrel swung toward him he jumped over it, snatched up the rope, and leapt back to safety.

Abigail was twisting and rolling in a way she had not before, turning sideways to the seas, the monstrous waves coming not so much on her bow as right amidships, and the ship in turn rolled further and further and the strain came on the rope as the gun reacted to the increasing slope of the deck.

But now Wentworth was ready. He jumped from the cabin top, clawed his way to the weather rail, the deck becoming more vertical, and just as the gun was starting to build genuine momentum in its slide he wrapped the rope around the beam that was the opposite number to the one Biddlecomb had used. The line came tight, the beam creaked under the weight, but the gun ceased its downhill slide.

Wentworth looked for Biddlecomb, hoping to share his triumph, but Biddlecomb was nowhere to be seen. *Has he abandoned his post?* Wentworth thought, but a motion above caught his eye and when he looked up he could just make out the figure of a man—Biddlecomb, he was sure—clinging to the mizzen shrouds above his head, one hand holding the shroud, the other flailing out with a knife, cutting the lines that held the sail lashed tight to the mizzenmast. With each line he cut, more and more of the sail, the mizzen sail, Wentworth believed it was called, spread to the wind, flogging and beating.

Abigail continued to roll. This was not like before, the dip and rise with the seas moving under. She was going over now, with the defeated feel of a ship that would not be coming back up. Wentworth clung to the weather shrouds and tried to keep his feet. The rope holding the gun popped and the gun slipped a few inches and Wentworth knew that it would not hold for long.

More ropes, more ropes . . . he thought, as coherent an idea as his mind could form. There was another, right under his hand, and he grabbed it up and let go of the shrouds. He half tumbled and half slid down to the gun. His shoes came hard against the carriage and stopped his plunge toward the lee scuppers. He wrapped the rope around the wheels, around the barrel, then turned and crawled back toward the weather side, crawled up the steeply slanting, wet deck. He clawed at the pin rail, pulled himself up. He hauled the slack out of the rope as best as he could and wrapped it around the beam where he had tied the other.

Biddlecomb was back on deck. He half slid down to the cabin's raised overhead, used it to break his slide, then scrambled aft. He climbed onto the smashed remains of the helm, reached up to the boom above his head, and yanked a coil of rope from a cleat there. With a deft move he tossed the rope so it payed out straight and draped over the cabin top.

"Haul on that, Wentworth, haul for all you're damned worth!" he shouted, his voice cracking with the effort, and then Biddlecomb laid into the rope, heaving it out with quick jerks, and inch by inch the corner of the flogging mizzen sail was dragged snapping and beating to the end of the boom.

Wentworth once again slid down the deck, stopping himself on the cabin top. He snatched up the rope and shouted in pain, confident the wind would whisk that show of weakness away. He pulled as hard as he was able, but Biddlecomb looked over his shoulder and shouted, "With me! Hey, ho!" and as he said "ho!" he jerked the rope.

"Hey, ho!" Wentworth caught on to the rhythm. "Hey, ho!" On that note they hauled away, the wildly beating sail coming under control. The *Abigail* was standing more upright. Wentworth had one foot on the deck now, one on the side of the raised overhead. The water was up to his waist but it was swirling away, rushing aft, crashing over the transom and the taffrail, spewing from the gunports.

"Hey, ho!" He had no idea why they were pulling this sail out, but they were, and it seemed to be helping. Then there were more hands on the rope, men swarming around, and Wentworth saw that the tarpaulins had come down from aloft and now they were putting their weight into the pull. Biddlecomb left off hauling and Wentworth did as well and soon the sail was hauled out, the line made fast.

Abigail's motion was much improved, her bow turned partially toward the seas, which broke around them and sometimes over them, sending the familiar rush of water along the deck, but she did not seem in danger of turning over, and she was not making so wild a corkscrew motion. He heard Biddlecomb use the words *lie to* and he guessed that was what they were doing, stopping, as it were, in the middle of the storm, letting the ship ride like a cork over the terrible waves.

And with that, Wentworth sensed the worst of the emergency had passed. A gang of men went forward, more went aft to examine the shattered helm.

No one was steering because there did not seem to be anything with which to steer. Biddlecomb, quite distracted by the many things that required his attention, finally noticed William once again at the mizzen weather shrouds. He took a step toward him. "Thank you, Mr. Wentworth, for your help," he said. William nodded, a humble acknowledgment of the fact he had doubtless saved the ship. Then Biddlecomb turned and made his way aft to the rudder head, leaving Wentworth to feel, though he would never articulate it, that more might have been made of his quick thinking and thoroughly seamanlike actions.

For two days they remained lying to as the storm blew itself out, and Jack Biddlecomb did not like to think on what a close run thing it had been. Such disasters, or near disasters, in this instance, were rarely the result of one big blunder. They were the result of little mistakes built upon little mistakes, like piling stones on a board when those worthies of old put someone to death by pressing.

He had, without a doubt, held on to the fore topsail longer than he should have, making every inch of progress he could on the proper course before he was forced to turn and run with a deep reefed foresail and main topsail and the wind betwixt two sheets. A bully driving captain he, eager to be known as a bold young blade, willing to keep the ship on her course long after more timid souls would have had her scudding. He had nearly killed them all in proving himself such a fine fellow.

And because he had held on to sail for so long, it called for nearly all hands aloft to take it in, and aloft they had been when the gun, the cursed gun, had torn free of the bulwark. That, at least, could not be laid at his feet. The lashings, which he had inspected, had held, tight and true, while the ringbolts put in by those poxed dogs in Philadelphia, who called themselves carpenters, had torn clean out of the side.

Wentworth had made a decent try of helping, Jack would not begrudge him that. But if he had had the sense to belay his line rather than trying to hold it in his soft, bare hands, trying to stop two tons of wood and iron from careening around the deck, then it might not have taken the helm clean out. And not just the helm. The damned thing, the damned vicious beast had smashed through the helm and taken out the tiller behind it. If the tiller had been spared they might have steered with the relieving tackles, but there was no more than a bare stub left projecting from the rudder head, and no relief to be found.

And thus, in a matter for thirty or forty seconds, the ship had gone from a vessel riding out a brutal storm in relatively good order to one with steering gone, turning sideways to the massive seas, rolling on her beam ends and beyond, with a two-ton cannon charging around the quarterdeck and all hands up aloft, save for two seamen and some macaroni of a landlubber.

They that go down to the sea on ships, and do their work on great waters . . .

Jack had never been aboard a ship that had come that close to rolling clean over. Lucas Harwar and John Burgess had been at the helm and he sent them forward to haul up the weather clew of the foresail while he set the mizzen in hopes that that balance of sail would turn the ship like a weather vane into the wind.

In truth, he had not thought it would work, or more accurately, he felt sure the *Abigail* would roll clean over and take them all down before the sails could have any effect. Even as he was slashing at the mizzen gaskets with his knife, Jack figured he was just killing time, amusing himself for a few seconds before that last wild ride as the ship rolled over, as he found himself clinging to the shrouds, the sea roiling around him, his own ship dragging him down. Would he kick for the surface? He could swim, an oddity among mariners, but would he have sense enough to not bother, to just take that big lungful of water that would end it all?

But that opportunity, that chance to discover what he was made of when standing on the threshold of mortality, would have to wait. Once they had hauled the mizzen out, the ship actually behaved as he thought she might, turning slowly up into the wind, shaking off the water that flooded her deck.

Two reasons now to hate the damned guns. The first, of course, was the way that one of that tribe had tried to smash every bit of deck furniture aft, and had taken the steering out in the attempt. The other was the bulwarks required to mount them. When *Abigail* had sported rails around her upper works the seas had washed right over her, unimpeded. Now the bulwarks held the boarding water in, like her deck was some sort of wooden mill pond, tons of salt water that left the ship wallowing and unresponsive as it slowly and laboriously cleared.

They had trimmed the mizzen, trimmed the main topsail, hauled up the foresail, set the fore topmast staysail and finally found the right balance of canvas that would keep *Abigail* shouldering the seas with her rudder gone. They were at the mercy of the wind and the breaking waves, driven in whatever direction the storm chose, and while Jack had only a rough sense of where on the watery globe they were, he was fairly certain that there were many hundreds of leagues of deep water between his ship and the nearest hazard to navigation.

There was no chance of moving the wayward cannon in those conditions so they trebled the lashing until there was a ridiculous amount of rope holding the thing in place, and preventing it from further movement. With that secured, they turned to the next most dire problem, which was the fact that *Abigail* had no means by which she could be steered.

In driving rain and winds that gusted to sixty knots, by Jack's well-practiced estimate, with seas still running feet deep along the deck, he and Burgess, who was a hand with tools, and Harwar and Tucker had pounded the stump of the old tiller out of the rudder head, had shipped the new tiller and rigged the relieving tackle. A four-hour job in fine weather had taken them two days, and just as the storm was rolling past and the seas returning to a human scale, they once again were able to steer the ship.

Jack had spent a majority of the storm on deck, in many instances as the only one on deck. When the ship was riding properly and no sails needed attending to, there was little reason for anyone else to be topside, save to man the pumps, which they did quite a bit. But by Jack's reckoning, the deck was where the captain belonged when the ship was in such peril, and standing watch while the others were below helped mitigate the guilt he felt at putting the ship in peril in the first place.

Two days, and then the wind began to back and blow with less force, leaving *Abigail* to wallow in a lumpy, confused sea. With the new tiller shipped and the wreckage of the steering gear cleared away, and Jack reasonably certain that no serious damage had befallen the rudder, they shook a reef out of the main topsail, set the fore topsail and foresail, and felt the motion of the ship change from something helpless and buffeted by storm to something making purposeful headway, moving of its own volition, pushing the seas aside with the insistence of life.

The sun emerged, and so did William Wentworth, though in truth he had made the occasional appearance on deck during the two days the ship had been lying to. He had stripped off the ruined, bedraggled clothes he had been wearing and arrived on the quarterdeck in a fresh shirt, coat, and breeches. He looked as if he was off to some gathering of the better sort on Beacon Hill, save for his hands, which were thoroughly wrapped in cloth bandages.

"Good day, Mr. Wentworth," Biddlecomb said. The fact that Wentworth's hands, which he was sure had never known a day's labor, had been so terribly torn up through the man's own ignorance delighted Jack to such an extent that he found himself capable of civility.

"Good morning, Captain. We are sailing, I see."

"Indeed we are," Jack replied. "And if ever the sun reveals itself I may be able to determine where we are, and in which direction we must sail. How are your hands this morning? Has Dr. Walcott's salve been of any use?"

Wentworth sniffed and looked at his bandages, which were absurdly bulky. Jack was certain that Israel Wolcott, ship's cook and surgeon when required, had deliberately wrapped Wentworth's hands in that way for the pleasure of making him look ridiculous.

"Ah, yes, Dr. Wolcott!" Wentworth said. "I should be curious to know which medical school he attended, one that does not require literacy, apparently. I suspect that his 'salve' as you call it was simply beef fat with something indescribably horrible added to it."

It was indeed beef fat, of that Jack was morally certain, but what the cook might have added to it he could not imagine, and did not care to. "You will not be playing the pianoforte for a while, I take it?"

"No," Wentworth said, "and happily there are no such marks of civilization about to make me long for it."

Any further sparring was interrupted by Charles Frost, who didn't so much step from the scuttle as burst from it, as was his way. He had not been much in evidence during the storm, which was fine with Jack. Passengers were better off below in foul weather. Save for his moment of glory, Wentworth had been an insufferable pain.

"Ah, Captain Biddlecomb!" Frost said in his expansive manner, arms wide as if embracing the world. "Tops'ls are set and drawing, God is in His heaven and we are under way, I see!"

"Conditions are much improved, Mr. Frost," Jack agreed.

Frost looked around as if looking for some familiar landmark, but there was nothing but lumpy gray sea. "Do you know where we are? Were we much blown off course?"

"I've had no opportunity for a sun sight," Jack said, "but by my dead reckoning I don't think we've lost much ground."

"Excellent! Glad to hear it!" He nodded toward the cannon, which still lay on its side on the quarterdeck, tied down like a rogue elephant. "This beast will be put back in its proper place soon, I'll warrant?"

"As soon as the seas are such that we can safely move it," Jack said, "I intend to push it over the side."

Frost frowned and his eyebrows came together, and then his face brightened again. "You are practicing on me, Captain, I perceive," he said.

"Indeed I am," Biddlecomb said. "As much as I would like to give it a burial at sea, it is still Mr. Oxnard's property and I will see it back in its gunport with ringbolts properly fastened this time."

"Good, good! There's not a moment to lose!"

"Indeed," Jack said, and then realizing that perhaps they were thinking of different things added, "Not a moment to lose doing what?"

"Why, exercising the men with the great guns! Drill, sir, gunnery practice."

"Gunnery practice, Mr. Frost?"

"Certainly, gunnery practice. I'm sure Oxnard told you that I had a certain expertise in these matters."

Jack searched back in his memory. Yes, Oxnard had mentioned it. Or so he thought. Either way, Frost was a particular friend of Oxnard, who was the owner of the *Abigail* and Jack's employer, and that meant Jack was not inclined to argue with the man.

"Yes, Mr. Frost, I do recall," Jack said.

"Well good. We're sailing into dangerous waters you know, French privateers, French navy for all we know, looking for the main chance to snatch up an American merchantman. Oxnard won't have it, and I am fully in agreement. We must defend ourselves."

"Defend ourselves . . ." Jack echoed.

"Exactly! So as soon as ever we can, we must get this gun remounted and we must begin exercising the men. Loading and firing, loading and firing. And then we'll be able to show Jean Crapeau what we are made of! What say you?"

13

Jonah Bolingbroke had been feeling like quite the clever blade, but he was feeling that no longer. Lying in a dark room, hands bound, body aching from various bruises, with no notion of why he was there or what fate might be his, it was hard to muster that cock-of-the-forecastle confidence that had generally carried him though most awkward situations.

The *Lady Adams* was bound to sail on the morning tide and he aboard her as second mate. And if he was not aboard her, as was currently the case, she would sail anyway, and leave him on the beach. He had been safe within her wooden walls, secure in the tiny closet that was his private cabin, private save for the sailmaker with whom he shared it. A cabin had once seemed a luxury beyond his dreams, but it had been his, until he decided to push his luck to the breaking point.

Second mate. That was a loftier position than he had ever aspired to, at least in the first years of his seagoing life. Eleven years old, sailing as ship's boy, his life had consisted of constant labor of the most vile, dangerous, and exhausting kind; barely edible food and not much of it; and a regular boxing on the side of the head by the various brutes in the forecastle.

That was a long time in his past. Since those days he had grown a foot and a half, put on 120 pounds, nearly all of it hard muscle, had learned to dominate a forecastle rather than cringe in the corner. With the authority concomitant with his new berth, the money from his advance on pay, and the considerable sum given him on his agreeing to injure Biddlecomb or kill him in an affair of honor, he had been feeling a flush of satisfaction, wealth, and power such as he had never known before.

As far as employment was concerned, the job of doing major hurt to Jack Biddlecomb was one of the better opportunities that had come his way. Indeed, he had envisioned doing such a thing for free for some years, though the main chance had never really presented itself. But then there it was, and the pay had been excellent.

There would have been quite a bit more, of course, if he had managed to fire a bullet into Biddlecomb's gut, but Oxnard had put a stop to that. Still, there had been enough in that first payment to underwrite several nights in the finest nunnery in Philadelphia, a place where he would have found no welcome before, but where, with specie in his pocket, they had treated him very well indeed.

His nights away from the ship carried with them considerable risks, and catching a dose of the pox was the least of them. Someone was looking to waylay him, he found, but who it was he did not know. There were a number of possibilities—Bolingbroke seemed to collect enemies the way some men collected artwork or butterflies—so he could not be entirely sure who the aggrieved party was. By his best guess, it was someone connected to this Biddlecomb business.

Bolingbroke, no fool or stranger to such things, saw them watching, following, as he made his way through Southwark. They nearly had him once, that night in the alley. That had put a real fear into him, and he did not leave the ship after that. Not, at least, until the night before they were slated to sail, when arrogance, lust, and the erroneous impression that the watchers had abandoned their posts allowed his passions to supersede his native sense of preservation.

The last time he had patronized that establishment they had been waiting for him—some big bastard, big as a bear, had chased him right through the door and down the basement steps. He kept a weather eye out the second time, moving cautiously, and the way had seemed clear. But it was not.

Bolingbroke had been halfway down the alley with its lantern above the nunnery door when one of them stepped from the shadows and called his name. There was light enough for Bolingbroke to see that it was not the same bear who had chased him before, which meant he might use his basement escape route a second time. He turned and flew up the brothel stairs and through the door, past the hulking doorman and through the parlor. There were not so many people there that night, making the way more clear as he leapt over the sofa and down the hall. He took the stairs to the cellar two at a time, leaping to the floor from three steps up and bounding along the way to the cellar door, a path that was always well lit since he was hardly the only patron who found need for a secondary exit.

He ducked under the lantern, around the various obstacles, out the back door, and up the few stairs to the street level. And then his considerable momentum was stopped cold, like a ship running aground. A blow to the stomach doubled him over, a blow so solid he was sure he had run into a hitching post or some such.

But then a massive hand grabbed him by the hair and pulled him straight, craning his head back at an unnatural angle, and he found himself looking into the face of the two-legged bear, an animal smart enough to not be fooled twice, apparently.

"Jonah Bolingbroke?" the man said, and Bolingbroke could not help but note the odd combination of thoughtfulness and menace in his tone. "A word with you, sir, if you please."

In the end, the words had been few. Indeed, if this fellow had wanted information from Bolingbroke, he had neglected to ask. Most of the communication was of a type with which Bolingbroke was more familiar; kicks, blows, curses, though far from the worst of those he had experienced. Bolingbroke was shoved to the floor of a carriage and brought around to the place where he was now. Where that place was, he did not know.

Nor did he know how long he had remained trussed and lying on the floor. Quite a while, it seemed, though time passed very slowly in such circumstances. There were a few things he could discern about his surroundings, despite the absence of light. He was lying on a carpet of some sort, and it was soft, and that told him something about the quality of the establishment. That and the smell. Or absence of smell. There was no odor of boiling food or unwashed men or smoky fires or any other sort of dank corruption, none of the sort of smells to which he was most accustomed. There was a hint of candles recently burned, wax candles, not the cheap tallow dips that gave feeble illumination to the miserable haunts he more habitually frequented, the sort of places where one was content with deep shadows and was not eager to see what was in those corners where the light could not reach.

Very well, some wealthy cove, then, Bolingbroke thought. He was not entirely sure how to feel about this revelation. Relief, on the one hand. The wealthy sort did not tend to dole out painful and bloody retribution, and he was pleased about that. On the other hand, pain was something he was accustomed to, and could endure to a surprising degree. The rich, he knew, could arrange for punishment far worse and of much longer duration. He feared men of power, because he did not know what they were capable of doing.

He was lost in that contemplation when the door opened and the sound made him jump. He shifted and turned his head in time to see a pair of well-worn shoes and wool stockings stepping up to him, and felt big hands grab him under the arms and lift him to his feet. It took a powerful man to do that, and this fellow, Bolingbroke noted, seemed to have not the least bit of difficulty.

A hand on the back propelled him toward the open door, into a room well lit with the wax candles he had guessed at, and a big man in a suit of clothes far finer than that of Bolingbroke's handler. He wore a waistcoat with some sort of embroidered pattern running around the edges, but no coat over that. His sleeves were rolled up and, for all his refinement, Bolingbroke could recognize a former seaman, a man raised on hard work who was now aping the gentleman. He would have recognized those characteristics even if he did not recognize the man, but recognize him he did.

"Mr. Tillinghast, you may free his hands, I should think," the seated man said. Bolingbroke felt the cold steel of a knife blade against his skin, an upward movement, and the lashings were cut free. He moved his arms gratefully, rubbed his wrists.

"Sit, Bolingbroke," the man said, and Bolingbroke looked around and then sat in the chair indicated, facing the man, while the one called Tillinghast, the two-legged bear who had been in his wake the past few weeks, stepped into view on his left.

"So, Bolingbroke, do you know who I am?" the man said, his tone flat, which was more frightening to Bolingbroke than anger would have been.

"Yes, sir," he said. "Yes, Captain Rumstick."

The big man nodded. "And no doubt you know that Jack Biddlecomb is my godson? Jack Biddlecomb who you tried to kill a fortnight past?"

Bolingbroke sat a little more upright. "Oh, I know. Everyone knows, no damned secret at all." He had intended to be silent, to yield nothing, but once he opened his mouth it was like the side of a ship stove in, the words gushed like green water. Rumstick was a powerful man, and he had influence and connections at which Bolingbroke could only guess. To save himself, Bolingbroke had to be clever, which he considered himself to be, all evidence to the contrary notwithstanding.

"If something happens to me," Bolingbroke went on, "there'll be no question about who to look to." It was a good play, he thought, though still his panic seemed to rise with every word he uttered. "It was an affair of honor, straight up, I did nothing wrong and Biddlecomb wasn't touched. Hell, we never even came to blows. Everyone knows it. I told the captain of the *Lady Adams*, I said, 'Anything happens to me, it's Biddlecomb's friends to look to, Captain Rumstick and them.'"

He stopped, panting, as if he had just sprinted three blocks. Rumstick and Tillinghast remained silent, looking at him. There was a clock ticking somewhere behind him; in the silence he heard it for the first time.

"Are you done?" Rumstick asked as if he did not actually care about the answer.

"Yes, sir."

"Good. Because I am really not interested in you, you miserable little worm. I want to know who paid you to challenge Jack to this *affair of honor* . . ." his tone suggesting, quite correctly, that honor played no part in the affair.

"No one paid me," Bolingbroke said, and felt some of the old defiance creep back into his heart. What, really, could Rumstick do to him? "It was an affair of honor," he spat. "Maybe you don't know how those things work."

For all his airs, Rumstick was still more forecastle than quarterdeck, Bolingbroke guessed, more whorehouse than counting house. In his younger days, Rumstick would no doubt have beat him to death, but now, precisely because he was trying to be part of a world to which he did not belong, he would do no such thing, and probably would not let Tillinghast do so, either.

Rumstick had the influence to see that Bolingbroke never shipped out of

Philadelphia again, or Newport, or maybe Boston, but there were seaports the world over, and an experienced mariner like him would never want for employment. No, what in truth could this whoreson do?

But Rumstick, far from being angry or offended, was smiling at Bolingbroke's defiance. "Honor, you say? Pray, tell me who paid you to suddenly discover this great store of honor, because I know damn well you did not hit on this idea of your own."

"If there was someone, I would not tell you, but there wasn't." Bolingbroke was sure if there was violence in the offing, it would have been hull up by now, but he saw none on the horizon.

Rumstick sighed. He and Tillinghast exchanged weary looks. "Bolingbroke, do you know of the British frigates, patrol off the Capes?"

Bolingbroke shifted, unsure where this was bound. "Yes . . ." The size and composition of the lurking squadrons changed, but there was generally some Royal Navy presence hanging off the Capes of the Delaware Bay. And the Chesapeake, and New York, and Boston, for that matter.

"Do you know why the captains do not molest my vessels, or those of my friends?" Rumstick asked next. "Let me tell you. It's because I see to it that they are amply supplied with seamen. If someone plays clever with me, then I arrange for him to be employed in His Majesty's navy. That makes the captains of those ships my dear friends. Would *you* care to serve the king, Bolingbroke? It's a job you may keep for life, however long that might be."

Bolingbroke felt a wash of fear go through him, and it extinguished any growing confidence that was smoldering there. Maiming or killing someone carried a considerable risk of being found out, and Rumstick likely did not want to chance having the law come after him. But this threat, this was different.

It was well within Rumstick's power, and it would indeed put him in the good stead of the commander of any British man-of-war. He, Bolingbroke, would disappear with never a trace. He might get a letter back to someone in the States, but what the hell good would that do? He would disappear into a torment far worse and more prolonged than a simple beating in a back alley. A cannonball through the gut would be the least of his worries, and the least likely fate to befall him. Flogging through the fleet,

hanging for insubordination, a slow death from yellow jack in the West Indies, those were the more probable outcomes of his being pressed.

"But . . ." Bolingbroke stuttered, flailing for some response. Unfortunately,
all he found was the stupidest of possible arguments, and even more unfortunately, he said it out loud. "But I'm an American!"

At that Rumstick and Tillinghast laughed. Not a cruel laugh, but one of
genuine mirth. "And so you are, Bolingbroke!" Rumstick said. "You have
papers to prove it?"

"I do," Bolingbroke said. No seaman would venture from an American
port without them, for all the good they might do.

"You have them on you, then?" Tillinghast asked. Bolingbroke looked
at him, looked at Rumstick, said nothing. He did not need to speak. They
knew the answer.

"Very well," Rumstick said, "that's enough of that. Tell us, Bolingbroke,
who paid you to do what you did."

Bolingbroke said nothing. Some might have felt honor-bound to keep
their mouths shut, but in Bolingbroke's case he was silent because he did
not know the answer to Rumstick's question. He did not know who hired
him. And he did not know how to make Rumstick believe that.

"Eight bells," Rumstick said. "Time's up. Mr. Tillinghast, pray take our
friend on a boat ride. My compliments to Captain John Carney, who commands the squadron presently at the Capes."

Tillinghast let out a low whistle. "Mad Jack Carney's there, is he?"

"The very man to teach young Bolingbroke here the ways of the king's
service."

Tillinghast grabbed Bolingbroke's collar and the words came tumbling
from Bolingbroke's mouth like a sluice gate had been opened up. "Stand
off, stand off, I'll tell you, damn you," he all but shouted. Tillinghast let go
of his collar. Rumstick leaned back and folded his arms. Bolingbroke glanced
around for no reason at all but to stall for a second more.

"See here," he began, "the truth is, I don't know who it was. Some vil-
lain from the docks. Not a talkative cove, I never even got his name. I don't
know who sent him."

Rumstick shook his head. Tillinghast grabbed Bolingbroke's collar. More words exploded from Bolingbroke's throat. "Wait! There was . . ." He reached back desperately into his memory, which was really rather good. "There was a name, this son of a bitch did say one name once, it's all I know. Ness. It was Ness. He said, 'Mr. Ness knows you'd fancy putting a bullet in Jack Biddlecomb, and he'll even pay you to do it.' That was the only name he said, and only the one time."

"This fellow who was speaking for Ness, where would we find him?" Rumstick asked.

"Don't know. I swear I don't know. Never seen him before or since." Bolingbroke was not sure what real, sincere truth sounded like, but he hoped that it sounded like the words he blurted out, because they were indeed the truth, and he knew of no other way to convey that fact. Rumstick and Till-inghast exchanged glances. Bolingbroke thought he saw Rumstick give a little nod, barely perceptible.

"Bolingbroke, I certainly hope you're telling me the truth," Rumstick said.

"I am, I swear to God I am," Bolingbroke said, too quickly and too emphatically to lay claim to any remaining dignity.

For a long and terrible moment Rumstick just looked at him, looked right into his eyes. Bolingbroke tried to hold his gaze, but it was like looking into the sun, too painful to hold for long. And then Rumstick said the words Bolingbroke most wanted to hear of any in the world, said them so low that Bolingbroke almost didn't hear them at all.

"Get out of here, Bolingbroke. And do not cross my path again."

And the next thing Bolingbroke could recall, he was running down the dark, predawn street toward the waterfront, the frantic dash from Rum-stick's parlor and out the door forever lost to his memory.

14

It had taken less than a minute for the aftermost six pounder on the larboard side to break free, and with the momentum of sixteen hundredweight of iron loose on a heaving deck, it took only a minute more to destroy the *Abigail*'s steering gear and tiller. It took nearly two days to get the hated thing back in place. Where the ringbolts had torn clean out, the bulwark had to be repaired and reinforced, no easy task on the still rolling deck, with spray like torrential rain flying aft as the bow shouldered the confused seas.

The first order of business was to sort out the steering gear. Happily, while the wheel, drum, and mounts had been torn clean out of the deck they had not been smashed to shivers, which made repairs a simple matter of remounting the helm and reinforcing it where it had suffered damage.

Abigail was too small to carry a carpenter, a single individual with the expertise and authority to take charge of this task, so every man aboard who knew which end of a saw to hold and could tell a piece of oak from a ball of oakum designated himself an expert, and appointed himself to the role of carpenter or carpenter's advisor. They hammered, sawed, argued, and undermined one another until Jack, who knew as much about woodworking as any man aboard, which was no great amount, stepped in and took personal oversight, and from there the work progressed much quicker.

Once the wheel was remounted they turned to the wayward gun and its gunport. Not only did the damaged bulwark need repair, but each of the other guns had to be unlashed and the ringbolts carefully inspected to see that such a thing could not happen again. When Jack was at last satisfied that all was well, and that they were reasonably safe from any further errant ordnance, they unlashed the truant gun and with handspikes and handy-billys they hove it back onto its wheels. Then slowly, carefully, laboriously they bullied it back to its assigned gunport.

In the course of the forty or so hours that that evolution took, the seas settled down, the wind came fair and dropped to a steady twelve knots, and the sun made a welcome appearance. Soon the *Abigail* looked more like a floating tenement than a ship, with clothing and bedding flogging in the rigging and drying in the blessed heat. Jack took a noon sight and found they had been driven a hundred miles or so to the northwest, not so bad as he had feared, and if the wind held they would lose no more than two days' sailing.

The loss of two days, however, seemed of great concern to Mr. Charles Frost, who hovered over Jack's shoulder as he walked his parallel rules across the chart and marked the fix with his pencil.

"Two days, you say?" Frost asked, not for the first time. "Two days delay in when we might make Barbados?"

"Two days. Maybe less. But you're no stranger to the sea, Mr. Frost. You know well enough there's no predicting these things. The winds are as re-liable as winds will be this time of year, but we could still have a calm that sees us wallowing for the better part of a week."

"Of course, of course," Frost said. He looked down at the chart again. "Your course will be what, then?"

The correct answer was "whatever damned course the wind will allow for us to get to Barbados," but Jack sensed that Frost did not want to hear that, so he traced an arced line with his finger from the latest fix to their destination, avoiding all obvious landmasses along the way. Frost nodded, and he seemed pleased. "Good, good, let the god of storms send us a fair wind, then!"

"Indeed," Jack said with what enthusiasm he could find. He was not at all comfortable with this, any of it. A ship's master, he felt, should maintain a certain degree of aloofness. Aloofness, of course, was not his nature. It was so much not his nature that he had had to purposely cultivate it when he became a first mate, an office that also required one to stand apart from both the herd in the forecastle and the better sort in the passengers' cabins.

Aloof captains did not discuss their navigation or intended routes with anyone, passengers foremost. Had Wentworth even asked to see the chart, Jack would have given him such a display of aloofness as the world had not yet witnessed. But Frost was different. He was, for one thing, a known friend of Oxnard's, which Wentworth was not. How much deference that should buy him, Jack was not sure.

And there was also the undeniable fact that he liked Frost, liked his open, jocular manner. But Jack also harbored a natural defensiveness, the result of his age and the fact that he was only a few weeks into his first command. He was sensitive, very sensitive, to any hint of Frost telling him how to run his ship. But thus far the passenger had said nothing to cause offense. It was a very confusing situation, social rocks and shoals through which Jack found the navigation tricky in the extreme.

The runaway six pounder had been secured, the men fed their dinner, the afternoon watch settling in to their stations, when Frost approached Jack with the suggestion that they begin exercising with the guns. Try as he might, Jack could think of no excuse to not do so, so he told Tucker to call all hands aft. The off watch was engaged in ship's work, so most of the company was already on deck or aloft, and it took little time for them to assemble just forward of the mizzen.

"See here, men," Jack began. "I suspect you've noticed that the *Abigail* now boasts a broadside of guns. We're standing into the Caribbean, and it's no secret the Frenchies have been making prizes of American ships. We won't let that happen to us. We'll defend ourselves. And to see we are able to do that, Mr. Oxnard has sent along Mr. Frost here, who you know, and who is a hand at the great guns. We will commence now with exercising them, and Mr. Frost will instruct you in what you need to know so you don't all end up rotting in some *parlez-vous* prison."

Jack looked out over his people, pleased with the degree of inspiration he had managed to bring to his words, confident that beneath the looks of vague indifference the men were genuinely ready to take on this new task. He looked to his right and saw Wentworth leaning against the bulwark, the expression on his face one of smug amusement, and Jack's good feeling collapsed like a waterspout. He was never too comfortable with rousing oratory, and he guessed that Wentworth found him ridiculous, and that in turn irritated him greatly. "Very well, Mr. Frost, I leave them to you," he said.

Frost stepped forward, clapped his hands and rubbed them together, and with that single gesture grabbed the men's attention as if he had hypnotized them, because Frost was a man who commanded attention. Jack could see all hands perk up with interest, and he knew Frost had several advantages over him. The men knew Frost and liked him, he having already made his presence felt fore and aft, and they had no reason to fear him as they had to fear their captain. He was a passenger. He had no authority.

What's more, this was a novelty, playing with cannons. As a rule, sailors did not much cotton to novelty, they did not care for anything with which they were not entirely familiar. Anyone who tried to serve them food that was hitherto unknown in the forecastle, for instance, would soon learn as much. The sea was changeable enough for any man; those who sailed it did not need other surprises visited upon them. But this was something else, because it involved firing guns and it took them away from the chipping of rust and tarring and slushing and rousing out casks of this or that, the daily tedium and bane of the sailorman's life.

And Frost knew how to instruct in the exercising of the great guns. In his grand, jovial, embracing way he took the men through the steps, set up a model gun crew, used them to demonstrate to the others casting loose the guns, leveling the guns, removing the tompions, loading with cartridge, shot, and wadding. When all was in readiness the gun was run out and Frost jabbed the priming wire down the vent, filled the vent with powder, touched it with the glowing match. With a shattering, satisfying roar the six pounder bellowed and leapt back against its breeching, blowing a horizontal column of smoke and flame and iron shot straight out over the sea, and the men, despite themselves and their studied cool, cheered as if Frost had performed an act unparalleled in the modern age.

Then, with his expansive bonhomie undiminished, indeed rather augmented by the men's enthusiasm, Frost took them through sponging the gun with the vent securely covered, which brought them right around to once again loading with cartridge. This the men were more than eager to do, eager to see the big gun roar to life again. But Frost had other plans, and rather than reload the gun, he divided the men into the gun crews so that they might each try a hand at the exercise.

This proved more difficult. *Abigail* had seventeen souls aboard, passengers included. Biddlecomb, as captain, had no business messing with the guns. For purposes of combat he designated Oliver Tucker as helmsman and set Lucas Harwar to join one of the gun crews. Barnabus Simon, the steward, was given the sponge for the aftermost gun, and the cook, Israel Walcott, was driven from the caboose and made to act the part of powder monkey, supplying the guns with the tight-filled flannel cartridges. This he did at a sullen, shuffling pace while issuing a steady stream of curses, protests, and invectives, loud enough to be heard, not so loud as to constitute insubordination.

With Frost joining in there were thirteen men to man a single broadside of three guns with a grudging powder monkey to supply them all. They could fire the larboard guns or the starboard guns, but not both at the same time, and even then they had barely enough to make the guns speak and no one left to see to the sails or any other task that might be required, but there was nothing for it. Oxnard, in the way of merchant ship owners the world over, wanted his ship protected but did not want to put out the money required to do so.

William Wentworth did not volunteer to join in. When Jack turned to him again, Wentworth held up his ridiculously bandaged hands, gave an ironic smile, and said, "My apologies, Captain, but, doctor's orders, you understand." Beyond that he did not utter a word during the entire exercise, simply watched the goings-on, and save for that one flash of amusement at Jack's speech, his expression was inscrutable.

In dumb show the men loaded, ran out, fired, sponged, reloaded. No gunpowder was burned, no match glowed orange, there was no sound save for the grunt of the men hauling the guns up the sloping deck, the squeal of the gun carriage wheels, and the eternal sound of slapping rigging, creaking spars, and water rushing down the sides.

Charles Frost had an impeccable sense for the mood of the men, and he gauged the moment perfectly when they were done with that nonsense for the day, when the novelty was gone, when the change of routine moved from engaging to irritating. When he saw that happen he ordered one last round, a live round, with gunpowder and shot, and once again the entire situation was changed up, the interest renewed. And when that one rolling broadside was fired, slowly, with ample precaution to avoid crushed feet or arms blown off, then the guns were secured and the men left wanting more.

And that was good, because more they got, the next day, and the next, and on after that as Frost drilled them in the afternoon watch, from the end of dinner to the start of the first dog watch. The men moved happily to their assigned stations, eager to see what new incentive Frost might offer up—a silver half-dollar to each man on the fastest gun, the chance to fire at an empty barrel with a tot of rum to the gun crew that first blew it out of the water.

This act of going to fighting stations, Jack knew from a long and often unwilling association with naval affairs, was called "quarters." A list of such stations, if he was inclined to make such a thing, which he was not, or if he thought it necessary, which he did not, would be called a "quarter bill." He knew that a quarter bill would designate some men to double as sail trimmers, some to go to the pumps if needed, some singled out for boarders. Such a thing might make sense aboard a man-of-war, with its crew numbering in the hundreds, most of whom were simply interchangeable parts like the components of a gun carriage or a treble block, but it did not make sense aboard the diminutive *Abigail*.

As it was, all this loading and running out and firing and general martial activity was getting far closer to the world of Isaac Biddlecomb than Jack Biddlecomb cared to get. He had quite purposely sailed a reciprocal course from the Great Man, a course on which he had been set by Jonah Bolingbroke not so many years before, though it sometimes felt to Jack like several lifetimes past.

The trouble had started at Jack's birth, or before that, possibly.

Whatever it was that made Isaac Biddlecomb the man he was, the hard and the soft of him, strength and weakness, brilliance and folly, that was the stuff of which his son Jack was made as well. The fact that they had been born into different worlds did not change that truth. Isaac, born to a former soldier turned farmer of a small part of Rhode Island's sandy soil, was orphaned at the age of twelve. His mother died in childbirth. His father, wrecked by grief, rejoined his regiment and took a French bullet at Quebec. Isaac was then taken under the wing of William Stanton, but Stanton did no more than give him work in the man's world of the forecastle until Isaac's native genius for driving ships and men had revealed itself, and he took his first steps onto the quarterdeck.

Isaac Biddlecomb was born in the British colony of Rhode Island and Providence Plantations. Jack was born in the state of Rhode Island in the United States of America, in the middle of a war to determine if those united states would remain a sovereign nation or return to their former status as colonies of England. Jack's mother, Virginia Biddlecomb née Stanton, William's daughter, was heir to a great fortune that the war did not diminish. Indeed, through the quasi-patriotic and thoroughly profitable enterprise of privateering, Jack's grandfather actually managed to increase his wealth during eight years of conflict.

By the time Jack was old enough to have some understanding of the wider world the war was over, his father was lauded as a great hero of that war, and his mother had somehow produced a baby sister. Jack would not come to appreciate until many years later just how comfortable their situation was, particularly in light of the great fiscal devastation visited on so many others by the War for Independency.

In his ignorance he enjoyed a childhood free from want. During much of his younger days his father was gone, off to sea, but when Jack was eight Isaac came ashore permanently to be with his family and oversee the growth of Stanton and Biddlecomb, Merchants.

Isaac, naturally, wanted everything for Jack that he himself had not enjoyed: a family home, education, social standing, and the graces expected of one who occupied that station. Jack, naturally, wanted none of it. Like his father, he longed for the sea. A series of tutors managed to plant the seeds of Latin, sprout translations of Caesar, the words of Shakespeare, husband the young shoots of an appreciation for music, but they found the soil rocky and inhospitable.

Mathematics alone took some hold, not out of any academic interest but because Jack understood that mathematics was central to navigation, and navigation was one of those things that separated the men who spent their lives heaving on capstan bars and hauling on braces from those who gave the orders to do so, and Jack knew enough to know he wished to be the latter.

And so, at the age of eleven, with his father despairing of his ever pursuing a more gentlemanly life, Jack was apprenticed to a ship's captain, a trusted friend of Isaac Biddlecomb. Virginia, despite being the daughter and wife of sea captains, or perhaps because of this, objected to the arrangement. Her objections manifested in her shrieking at her husband and hurling various *objets d'art* at him, weeping, and directing the same barrage at her father, who sided with Isaac on this issue. It was the only time before or since that Jack had seen such behavior from his mother, the only time he had ever seen her lose that composure and air of cold command that he would later come to admire in the better ship's masters under whom he served.

Eventually Virginia was convinced by Isaac and by William Stanton that Jack was of such a temperament that if he was not sent to sea with someone they could trust he would run away to sea and find himself in a situation far worse. This was true; Jack was already making alternate plans if his father should fail to win the day; and when Virginia saw the truth of it she relented.

As his peers among the sons of the Rhode Island gentry were stuck with their *amo, amas, amat*, Jack and his three trunks of gear, his notebooks, sextant, portable writing desk, ditty bag, oilskins, envelopes, sealing wax, all the things that a mother deemed her young apprentice to the sea might need, were delivered up to the 354-ton merchant vessel *City of Newport*, tied to a wharf in her namesake town.

The master of the vessel was a venerable man named Amos Waverly, whom Isaac had known for many years, they both being members of that exclusive fraternity of respected Rhode Island seafarers. Waverly stood on his quarterdeck as they approached, tall and rail thin, white hair like a dandelion in seed under a tall hat. His hands were clasped behind his back, his face was locked in an expression of serious intent. He looked more like the ship's figurehead than its master. They went aboard, Isaac and Jack, at Waverly's invitation, down the ladder to the great cabin, where a somewhat cowering young steward served the men wine and Jack a cider royal.

The three of them, Isaac, Jack, and Captain Waverly, discussed the coming apprenticeship, the places to which they would voyage, the things that would be expected of Jack, the things he would learn. "We'll see young Master Biddlecomb brought up to the sea as a gentleman should be," Waverly assured Isaac, and both Biddlecombs knew that whatever their particular wishes might be, such an approach was very much what Virginia Biddlecomb wanted, and so there they were.

The ship was Jack's classroom, from the keelson to the truck of the mainmast, and there he would learn all the sailors' arts. He would be taught to hand, reef, and steer, to long splice and short splice, to draw and knot yarns, make spun yarn, foxes, and sennit, to box the compass, to set, trim, and take in sail, to navigate with deduced reckoning and lead line and sextant. He would learn bills of lading and keeping a log and the fine art of negotiating for a cargo in a foreign port. His penmanship and table manners and clothing would be attended to as well. In short, all the things that would make him a competent mariner and a gentleman would be passed on in the time-honored tradition of master and apprentice.

And Jack was a willing student. For all his bold talk he was as frightened as any eleven-year-old boy would be to leave everything he had known and sally forth into the world of men, ships, and the sea. Waverly made him less frightened. The idea of not being thrust into that world so much as ushered in by the likes of such a man as Waverly made the entire thing less terrifying.

Being a ship's master, Waverly lived a life removed, both physically and spiritually, from the men under his command. A captain sensitive to the moods of the men, the atmosphere of the ship, can know a great deal about how things are acting, even when no one will tell him what specifically is taking place, which is nearly always the case.

But Amos, Jack would discover, was not a sensitive man. His only concern was that the ship's work be done, done right, and done quick. He was exacting and he was a driver and he had shipped a mate who saw those wishes carried out, who made manifest Waverly's philosophy that the men before the mast were not to be coddled in any way. Waverly had little sense for the attitude in the forecastle and cared even less. This much Jack would discover, months later, and to his profound regret.

15

The education of Jack Biddlecomb, ship's boy, green hand, apprentice, began immediately, before the *City of Newport* even was under way, bound for Lisbon with salt cod, rum, ginger, and general merchandise. With a few words of encouragement and a manly handshake his father left him in the care of Captain Amos Waverly, who was still below. Isaac took his leave to return to the family home in Bristol, where Virginia remained, having made her tearful, thoroughly dramatic good-byes there, thus sparing her son the humiliation of doing so dockside.

Jack was left alone on the quarterdeck, and he remained there, unsure of what to do, for a full twelve minutes before he decided a climb to the main topgallant would be in order.

For all his lowly status as boy, his rating of apprentice, Jack was no stranger to ships. Indeed, he knew quite a bit for a boy of eleven, having made several short coasting voyages with his father and Uncle Ezra, both of whom had been eager teachers, and having sailed boats in Narragansett Bay and read whatever he could lay hands on, including Mountaine's *The Seaman's Vade-Mecum* and Falconer's *Universal Dictionary of the Marine*. He had been aloft more times than he could ever count, but his familiarity with a ship's rig had not been so obvious to the mate who ordered him down in a volume and tone of voice that made his displeasure clear. Waverly used the same tone, though quieter and thus more intimidating, when Jack reported to supper a few hours later in torn stockings and tar-stained clothes.

"Master Biddlecomb," Waverly said, his words were like those of a strict schoolmaster, not the kindly sort, "you have no business climbing aloft unless you are ordered aloft, and when you are quite ready you will be ordered aloft for work, not for skylarking. You are a gentleman and your place is aft and I'll thank you to not forget that."

"Yes, sir," Jack said, sensible enough to say no more.

They were under way with the next tide, and with the boat away passing the warps to the warping posts, Jack was eager to lend a hand at the windlass, but Waverly restrained him. "You stay on the quarterdeck," he ordered, "and see how this is done. Heaving on a handspike is not a gentleman's work."

And so Jack remained on the quarterdeck and watched an evolution with which he was already quite familiar, and danced from one foot to another in his eagerness to jump in and lend a hand. But even when the order was given to loosen sail Jack was not allowed to the topgallants, which were boys' work, but had to remain aft while the single boy in the forecastle, a biggish fellow a few years Jack's senior named Jonah Bolingbroke, and another rated boy though he would certainly never see twenty again, made the long climb up to the light yards.

As the *City of Newport* plowed her way east and south, so Jack's education was also full under way, with Waverly driving that as hard as ever he drove his ship. As much as Jack would have wanted that education to include the most tarry, marlinspike aspects of seamanship, Waverly's philosophy ran more toward navigation, mathematics, and even, to Jack's chagrin, a smattering of Latin translation and literature.

The days passed, and then the weeks, and the crew settled into their watches, and bit by bit Jack was able to find release from his books in the great cabin and engage in those lessons in which he had real interest. For this Waverly put him under the care of the boatswain, a Boston man named Henry Hacking who was everything Jack thought a boatswain should be; old for a seaman, gruff, generally unpleasant, thoroughly competent with anything that fell under his purview; willing to teach if he did not have to even pretend to be kindly while doing so.

Jack soaked it up with the enthusiasm of his youth. He had come aboard thinking he knew quite a bit. He soon learned that he knew practically nothing, but he worked hard to change that. Three weeks into the voyage he turned twelve, but he did not mention it to anyone because one of the things he had learned was that no one would much care.

But for all the progress Jack was making in his seagoing education, he was still just a boy, one who had grown up in privilege, well sheltered from the worst that the world had to offer. He had no sense for how the company of the *City of Newport* felt about him. Since he generally liked everyone, he assumed everyone generally liked him, and it did not occur to him that he was looked on as the spoiled, pampered son of a great war hero and wealthy merchant, a silk-stocking little puke who spent most of his time on the quarterdeck or in the great cabin and played at being a sailor-man while they were worked near to death by Waverly, the hard driver, and the mate who enforced Waverly's will.

Indeed, Jack would have been shocked to know they felt that way, since he himself hated standing aloof on the quarterdeck or poring over Latin texts or trigonometry in the great cabin. The times he was most happy were those times he was doing the meanest or most dangerous tasks, side by side with the men.

They were still a couple of hundred leagues shy of Lisbon when Jack came to understand the reality of his place aboard the ship. He had spent the morning with pages of Cicero and it was a great relief to take his ditty bag up into the foretop to replace ratlines that had become dangerously worn. There he found Bolingbroke, already at work.

For some time now Jack had the idea that he should speak to Bolingbroke, seeing as they were near in age and were the only boys aboard, save for the one older green hand rated boy. They had had few interactions, because Bolingbroke was generally off doing some lowly job and Jack, by Waverly's orders, was not allowed into the forecastle. Bolingbroke seemed to be shunned by the men forward—Jack had seen him cuffed and kicked on more than one occasion—and Bolingbroke never seemed as if he would welcome any sort of contact.

Jack pulled himself into the foretop, hung his ditty bag from the stretcher, cut the seizing of the old ratline away, and worked the clove hitches loose with his marlinspike. "Are you from Rhode Island?" he asked Bolingbroke, by way of conversation.

"No," Bolingbroke said, and he said no more.

Jack was seizing the new ratline on and trying to come up with some other approach when Bolingbroke spoke at last. "You are, ain't you? From Rhode Island?"

"Yes. Bristol."

"Of course," Bolingbroke said, with a sneer in his voice that took Jack by surprise. "Son of the great Captain Biddlecomb, of the War for Independency."

Jack felt himself flush. "Yes. That's right," he said at last. He was not sure why he should be embarrassed by that, but he was.

They worked in silence. Then Bolingbroke said, "Your father paying Waverly for you to be here?"

"No," Jack said, alert now to danger of some kind. In truth he did not know what arrangement his father had made.

"But you ain't a sailor," Bolingbroke continued, "with your books and your white stockings and all."

"I'm a sailor," Jack said. "I'm just not a dog, to be kicked and boxed around the deck."

Now it was Bolingbroke who flushed red. He turned from his work and looked Jack in the eyes. "Are you saying I am?"

Jack shrugged. He turned and worked the new ratline into a clove hitch around the shroud. He heard Bolingbroke turn back to his own work. They were silent for some time, knotting, splicing, seizing, as the foretop moved through its easy sway and roll and the *City of Newport* made easting under all plain sail. Jack pulled a length of spun yarn from a ball he had carried aloft, ran his eyes over Bolingbroke's work. "Where that clove hitch crosses, it wants to be outboard and slant up, aft to forward," he said helpfully. But Bolingbroke was not looking for help, apparently.

"Shut your mouth," he said. That minor conflict, unpleasant as it was, might have been no worse if Henry Hacking had not chosen that moment to appear over the rim of the foretop, take one quick look around, then cuff Bolingbroke on the side of the head and explain to him, in a voice loud and studded with profanity, that the clove hitches had to slant up from aft forward. "Like Biddlecomb there done it."

Jack made no comment. He did not have to. And it would be some time before he understood how completely Bolingbroke's enmity had been cemented at that moment.

As Jack continued to subtly liberate himself from Waverly and the great cabin, so he came increasingly into contact with Bolingbroke. In the merchant service as well as the navy there were certain jobs that were designated as boys' work. Those jobs—sweeping fore and aft, coiling down the lines, slushing the masts, loosening or furling the light sails, and a dozen other tasks—were too trivial or mean for the able-bodied men, or even the ordinary seamen, to bother with, at least if a boy was available when the work needed doing.

More often than not Jack was not available, being in the care of Captain Waverly and set to more erudite tasks. But when he was about ship's work, he and Bolingbroke might find themselves side-by-side in the slings of the yard while reefing topsails, or high aloft, laid out on the topgallant yards, loosening off those sails or wrestling the canvas back onto the yard, a job that called for a degree of cooperation that increasingly neither felt like giving.

They worked high above the deck or deep in the hold, places where conversations could not be overheard, and Bolingbroke probed and pulled and worked his way into Jack's spirit like a gale of wind tugging at a furled sail, looking for that flaw in the stow that would allow it, with relentless malice, to pull the canvas from its gaskets and shred it to ribbons. He needled Jack about his family's wealth, about his father's fame, about his education, about how easy Jack had it as a child. They cut Jack, each of these thrusts, but Jack turned them aside with his own verbal parries before the wound was deep.

But when Jonah suggested that Jack was little more than a passenger aboard the *City of Newport*, that his place had been secured by privilege and not merit, that he was only playing at sailors, his blade found its mark. Bolingbroke, sensing as much, continued in that vein, waxing on about how he himself had been hired on with no assistance from anyone, having no one in the world interested in helping him, whereas Biddlecomb was aboard through the influence of his father and would never be able to shift for himself, were the apron strings cut free.

Jack had little to say in response because secretly he worried that it was true. Certainly his father had secured his position aboard the ship, and he was not treated like a foremast hand or a typical ship's boy. No one in the forecastle, or indeed any of the mates, would dare to cuff him as they cuffed Bolingbroke. Naïve and generally unaware as he was, this came as a startling revelation to Jack.

Worse was when Bolingbroke assured Jack that he was despised by the foremast hands for the privileged place he held aboard the ship. And with that came Jack's sudden appreciation for the subtle, muted disrespect, bordering on loathing, with which he was indeed held. Jonah had pulled a curtain back. Jack did not like to look at what was behind it.

Years later, thinking back on that time, after the memory of his apprenticeship aboard the *City of Newport* had dulled enough that he no longer tried actively to forget it, Jack understood that it was Waverly the men hated, not him. It was Waverly, with discipline so taut it approached maniacal, and a mate who delighted in enforcing it. Waverly, who rarely gave a Sunday off at sea or a run ashore in port, who laid in food that was remarkable in its badness and paucity, who was never satisfied and not shy about saying so.

Jack's only experience with shipmasters up until that voyage had been with his father and Rumstick. Watching Waverly in command, thinking Waverly the very model of the ideal master, he had concluded that his father and Rumstick had been too easy on their men. It would take some years at sea, and the experience of serving many sorts of captains, before he understood that the opposite was true.

But more than his hard driving, it was Waverly's attitude that set the men off. Seamen could stand a driver, they could stand a screamer and a mean son of a bitch. Any man who had gone to sea for any length of time had seen all those and more. But Waverly's imperious quality, his utter disdain for the forecastle, worked on them. No sailor expected to be treated as an equal, but neither would he tolerate being regarded as a slave. Aboard the *City of Newport*, however, the great cabin was very much the big house, Waverly was the master, the mate the overseer, and those forward little more than field hands.

The same attitude that made Waverly seem the gentleman mariner ashore made him the insufferable tyrant afloat. And Jack Biddlecomb, in the eyes of the foremast hands, was Waverly's boy, a young gentleman there to be molded in the image and likeness of the master.

All this Jack would come to understand years later, but at the time it was a mystery to him, bewildering and heartbreaking that he was so shunned by the men he longed to join. And when his verbal sparring with Bolingbroke finally and inevitably turned to violence, there was no one there to stand with him.

They were in the cable tier, sweeping. It was hot, the work was dusty, the dust clinging to the sweat on their faces, getting under their shirts. Bolingbroke was going on about the rotten food forward and asking Jack about the dinner he had enjoyed aft in the great cabin. Jack, done with the nasty insinuations, turned and hurled his broom at Bolingbroke, and had the satisfaction of seeing him flinch in the dim light, seeing the handle of the broom glance off his head.

"You little shit!" Bolingbroke hissed. "You wait until we get a run ashore, I'll do you for this!"

"Why wait?" Jack asked. "You want satisfaction, well, come along and I'll give you satisfaction!"

"Sure, and one scream from you and here comes the mate to box me good, and carry you back to the great cabin!"

"All right, then, you tell me where."

There was only one place aboard that small merchantman that might be reasonably secure from Waverly and the mates, where two men might beat each other senseless with no interference. That was the forecastle, the forbidden place, forbidden to Jack. But he was in the grip of anger and despair now, and the boundaries set by Waverly were the last of his concerns. And so, just minutes after eight bells had rung out in the night watch, after the larboard watch, Bolingbroke's watch, was relieved, Biddlecomb made his silent way out of the cabin he enjoyed aft, crossed the dark and rolling deck, and climbed below to the forecastle, his first visit to that wicked den.

There were half a dozen men there, just the off watch, and the steward and cook who had heard about the fun and turned out to watch. Biddlecomb clenched his fists so that no one would see his hands shake. He hoped he would not puke. He had never been more frightened in his life. Climbing aloft at sea for the first time was nothing to this.

Jack's feet hit the deck and he turned and looked around the fetid space. There was one lantern hanging from the overhead, spilling a feeble pool of light on the planks underfoot and leaving most of those quarters, the berths and the sea chests and the gear hanging from hooks, in deep shadow.

Bolingbroke stood on the other side of the patch of light. He looked bigger than Jack remembered. But Jack noted with some satisfaction that he stood alone, that the rest of the crew seemed not much interested in his success or failure. If he, Jack, was an outcast here, if the men were indifferent to his fate, then the same apparently was true for Bolingbroke.

Jonah took a step toward him. "I'll give you a chance to apologize to me, here, in front of the others," he said.

"Sod off," Jack said, the most foul invective he could make himself say, though by then there were few profane words he had not heard.

Bolingbroke took a step forward and swung and Jack stepped back and made a feeble swipe in return. Bolingbroke dodged it with ease, stepped in again. He made a jab with his left, which Jack deflected. Then Jack felt Bolingbroke's right fist connect with his stomach, connect with enough force to lift him from his feet, and he knew he was in trouble.

He landed, doubled over, and staggered back until he hit the bulkhead, which helped hold him upright. He knew he had to stand, to get his arms up to ward off the next blow, but he could not make his body do that, and so Bolingbroke's fist was unimpeded as it struck him right across the face, twisted him around, and deposited him on the deck.

The pain was radiating out from two points now, and Jack had the idea that he might lie there on the deck a bit, but Bolingbroke's shoe connected with his stomach and blew the wind out of him, so that now along with the agony of the blows he was gasping for breath, flailing to draw air into his lungs. Another kick, this time to the chest, and Jack was curled up in a ball.

He opened his eyes and from that odd angle saw Bolingbroke coming at him again, but before his cocked leg could deliver another blow he was grabbed by a few of the others and dragged back. Jack heard someone say, "That's enough, you beat him too bloody, that son of a bitch Waverly will have us all for it."

There it was. The foremast jacks would see him spared because he was Waverly's boy, under Waverly's protection. Jack felt a rage run through him that drove him to sit up, drove him to gain his feet and, with blood spewing from his mouth, still half hunched over, fling himself at Bolingbroke once again.

He did not get far in that, maybe two steps before he was grabbed by the watching men as they had grabbed Bolingbroke. "Well," someone said, "ain't he the little hero, just like old daddy!" They shoved him up the ladder and they were laughing as they did. The fight had earned him no respect in the forecastle, and when Waverly asked him about the bruises, and he swore to all that was holy he had fallen down a hatch, that bought him no respect, either.

He earned only one thing from that fight and that was a nickname, Little Hero. From that night on, whenever he was out of the earshot of Waverly or the mate, he was Little Hero, a mocking, hateful sobriquet. Little Hero. Isaac Biddlecomb's son, Amos Waverly's boy.

It was humiliating and intolerable and there was only one way out, one way that would relieve him of that awful name and the self-doubt Bolingbroke had so skillfully and viciously planted. He could think of only one course by which he might discover if he really was no more than the son of Isaac Biddlecomb, child of privilege, unable to navigate the wicked world as Bolingbroke did, or whether he could make his way on his terms alone.

The passage had not been unfruitful. Jack now had knowledge enough to ship as an ordinary seaman, and he would do so once he had the years and the size. Until then, boys who knew the head from the halyard were always wanting aboard. He was encouraged, as they stood into the harbor in Lisbon, to see the vast array of shipping at anchor there, and the number of vessels of all size that flew the Stars and Stripes at the mizzen gaff.

In casual conversation with Waverly he discovered that they would not be lightering the cargo off but rather warping alongside a dock, when the space was ready to receive them. When they did, and when Waverly had gone ashore for business or drinking or whoring, Jack did not know which, Jack packed up one suit of decent clothing, his ditty bag, his blue jacket and his tarpaulin hat, a blanket, and eating utensils, wrapped them all in his oilskins and bound them well.

Knowing where Waverly kept the specie he carried for business purposes Jack paid himself what he reckoned were fair wages for the work he had done. Once it was well dark and he was sure the steward would not surprise him, he climbed out the stern window, and from there it was easy enough to reach the after dock fast and climb, monkeylike, to shore.

In canvas trousers and a checked shirt, a tarpaulin hat on his head, Jack was all but indistinguishable from the hundreds, perhaps thousands, of other sailors who roamed that port city, who moved with ease from ship to ship, forecastle to forecastle, with nothing but their labor and knowledge to sell, no community to which they must answer, save for the free-flowing community of mariners who washed up in every place that bordered salt water. The seamen's cocky swagger, the way they wore their clothes, cocked their hats, the way the half-fathom of ribbon on the hat's crown hung over their left eye, these were not things that could be faked, but Jack was a full-fledged member of that tribe now, and there was nothing false in his carriage.

He headed off down the quay, determined to remake himself, authentically, in the image he had embraced.

16

The storm that swept up from the Caribbean and wrenched the after six pounder from its new-made gunport on the *Abigail*'s side visited destruction on a number of other vessels unlucky enough to also be at sea and in its path.

A dozen fishing boats, whose captains thought they had time enough for one last haul of the nets before racing for the sand-fringed safety of their harbors, were lost without a trace, vanished as if they had never existed. A Spanish snow carrying sugar, rum, and fruit was dismasted. Her listing hulk was seen three days later by a homeward-bound Englishman and towed into Antigua, her crew insensibly drunk, most of them passed out amid wine bottles, pools of rum, and piles of plantain skins.

And the small French corvette *L'Armançon*, originally attached to the naval base at Brest, now making its home at Port-au-Prince, lost her main topmast and main topsail yard. More inexcusably, her foresail was pulled from its gaskets and beaten to rags before any of the reluctant, argumentative crew, illiterate seamen now marinated in revolutionary fervor, could be made to lay aloft and restow it.

But unlike the fishing boats, the generally well-found corvette had survived the storm, and with the seas gone down and the Caribbean sun once again baking the white planks of her deck, repairs were well under way. By the mizzen fife rail, silently watching the progress aloft, stood Captain Jean-Paul Renaudin. Once, as a prisoner of the English, Renaudin had seen a Punch-and-Judy show, and he had to admit that the work going on in *L'Armançon*'s maintop resembled nothing so much as that.

At another time he might have found himself fully engaged in the frustrating, ultimately futile task of trying to get the men to move faster. They had been hours just getting the topgallant mast and yard down, and another hour sending the remains of the old, shattered topmast to deck, an absurd waste of time. But in this instance he did not look on it as his particular problem.

Pierre Barère, *L'Armançon*'s first lieutenant, had taken it upon himself to drive the men on, shouting orders from the deck, personally taking a bar on the capstan to raise the shattered mast enough to remove the fid, reminding the men of their duty to the Revolution. Renaudin could not help but smile. Five months before, Barère had been a chief mate aboard some miserable, inconsequential merchantman. He had been given this great elevation to naval officer, and a first lieutenant, no less, more for his revolutionary zeal than for his seamanship, which was minimal, or for his fighting prowess, which was untested. Barère did not know what a real man-of-war's crew was, but it was not this.

Now Barère left off the supervision and came aft. "*Citoyen* Renaudin," he said, and Renaudin was certain he said it as much to irritate as to solidify the egalitarian nature of the ship. "I think we shall see the topmast down directly. We were fortunate we did not lose more top-hamper in such a storm."

"The topmast was rotten," Renaudin said. "It was rotten when the dockyard put it in."

Barère made a disapproving face. With the naval dockyards fully under the control of the revolutionary government, he did not like to entertain the thought that those in charge might be corrupt, incompetent, self-serving malicious swine, even though they clearly were. He certainly did not care to have that suggestion spoken out loud.

Renaudin wished very much to be rid of Barère, but he had no idea when or how that might happen.

L'Armançon had sailed from Brest late in the season in '93, just as *La Terreur*, the Terror, was spreading out from Paris like the cancer it was, before the *sans-culottes* of the Parisian *Armée Révolutionnaire* had arrived in Brest to set up their Surveillance Committee and their Revolutionary Tribunal. That timing had been fortuitous. Despite his years of good service, Renaudin was not sure he would have survived long in that fetid atmosphere. Not because of who he was—a good, active, and experienced naval officer—but because of who he had been born.

When *Citoyen* Renaudin had begun his naval career and his impressively quick rise to command, he was still known as Jean-Paul, Chevalier de Renaudin, a title he no longer flaunted or even mentioned, the better to keep his head firmly mounted upon his neck. His career had begun with his appointment, at age fourteen, as *enseigne de vaisseau* aboard the 104-gun ship-of-the-line *Ville de Paris*, commanded by François-Joseph Paul de Grasse-Rouville, Marquis de Tilly, Comte de Grasse, a dear friend of Renaudin's father, the Comte de Renaudin.

Young *Enseigne* Renaudin had served as signal officer during the Battle of the Capes, that great melee that had ultimately decided the American War for Independency. He was still aboard *Ville de Paris* during the less successful engagement called the Battle of the Saints, and had spent some small time as a prisoner of war to the British before being paroled back to France.

Barère was talking again. "I have explained to the men what our mission is, its importance, and now they work faster," he said. "Free men will work hard if they know the reason of it."

They'll work hard if they know there's a damned good flogging waiting for them if they don't, Renaudin thought, but he did not say as much. Instead he said, "Perhaps you should tell *me* what our mission is. Then perhaps I'll work harder as well."

Barère smiled, that insufferable smile of his. "Ah, *Citoyen* Captain," he said, "you know what you need to know, and any more would only serve to distract. We must find the American, that is what you need to know."

Renaudin just nodded and said nothing. He was not really listening to Barère's words. He was too distracted by the anodyne thought of shooting him in the head. He had seen enough men shot that he could picture it perfectly; the hole in the forehead, the instantaneous look of wide-eyed surprise, the spray of blood and bone from the back of the skull. He found the image lovely and comforting.

Unfortunately, the warm feeling that came with such daydreams was cooled by the knowledge that he would not really do such a thing, because doing so would likely lead him right to the guillotine. Unless it was done under the cover of a desperate battle.

Barère was more than just a first officer. He was the handpicked representative of the revolutionary government, the *Directoire*. He was there because men such as Renaudin presented a dilemma for the Jacobins. Through bloody trial they had found that any man who could march, who could be filled with the fire of revolution, and was not a complete imbecile could be made into a soldier. But that was not the case when it came to manning the ships of the French navy.

It took years of experience to make a good sailor, and more to make a good naval officer. But the French navy, even more so than the British, had been officered by the aristocracy, and they had made themselves scarce when the Revolution turned ugly. Most of Renaudin's fellow captains (as well as most of his family) became *émigrés*. In post-revolutionary France, experienced naval officers were rare birds indeed.

Renaudin remained part of that small and endangered flock. He was a good officer who rose to *capitaine de frégate* under the *Ancien Régime*. Having absorbed a good deal of the philosophy of the rights of man while on the American station, and having seen George Washington himself when the great man visited de Grasse aboard the flagship, Renaudin had genuine republican leanings. He supported the Estates General in 1789 and the National Assembly after that. Renaudin was second cousin to the Marquis de La Fayette though he was no more likely to mention that relationship now than he was to mention his title. Years before he and the young hero had enjoyed long conversations about questions of liberty and equality and all that. La Fayette had had a big impact on Renaudin's thinking.

By the time the fleets of Great Britain and revolutionary France engaged in what the British called the Glorious First of June, and to the French was known as *Combat de Prairial,* Renaudin was thirty-one and commander of the lovely 620-ton, twenty-eight-gun frigate *Médée*. Being a frigate, *Médée* did not stand in the line of battle with the great capital ships, but rather hung on the flanks and relayed signals and got in what blows she could. Still, some glory from that engagement, in which both sides claimed victory, shone upon Renaudin.

It shone, but not so very brightly. Bright enough, perhaps, to keep his neck out of a guillotine at a time when so many of the Second Estate were being loaded into the tumbrels and rolled off to the city squares. Through it all

Renaudin remained true to what he was, a naval officer of France. At first he remained because he believed in the Revolution. Later, when he could no longer deny the grotesque turn the movement had taken, he stayed on because he still loved the naval service as he loved his home.

And finally, though he would not admit it to himself except in the most oblique and cursory way, he remained because he was afraid to go, afraid to stay, paralyzed by an inability to take a bold step in any direction.

The *Directoire* did not trust men like Renaudin but they needed them, because Renaudin knew his business. Being stationed in the Caribbean had spared him the worst of the horrors on French soil, *la Terreur*. Indeed, the fact that he now commanded a vessel as insignificant as *L'Armançon*, a corvette mounting ten twelve pounders and two sixes on the bow as chasers, a punishment for his suspect heritage, may have helped him escape notice. Every year or so some unnamed bureaucrat in the naval administration sent a new first officer of known allegiance to the revolutionary government to replace the previous one who had been recalled, or died of yellow jack, or met with some other fate. That new officer would assiduously monitor Renaudin's loyalty and that of his men, until something untoward happened to end his commission.

Barère was the latest of these but he was different, in that he carried not just orders but secret orders. Whether he was genuinely instructed not to share them with Renaudin until he felt it was necessary, or if he was doing so just to plume up his own importance Renaudin did not know, but the end result was the same.

"We have not lost sight of the launch, have we?" Barère asked. Renaudin looked at him with curiosity. He seemed to be growing increasingly anxious, waiting for the events he had put in motion to unfold. Renaudin did not know the man well, so he did not know if this was a genuine character flaw, or if his mission was such that failure was a path to the guillotine.

"Masthead, there!" Renaudin shouted. "What do you see of the launch?" The most that Barère would reveal was that they were to patrol the Mona Passage and keep watch for an American merchantman. To cover more territory Renaudin had sent his second officer, René Dauville, off with the launch, with instructions to stay within sight of *L'Armançon* and keep an eye on the far horizon.

The lookout was settled on the fore topgallant yard, now the highest spot aboard the corvette, and he swung his glass off to the north. There was a moment's pause before he reported, "Launch is making for us, it looks like."

Renaudin pressed his lips together and stifled an almost physical need to scream his displeasure aloft. The idiot on lookout should have reported the very instant the launch altered course to intercept *L'Armançon*, but he was likely dreaming of the day when the leveling effect of the Revolution would see him made an admiral, and wear shoes on his feet, and so was not paying attention. Revolution, republicanism, these things were tailor-made for the malingerers, whiners, and sea lawyers of the lower deck and they took to it like they took to salt water.

"The launch is making for us?" Barère asked. "What could this mean?"

"Many things, *Citoyen* Barère," Renaudin said. "They may be out of food or water. There may be someone chasing them. Or they may have seen your American. Patience, patience, *Citoyen*."

That last Renaudin said specifically to annoy Barère, because he knew that Barère's patience was severely limited, at least where this mission was concerned. The lieutenant looked out toward the direction of the launch, which was not yet visible from the deck. Even with the tolerable breeze blowing it would take hours for the open boat to reach them. "Should we not close with the launch?" Barère asked.

"We should, but . . ." Renaudin said, looking up at the main topmast and giving a shrug. "Perhaps if you lead the men in a chorus of 'La Marseillaise' it will inspire them to work faster."

"Perhaps, *Citoyen* Renaudin, you are not as loyal to the *Directoire* as one might wish," Barère replied, a thin veneer of calm over the rage and anxiety. "Perhaps this lack of cooperation might be of interest to Paris."

Renaudin smiled. "Perhaps it would," he agreed. "But first let me see if I can inspire the men to move a bit quicker." He stepped forward and looked aloft. It was not fear of Barère or the *Directoire* that drove him, but rather a genuine sense of duty, and the understanding that his petty lack of cooperation was childish, no more.

"Gohier!" he shouted up to the boatswain, who was facing off with the captain of the maintop, gesticulating wildly to make whatever point he was trying to make. "Why in all bloody hell is that damned topmast not in place?

What sort of whoreson incompetent blunderer are you? Get it up now, you miserable son of a bitch, or by God, I'll know the reason why! I will set that main topsail in twenty minutes and the halyard will be wrapped around your neck if it is not ready!"

The boatswain, Gohier, had been in the naval service long enough that he responded to such commands like a dog that has been trained with a stick, all thoughts of *Liberté, Égalité, Fraternité* quite forgotten. Renaudin wished that his second lieutenant, René Dauville, was there to drive the work along. Dauville was a good officer and a thorough seaman, which, of course, was why Renaudin had sent him off in the launch. That, and because Barère would not have gone, for fear of some mischief in his absence.

Still, Renaudin's sharp words, in the old-school manner, inspired the boatswain and the others aloft to work at a less leisurely pace. Renaudin altered course to the northward and set the mizzen topsail, and half an hour later the main topsail went up, Gohier's neck well clear of the halyards. *L'Armançon* and her launch were on converging courses, and it was less than an hour after that that the big boat swooped up alongside the corvette's leeward side and Dauville scrambled up the boarding steps, his blue coat black with the spray they had taken over the launch's rail.

Dauville saluted Renaudin and began his report in the same instant that the wildly impatient Barère said, "Well, *Citoyen*, what do you have to say?"

"Gunfire to the northwest, sir," Dauville said, directing his words to Renaudin and eschewing the "*Citoyen*" nonsense that he knew Renaudin hated on shipboard. "But not a sea fight, sir, I don't believe. Too regular, too measured. Three shots at a regular interval, a pause, three more, and then again."

Renaudin nodded. Gunfire in battle was more chaotic, irregular. This sounded more like a salute, or a ship exercising the great guns. He turned to Barère and could not help but notice the look of satisfaction on his face. And relief.

"What do you think, Lieutenant?" he asked.

"I think this is our American," he said. "I think we had best beat to quarters, *Citoyen*, and clear for action."

17

his is damned tiresome, Jack thought as he watched the men move with notable reluctance to the great guns, cast off the lashings, remove the tompions. The cook was particularly slow about his powder monkey duties, his surliness and distaste for the work evident in every shuffling step. Even Wentworth, the absurd bandages now removed from his hands, seemed to have lost his enthusiasm for ironic detachment.

Only Charles Frost retained his unbounded delight in running the exercise with the great guns. His rumbling voice, like a gun truck rolling across a deck, called out, "Cast loose your guns! Level your guns!" and the force of his words seemed to be the only thing pushing the men forward.

They ran out the guns, primed and pointed, fired and sponged on Frost's command. Every day since the wayward gun had been replaced, Frost had them at it, and for most of that time their interest had remained rather high. But the novelty was gone now, and even live firing was just one more chore in the never-ending rotation of chores that was the lot of the sailorman.

That is not to say that they had not improved in their gunnery, indeed they had improved quite dramatically. From the comedy of errors that was the very first exercise, the men had quickly picked up the rhythm of the work, the fast and orderly progression of loading and firing. These were able-bodied seamen for the most part, smart and competent men, the cream of the American carrying trade. Such a thing as gun exercise came natural to them, and soon they could load and fire as well as any man-of-war's men, or nearly so.

Jack had come on deck at first light determined that they would not exercise the great guns that day. The men had had enough of it and were making that clear with every disgruntled effort. What's more, the constant wreaths of smoke were playing havoc with the paint. The masts needed scraping and oiling, the number-one fore staysail had blown out a seam that called for restitching, and there was running gear to overhaul, but with the great guns nonsense added to the regular day's work and the effort required just to maintain their forward progress, there was never a moment for any of it.

"Good morning, Mr. Frost," Jack said, crossing the deck to where his passenger stood looking out to sea. Frost was always respectful enough to keep to the leeward side of the quarterdeck when Jack was about, unless invited to the windward side.

"Good day, Captain, and a fine one, too, I reckon!" Frost said. His *joie de vivre* seemed not to be affected by any outside influence. Like some eternal flame it just burned on and on.

"So, Mr. Frost——" Jack began but Frost cut him off, or rather bowled him over, rhetorically.

"Forgive me, Captain, but I took the liberty of casting an eye over the charts, and if I do not mistake it we are entering into the Mona Passage now, are we not?"

"We are, indeed," Jack said, feeling that old discomfort rising up.

"Notorious place, notorious," Frost said. "It's like a funnel, do you see? American merchantmen just funneling through, and those damnable Jean Crapeau privateers hovering. Like vultures, I say. I think some extra exercise with the great guns is in order today, what say you?"

Jack said little. Frost's enthusiasm, his insistence, and mostly his close friendship with Oxnard left Jack relatively speechless, certainly too speechless to object. So, despite all earlier resolutions, he found himself informing Oliver Tucker that they would be starting the great gun exercise in the forenoon watch and continuing on until four bells in the afternoon watch, at least. Tucker, good mate that he was, said nothing but "Aye, sir," and showed just the slightest hint of dismay.

Abigail was sailing on a bowline, yards braced hard around, the deck steeply slanted, the ship heeled to the fresh breeze. That gave the men a hard pull as they heaved the loaded guns up to the ports, and soon they were sweating, smudged black with powder residue, and cursing, first under their breath, and soon quite audibly.

"Sponge out, sponge out well, there, Maguire, do you want to blow your damned hand off?" Frost shouted and a grumbling Maguire shoved his sponge in the bucket of filthy water and swabbed out the hot barrel once again.

The last of the rolling volley was still dying away when the masthead lookout called down, "Sail, ho!"

Sail, ho! Jack felt a twist of emotion at those two simple words, words he had heard countless times before, but never so fraught as they were now. Perhaps it was nothing, another merchantman as worried about privateers as he was. Or a British man-of-war who might be looking to augment its crew with ostensible deserters shipping aboard a Yankee merchantman. Or a French privateer hunting for easy prey. Whatever it was, it would at least mean an end to the damned exercise with the great guns and that was one good thing.

"Stand by your guns!" Jack called, then, "Aloft, there, where away?" Jack had sent Lacey aloft, allowing him to skip his trick on the guns, over Frost's objection, because he wanted a good hand keeping an eye on the horizon.

"Nor'east, sir, just t'gan'sls is all I can see!" Lacey had been sent aloft with a glass, an unusual practice, but these were unusual waters

Northeast. She was to windward of the *Abigail*, and still hull down, which put her a good ten or fifteen miles away. Jack stared off to the northeast, not in any hope of seeing her, but just as a place to focus his eyes as he considered this.

"Do you make out her course?" Jack called aloft.

"Looks to be she's making easting, sir," Lacey called out, "but it's damned hard to see for certain."

Biddlecomb thought about that. *Easting* . . . They were on something like a parallel course. What this unknown ship did in the next hour or so would tell them volumes. "If she makes any change of course, you sing out, Lacey, you hear?" Biddlecomb shouted aloft, and was greeted with, "Aye, sir!"

"Mr. Frost, pray secure the guns, that's all the noise we need to make this morning," Jack said.

"Indeed, sir, indeed," Frost said, and with a word the men sponged out, rammed powder and shot home, reinserted tompions, heaved the guns up the deck, and secured them, loaded and ready for action, staring out over the empty horizon.

The time crept on, five bells, six bells, seven bells, and never a word from Lacey, save for the occasional report that the strange sail had not altered course. Its course, however, was not what Lacey had first thought. The stranger was not sailing parallel to *Abigail* but somewhat lower, meaning that if both vessels kept on their present track, and the other ship was faster than *Abigail*, then they would ultimately converge at some point far out ahead.

Wentworth appeared on deck, pretty much the last person Jack wished to see, but there was something odd in his demeanor, not the usual detachment, but an engaged quality that made Jack wonder if he had been drinking again.

"Captain Biddlecomb, what news of this stranger?" he asked. His tone was friendly, the note not quite right, like someone speaking a foreign language in which he was not entirely fluent.

"Nothing yet, Mr. Wentworth, nothing yet. Sailing roughly the same direction as us, no change of course or sail."

Wentworth nodded, frowned, and seemed to consider this information. "I see," he said. "And do you attach any significance to this?"

Jack allowed himself an audible sigh. "Well, it would seem he's not chasing us, which could rule out his being a privateer. He's also not running, which means he has no fear that we may be a privateer. It could be a British frigate, or a sloop-of-war. I hope you have your papers handy, Mr. Wentworth, I should hate to see you pressed into the Royal Navy."

"You would delight to see me pressed into the Royal Navy, Captain Biddlecomb, but, alas, my papers are quite in order."

"Well, then, if we have no fear of losing you to King George, we shall press on and see what becomes of this."

They did press on, another fifteen minutes, until Jack felt he must see this strange ship for himself or explode with the pressure of curiosity. He pulled off his hat and coat and took his best glass from the binnacle box. "Mr. Tucker, I am going to the masthead to have a look," he said.

"Very well, sir," Tucker said. Jack moved toward the main shrouds on the weather side but made it no further than the mizzen fife rail when Wentworth stopped him.

"Captain . . . you are climbing up the mainmast, I take it?"

"Yes," Jack said, unsure where this was going.

"Might I join you?" Wentworth asked, in a more humble and hesitant tone than ever Jack had heard him use before.

Jack took a long look at Wentworth before answering. He was not sure what he was seeing here. Wentworth, the bored young man of privilege, quite uninterested in anything of a nautical bent, anything that smacked of a trade, now asking to risk his silk stockings on the rough, tarred shrouds? Jack did not much care for Wentworth's company, on deck or in the rigging. On the other hand, he saw a most excellent opportunity to let Wentworth humiliate himself.

"Well, Mr. Wentworth, a climb aloft will do your fine clothing no favors. Nor have I time to see to your safety and instruction."

"The clothes are of no concern, I have more," he said, and Jack could not help but think that the suit that Wentworth was about to ruin likely cost more than the wages that any of the foremast hands would earn on that voyage. "As to instruction, I'm sure I will be fine if I just follow you, and do as you do."

Jack thought about this for a moment more. "Very well," he said. "But I have no time to slow and wait for you."

"Pray, do not wait for me. I'll be right behind. In your wake, I believe is how you tarpaulins put it."

Jack grabbed on to the aftermost main shroud, pulled himself up on the pin rail, and swung outboard. He stepped up on the stretcher, hands on the thick shrouds, and headed up the ratlines, moving as quickly as he could, faster, he hoped, than Wentworth could follow.

He reached the futtock shrouds that angled outboard to the edge of the maintop, paused and glanced down. He hoped to see Wentworth struggling at the bottom of the shrouds, or, in a perfect world, frozen in terror halfway up. But far from struggling, Wentworth was directly below Jack and waiting for him to proceed, and Jack nearly kicked him in the face by accident.

"Mind yourself here, this is a bit tricky," Jack said to cover his surprise as he grabbed on to the futtock shrouds and made his way up, waiting for the ship to roll to leeward and give him that bit of momentum that sent him up and over the edge of the maintop.

He did not break stride as he continued on up the main topmast shrouds. To his disappointment, he could feel in the vibration of the rigging that Wentworth was just below him, having apparently had no difficulty at all in negotiating the climb around the top.

Up he went, with the topmast shrouds coming closer together as they converged on the masthead, and then up and over the main topmast crosstrees and up the topgallant shrouds, even closer than those of the topmast and twisting under his weight. The motion of the vessel as she plunged along close hauled was more pronounced at that height. The topgallant sail, topsail, and mainsail were billowing out, hiding the starboard side beneath their smooth press of cloth, and forward, the foremast held the same pyramid of canvas.

He felt the topgallant mast jerk as Wentworth came up over the crosstrees and climbed up below him, until his shoulders were level with Jack's feet. Not only had the climb presented no difficulty to Wentworth, but to Jack's great annoyance he realized that Wentworth was not breathing as hard as he was.

"All well, Mr. Wentworth?" Jack asked.

"Very well, Captain, very well, indeed." He was smiling. Jack was not sure he had ever seen him smile.

But that was all the time Jack had to spare for William Wentworth of the Boston Wentworths. He took two steps more and then stepped onto the slings of the main topgallant yard, on the weather side, Lacey having retreated to the leeward side on Jack's arrival.

"There, sir," Lacey pointed off to weather. Jack followed his finger. A ship, and not so distant now. Hull up from that height, and her topgallants would soon be visible from the *Abigail*'s deck, if they were not already. Jack reached for the telescope that was hanging by a strap around his shoulder, put it to his eye, and twisted the tube to bring the ship into focus.

He looked first at the peak of the gaff, the mastheads, looked for a flag of some sort, some mark of nationality, but there was not a bit of bunting to be seen. Not so odd; *Abigail* had no flag flying, either. Half the Western world, it seemed, was at war, international alliances and hostilities a convoluted mess, and there was every reason to not advertise one's country of origin, at least until one knew who was in the neighborhood.

"No change of course, Lacey?"

"None, sir. Steady on, just like us. Sailing lower than us, like you can see. Since I first seen her, she's closed quite a bit. Four or five miles, I should think."

Jack nodded. The two ships were sailing at nearly the same speed down the legs of an acute angle, and somewhere out ahead was the vertex of that angle, the watery point where they would meet. He could ease *Abigail*'s helm, sail further off the wind, widen rather than narrow this angle. He could turn and run. But every mile he lost to leeward would have to be made up with a hard slog to weather, and he did not care to lose an inch if he did not have to. And this fellow was posing no threat. Not yet, at least.

Jack swept the glass over the distant ship's top-hamper. Main topsail and foresail were whiter than the rest, newer, Jack guessed. *The old suit damaged in the late storm, perhaps?* he wondered. Perhaps. *Poor seamanship? Inadequate crew?* Perhaps.

He ran his glass along the hull, slowly, a tricky business holding the distant ship in the telescope, a moving target that he was observing from a moving platform, but he had years of experience in doing just that, and the object in the primary lens did not waver. Like *Abigail*, she was on a larboard tack, and he was looking at her starboard side, which meant that she was heeled toward him and much of her hull was hidden from his view. Still, there was a quality to her, the shape of her hull, the steeve of her bowsprit, the flat cut of her topsails, hardly any roach at all in the foot.

"Well, Captain, what say you?"

Jack nearly jumped in surprise, so focused was he on the ship in his glass. He thought at first that Lacey had asked that impertinent question, a shocking breach of shipboard decorum, but when he looked up sharply at Lacey he saw only horror on his face. Then Jack recalled Wentworth, who had climbed high enough to see over the topgallant yard. He stood with feet on the ratlines, elbows on the yard, just a few feet from where Jack was perched. "What can you make of her?" Wentworth persisted.

We are becoming far and away too informal aboard this damned bucket, Jack thought, but he was not sure how to stuff that cat back into the bag, so he said, "It's a ship, Mr. Wentworth."

"Well, yes, but what sort of ship, Captain? Privateer? Some marauding buccaneer?"

"One can't be certain, at least not from this distance, and with never a flag flying," Jack said, drawn once again into giving more explanation than he cared to give. "But my guess is that she is a man-of-war of some description."

"Indeed? But whose you cannot tell?"

"I cannot. Until she shows a flag or hails us or draws close enough for us to see if her men are mustachioed."

"Oh," Wentworth said. "So what will you do?" From the deck far below they heard the ship's bell ring out, eight times.

"I believe I will have dinner," Jack said. He climbed down ahead of Wentworth, allowing Wentworth to observe and copy the manner in which he did so. Had Wentworth not been with him, Jack would have slid down a backstay, but he did not want to encourage Wentworth to try that trick. One had to place one's feet just so to avoid tearing flesh from hands, and Wentworth had had a good flensing there already.

They made it to the deck unscathed, though predictably Wentworth's stockings were shredded and his breeches beyond hope of salvation. His shoes, too, would never see another cotillion in Boston's finer homes. Wentworth seemed not to care, or indeed even to notice.

There was nothing Jack wanted more at that moment than to disappear into the great cabin, to dine alone, unwatched, free from the ship's company, who were waiting for him to decide on a course of action. But somehow, because of the situation they were in, this odd vessel out to windward, its intentions unknown, and the intimacy his passengers had forced upon him, he felt compelled to invite Frost and Wentworth to join him. Jack had always craved the autonomy he believed command would provide. The master of a vessel at sea, he thought, could do as he wished, at least with regard to such things as who would share his table. But now he was finding that that, too, was an illusion.

Twenty minutes later they were seated at the crowded table in the diminutive great cabin. The enthusiastic Wentworth of that morning seemed to have been left on deck, and in his place was the Wentworth with whom Jack was more familiar; disdainful and ironic. Indeed, he seemed to elevate that attitude to new heights, as if embarrassed by his earlier, unseemly enthusiasm, as if he hoped to wipe it away with some notable unpleasantness.

The meal, to be sure, was a thing worthy of disdain. Anything Maurice had prepared prior to the voyage was long gone, and though much of the excellent cabin stores Virginia had laid in remained, much had been ruined in the storm. In any event, Walcott had no idea what to do with any of it other than boil or fry it, so boil and fry he did.

Jack was famished, and not too particular in his tastes, so he tore into the meal with relish. Frost made a noble effort, but Wentworth gave the offering a cocked eyebrow, poked at it with a knife, and then poured himself a glass of wine. "Dr. Walcott seems to have discovered some hitherto unknown species of meat, and then charred it beyond all recognition," he observed. "Such a loss to the world of natural science."

"So, Captain," Frost said, gesturing with knife and fork, "this fellow to windward, what do you make of him? Now that we have some privacy?" Jack had hoped to maintain the taciturnity he thought proper for a ship's master, but Frost would not be put off.

"Well," Jack said, "It is hard to tell, of course, I never did get a proper look at her, but she looks to be a man-of-war to me."

Frost nodded and considered that. "Man-of-war? Indeed. No indication of whose man-of-war she might be?"

"French, perhaps?" Wentworth said. "Captain Biddlecomb didn't do me the honor of offering the use of his glass when we were aloft, so I could not see, but was there a guillotine on her quarterdeck, at all, captain? That's how you can tell. Or perhaps heads rolling about the deck?"

Frost gave Wentworth a sharp look. He turned to Jack. "Not sure which would be worse, French or British. British, they might press half your crew. French are taking prizes, but it's the privateers, you know. A man-of-war, she'll leave a merchantman alone. However the *Directoire* feels about America's carrying trade, I don't reckon they're ready to start a war."

"I can't say I agree," Wentworth said, refilling his glass for the third time by Biddlecomb's count. "It seems to me they've had such a jolly good time killing one another that now they will insist upon exporting their *liberté, égalité*, et cetera, et cetera to the rest of the world at the point of a bayonet."

"Mr. Wentworth," Frost said, exasperation creeping into his perpetually cheerful tone, "you are no great friend to the French, I take it?"

"The cheese-eating, duplicitous, Gaulish, papist French? Not really, no."

"Well," said Frost, "I will not ask Captain Biddlecomb his opinion, as such things are not the proper topic of *civilized* discussion."

Wentworth raised his glass. "To civilization. May we see it again."

Jack was not listening in any meaningful way. He was focused instead on the skylight above their heads and any word that might come filtering down through it. Unthinking, he sawed at his meat with his knife, lifted it to his mouth, and chewed it laboriously as he listened for any report from aloft, his mind sifting out the meaningless sounds of his guests' discourse. And so Jack was perfectly prepared to hear Lacey's voice come ringing down from the main topgallant, shouting "Deck, there! Ship to weather's falling off! Oh, there she goes! Looks to be making right for us!"

Jack was on his feet in a flash, knocking his chair over, and was halfway to the door before it hit the deck. "Excuse me, gentlemen," he called over his shoulder, but by then he was too far along to be heard.

18

For all his time at sea, Jack was still astounded at how quickly things could change. The moment before Lacey's shout from aloft they had been peaceably sailing in company with some unknown man-of-war. Now, as he emerged into the sunlight of a Caribbean afternoon, less than a minute after the hail from on high, certainly, he found his ship and men under genuine and immediate threat.

The man-of-war was hull up from the quarterdeck, had been for some time, but it was appreciably nearer now than when Jack had led the way to dinner. More significantly, it had altered course by seven points of the compass, so that rather than sailing a near parallel track with *Abigail* it was sailing almost directly at her, making for the nearest point where their paths would intersect. She was setting studdingsails, and Jack thought, *A Frenchman, then* . . . though he did not know why he thought that, and he was too occupied with his own ship to wonder.

"Hands to the braces! Burgess, fall off, there!" he called to John Burgess at the helm. "Come around to south by east!"

"South by east, aye," Burgess shouted, spinning the wheel as the lee braces were cast loose, the weather hauled upon, with Wolcott hurrying out of the galley to attend the foresheet.

"Stuns'ls, aloft and alow!" Jack shouted, and he had not breathed the last syllable of that order before the men were leaping into the shrouds and racing aloft.

Studdingsails . . . Jack looked across the water at the man-of-war, closing fast. They were just sheeting home the fore lower studdingsail on the leeward side and he realized that that was how he knew her to be French. He had seen British men-of-war flash out studdingsails, and it was a wonder to see, the speed and precision, like a magic trick, one moment they were not there, the next moment they were. In comparison, this fellow was slow and awkward, the sails coming out in no particular order, as if the topmen were setting them as the mood struck.

Could be Spanish . . . Jack thought, but a Spaniard would have no reason to come swooping down on a poor Yankee merchantman that way, nor would they be so sloppy in setting sail. The tales told in the various ports in the Atlantic carrying trade were of a French navy infested with republican thinking on the lower decks, and any man who had spent any time at sea could guess how well that would work, and what the end result would be. And here it was, on display.

"So, a Frenchman, Captain, by the looks of it," Frost said. Jack had not seen or heard him come on deck, but he was standing just behind and staring in the same direction Jack was, the same direction every unoccupied eye aboard was staring.

"By her actions, and the way they get the stuns'ls on her, I would think so," Jack said. "The dog, she's been inching closer to us for hours, and fool that I am, I just let her." Those last words came out more bitter than Jack had intended, but they reflected well the way he felt, his anger at his own naïveté. *I am like a boy playing at being a ship's master,* he chided himself.

"Well, if he fooled you, he fooled us all," Frost said kindly. "I'm no stranger to these waters, nothing like, and I did not suspect. But see here, you still reckon her for a man-of-war, or might she be a privateer?"

"I'm not so sure, now," Jack said. "If she's a privateer, she's a damnably big one." Fast schooners or brigs were more often the choice for privateers; they were cheaper to build, cheaper to man. To see a privateer as big as what the British navy would call a sloop-of-war, or the French would call a corvette, was unusual. But not unheard of.

"She is big, for a privateer," Frost agreed. They were quiet for a moment, watching the onrushing ship, now directly in their wake and about a mile and a half distant. "And fast, I fear," he added at length.

Jack nodded. *Fast, indeed* . . . The Frenchman's studdingsails were set and drawing now, to weather and lee, aloft and alow, just like *Abigail*'s, which had been set with considerably more alacrity. But this distant ship was longer on the waterline than *Abigail*, which would make her faster, and being French-built they could count on her having a finer entry and a cleaner run aft than the apple-bowed, stubby American merchantman built to haul a maximum of cargo at a reasonable but not remarkable speed. Jack looked up at the sun. It was late spring and they were well to the south. Darkness would not be on them for many hours.

It is only a matter of time . . . he thought. They could not outfoot this damned Frenchman. They could not lose him in the dark

"Your papers are in order, I would assume," Frost said. "Bills of lading, clearing manifests, invoices?"

"Yes, the papers are in order," Jack snapped. He was fully engaged in self-flagellation, and he did not need any prompting from Frost to do it better.

"And your *rôle d'équipage*, of course," Frost added.

Jack felt a sensation in his stomach that was much like what he imagined swallowing a grapeshot would feel like; a sudden and unnatural weight, nausea, the certain knowledge that something was terribly wrong. The *rôle d'équipage*! How many times had he pestered Oxnard for it? And every time Oxnard had assured him he was pulling it together, and in the end he had sailed off without it.

"You do have a *rôle d'équipage*, do you not?" Frost asked, sensing something was amiss, because Jack was not at all the stoic, unflappable character that he wished himself to be.

"No, I do not have a damned *rôle d'équipage*," Jack said. "Oxnard . . . Mr. Oxnard had said repeatedly he would take care of that, but in the end he forgot. As did I."

"Oh, dear . . ." Frost said. They remained quiet for some time, watching the man-of-war in their wake plunging on, relentless and fast. Jack felt a slight veer in the wind and he ordered the braces trimmed just so, but it was pointless and he knew it. Even if the Frenchmen sailed their ship like a Portuguese bumboat she would still have a knot or better on the *Abigail*. If she did not carry any spars away—unlikely in that wind—then she would be up with them in just a few hours.

"If she is not a privateer," Jack said, "then perhaps she is not on the lookout for a prize. Perhaps her intent is not hostile." He wanted to confer with

Frost now, wanted the older man's input and suggestion, this friend of the *Abigail*'s owner, he was happy to look on him now as Oxnard's surrogate. Jack wanted Charles Frost to take the cup from his hand, or at least help him bear it, and he loathed himself all the more for feeling that way.

"This looks to be the actions of a ship bent on taking a prize," Frost said, his voice lower now, conspiratorial. "We don't know what has happened. New orders from Paris? We may be in full-fledged war with France, for all we know."

Jack nodded. Frost was not offering much in the way of comfort.

"But see here, Captain," Frost said, speaking lower still and taking a step toward Jack. "I have no say aboard this ship, I know that. But Oxnard and I are friends, and we talked of this quite a bit these past months, so I think I know his mind. This . . ." He nodded toward the Frenchman astern. ". . . this is the very reason he put those guns aboard your ship. The reason he asked me, if I was to take passage with you, if I would train your men in the use of them. Oxnard does not want to lose a ship, and her men. He wants to make a stand. And that, my boy, is why he wished you to take command. Because he knows a fighting man when he sees one."

Jack did not take his eyes from the Frenchman. He waited for the inevitable reference to his father, the apple not falling far from the tree, chip off the old block, like father like son, et cetera, et cetera, but Frost apparently had said all he meant to say on that point, and said no more. It was Jack's turn to speak.

"We have six guns, and men enough to man three of them, if we have no need to trim sails," he said, also speaking low and conspiratorial. "I could not count the men or guns aboard this fellow, but I'll wager it's a damned lot more than we have."

"Of course you're right, Captain Biddlecomb," Frost agreed. "And I would not interfere with your decisions. *Abigail* is your command, no one else's. But I look at it this way. We can't outrun this fellow. We have no *rôle d'équipage*, which, if he means to take us as a prize will give him cause, at least by his lights. But he won't expect a fight, will he? One or two broadsides, we carry away some of his top-hamper and we're off for the horizon, leaving Jean Crapeau knotting and splicing in our wake."

Jack looked out at the Frenchman, visibly closer now. He pictured the chart on his mind. They were well through the Mona Passage, with Puerto Rico and Santo Domingo, which was now a French possession in any event, to windward, offering no hope of sanctuary. No sandbars in the offing; he would not be repeating that business west of Montserrat.

"You'll take command of the guns?" Jack said to Frost, his eyes still on their pursuer.

"Indeed I will," Frost said, and Jack could hear the smile in his voice.

Captain Renaudin considered ordering Lieutenant Barère to scrub *L'Armançon*'s heads.

What would you do, you damned popinjay, you strutting little bantam? he wondered. Would he refuse a direct order from the captain? Would he tell the men that such work was beneath him, the ship's first officer, even though *they* were expected to do it? Is that how a paragon of republicanism such as Barère should act?

He watched Barère strutting back and forth across the quarterdeck as if it was his quarterdeck, looking beyond the bow at the American merchantman ahead and nodding and smiling in his insufferable, self-satisfied manner. *Yes, it would be an amusing little conundrum for you, Barère*, Renaudin thought.

But of course he could not do that. He could not humiliate a fellow officer, a lieutenant in the French naval service, no matter how lowly his origins or intolerable his demeanor.

Barère turned as if he could read Renaudin's thoughts, except he was smiling, which told Renaudin he could not, and that there was still some place the *Directoire* had not infiltrated. They had been watching the American set studdingsails, an impressive display by Renaudin's thinking. This merchantman could not have more than a fraction of *L'Armançon*'s crew, yet they had set their studdingsails faster and seemingly with less fuss than his own men had.

The crew of *L'Armançon* was almost to a man members of Brest's Jacobin Club and they treated the ship as if it was a venue for their revolutionary gatherings. Renaudin would not have been surprised to hear they had called a meeting to discuss whether or not they should set the studdingsails. The evolution could hardly have been done more slowly or in a more lubberly fashion if they had.

"The Americans have stuns'ls set, but I do not think they will outrun us," Barère said. "An hour or so and we will be up with them."

"So this is our plan, *Citoyen* Barère? To take this American, this unarmed merchantman, as a prize?"

"Yes," Barère said. "But she is not unarmed. She will put up a fight." He spoke a bit louder than necessary. Renaudin imagined he wanted the men to hear and to be impressed by the depth of his knowledge, to understand that he was a man accustomed to intrigue, privy to its inner circles.

"I see," Renaudin said, by which he meant that he saw several possibilities. One was that Barère was a liar trying to puff himself up. He hoped that was the case. Because if it was not, then it meant that *L'Armançon* was part of some great web of conspiracy about which he, Renaudin, her commanding officer, knew nothing. And Barère did.

"But see here, *Citoyen* Renaudin," Barère continued, "this is a delicate matter. I have spoken to the men about this, and I will speak to you. We must fight them, and we must let them get their blows in, let a few of their shots strike home, before we capture them."

"I see," Renaudin said once more. "And why is this?"

"The wishes of the *Directoire*," Barère said, in the arrogant tone of one trying not to sound arrogant. "We play our small parts in the greater glory or France."

"Very well," Renaudin said. "Then we must clear for action. And *Vive la France!*"

"*Vive la France!*" Barère repeated, quite missing the irony in Renaudin's voice, which was probably just as well.

Abigail was cleared for action, her men at quarters. Such as it was. Those phrases Jack remembered well from his father's stories, when he used to beg his father and Uncle Ezra to tell them, again and again. *Cleared for action . . . quarters.* He toyed with those words because they were so absurd, applied to the little handful of men he had, huddled around the guns or standing by the braces, Tucker at the helm, Frost prowling the quarterdeck.

Jack looked astern. The Frenchman was three quarters of a mile behind, right in their wake, and at the rate he was closing Jack gauged there were perhaps thirty minutes before he would make his move, his one, desperate move.

He had heard about this, it was a common theme in the old stories, how the waiting was far and away the worst part of it. And that seemed to be true enough, though he had yet to experience the other part, the part when the iron began to fly and the blood began to run over the deck. He did not think the few shots from the privateer during that business west of Montserrat qualified as a real sea fight. Though, to be sure, neither would this, if things went as he hoped.

He turned back in time to see William Wentworth emerge from the scuttle. He wore plain wool stockings and breeches, a waistcoat, no overcoat, his head uncovered, a musket in his hand. His presence topside was something of a surprise. After the initial excitement that had curtailed their dinner and brought them all on deck, Wentworth had gone below and not reappeared. Jack imagined he would retire to his cabin, or the cable tier, until the shooting was done. But here he was with a long gun and a cartridge box over his shoulder.

"Ah, Captain!" he said on seeing Biddlecomb. "If I am not mistaken, it is the custom in a sea fight to have men with long arms stationed in the platforms up there, inflicting what damage they can on the enemy. With your permission I thought I might fill that function today."

Here was even more of a surprise, and Jack tried and failed to hide it. "This is your own musket, I take it?" He thought there might be a musket on board, but he was not certain where it was located, and in any event, it was not so fine a weapon as Wentworth's.

"Musket? Oh my dear sir, no! This is a Jover and Belton .62 caliber rifle, the finest London has to offer. There aren't half a dozen of its like in the United States, I assure you."

Jack's eyes moved over the gun. The silver side plates blazed in the Caribbean sun, the barrel glinted, the lock was kept up such that it showed no sign of ever having been used. He could see there were fine engravings on all the metal parts, though what they were engravings of he could not tell.

"Very nice," said Jack. "And you know the use of it?"

"I do," Wentworth assured him. "One does not behave as outrageously as I and live to the venerable age of twenty-two without being an expert with gun and sword."

Jack nodded. That made sense to him. "Very well. You may take station in the maintop. There." He pointed. "But under no circumstances are you to fire before I order the great guns fired, do you hear? Once I fire on the Frenchman you may assume we mean to kill as many as we can, but you are not to shoot before I do."

"I quite understand, Captain. 'Aye, aye,' I should say," Wentworth replied, slinging his rifle by a strap over his back, then turning and heading for the main shrouds, which he had climbed for the first time that morning. He seemed once again to have that buoyant mood he had displayed earlier, a course change from his attitude at dinner. Jack wondered if he ever became dizzy, with his demeanor spinning so quickly.

And then he had no more time to spare a thought for William Wentworth. He heard a dull, heavy noise astern, like a big hatch cover dropped in place, and then the scream of roundshot that he recognized from that earlier voyage, and before he could turn around he saw the spout of water as the ball plowed into the sea, well ahead of *Abigail* and well to larboard.

The last wisps of smoke from the Frenchman's bow chaser were still being pulled apart by the breeze when Jack turned and looked astern. The Frenchman was all but directly to windward and less than half a mile behind. The starboard chaser went next, the horizontal blast of smoke, the sound of the shot passing far wide of *Abigail*'s stern. *That's a warning, a signal to heave to,* Jack thought. If they had been trying to score a hit they would have turned aside to bring the gun to bear, but they likely did not want to lose even an inch of distance.

"That's but a warning," Charles Frost said, stepping up to Jack's side. "They wish you to heave to, and good luck to them, I say!" Frost seemed to be enjoying this in the way that Jack had always imagined the truly fearless enjoyed such things. It was a pleasure he could not seem to muster.

"Another ten minutes, Mr. Frost, I should think. All is ready with you?" Together they turned and looked at the small cluster of men at the guns, two guns, because that was all they could man and still have hands enough to haul the braces, with Tucker on the helm and Jack tending to the pin rails on the leeward side.

"All is ready, Captain, and we'll give them what for, let me tell you!" They looked astern again. Closer, closer, Jean Crapeau was coming up in their wake. *Now why did I not move any guns to the stern?* Jack thought. If they had been firing away with stern chasers they might have taken out one of the Frenchman's topmast by now and he would not have to risk everything on this ridiculous plan of his.

My plan? Or Frost's? Whose damnable idea was this, anyway?

And then he smiled. He could not help it. Because he had spent nearly all of the past decade trying to not be his father, trying to be Jack Biddlecomb, not the son of Isaac Biddlecomb. And now here he was, in command of a merchant vessel, about to try some bold but blockheaded move against an enemy far more powerful than he was.

If he managed to pull it off, and lived to tell the yarn, what would they say? They would say the most obvious thing, the most trite, shallow, obvious, and irresistible thing. He could hear it already.

And so he smiled because if he did not he would scream and he did not think his screaming would do much to bolster the courage of his men.

19

The Frenchman surged up in *Abigail*'s wake, and Jack Biddlecomb did not feel like screaming anymore. He did not want to open his mouth at all because he felt certain he would vomit if he did. The tension was unlike anything he had ever experienced, like the whole world was waiting on him. His word, spoken at the moment of his choosing, would unleash a nightmare of shrieking iron and choking smoke and spilled blood. Men might die—his men—because he spoke the word.

The Frenchman was a few hundred yards astern now. From his quarterdeck Jack could see the gun crews at the forward guns, the occasional glimpse of a blue uniform aft. He felt the words of command rise in this throat and he swallowed them down. He had heard of men, sentenced to be hanged, who had been allowed to give the order themselves that would see them hauled up to the yardarm; those men had been unable to speak the words, "Haul away." He understood that now. He could not give the command. Indecision had never been part of his makeup, if it had, he would not be in command of a ship. But this was different.

He could feel the eyes on his back, thought he heard Frost make some small noise. The wind hummed in the rigging, the water made its rushing sound alongside, the tiller ropes squeaked a bit as Tucker made small adjustments to the wheel.

Then the Frenchman turned, swung through two points of the compass and her larboard bow chaser went off, the dull boom of the gun, the smoke, the scream of the shot all mixed into one terrible sound and Jack spun around and shouted, "Now! Now!" He had no idea he was going to do that; he gave the order with no decision aforethought. It was as if the shot had released him, the way a fuse releases the innards of a hand grenado, all the tension blown out of him, his mind sharp and ready.

Tucker spun the wheel and Jack leapt to the pin rail and took up the braces for the yards on the mainmast, belayed to a single pin, and held them all in his hands. *Abigail* heeled hard to starboard as she slewed around, turning ninety degrees to the Frenchman, presenting her larboard battery. Forward, the ridiculously small number of men designated as sail trimmers braced the yards around.

"Mr. Frost, quickly, if you please!" Jack called out. Frost was hunched over the aftermost gun, directing two of the men, who levered the carriage with handspikes, but there was not time enough to be so fastidious. Frost stepped back and brought his match down on the vent and the cannon roared out and flung back against the breeching, a familiar sound now, after so much gun drill. Jack was instantly engulfed in the smoke, the smell of the burned powder blotting out all other smells for the instant before it was gone to leeward.

Jack turned back to the Frenchman. He saw the ship's inner forestay part, the upper end swinging inboard, the sail that was hanked there collapsing in a heap over the bowsprit cap and the slings of the spritsail yard. A ragged hole appeared in the foresail behind it, and Jack shouted, "Well done, Mr. Frost!" But it would take more than a forestay and a jib. It would take a topmast, at least, to cripple this bastard enough to allow them to run off.

Frost was on to the next gun as the crew of the first flung themselves into the reloading. The Frenchman was turning, following *Abigail* around in her wheel to larboard, and presenting more of a target as she did, so Frost did not have to spend so much time in aiming. He brought the match down, the gun roared, leapt clean from the deck, and slammed inboard. Another hole appeared in the Frenchman's foresail.

Two shots, some inconsequential damage, and then the Frenchman replied in kind. Her starboard bow chaser went off first, the ball punching a hole through the bulwark just forward of the caboose, ripping the longboat apart in its flight and leaving Tommy Willoughby of Philadelphia, new to the *Abigail* and rated able-bodied, struck dumb and staring at the ragged hole, but otherwise unhurt.

The splinters from the longboat had not yet all fluttered to the deck when

Frost's third gun went off but Jack did not have the luxury of being able to watch the fall of the shot. "Stand by to wear ship! Stand by to wear ship!" he shouted. "Main lower stuns'ls in! Haul up the mainsail, now!"

The lower studdingsails came flying in and eager hands hauled away, clewgarnets and leechlines and buntlines. The big mainsail rose up like a curtain in a theater and Jack ordered Tucker to put the helm over. As *Abigail*'s stern turned through the wind, the ship swinging from a larboard tack to starboard, the gun crews scrambled across the deck to what would now be the weather side, the engaged side, once they had come around. They left off the guns for the time and heaved away on the braces while Jack dashed across the deck and tended the lines to larboard as he had to starboard. It was a well-choreographed performance, falling out just as planned, the sort of evolution possible with a crew such as that which their ship boasted.

Abigail swung off to starboard, turning through 180 degrees as she came around on the other tack and bringing the starboard guns, already loaded and ready, to bear on the Frenchman. Six shots, that was the plan. Three from larboard, wear around, three from starboard, and with any luck at all some part of the Frenchman's rigging would go by the board and they could sail off in peace.

The ship was still turning, her motion quick and nimble in the fifteen knots of steady breeze. Biddlecomb looked astern. He had expected the Frenchman to follow him around, to turn as he did, so they could continue to fire into Jean Crapeau's bow, and the Frenchman with nothing but bow chasers with which to answer. But the Frenchman was holding his course, sailing perpendicular to *Abiguil*, crossing her stern, which was now presented like an offering to their broadside.

"Oh, damn you . . ." was all Jack had the chance to utter when the guns went off, one after another, a rolling broadside with less than a beat between each big gun. He had time enough to note the deep boom of the Frenchman's ordnance, deeper than the bow chasers or *Abigail*'s own six pounders, and then his world became one of smashing wood and falling gear and the scream of roundshot and a dull, blank unreality.

He saw the bulwark along the stern blow apart and watched, transfixed, as a great section of wood came spinning through the air. It seemed to move slow, and the sound seemed oddly muted, and then it struck his upraised arms and swept him clean off his feet, just as the gaff and mizzen sail collapsed onto the very spot he had been standing before the bulwark knocked him aside.

He fell against the raised overhead of the great cabin and rolled off onto the deck. Five feet away Frost touched off the aftermost gun and it came charging inboard and ordinary seaman Ratford was staring at the place where his arm had been, which was now ragged bone and a great torrent of blood. It all seemed to be swirling around before Jack's eyes and it made no sense and Jack thought he might just go to sleep.

"Captain! Captain!" Here was Maguire, come aft, lifting Jack to his feet, massive hands on Jack's collar. He set Jack down on the cabin top, said, "How are you, boyo? Did you get knocked galley west, then, by that great bit of bulwark?"

Jack looked around. Frost was firing the second of the great guns, starboard side. The Frenchman's aftermost gun went off, the shot passed overhead, and Jack and Maguire ducked as a section was ripped from the mizzenmast like a shark had bitten it clean away. But Jack's head was beginning to clear, and he stood and looked around.

The gaff was lying across the quarterdeck and the sail like a blanket of new snow covered the larboard side. But Tucker was still at the wheel, the helm appeared undamaged, and the guns were still upright. Ratford was down, dead or near to it, but Jack could not see anyone else wounded or killed.

Abigail was on the starboard tack now, having worn around, and they were supposed to be taking their last shots at the Frenchman and running for safety, but the Frenchman was not cooperating. Jack, an avid fencer, a passion picked up from his father, had learned early on that it was not enough to think of what you were going to do to win a fight, you had to think about what your opponent was likely to do as well. The moment you started working out your indefatigable strategy was the moment your opponent would drive the point of his foil into your chest.

And so it was with a sea battle. He could see that now. All the careful thought he and Frost had put into this was so much flotsam because the Frenchman was wearing in their wake, a move they had not anticipated, and would bring his other broadside to bear and there was nothing Jack could do. If he wore again back to a larboard tack then Jean Crapeau would have another go at his stern. If he bore up the French would bear up with him. If he ran the French would soon be alongside and beating them to matchwood.

Then Frost was there, with an expression Jack had not seen him wear before, and he did not care for the look of it. It might be described as regret, resignation. Whatever it was called, it was not good. "Forgive me, Captain, if I had any influence on your decision to fight. It seemed the proper thing to do, but we are defeated. I don't see how we can stand up longer."

Jack felt sick. With the action begun, the fear had gone, the uncertainty washed away, but now it was back, sparked by Frost's plain statement. *We are defeated* . . . Indeed, how could they fight? If Frost, the most bellicose, eager, and experienced man aboard thought it hopeless, what more was there for it?

The Frenchman was wearing around as *Abigail* had done, turning in the merchantman's wake and bringing his fresh larboard battery to bear. The bow chaser went off and Jack felt a shudder underfoot as the ball hit the hull below. He wondered what horror had been inflicted on his great cabin. A few seconds more and the Frenchman's broadside would bear and the great guns would be unleashed on them, and there was nothing meaningful they could do in return. The *Abigail*'s two gun crews were loading, the aftermost gun already running out, but those six pounders, which seemed so grand on the wharf in Philadelphia, seemed pathetic now.

And then the Frenchman seemed to stop in the middle of his elegant, sweeping turn, as if he had changed his mind. The corvette's bow sagged off, her sails, full in her turn, flogged as the ship seemed to slump to leeward. The lower studdingsails had been coming in in some reasonable order, but now they twisted and collapsed in confusion. Her larboard broadside would no longer bear and her starboard guns were not yet reloaded and in that unexpected bit of clumsy sailing, Jack saw a gift from God, and he saw salvation, all at once.

Maintop . . . William Wentworth thought, *maintop . . . not a platform . . . must remember that* . . . He did not really care about the jargon of ships, but even more he did not care to display ignorance on any subject. Under most circumstances he could just express disdain for anything he did not understand, and that covered him well, but now he was under the necessity of using the dialect of the tarpaulin, and he wished to get it right.

Climbing up to the maintop was a bit more difficult with the gun over his shoulder, but not markedly so. The motion of the ship had changed from earlier, more pitching front to back and less rolling side to side, and that, too, made the climb a bit more difficult as the vessel was no longer leaning over in that convenient manner that made the rigging less steep.

Still, it presented little problem. Wentworth was naturally athletic, an active person with virtually unlimited free time to indulge his pastimes. Riding, fencing, swimming, hunting, shooting, dancing, even boxing, he enjoyed them all and excelled in each, as he did in most things to which he sincerely put his hand.

He even enjoyed the occasional duel, the odd affair of honor, a sport at which the stakes were much elevated and thus the thrill of the thing that much enhanced. He enjoyed it, in fact, a bit too much, one of the few aspects of his generally reprehensible behavior which he himself found troubling. He knew that men could get addicted to dueling, as they could to drink. And he could see why. It was not so easy for a young man in his circumstance to get his heart pounding, his blood flowing, to get that clarity that comes with the genuine possibility of losing one's life.

He reached up over the edge of the top, got a good grip on the topmast lanyards, and hauled himself up and over. He swung inboard and found his footing on the small, crescent-shaped structure, steadied himself with a hand on the topmast shrouds, and surveyed the scene. Things had not changed in any material way since he had left the deck. The Frenchman was mostly hidden by the sail on the aftermost mast, but he could see the ship was still astern of them and getting closer, and Biddlecomb was still running like a dog with its tail between its legs.

"You'll have to do some bloody thing soon," William said, pleased to be able to speak out loud where no one could hear, a luxury he had generally taken for granted before being thrust aboard the tiny, tight-packed *Abigail*. Talking to himself was one of his great outlets, and he missed it terribly.

He crouched down and leaned outboard, but with the ships as they were he could not get a shot at the Frenchman without shooting a hole through the sail, which would not be welcome, he guessed, nor would it be very effective. It was one thing to fire roundshot or a stand of grape without careful aim, it was another to shoot a tiny .62 caliber ball. In any event, he could not fire until Biddlecomb did, because in this instance anyway Wentworth had decided to follow orders.

Wentworth widened his stance, let go of the shroud, and grabbed up the powder horn, silver inlaid with a brass measure on the end. It was a familiar gesture; he had owned the gun for eight years and with it had terminated the existence of many living things, though never a human. He poured a measure of powder down the grooved barrel. He held the gun up, removed a greased patch from the patch box in the butt of the gun, and pulled a smooth, cool lead ball from his shot pouch. He laid the patch over the muzzle of the gun and it blew away in the breeze. He cursed, pulled another patch from the box, held it in place with his thumb as he positioned the ball on top and shoved both of them partway down the barrel.

With a practiced flip of his wrist he pulled the rammer free and began to bang the ball and patch down the barrel. The patch would grab the rifling as the ball came out and impart a spin to it, giving the gun its legendary accuracy, but it made for hard going as he loaded. And it would only get worse as powder residue built up and made the fit tighter still.

After some pounding he felt the bullet was home, so he pulled the rammer out and returned it to the slot under the barrel. He flipped open the frizzen, primed the gun, and closed the pan. He rested the butt of the gun on the wooden slats of the top and looked astern once more. Nothing had changed.

"You damn well better do something bloody soon," he said. Having seen Biddlecomb in command during the storm, Biddlecomb, who stood unflappable as the ship seemed to come apart around him, who charged into the rigging to cut the sail free as the ship was going over, who ordered men aloft into the maelstrom with never a second thought, who had leapt like a cat onto the loose cannon, Wentworth had come to think of the man as bold and decisive. He might even have seen in himself a touch of envy if he had explored his feelings that deeply, which he generally did not.

But now Biddlecomb appeared to be immobilized by indecision; this Frenchman was a snake, and Biddlecomb a rabbit transfixed by its stare.

And then around the edge of the sail Wentworth saw the Frenchman alter course, swinging off to one side, and as he did, one of his cannons blasted out, and through the rumble of the shot came the sound of rent wood below. He stepped to the forward edge of the top and looked down. He could see a straight line of destruction through the boat on the hatch directly below him, delineating where a roundshot had passed clean through. And then he saw the hole in the bulwark where it had first made landfall aboard *Abigail*. A sailor was standing by the hole, the ball having only by inches missed cutting him in two.

From below and behind he heard Biddlecomb's voice shout out, and suddenly the ship, which had been like a frozen tableau, exploded into action. The sails began to wheel around as men on deck hauled away, the sails that Biddlecomb called "stuns'ls" disappeared, the big sail just below Wentworth's feet was hauled up, and the ship slewed around to larboard. It happened so fast, and was so unexpected, at least to Wentworth, that he had to lash out and grab a topmast shroud to avoid being tossed from the maintop.

Then the guns went off, one, two, three, in a great and satisfying concussion and Wentworth shouted over the blast, "Cry havoc! And let slip the dogs of war!" He was grinning, an unseemly expression, but there was no one there to see so he kept right on.

He recalled then that he was not supposed to be sightseeing, that he had "laid aloft" with a purpose, and the blast from the great gun was his signal to fire at will. *Abigail* was presenting her larboard side to the Frenchman, so he stepped to the larboard main topmast shrouds and thrust the rifle between them, resting the barrel on a ratline of a convenient height. He looked down the length of the winking steel tube toward the enemy beyond. The great blankets of sails, *Abigail*'s and the Frenchman's, made it damned hard to find a target.

One of the Frenchman's sails, one of those forward, had collapsed, perhaps shot down by *Abigail*'s broadside, and Wentworth could see a figure in white duck pants and a checked shirt making his way along the bowsprit, laying out to do something or other, secure the sail or cut it away or fix the rigging. Wentworth had no idea of what he was about, but the man was a target, and he could find no other.

He lined the end of the barrel up with the man's checked shirt and let his breathing settle, tracking him with the gun as he moved along the bowsprit. The French ship was plunging up and down and the *Abigail* was rolling and the man was moving outboard; three separate motions for which to compensate, a shooting conundrum that Wentworth had never encountered.

And another problem he had never had to consider before. This was a human being at which he was pointing his gun, a gun with which he generally did not miss. When Biddlecomb unleashed his cannon fire, he was killing randomly, anonymously, aiming at a ship and killing anyone who happened to be in the way. But Wentworth was picking the individual he meant to shoot, and if he succeeded he would see him die, the direct result of a conscious decision.

Wentworth had wounded men in duels, but never killed one. He had often considered how he might react to taking a man's life. He never thought it would bother him. But now he was not so sure.

He finger eased against the trigger. The French ship plunged down and the man on the bowsprit grabbed hold and Wentworth tracked him, putting more pressure on the trigger. Then he heard Biddlecomb shout again from below, felt the *Abigail* turning once more, a new element of motion in this world where everything was moving. He cursed, lined the gun up with the target, and pulled the trigger as *Abigail* rolled away to leeward. He saw the heavy black line above the French sailor's head cut nearly in two, saw the man look up sharp toward the *Abigail*'s rig, then turn and race back inboard. A few seconds more and the sailor and the Frenchman's bow were lost from sight as the *Abigail* turned.

"Damn it!" Wentworth said out loud. Any moral qualms he might have had about shooting the fellow were lost in his frustration at missing. Indeed, the alacrity with which the sailor had raced off the bowsprit would have been funny if Wentworth had not been so annoyed.

He threaded an arm through the shrouds to steady himself and went through the process of powder, patch, and bullet once again. He primed the gun and looked up, ready for another go at the Frenchie, but the Frenchie was gone. For a moment Wentworth stared dumbly at an empty ocean. Then he swiveled around and saw the Frenchman on the starboard side and realized the *Abigail* had turned a half circle while he was focused on loading his weapon.

He stepped across the maintop and rested the gun on a ratline on the starboard side and looked over the barrel as he swept the deck. There were any number of men there, standing ready to haul at the lines or working the guns, which were not below decks as Wentworth had seen on larger ships but right there in the open. The crew was considerably bigger than that of the *Abigail*, but that was how things were, he understood. Penny-pinching merchant ship owners would scrimp in every way they could: the fewest men, the cheapest food, the minimum of maintenance to their ships, if it meant an extra sou in their pockets. The navy, in turn, fed at the trough of public money and did not care how much it consumed.

Wentworth ran his eye over the Frenchman's crowded deck, let his arms and legs absorb the motion of the ship, let the gun sway naturally. The trick, he could see, would be to work with the combined motions of the ships, not fight them. Let the gun move into the firing position, pull the trigger a fraction of a second before the sight was on the target.

"Now, which one of you bloody damned Frenchmen should die first?" he asked out loud. *Abigail* was turning but the Frenchman was sailing on, and it seemed to Wentworth that in a moment the Frenchman would be able to fire into *Abigail*'s stern, and *Abigail*, with never a gun pointing in that direction, would be helpless.

"That can't be a good thing," he said. Standing behind one of the guns was a figure in a blue uniform and he seemed a likely target. Certainly it would be more advantageous to kill an officer, Wentworth thought. He felt the ship move under him, lined the gun up with the Frenchman in blue. *Abigail* rolled and the Frenchman rolled and the gun swept past its target, paused and began to roll back.

A poor marksman, even a mediocre marksman, would have fired when the rifle was aiming at the target, but Wentworth was neither of those things. He understood that the target would continue to move as the bullet sailed across the space separating him from the gun. He paused as the French ship rolled toward him, and he squeezed the trigger while the rifle was still pointed at the Frenchman's deck, a foot to the right of the man in blue.

Such niceties would have been a joke with a musket, and even with most rifles, but the shot from the Jover and Belton was straight and true. The spinning bullet traversed the space between the ships in a fraction of a second, and in that fraction of a second the French ship rolled to leeward and carried the officer, quite unaware of the flying lead, right into the path of the bullet, which struck him square in the chest.

From his perch in the maintop Wentworth saw the man knocked from his feet and flung back on the deck, and he was close enough and the planks of the deck were white enough that he could see the streak of blood that landed there in the wake of the bullet.

He straightened and smiled, satisfied with that damned fine shot, not struck in any profound way by the fact that he had just ended another man's life. Then the forward-most cannon on the Frenchman's broadside fired, a deep boom, much deeper than the previous guns, or *Abigail*'s, and a great jet of gray smoke shot from the muzzle, and then the next gun and the next. From his perch he had a good view of *Abigail*'s quarterdeck, the starboard side, in any event, the larboard being hidden by the sail they called the mizzen. Wentworth could see significant chunks of wood torn from the rails as one after another the Frenchman's guns fired into the *Abigail*'s stern, and *Abigail* unable to fire back.

He watched, astounded. The Frenchman seemed to be tearing the *Abigail* apart. The rail behind the helmsman exploded in a burst of shattered wood and Biddlecomb went flying back across the deck and landed splayed out on the cabin top.

"Oh, dear God!" Wentworth shouted and then the mizzen sail and the spar that held it collapsed to the deck, falling in a great heap of canvas and wood and rope and Wentworth stood there, feeling impotent, his ship being blasted apart and not a thing he could do about it.

"You have a gun, you damned idiot!" he said to himself and his hands moved swiftly through the familiar drill: powder, patch, ball, rammer. After the fouling from two shots the patch and ball were harder to pound down, and Wentworth was sweating by the time he felt the charge hit the bottom of the barrel. He replaced the rammer and looked up again. Once more the entire situation had changed. The Frenchman was still to windward of *Abigail* and turning, bringing the guns on her other side to bear. They were taking in their own lower studdingsails and hauling up the big mainsail, and this opened up Wentworth's view of the deck, allowing him to see clean aft to the quarterdeck.

There were several men there who looked to be likely targets, men in blue uniforms, cocked hats on their heads. They strode back and forth, but slowly, as if this was an outing aboard a yacht, and Wentworth did not think it would be so much of a problem to drop one of them, at least.

He set the gun on a ratline and once again looked over the barrel, sweeping it along the quarterdeck. And then he noticed, behind the officers, the two seamen at the helm, one on either side of the wheel and turning it as the ship turned under them, but remaining otherwise rooted in place.

"Perhaps one of you would make a more efficacious target," Wentworth said and shifted his aim. He had the feel of it now, the way the two ships moved, the extent to which he had to let the motion of the vessels dictate the moment he squeezed the trigger. He lined up on the helmsman on the starboard side, having a somewhat clearer sight on him, let the ships roll away, let them begin their slow roll back. The rest of it, the battle, Biddlecomb's apparent death, the fact he had just killed a man, it was all gone from his mind, and every part of him, conscious and unconscious, was absorbed in that moment, that geometric problem of motion and distance, velocity and time. His world had closed down to that invisible line between the muzzle of his rifle and the man at the Frenchman's helm.

And just as the ships were rolling into the proper alignment, the helmsman on the larboard side stepped forward, arm outstretched as if reaching for something, and in that instant he broke the line between muzzle and target and Wentworth gave a little smile and squeezed the trigger. The smoke whipped away and Wentworth saw the larboard helmsman knocked sideways and the starboard helmsman blown backward as the spinning .62 caliber round passed through the first man and lodged in the second.

"*Égalité, fraternité, ou la mort . . .*" Wentworth said. "Sorry, gentlemen, I seem to have made the choice for you."

As he watched, it seemed to Wentworth that the result of what he had to admit was a spectacular shot was nonetheless quite out of proportion with the loss of two miserable French sailors. The officers were suddenly running around the quarterdeck, the other sailors aft were running around, everyone was waving his arms in the French manner. The wheel was spinning out of control and the ship was checked in her turn to starboard and began swinging back the other way. One of the officers spun around and grabbed at the wheel. Wentworth saw two seamen run up and take the places of the men he had dropped, but that did nothing to check the chaos on deck.

Then Wentworth heard shouting below him, on *Abigail*'s quarterdeck. He looked down. Biddlecomb was back on his feet and he was shouting orders in that tarpaulin jargon of his and the Abigails, like the Frenchmen, were all rushing about like ants in an overturned mound. Wentworth wondered what exactly he had done. More surprising still, he found he was relieved to hear Jack's voice, to know that so brash and unsophisticated a blade was once again in command.

20

They have lost steering," Jack said out loud, and to no one in particular. All that had happened seemed mixed up in a great amorphous swirl of events: the hellish raking from the guns, his being struck down by the section of bulwark and lifted again by Maguire, the mizzen sail coming down, the Frenchman falling off. He could not think clearly enough to form a coherent thought beyond that one statement.

But this was too good, like an unanticipated gift. Even if this sea fighting was some brave new world, Jack had long ago developed an innate sense for ships and the way they moved and the way they were able to move. He could look at the Frenchman, at *Abigail*, at the wind and sea and know in his gut how they might maneuver in relationship to one another. Even if he had not learned to anticipate where an enemy might wish to go, he could see exactly where he *could* go, and where he could not.

Whatever problem the Frenchman had experienced to make them falter in their turn would buy the *Abigail* a minute or two, no more. "Burgess!" Biddlecomb called out. "Burgess, lay aft!" As he spoke it occurred to him he did not know if Burgess was alive or dead, but the boatswain came charging down the deck, clambering over the mizzen sail.

Jack looked up toward the mizzen top. The throat of the mizzen gaff was still in place; just the peak halyard had been shot through, dropping the sail to the deck.

"Burgess, we are going to come about and we'll need all hands, but once we do you must get the mizzen set as quick as ever you can."

"Aye, sir," John Burgess said and said no more, racing for the foredeck, there to take up the headsail sheets.

Abigail was full and by on a starboard tack, moving away from the French ship, which had now fallen to leeward of her. Once the Frenchman got himself straightened out and was in her wake again, then they would be no better off than they were. He had one chance now, only one, but this time it did not depend on naval tactics, of which he knew nothing, but seamanship, of which he had made his life's study, brief as that might be.

"Hands to stays!" he shouted. "Mr. Frost, I will require your gun crews, but once we have come about you may have them back to engage with the starboard battery! Lacey, relieve Mr. Tucker at the helm. Mr. Frost, I shall need you to tend to the fore clewgarnets, Mr. Tucker will show you where they are."

They moved fast, Tucker, Maguire, and Burgess to the foredeck to handle sheets, bowlines, and the fore tack, Tommy Willoughby and Adams as well as a couple of ordinaries amidships attending to the main tack and topsail bowlines, with second mate Lucas Harwar to see the lee fore and main braces clear and ready for letting go. Israel Walcott shuffled at twice his usual speed to the foresheet and Barnabus Simon tended the main.

"Ready about!" Jack shouted. His voice was loud, his tone commanding, but there was no note of excitement, trepidation, or panic in it. He could wish for a bit more speed, and he could wish for the mizzen to help kick the stern around, but he had neither, and he likewise did not have a moment to spare worrying about it.

"Helm's a'lee!" Lacey, a good hand at the wheel, turned the ship up into the wind, fast but not too fast, not enough to check her forward momentum. On the foredeck the headsail sheets were let go, the jibs and fore topmast staysail flogging in the breeze. Up, up into the wind *Abigail* turned until the wind was blowing directly upon the leeches of the square sails and those began to flog as well.

"Rise tacks and sheets!" Hands heaved away at clewgarnets and the corners of the foresail came up in a jerky fashion, with Frost heaving on the larboard side and looking incongruous in his long blue coat and breeches. The Frenchman fired, and before Jack could turn and look he saw the streak of the ball passing six feet above the deck, clipping the smokestack off the caboose in its flight but doing no more damage.

He wanted to turn and see what the enemy was about, but this was the crucial moment, the ship passing through the eye of the wind, the moment where missing stays or not would quite literally decide life or death.

"Mainsail haul!" The mainsail's lee brace and the crossjack's weather brace were both let go and hands laid into the lines on the opposite sides. The main and mizzen yards swung around as the wind caught the sails on the foremast aback and pushed the bow through the wind. The Frenchman fired again. Jack felt the deck jump underfoot as the roundshot hit the side of the ship. Happily there was no one below, because *Abigail*'s thin scantlings could hardly even slow the flight of the shot, much less resist it.

He looked forward again and felt the breeze on his face. The bow was through the wind, the backed foresails pushing it around. Jack opened his mouth to shout an order and the Frenchman fired and the mizzen sail, still draped over the quarterdeck, jerked and an ugly hole appeared in it.

"Let go and haul!" he shouted. *Abigail* was through wind, she had not missed stays despite the loss of her mizzen, and now she was falling off on the larboard tack. "Steady, meet her!" Jack shouted at Lacey. He looked over the starboard side. While the Frenchman was flailing about they had effectively sailed around him, and now Jack found himself looking at her stern, close enough that he could see the blue-coated officers on her quarterdeck, the name *L'Armançon* painted across her transom, and the delicate glass of the great cabin windows below it.

You'll not have those for long, I reckon, Jack thought, then called out, "Gun crews, lay aft! Mr. Frost, starboard battery, if you please, fire as you will!"

The men who had been pulled from the guns left off what they were doing and tumbled aft and John Burgess followed behind to see to the fallen mizzen. Jack lent a hand as they pulled the canvas free from the ordnance. The Frenchman was turning up into the wind, trying to follow *Abigail* around, but Jack kept his ship falling off, sticking to the Frenchman's unprotected stern, turning downwind as he turned up, the two ships turning together.

Frost came huffing around the cabin roof with the smoldering match in his hand. He did not bother checking the aim of the gun; the Frenchman was so close that aiming would not be required. He brought the match down on the vent and the gun roared out, the noise stabbing Jack's inner ear like a thin blade, and the fine stern windows of *L'Armançon* were blown apart. He saw one of the blue-clad officers jump in surprise, a reaction that struck Jack as not being particularly officer-like.

Frost was on to the next gun and Jack called, "A bit more elevation, Mr. Frost! Destroying their great cabin will be of no help to us!" Frost nodded and one of his men thrust a handspike under the barrel and heaved it up. Frost pulled the quoin halfway out and the barrel was set down again. Frost touched the match to the priming and the gun went off, loud as the first. Half *L'Armançon*'s taffrail blew apart and the roundshot took the head clean off the starboard helmsman and continued on, tearing a sizable section out of the mizzenmast.

"Dear God!" Jack shouted, forgetting again to maintain the quiet stoicism of a proper ship's master. The image was frozen there, like the ghostly vision of a candle flame imprinted on the eye; the helmsman's back, checked shirt, a black tarpaulin hat on his head, and then his head was gone and Jack was sure he'd seen a spray of blood, the jagged neck, and then the body was tossed forward by the impact.

"Dear God . . ." he said again, softer, to himself.

The gun crew, well trained after the week or more of Frost's relentless badgering, was hauling the first gun back out, having reloaded it with creditable speed. In the moment of relative quiet Jack could hear orders shouted out along the Frenchman's deck. What was being said he could not tell because the distance was too great, his hearing was dulled by the cannon's blast, and they were speaking French, which he did not.

But he had a good idea of what they were saying, one of two possibilities. Either they were going to tack and try to chase *Abigail* around, come behind her as she came behind them, or they were going to wear around and try to engage that way. *Abigail* was hanging on their stern like a dog nipping at a bull's ankles and they had to shake her. But they would not be able to shake her, of that Jack was fairly certain. Because he had seen their seamanship, and it was not exceptional, and his was.

"Keep bringing her around, steady on," Jack said to Lacey, then shouted down the deck, "On the braces . . ." But he got no further before the aftermost gun went off, fifteen feet from where he stood, blotting out all other sound. The Frenchman's spanker boom was cut in two, the bulk of it falling to the quarterdeck, and Jack thought it might even have hit one of the officers on its way down.

L'Armançon continued her turn, her bow swinging to windward. Looking down the length of her deck, Jack could see her headsails flogging as the sheets were let go.

Tacking, then, he thought. The Frenchman was taking the bolder of his possible courses, turning through the wind, risking getting caught in irons.

"Stations for stays! Ready about!" Jack shouted. If the Frenchman was going to tack, then they would have to tack as well, keeping right on his stern quarter where he could not hit back with his big and numerous guns.

"Mr. Frost, leave off the guns until we've come about!"

The gun crews dropped their tools and scrambled forward to take up sheets, braces, bowlines, and clewgarnets. "Stand ready, Lacey, we'll follow them around," Jack said, his eyes on the Frenchman's stern as the bigger ship turned up into the wind. The quiet seemed unnatural, the familiar sounds of water and ship out of place. Then Jack heard a crack from aloft, a sharp sound, as if something under strain had parted, but before he could turn and look he saw the remaining helmsman at the Frenchman's wheel pitch forward and the wheel begin to spin out of control. Jack looked aloft. Wentworth was there, in the maintop, still looking over the barrel of his rifle, lifting his head from the firing position to see through the small cloud of smoke that was quickly whisked away to leeward.

Wentworth . . . Jack thought. He had completely forgotten about the man. *That was a damned lucky shot . . .*

Luckier, in fact, than Jack even realized. With no hand on the helm, *L'Armançon* slowed in her turn to weather, her square sails shivering, her jibs flogging, the momentum of her turn dying with every foot. They would miss stays. They would turn into the wind and stay there, sails aback, immobile.

"We're going to heave to," Jack said to Lacey. "Stand ready to put your helm a-lee." He shouted down the deck, "We shall heave to, main topsail to the mast! Rise tacks and sheets! Heave away the weather main braces! Helm's a-lee!"

Many a crew that Jack had known would have been stunned into paralysis by that quick shift of orders, but these men were too good for that, and they did not hesitate a second as they acted on these new commands. The main yards came slowly around, the main topsail and topgallant flogged as the wind struck their leeches, and then lay quiet as the wind got on their forward face and pressed them back against the mast. *Abigail* slowed as the way came off her, and then she stopped, fifty yards from *L'Armançon*'s larboard quarter, *L'Armançon* with her sails in disarray, flogging in the wind, the ship motionless, her crew running fore and aft and shouting as they did.

"Mr. Frost! Man the starboard battery, if you please!"

Once more the gun crews came rushing aft and took up their positions. All three guns had been left loaded and run out, and in the odd quiet Frost's voice seemed overloud as he ordered the aftermost gun levered around, the elevation adjusted, then touched off the powder. He could hardly miss at that range, and he did not, the ball plowing into the bulwark around the quarterdeck, striking it lengthwise and tearing out a great long section in its flight.

Frost was already on to the second gun, fired that as well, and another shark bite was taken out of the mizzenmast. The crew of the aftermost gun had begun ramming home a new charge when Frost fired the farthest forward, the shot striking the mizzen chains with a screech of rending iron. The mizzen channel blew apart in a cloud of splinters, twisted bits of metal flew fore and aft, and several shrouds swung free.

Frost hustled back to the first gun, linstock held high, the match glowing. Jack could see the French crew rushing about, backing the jibs, bracing the mainsails back to a starboard tack in a desperate attempt to get the ship to fall off, to gather way so they could turn their broadside on their tormentor. Jack wondered how long he could keep this up, how long he could hang on the Frenchman's stern. He was like a man riding a tiger—safe where he was, but if he tried to get off he would be torn apart.

And then he saw *L'Armançon*'s mizzenmast leaning to one side.

Until the moment when both helmsmen were shot, by a single bullet, no less, Captain Jean-Paul Renaudin was feeling relatively optimistic about things.

The American was well handled, he was quite willing to admit that, and even with all the men he had aboard *L'Armançon* he could not get his stud-dingsails set or taken in as quickly as the little merchantman. But that would not matter, because, indifferent as his crew might be, Renaudin knew he could coax considerably more speed out of his corvette than the Americans could ever find in their tubby vessel.

Barère had told him the Yankee would mount six pounders, and by the sound of it, he was right. The Americans had made their one bold move: turned, fired, wore around and fired again, and for their effort they managed only to take out *L'Armançon*'s jib stay, certainly far short of the result for which they had hoped. That, and someone had shot *Enseigne de Vaisseau* Lessard, who had been amidships supervising the guns. The Americans might have thought that the death of the young officer was a wicked blow, but in fact it was something of a relief to Renaudin to be rid of that inept fool.

What the Americans' plan might have been beyond that, Renaudin could not imagine. He had to admire their boldness, bordering on stupidity, in trying to fight back against such odds rather than striking when the first bow chaser went off. As deftly as this Yankee shipmaster might handle his vessel, however, he clearly did not understand the most basic aspects of ship-to-ship combat. He had sailed off, leaving his stern exposed to *L'Armançon*'s full broadside, and Renaudin had taken advantage of that, firing from so close that his gunners could hardly miss.

The Americans' mizzen sail was brought down, and Renaudin could see the Yankee's rails were well torn up. There seemed to be no material damage beyond that, but no matter. It would be simple enough to keep alongside the American or athwart her hawse, and beat her, weak-sided, frail, poorly armed thing that she was, into bleeding submission.

"Now see here, *Citoyen* Renaudin," said Barère, standing at Renaudin's side. On so small a vessel as *L'Armançon*, the first officer should have taken charge of the guns, but the little man chose instead to stand beside Renaudin on the quarterdeck during the action and offer his wisdom concerning a sea fight, wisdom he had garnered from serving several years in the carrying trade.

It further annoyed Renaudin to think that if Barère had been in his proper place, it would have been him, and not Lessard, who had taken that bullet.

If it had been René Dauville killed in Barère's place, Renaudin would have been truly furious.

Barère was still talking. "We are not to ruin them with a single broadside, they must get their shots in, it must seem as if they have put up a good fight, do you see?"

Renaudin ignored him. He would not bother asking why they had to enact this charade, because he knew Barère would only give some cryptic and unhelpful answer involving the wishes of the *Directoire*. More to the point, Renaudin's mind was occupied with handling his ship, calculating course and speed and what this American might do next, how quickly they might stay or wear, and how easily *L'Armançon* might draw alongside. Any part of his mind not given to that task was taken up with self-loathing at his own cowardice, that he would allow himself to endure this humiliation rather than take the honorable way out, which at this point could only mean shooting Barère in the head and then stepping unflinchingly up to the guillotine.

"*Citoyen*, do you attend?" Barère asked, peevishly.

"Yes, yes," Renaudin said. "Well, they've gotten their blows in, Lessard is dead, might we knock them on the heads a bit?"

Before Barère could answer, Renaudin turned to the second officer, Lieutenant Dauville, and said, "We will bear up now, bring the larboard battery to bear. Shift some of the men over to the gun crews on that side and send the sail trimmers to the braces." If they did not turn they were in danger of losing the weather gauge and the advantages that went with it.

"Aye, sir," Dauville said and relayed those orders to a boatswain's mate, who put his call to his lips and trilled the command, then moved forward, shouting out additional orders. Barère was nearby, shifting nervously. He opened his mouth to speak again when Renaudin interrupted once more, quite on purpose, telling the helmsmen, "Bear up now, bear up, follow this Yankee dog around." The helmsmen, one on each side of the big wheel, put the helm slowly a-lee and *L'Armançon* came closer to the wind as the yards were braced around to meet the new course.

"See here," Barère said, barely able to contain himself, when the helmsman on the larboard side, seeing something amiss in the binnacle box, apparently, stepped forward, arm outstretched. And then he was flung aside as if swatted by the hand of God, and behind him the second helmsman fell back, his eyes wide, a great and spreading wash of blood on his shirt.

It happened so fast, and was so completely unexpected, that for a second Renaudin could do nothing but look with confused wonder at the two men sprawled on the deck. The wheel, which had been nearly hard over, began to spin back the other way and *L'Armançon* faltered in her turn. Renaudin leapt across the deck toward the unmanned helm as Barère fairly shrieked, "The helm! Get the helm, damn your eyes!"

Renaudin kept clear of the spokes, spinning at lethal speed, and used his palm to slow the turns until he had control of the wheel. One hand on a spoke, he turned and looked forward. *L'Armançon* had fallen back to her original course, running downwind of the American, and the American, no fool, was taking the opportunity to get to windward of her. "Beaussier! Ouellette!" he shouted to the seamen tending the lee main brace, "come and take the wheel!"

With the new men at the helm and Barère shouting something or other, Renaudin stepped forward and looked down the length of the deck. The hands were still at stations for bracing around, half the gun crews had moved to the larboard side, ready for *L'Armançon* to turn and bring those guns to bear. There was a collective look of confusion. No one had any notion of what was happening.

"Man the starboard battery!" he shouted, and then, when no one moved, "Starboard, damn you, starboard!" But they only looked at him, uncomprehending.

"Fire as you can, starboard battery!" That last seemed to move them, and the men who had gone to reinforce the larboard side returned to the starboard and began to reload the guns with acceptable alacrity. Renaudin turned to Beaussier on the helm. "Helm's a-lee, easy now." Forward again. "Sail trimmer, brace up, starboard tack, brace as she comes around!"

"He's tacking, the American is tacking!" Barère shouted, his voice pitched a bit higher than before.

I can see he's tacking, you little puke, Renaudin thought, but in another part of his mind he was considering what the American was playing at. He had expected him to run off as fast as he could to windward, in the hope that his ship was quicker on a bowline than *L'Armançon*. But he was not. He was coming about and he would cross to windward and if, please God, he missed stays he would be done for as *L'Armançon* followed him around.

To starboard, the faster of the gun crews were running out, and first one, then two of the guns went off. Renaudin watched the shot fly across the American's deck, but he said nothing because he was content to let them shoot high. It was his most profound hope that they would bring down one of the merchantman's masts, which would end this quicker than anything.

The American turned up into the wind, the headsails were let go, the main and mizzen yards braced around. Renaudin wished with all his heart that they would miss stays, that they would find themselves pointed help-lessly into the wind, motionless and vulnerable, but he could see they would not; they would turn nimbly from starboard tack to larboard, even as his own ship was struggling to get headway enough to follow them around.

"Damn them!" Barère shouted. "Very well, *Citoyen* Renaudin, you may bring them to now, you may defeat them as soundly as you wish."

"Thank you for that kindness, *Citoyen*," Renaudin said. Unfortunately, the path to such a victory was not as obvious as it had been even five min-utes earlier. The American had come about and was taking position on the starboard quarter, at a place where none of *L'Armançon*'s guns would bear, and Renaudin had a good notion of what would come next.

And it did, just as he had imagined, the American's starboard battery firing into *L'Armançon*'s unprotected stern. The first gun went off fifty yards away, loud, but not so loud that Renaudin could not hear the glass in his aft windows shattering, the sound of the roundshot doing untold damage to the great cabin he had so finely fitted out over the long and dull commis-sion. He saw Barère jump in surprise, was certain the man's feet had cleared the deck, and he smiled.

"Monsieur Dauville!" Renaudin called to the first officer. "Stations for stays!" They would have to tack as well, follow the American around, try to get their broadside to bear and finish this impudent son of a whore off. He watched with satisfaction as the first officer drove the men to their sta-tions, displaying the kind of discipline that could almost make Renaudin imagine he was back in the navy of the Old Regime.

The American fired again and Renaudin felt the hot wind of the ball's passing and saw it tear a nasty chunk out of the mizzenmast. He felt a warm spray and looked down at his hand and saw it was splattered with blood. He turned in time to see the helmsman, Ouellette, *sans* head, topple forward, adding to the great pool of blood already left in the wake of the two men before him.

"Someone get aft and get this man clear!" Renaudin shouted, then to Beaussier, "Helm's a-lee!" *L'Armançon* began her turn up into the wind, the hands on the forecastle, experienced men, letting go the headsail sheets. The sails flogged and the ship surged around, but to Renaudin's mounting frustration, the damned Americans followed her turn, keeping on her quarter as if secured there by some unseen cable.

The American fired again, the ball screamed past. Renaudin felt the concussion of its passing and then it struck the spanker boom, nearly at the center of the long spar. A great ragged hole was torn in the wood. The boom hung for a second as the last, tenacious fibers parted. Renaudin shouted, "Stand from under!" and he stepped forward and shoved Barère in the path of the boom just as it gave way. The heavy spar, a foot thick, came crashing to the deck, taking Barère down with it, and Renaudin thought, *Very well, I'm free from that distraction.*

Beaussier had continued to hold the helm hard over, and properly so. *L'Armançon* turned to windward like a weather vane, so far up into the wind by then that she would have to tack or get all aback. And the American, the cursed American, was still hanging on the quarter, within a pistol shot but beyond the reach of any of *L'Armançon*'s great guns.

"Mainsail haul!" Renaudin shouted and he turned to give instruction to Beaussier when the man's chest seemed to explode in a spray of blood. Renaudin saw the wide eyes, the look of surprise, and then Beaussier crashed against the binnacle box as the force of the shot flung him forward and the abandoned wheel began to spin.

"You bastard!" Renaudin shouted, the curse directed at the American. Four helmsmen! They had killed four helmsmen, Renaudin had never seen the like.

And he knew in his gut what this meant. Even as he again leapt for the unattended wheel, the second time that day, he knew they were in irons. He grabbed the spokes and steadied the helm and looked forward. The headsails were flogging, the mainsails shivering, the momentum of the turn all but gone. They were stopped dead, and there was the American, still on the quarter, like one of Satan's minions sent to torment him.

If there was one consolation, it was that the men of *L'Armançon* reacted as seamen should. He could hear Dauville shouting orders, could see the men flatting in the headsails to bring the bow around again. Two men came racing aft to take up the helm, despite its being, apparently, the most dangerous position on the ship. They dragged Beaussier's body out of the way and relieved Renaudin of the wheel. Barère had not moved since the boom had come down on him, and there was every reason to hope he was dead.

The American fired again, the shot ripping down the length of the quarterdeck bulwark and tearing it apart. Dauville shouted for the men to haul the main braces back around to a starboard tack. Another gun from astern, and another bit of the mizzenmast gone. The American had hove to, stopped dead in the water, right astern, and was pounding away to the extent that he could, with the three pathetic six pounders in his broadside.

Pathetic, but at least he can hit me, Renaudin thought, and then as if to demonstrate, a roundshot struck the mizzen chains on the larboard side with a shower of wood and screech of iron hitting iron. Shattered bits of deadeyes and chainplates were hurled forward and two men who were tending the fore brace were struck down.

Renaudin wanted to shout out to Dauville to get the ship turning but the officer was doing everything he could so Renaudin clenched his teeth and remained silent. He could feel some motion underfoot, the bow starting to swing off the wind under the pressure of the backed headsails. *Very well, very well*, Renaudin thought. In a moment or two the larboard battery would bear on the American and then they would end this nonsense.

But something was out of alignment and it caught his eye, something about the ship was wrong. Renaudin did not realize what it was until he saw the mizzenmast leaning farther and farther to larboard, the beautiful symmetry of masts and rigging ruined. The leaning stopped as the starboard shrouds took up the strain and held the mast in place, checking the momentum of the collapse.

But the shrouds did not check the momentum for long. The leverage exerted by topmast, the topsail yard, and its attendant gear, not to mention the topgallant mast, yard, and sail on that lofty rig, was far more than the lower shrouds could bear. First one then the other tore from the channel with a horrible wrenching sound. Men at the base of the mast shouted and raced away and two topmen came sliding down the backstays just as the entire thing fell slowly to leeward, picking up speed in its tumble to the sea. It went by the board with a great splash as the topmast and topgallant hit the water, and the mizzen lower mast crushed the bulwarks on the larboard side of the quarterdeck as it fell across them.

L'Armançon was stopped dead and would remain that way for hours, until she had cut the wreckage clear and could limp away. The Americans would be free to continue their cannonade if they wished, perhaps even to try to beat *L'Armançon* into surrender, a thing that would not happen as long as Renaudin was still alive. He pulled his eyes from the wreckage and looked astern. The Americans were done fighting. They had already hauled their wind and were racing off with larboard tacks aboard.

Renaudin stepped over to Barère's inert form and kicked him hard in the stomach. "I may defeat them soundly now, eh, you whore's son, you bastard?" he shouted, and to his further and profound dismay he heard Barère groan in response.

21

A ship fogbound at sea is in no particular danger. A ship fogbound in soundings is quite a different matter. Making way with visibility so poor the master cannot see from the quarterdeck to the jibboom end, or perhaps not even to the foremast, is a dangerous and unnerving situation. In such a thick fog there is no chance of seeing fore or aft, to weather or lee, no point in seeing up, and so the only way of determining position is to look down, or, more correctly, to feel what is below by means of a lead line.

To sound with a hand lead, a man stands on the fore chainwale, secured by a breast rope, and throws the lead forward, allowing the line to run out until he feels the weight hit bottom. The line is marked off at various fathom intervals, and the man in the chains sings out to indicate the depth at which the weight found bottom; "By the mark, five!" or "And a half five!" or "By the deep six!" A master who knows the waters can thus feel his way through the fog by measuring the depth, relying on his knowledge and intuition honed by years of experience.

It was in a similar situation that Ezra Rumstick found himself now, feeling his way through the fog, though in this case it was obfuscation and treachery, and not mist, that obscured his way. The interview with Bolingbroke had parted the fog a bit, but only a bit. Jonah had confirmed that the duel was a concocted affair, arranged for reasons unknown to him by men far more powerful than he. Bolingbroke had given them one name: Ness.

Between Rumstick and Tillinghast they knew two men of that name. One was a blockmaker in the Northern Liberties. The other was secretary to James McHenry, who was secretary of war to President John Adams, a holdover, as most were, from the Washington administration. Both Rumstick and Tillinghast had a pretty good idea of which was the Ness to whom Bolingbroke referred.

"This whole thing," Rumstick said, making a wide sweeping gesture to encompass the whole affair, "it's like French philosophy or some such, it doesn't make any kind of sense."

Tillinghast nodded. It was the morning after they had let Bolingbroke go, and so, fortified with coffee and a substantial breakfast, they met to discuss their next move. Rumstick liked discussing things with Tillinghast, who could usually see when Rumstick was getting far off course and was not afraid to say it.

"No sense," Tillinghast said. "At least none that we can see. Yet."

"Oxnard's no friend of the administration," Rumstick said, trying to put things into some logical framework. "Far from it. He's an associate of that whore's son Benjamin Franklin Bache and all those Jeffersonian disciples."

"And Ness is part of the administration, and they hate Oxnard and his lot as much as Oxnard hates them," Tillinghast supplied.

"Right. So if Ness tries to get Jack killed, he robs Oxnard of a good captain. Hurts him," Rumstick suggested, but Tillinghast just frowned.

"True enough," Tillinghast said. "But it don't answer. Someone from Adams's administration having the son of one of Adams's biggest supporters in Congress killed just so Oxnard loses a good captain? Be more effective to burn his ship. No. It's got to be something more than that."

Rumstick nodded and leaned back. Tillinghast was right. This was more complex by half.

"If there is one thing I learned back in the war," Rumstick said, a turn of phrase he used quite often, there being many things that he learned back in the war, "it's that the bold move is generally the best move, do you see? None of this tacking and wearing and weather gauge nonsense. It's always best to go right at them."

"Except those times when it ain't," Tillinghast said.

"Well, certainly, except those times. But generally, right at them, I say."

So that was the strategy they agreed upon, if strategy it could be called. Right at them. And by "them" Rumstick meant "Ness," because Ness was the only target in sight.

Ness, Jonathan Ness of North Carolina, who had been with Nathanael Greene during the brutal hit-and-run fighting against Cornwallis in his home state and had fought at Guilford Courthouse, was now getting corpulent in his older years, comfortable and prosperous. He dined nearly every day at the City Tavern, and Rumstick, who also dined there on occasion, would generally see him there. They had a nodding acquaintance, and so Ness was in no way surprised to see Rumstick step into the big, low-ceilinged room and make a gesture of greeting. He was more surprised when Rumstick crossed the room to his table, just to the right of the fireplace, unused now in the warming days of spring, and, uninvited, pulled out a chair and sat opposite him.

"Captain Rumstick, good day, pray have a seat," Ness said as Rumstick settled himself. Rumstick had had chairs collapse under him, and he always sat with care.

"Mr. Ness, good day," Rumstick said, and seeing Ness had been perusing the pages of Bache's *Aurora* said, "You've gone over to the other side, I see."

Ness looked at the paper as if surprised to see it there. "No, nothing of the kind. But I do like to keep up with what that seditious dog is printing. It's the only way to stay ahead of the vermin, you know, though I do feel the need for a damned good washing up after touching the thing."

One of the tavern girls brought a pewter mug of ale, because Rumstick was well enough known that they did not need to ask his preference. He thanked her, took a moment to regard her with some admiration, then turned back to Ness. "Quite right, know your enemy and that," he said. "Say, I had the chance to speak with a friend of yours just yesterday, Jonah Bolingbroke. He sends his regards."

Ness frowned. "Jonah Bolingbroke? Do I know a fellow of that name? I don't recall." There was nothing disingenuous in the reply, no note of mendacity, at least not that Rumstick could hear. He wished, as he often did, that Isaac Biddlecomb was there, because Isaac was much more adept at detecting such things. But he did not want to bring Isaac into this, not until he had a better sense of what was acting.

"Bolingbroke?" Rumstick said. "Do you not know him? A seaman, of sorts."

"No," Ness said. "I know few seamen, I must admit. Yourself and Captain Biddlecomb, of course, and a few others. Captain Barry. If one properly calls men of your status 'seamen.' I recall no Bolingbroke."

"Captain Biddlecomb . . ." Rumstick said. "Funny you should mention him, because this concerns him. Not Isaac, mind, but Jack, his son. Jack Biddlecomb. Just made captain of the ship *Abigail*. Owned by Robert Oxnard, of all people."

"Really? Oxnard? I should not think Robert Oxnard would do any favors for the son of Isaac Biddlecomb," Ness said, but this time Rumstick was sure he heard something, some catch in Ness's voice, some note that was off, just a bit, as if Ness could suddenly see where this was heading.

"No, I would not reckon Oxnard would do any favors for Isaac, though Jack's a damned fine seaman, make no mistake, and a good choice for master." Rumstick leaned closer, and let his voice drop to a more conspiratorial level. Time to cast the lead. "But here's the thing, Ness. Someone, it seems, did not care to see Jack sail, and he paid this rascal Bolingbroke to engage Jack in a duel to stop him. Do you have any notion of who might have done such a thing?"

"Why in God's name would I have any idea of who would do that?" Ness said, but now the note in his voice was unmistakable, and even Rumstick, who could be thick as a first rate's main-wale, and knew it, could see Ness knew more than he claimed to know. Indeed, he could hardly know less.

Rumstick leaned back, held up his hands. "Of course, of course, I did not mean to suggest anything. You could not be mixed up in this bloody business, I'm sure of it. But this Bolingbroke cove has become pretty talkative of late, with some persuasion, mind you, and though he certainly did not say you were in any way involved in this, he gave me the idea that some pretty important people might be. And sure, you are the most important fellow I know, in the government line."

Ness gave a wave of his hand, a gesture of dismissal. "I am no one of any importance, I assure you," he said, sounding a bit flattered nonetheless. "But I'm afraid I know nothing of this affair."

"Very well," Rumstick said. "I reckoned I should speak to you first, and now I've done so."

"First?" Ness said. "To whom else might you speak? If you'll forgive the inquiry."

"Never think on it. The sheriff, I suppose, is the fellow to see about this. There's something acting here, and I'll warrant it's criminal."

"The sheriff?" Ness said, his stoicism slipping a bit further still. "Not a discreet man at all."

"No, he's not," Rumstick said. He tapped the copy of the *Aurora* lying on the table. "Sometimes I think he goes direct to that whoremonger Bache with everything that comes his way. If I go to him, it will be all over this paper, and I don't reckon Bache will be singing the praises of the administration. Hell, he'll damn Adams and those who serve him for nothing, but if it happens they have some connection to this thing with Jack, I reckon Bache will find it, and then the cat's out of the bag. But there's nothing for it."

"Now see here, Rumstick," Ness began, but then with some effort altered the tone of his words. "I may be able to make a few inquiries, ask around. People hear things, you know. Before you speak with the sheriff, I may be able to find some hint of what this Bolingbroke was about."

"I would be very much in your debt if you would," Rumstick said, and he held Ness's eyes in such a way as to convey the very earnestness of his threat. "I would be very much in your debt if you was to find something out tonight, and tell me what you know on the morrow. Here. This same time." He tapped the *Aurora* with a beefy finger. He stood and left Ness open-mouthed but with nothing more to say.

It was another two days before *Abigail* dropped anchor in three fathoms of clear, aquamarine water, under the leering guns of a British seventy-four. They were not in Barbados, their intended destination. They had not even tried to reach Barbados. Rather, after hearing the persuasive council of Charles Frost, Jack had opted to run for English Harbour in Antigua. It was a place where Frost was well known, or so he insisted, a place where he knew the right people, people who could be of great service in getting *Abigail* safely to her stated destination.

With that one happy shot into *L'Armançon*'s mizzen chains, *Abigail* had brought down the Frenchman's mizzen and crippled her, and Jack knew she would remain crippled for a quarter of an hour at least as they cleared the wreckage away. Jack's blood was up by then, and his ship was hove to where the Frenchman's guns could not reach and for a moment he considered remaining where he was, pouring shot into her, beating her into surrender.

And then he realized that was madness. *How am I to take her as a prize, how would I secure the prisoners?* he wondered. But even that question was insane. *Prize?* he thought. *What in hell am I thinking? We're not at war with France, but if I keep shooting at this fellow, we damn well will be!*

He had no notion of what *L'Armançon* was about, attacking them as she had, but whatever it was, he did not care to make it worse. He ordered the sails trimmed, the helm put down, and they left the shattered Frenchman in their wake.

Abigail had not come through the encounter unscathed. Far from it. A roundshot through the great cabin windows had made a direct hit on Jack's sideboard, obliterating all of the fine dinner service his mother had insisted he take and spilling half his wine stores on the deck, so that it looked like a butcher had been at work on the painted canvas floor cloth. The chimney on the caboose had been blown clean over the side, the mizzenmast was badly wounded, and a surprising amount of rigging had been torn up.

Of greater consequence, one of the shots from *L'Armançon*'s broadside had smashed a hole through *Abigail* betwixt wind and water, but considerably closer to water than wind. Indeed, it entered just inches above the waterline, which made for a prodigious inflow when she was on a starboard tack. They managed to patch it after a fashion, but it still required hands at the pumps for an hour and a half during every watch.

Ordinary seaman Ratford was long dead by the time anyone had a moment to think of him, his arm lying a few feet from his body, his white face staring up at the sky, a shocking amount of blood pooled around him and running down into the scuppers. They draped a tarpaulin over him until Lucas Harwar was able to sew him up in some spare canvas, with two of the six pound balls at his feet. Jack read the burial at sea, words he had heard on a few occasions but had never uttered himself, and Ratford's earthly remains were tipped into the Caribbean. Any enthusiasm the men might have felt at their narrow and well-executed escape was muted by that grim task.

They set sail and they knotted and spliced and pumped and they made easting. Jack took Wentworth's hand and shook it with enthusiasm when the Bostonian regained the deck, rifle over his shoulder, his face smudged with powder residue in a way that would have seemed unthinkable the day before.

"Well done, Mr. Wentworth," Jack said. "An excellently placed shot."

"Thank you," Wentworth said. "To which shot do you refer?"

"Why, the one that struck down the helmsman. At just the right moment."

"Which helmsman do you mean? I seem to have bagged a covey of them."

Jack released Wentworth's hand. "Just as the Frenchman was coming about, you shot the helmsman like some poacher on the king's preserve."

"Ah, yes," Wentworth said. "And two others, you know, earlier. Two with a single shot, I dare say, though I was aided by the second fellow stepping into my line of fire at just the right moment."

"Ah, very nice," Biddlecomb said. Here he was, gracious enough to give the man his due for a well-placed shot, but that of course was not enough for William Wentworth of the Boston Wentworths. No, he had to lay claim to having shot two other helmsmen as well, and with a single bullet. In another two minutes he would be claiming that it was he and his rifle that took down the Frenchie's mizzenmast.

As to their own mizzenmast, it was fished under the careful supervision of Jack and John Burgess; additional stays were rigged, and the entire lash-up was treated as tenderly as possible as they made the best of their way to Antigua. They raised the island with only a few hours of daylight left, hove to and rounded Point Charlotte late the next morning, standing in under the fore topsail and coming to anchor half a mile from the Royal Navy dock-yard.

It was hot and still in the harbor, and all around them the hills rose up from the water's edge, dry-looking despite the thick vegetation that covered them. The white boats of the men-of-war at anchor plied back and forth, and the still air was filled with the tap-tap-tap of caulking mallets and the pounding of beetle hammers, the echoing sound of something heavy dropped into place and the occasional order shouted by a frustrated boat-swain, shipwright, or officer.

The men of the *Abigail* were not fond of being so close to the Royal Navy, for even though they were all Americans with the papers to prove it, the navy was not always so particular when they needed men. But Frost assured them they would be unmolested, so they grumbled and muttered but said no more.

The second shot from *L'Armançon* had shattered *Abigail*'s longboat, but happily the bumboats swarmed like mosquitoes once her anchor was set, and Frost had little difficulty in securing passage to shore.

"Captain," he said to Jack, taking him aside, "I pray you'll forgive me this liberty, but I must go alone. These negotiations are . . . delicate. We've no quarrel with England now, at least not officially, but still it's not in the interest of an officer in His Majesty's Navy to be seen helping an American, if you understand. Now, these dockyard fellows, they can be persuaded, but they're shy around those they don't know."

"I understand," Jack said, happy to turn this over to Frost, as he had no idea of what he might say to persuade anyone in English Harbour to give them aid. He would not expect help from any place called English Harbour.

"If you can manage it," Jack added, "we don't need to careen, just to heave her down a bit to get at that shot hole. A new mizzenmast is far too much to ask, but if we can get the timber to fish it proper we can make due. We could use water, and some casks, after the damage from that shot that holed us down low. And a boat, if one is to be had."

"A formidable list," Frost said, "but these British may be inclined to help one so battered by their enemy."

"I have money, of course," Jack added. "Mr. Oxnard provided money for expenses, but I have no great store of it. If they are asking a dear price we'll have to get it on Oxnard's credit, or do without."

"I shall see what I can do," Frost said, and with a conspiratorial wink he climbed down into the waiting bumboat and was gone.

Jack set the men to work, sending down the top-hamper in preparation for a partial heaving down, unbending the mizzen, which still needed various shot holes patched, and fashioning a new stovepipe for the caboose. The remains of the longboat were broken up and stowed down in the kindling box.

When that was done the Abigails stood down to an anchor watch, which was not particularly watchful, with most of the men asleep in whatever bits of shade could be found on deck. Jack was happy to give them the rest. There were some masters who would keep the men at their tasks even when there were no tasks that really needed to be done, but he could never see the percentage in that. As often as not a resentful crew would work Tom Cox's Traverse, a silent protest in which they did every job in the slowest, clumsiest, most lubberly fashion they could, until the master, driven to distraction by the frustration of it all, relented.

Nor was Jack adverse to a respite, now that the ship was safe in harbor and protected from the French by the massive guns of the British navy, an odd turn of events for the son of a hero of the War for Independency. He was seated on the taffrail in shirtsleeves and a straw hat, the sun approaching the high ground to the west, when Wentworth came aft, his step hesitant, as if trying to make it seem a great coincidence that he and Jack should find themselves on the same quarterdeck at the same time.

"Captain Biddlecomb," Wentworth nodded in greeting.

"Mr. Wentworth."

They were quiet for a moment after that, both looking out across the water at the massive ship-of-the-line moored by the dockyard, her rig sent down to lowers. "That ship there," Wentworth said at length, speaking quietly as the evening seemed to demand, "is that what one calls a 'first rate'?"

"She's a seventy-four, Mr. Wentworth," Jack explained. "Seventy-four guns, at least that is what she is designed to carry. As often as not the captain will crowd a few more on for good measure. But she is a third rate. A first rate would have a hundred or more guns."

"Indeed? A mere third rate. And yet there is nothing in the American fleet to match her?"

"There is not really an American fleet at all," Jack said. "The *United States* just launched, of course, we saw her on leaving Philadelphia. *Constitution* and *Constellation*, still on the stocks. We call them frigates, though the British might call them fifth rates. In any event, they would not stand in the line of battle, not with great beasts like that one yonder."

"Fascinating," Wentworth said. "I know absolutely nothing about such things, but I'll warrant it's a fascinating business."

Jack gave a twisted smile, despite himself. "Perhaps so. I was weaned on it, or at least talk of it. The novelty is quite gone."

They were quiet again for a bit, then Wentworth said, "I meant to say,

Captain . . . and I did not care to embarrass you, speaking so in front of others, but I was quite impressed with the way you handled the ship against the Frenchman. I'm no judge, of course, but it seemed to me quite the thing."

"Thank you, Mr. Wentworth, I appreciate that," Jack said. And he did appreciate it, with reservations, since Wentworth still put him on edge. He felt Wentworth was incapable of sincerity, though admittedly he seemed sincere enough in this instance. Still, Jack belied the sincerity of his own response by waiting a beat too long before adding, "And I am grateful for your fine marksmanship."

"Yes, well . . ." Wentworth said, and then fell quiet again for a moment. "It's a very odd thing, you know, this shooting a man. I've been in many affairs of honor. More than I can recall, a dozen certainly, if not more. I've shot men and I've drawn blood with cold steel, but I've never killed anyone. And to be sure, these were just Frenchmen, but they were *men*, do you see? A very odd thing, aiming at a man, seeing him fall. They were too far to see any more than their shapes, of course, but still one knows it's a human one is shooting. I can't seem to shake that image, or to stop seeing it in my mind."

The words tumbled out as if Wentworth had been waiting for the chance to say them out loud, as if he had been mulling them, adding thoughts, refining them as he looked for the main chance to tell someone. Jack listened, nodded, felt as thoroughly embarrassed at hearing the confession as Wentworth seemed to feel having given it.

"Well, in any event," Wentworth said, "we are much beholden to you for keeping us out of the Frenchman's grip. Now I believe I shall go below stairs . . . have my watch below, as you tarpaulins would say." There was a note of the old irony there, but it sounded as strained as did Wentworth's go at sincerity.

"Well, sir, I trust you'll have a good rest. And I believe I'll wait for Mr. Frost to return. You can imagine I'm eager to hear what he has managed to arrange."

They made their good nights and Jack remained aft, enjoying the evening on the quarterdeck. When Frost did not return after a few more hours he retired to the great cabin with a glass of wine from one of the few unshattered bottles left. And when Frost still did not return he changed to his nightshirt and crawled into his berth, exhausted from the day's labors.

The next morning, as John Burgess set the hands to scrubbing down, Frost still had not returned, and he had not returned by the time they began rousting out the shattered water casks from the hold. It was not until dinner was an hour past that Jack saw a longboat pulling for *Abigail*, the paint on her freeboard so white he could hardly look directly at it in the afternoon sun, six men-of-war's men pulling at the oars and Frost, large and seeming even larger than before, seated in the sternsheets.

They hauled up alongside and the bowman hooked on to the main chains, and Frost came aboard, and to Jack's surprise the British sailors did as well. This caused a wave of muttering to sweep through the assembled Abigails, but the British tarpaulins stood silent and respectful and caused no further alarm.

"Fine boat, isn't she, Captain?" Frost asked with his accustomed enthusiasm.

Jack glanced down at the longboat bobbing alongside, an excellent example of the boatwright's craft, to be sure. "Lovely boat," he agreed.

"She's ours," Frost said. "And these fine fellows, sent out to assist as long as ever we need."

"Assist with what?" Jack asked.

"Well, here's the thing," Frost said. "I had a most excellent meeting with the superintendent of the dockyard here. Fine fellow. Insisted I stay the night, and to tell the truth, with all the wine he plied me with, I don't know that I would have trusted myself to a boat. But here's the thing. This fellow will do anything, help anyone who wishes to knock a Frenchman on the head. Enemy of my enemy, that sort of thing. Astoundingly generous, astounding. Water and casks will be no problem, heaving down to get at the shot hole is being arranged as we speak."

"What of the mizzenmast?"

"Ah, yes, well he has no stick that will serve for new, but he'll be happy to help us fish the old one as best as can be done. But here's the part that's above and beyond the call. He's agreed to give us the use of another six six-pounders, and have his ship carpenters mount them. And you can bet they'll do a damned sight better job of it than those thieves in Philadelphia. It'll be a bit crowded topsides, I'm not saying it won't, but if we make that main hatch a bit narrower, that should answer. Then this fellow says he'll give us the powder and shot we need, and even lend us experienced hands enough to work the guns!"

Jack felt the sick twist in his stomach, which was becoming all too familiar. "Now, see here, Mr. Frost," he said. "I had thought you were going to see about getting what we need to set the ship to rights, enough to get us to Barbados. I hardly thought you were going to arrange to turn us into some kind of damned man-of-war." Even as he spoke he felt the shame of his failure. Had Frost ignored his instructions? No. He had given Frost no instructions, he had ceded his authority, he had allowed Frost all the latitude he wished.

"My dear captain, it's quite beyond that now," Frost said, not unkindly. "Robert . . . Mr. Oxnard . . . made it clear enough that he wishes the ship to reach Barbados, not end up as some prize to the French. We tried sneaking through and were caught up. Now, after the drubbing you gave Monsieur Crapeau out there, every privateer and man-of-war will be on the hunt for us. Forgive me, Captain, if I have overstepped my bounds, but the simple fact here is this . . . if we are to reach Barbados, we must fight our way there."

Jack nodded. Frost had said nothing with which he might argue or disagree. Frost seemed have a knack for doing that. But still Jack felt as if this business was spinning out of control, and he with no way to stop it, or even slow its momentum.

22

Boston in the summer could be beastly hot, or so William Wentworth had always believed. In truth, as he now realized, he had had no notion of what real heat was, but he was starting to. It had been hot enough at sea, but there had generally been a breeze of some sort that had tempered the heat considerably. There was little breeze to be found in English Harbour, however, where the sun beat down like a blacksmith's hammer, and every sound seemed unnaturally loud in the still air.

And, dear Lord, it's only . . . Wentworth had to think on it for a moment. *It's only May 22 . . .* What must happen, he wondered, when the really hot season arrived?

From a spot by the mizzen fife rail, a good place to observe yet stay well out of the way, Wentworth watched as they made ready to tow the *Abigail* alongside the quay. The degree of interest he took in the procedure still surprised him. A massive ship's boat came up under the bow, thirty feet long and expertly rowed by hardcase British men-of-war's men, pigtailed and straw-hatted, powerful arms with muscles that rippled under tanned skin. Watching them at their work gave Wentworth a vague feeling of inadequacy, and he reminded himself that they were seamen of the Royal Navy: poor, mostly illiterate, bound to the service, little better than slaves, while he was a Wentworth of the Boston Wentworths.

They took a towline that Burgess and a gang under his supervision had rigged from the *Abigail*'s bow, and once *Abigail*'s anchor hung dripping and muddy from the starboard cathead, they laid into the oars and towed the merchantman alongside the stone quay. A blue-coated officer sat in the boat's sternsheets, hand on the tiller, but if he ever gave an order, Wentworth did not hear it.

Once *Abigail* was secured alongside, her men and the dockyard's men and more men from the British men-of-war appeared and began hoisting the six pounders off her deck, which seemed an act of disarmament, but at the same time ship's carpenters appeared and as far as Wentworth could tell began cutting holes in the bulwark for even more guns to be set in place.

It was all something of a mystery, since no one had told him anything of their current plans, and so on the second day of that furious activity, when Biddlecomb seemed to be unoccupied for a rare moment, Wentworth approached him. They had not spoken more than a few words since Wentworth had confessed to his discomfort about killing the Frenchmen, an embarrassing and regrettable admission, and it took a considerable degree of curiosity to overcome his reluctance to speak to Biddlecomb now.

"Captain, forgive me, but could I inquire as to what's going on here?"

Biddlecomb looked at him with an odd expression, part annoyance and part surprise that he should ask such a question, as if Biddlecomb expected him to know quite well what was going on.

"We are getting the guns and stores off her, getting her ready to heave down," Biddlecomb said, unhelpfully.

" 'Heave down'?"

"We'll make a block fast to her mainmast head, a great four-part affair, and run the fall to a capstan and heave away, roll the ship on her side. Not all the way, just enough to get at that hole the Frenchie gave us, so that we might repair it."

"Ah . . ." Wentworth said, now partially enlightened. "And these other fellows?"

"Are cutting new gunports for the additional guns we're to mount. Now, please forgive me, but here's the last of the water casks hoisted out and I must see if we have any damage below that was not obvious before."

And so William Wentworth was left alone for that day, and the next, being, apparently, the only man in English Harbour, or perhaps on all of Antigua, who did not have one damned thing to occupy his time. He watched them heave the *Abigail* down, which was certainly interesting, and watched the rest of the preparations, which became increasingly dull with each passing moment. He managed to extract information from Frost, not much, but enough to give him some sense for what was going on. Or at least some sense for what Frost wished him to believe was going on. William Wentworth was many things, many of them unpleasant, but naïve was not one of them.

By the third day he had had his fill of dockyard procedures and decided to see if there was any shooting to be had on the island, so he collected up his rifle, powder horn, and shot bag and made his way down the gangplank to the quay.

It was all new, all utterly new and foreign to him. In twenty-two years he had left Massachusetts all of six times, and of those, New York was the farthest afield he had gone, save for his passage to Philadelphia to meet the *Abigail*. William Wentworth had never been one for travel, for novelty and new experience. He had never seen the appeal.

But standing on the quay, under a sun such as he had never felt before, surrounded by a place the likes of which he had never seen, he was nearly overwhelmed by the sensation, the strangeness of it. He was Adam waking in this new-made paradise. Palm trees—palm trees!—were waving as if in greeting. Bright-plumed birds unlike anything in his experience flickered past, making the cardinals of his native New England, perhaps the gaudiest of birds found there, look dull in comparison. A lizard, five inches long, stood in his path as if daring him to proceed.

A few hundred feet away stood the buildings of the dockyard, stone and brick and rough-hewn wooden beams. They looked out of place in their familiarity, stolid, humorless British architecture set down in this frivolous land. Worn paths, or perhaps they might be called roads, ran from the quay in various directions, dusty and paved with a layer of broken shells. One ran past a three-story stone building punctuated by a series of windows along its face, a flagpole with the Union Jack waving in a lazy, desultory way.

William took this building to be a barracks of some sort, a place for the officers to live when ashore, perhaps. A trellis stood to one side of the building; a profusion of vines and massive vivid flowers covered the wooden frame, giving some blessed shade to the four men at the table below it. British naval officers. They were in shirtsleeves and waistcoats. Their blue uniform coats were draped over the backs of their chairs and there were half-full glasses before them, a half-empty bottle amidships. They seemed to be taking their pleasure in a quiet, unhurried way, the only way that seemed right in such heat.

Their presence reminded William of yet another unique aspect of his situation, another novel thing after a lifetime of studiously avoiding novelty. He was now in a foreign land. He was in a colony of the British Empire. He had of course been born in a colony of the British Empire, had been British himself for all of ten months before the Congress declared independence and his father, among others, had fought to turn that declaration into a political reality.

William's father, Charles Wentworth, was never a wild revolutionary, despite having shot at Englishmen and having been shot at by them in return. *Père* Wentworth was not one of those who came to hate the mother country. Quite the opposite; he continued to admire the British and dislike the French, and his dislike of the French had expanded exponentially with the outbreak of their revolution, which, unlike that of the Americans, exhibited a hedonistic liberality of which he did not approve.

These attitudes, like wealth and a somewhat prominent nose, he had handed down to his son. William Wentworth would normally have felt an affinity for British naval officers. But at that moment, he was not so sure.

Standing there on that dusty road, wearing only a loose cotton shirt, rumpled from having been crammed in a sea chest and already wet from perspiration and quite wilted, wool socks and shoes that had suffered much from their sea voyage, and a straw hat such as a foremast jack or a field hand might wear, Wentworth was feeling every bit the Yankee Doodle Dandy. For all the heat, the officers under the trellis did not seem to be in the least discomforted, and their waistcoats and shirts were white and smooth as if fresh from the laundry, the buckles on their shoes glinted when the sunlight found them through the vines overhead.

Wentworth sighed. There was nothing for it. He would have to walk past them, secure in his knowledge that in wealth, breeding, or learning he was the equal of any of them. He put his rifle over his shoulder and walked on, he shoes crunching over the shells underfoot, the birds making weird noises from the cover of the thick and pungent vegetation.

He could feel the eyes on him as he walked past, and he was not entirely surprised to hear one of the officers call out, "I say! You there, I say!"

Wentworth stopped. He could feel the color rising in his face, felt the familiar sensation of growing resentment, of smoldering offense. What would happen if he was insulted? In Boston the answer would be as obvious as his reaction would be swift. But here? What would happen to him, or the men of the *Abigail*, if he were forced to call one of these fellows out and put a bullet in him?

But there was no time to think that through, to weigh the various possibilities. One of these fellows had called to him, and he could not ignore him. He turned on his heel. They were all looking at him, all four officers, three near his own age and one a decade or more older. It was one of the younger men who had called out, and he was now regarding Wentworth with considerable interest.

"I say," the naval officer continued, his tone one of surprise and admiration. "Your rifle, sir, is that a Jover and Belton?"

The question took Wentworth full aback, completely disarmed him. He approached the men, handed the weapon over for their inspection. The fellow who had called to him took it up with respect, held it at various angles to admire it, handed it off to his fellow officers, then insisted that Wentworth join them in a drink.

The shade was a blessing, a soft breeze had come up. The wine, which was Madeira, was actually cool, made so through an evaporative process that the officers explained to Wentworth as they opened a second bottle. The officer who had first called to Wentworth introduced himself as Lieutenant Thomas Chandler, fourth officer aboard the seventy-four *Warrior,* Sir James Wallace commanding, the very ship about which Wentworth had been asking Jack. Chandler told Wentworth that he owned a fowler by Jover and Belton and a brace of pistols, and he recognized the craftsmanship right off. They discussed the merits of the guns for a few animated moments, with the enthusiasm of the true *aficionado*, the sort that those outside the club find hard to fathom.

The older man, who was second aboard *Warrior,* said, "We were about to have a bite, cheese and fruit and cakes, nothing extraordinary, but we would be most pleased was you to join us."

"Delighted, sir, thank you," Wentworth said. The thought of fresh fruit and new company, enjoyable company, was powerfully compelling. He sipped his Madeira, sweet and cool. He took the ridiculous straw hat from his head.

"Beastly hot, and only going to get worse," the older man observed.

"You are from this American merchantman, I presume?" Chandler said. "Must be, we haven't seen a new face around here in weeks, not until you sailed in. It's tedious in the extreme, sitting out here, no one to look at but these three. God, but their conversation can get dull."

"Dull, you say?" said one of the officers. "Ah, my dear Chandler, you are always the whetstone to our dull discussions. By 'whetstone' I mean to imply that you are coarse, rough, and quite unpolished."

Wentworth wondered if this was going to grow more heated, how ugly it might become, but then he saw that this was simply how they talked with one another, men so familiar with each other's company that they could toss out insults of that nature and give no offense. Wentworth had seen that before, though he had never personally had such a connection to anyone.

The food and more drink were brought out by a young black man in bleached white slop trousers and shirt. The second officer said, "So you were in that action with that corvette, that *L'Armançon*, or so goes the rumor flying around here. Pray, tell us more."

Wentworth could see the men leaning a little closer in, more interested now that the discussion had turned to the topic of their profession, and he knew he was about to disappoint them. "Forgive me, gentlemen, I'm a passenger aboard *Abigail* and remarkably lacking in knowledge, even for a landsman, but I'll relate what I can."

He started in, describing the fight as best he could, from their first sighting of the Frenchman to their sailing off with the battered enemy in their wake. The officers asked a few questions, but Wentworth's stumbling, partial answers discouraged them from asking any more that required expertise of a maritime nature. But he managed a credible recounting, suitably humble, of the part he played, firing from the "maintop," savoring the use of one of the few nautical terms he remembered.

"Ho!" said one of the officers, "you made a one-man contingent of marines! Well done!"

"In a sea fight we will station the marines in the tops," Chandler explained, "to fire on the enemy's deck. I would we could equip them all with small arms from Jover and Belton."

"Jover and Belton or not," one of the others said, "that's a damned fine shot. And to take out the helmsman just as they were rising tacks and sheets, or so I gather from your description, well, I dare say that won the day for you."

"Just like a Frenchman, ain't it," another observed, "to have but one man at the wheel during a sea fight?"

The others nodded. Wentworth thanked them for their kindness. He did not tell them about shooting the two helmsman with a single shot. He feared they would not find that entirely credible, just as Biddlecomb clearly had not.

Wentworth's original plan to go shooting was lost in the languid, pleasant afternoon and evening, eating, drinking, conversing, and Wentworth had all but forgotten about it when Chandler asked, "Say, William, were you off for a bit of hunting when I so rudely stopped you?"

"Yes, I suppose I was," Wentworth said, recalling those intentions like some long-ago dream. One of the other officers snorted.

"Best of luck to you. Not a damned thing on this island worth shooting at."

"Maybe we should stock the hills with some Frenchmen," another suggested.

Chandler, an avid hunter, had to second his fellow officers, but he offered to meet Wentworth the next day so that they might go shooting together, an arrangement that Wentworth accepted with pleasure.

Wentworth was back on the quay just after sunrise the following morning, and as he approached the stone barracks Chandler appeared, wearing a white linen shirt and straw hat similar to Wentworth's. He had no rifle or powder horn, which struck Wentworth as odd, until two seamen appeared from the dark interior behind him. One carried a rifle, powder horn, shot bag, and a haversack that bulged with some unseen contents. The other carried two haversacks, the straps crossed over his chest, and some other odd-shaped item bound in a cloth and resting on his shoulder.

"William! Good morrow! Here, let my man carry your gun and such!"

He took the rifle from Wentworth's hands and passed it to the seaman, who shouldered it beside the gun he already carried. "Mind that gun, Kipfer," he said, "it's a Jover and Belton, worth more than you'll see in wages and prize money this year, I'll warrant."

"Aye, sir," Kipfer said, giving the weapon a loving pat, and Wentworth thought, *This naval service, this seems a damned fine, civilized occupation . . .*

"Good man with guns, Kipfer," Chandler said to Wentworth. "Mine is a Wilkinson, a decent gun, but you've inspired me to bring the Jover and Belton next commission. Thigpen there has our dinner," he continued, nodding toward the second man, "along with a couple of bottles of a passable Bordeaux. One of the few benefits of being stationed in the West Indies, you know. Surrounded by Frenchies. They won't fight, damn their cowardly hides, but they'll sell us wine quick enough."

Chandler led the way across the dockyard, then along a narrow road that ran into the interior of the island, finally turning onto a path that led up to the higher ground. He explained as they went that there was virtually nothing to hunt on Antigua save for the feral goats, but they could be quite wily, as was their nature, and that made them worthy adversaries.

They spent a few hours circling up into the higher country as the sun climbed aloft and the day grew hotter. Chandler located a small herd of goats with his pocket telescope. They worked their way to leeward of them, but the herd spooked and ran, and they were another hour in getting back up with them. Finally, from seventy-five yards, hidden by the scrubby brush, they dropped two respectable bucks, firing almost simultaneously.

They found their vanquished quarry on a spot of hill that enjoyed an unparalleled view of dipping valleys and the higher, scrubby green hills of Antigua rising and falling like ocean swells to the north, the ring of white beach, the great spread of blue sea beyond. Not the heavy, serious blue of the deep ocean but a lighter, more benign, warmer blue. Far below they could see English Harbour and the great bulk of the *Warrior* at her moorings. With Chandler's glass Wentworth could see *Abigail*, now hove down and listing at an unnatural angle.

Chandler ordered Kipfer to field dress the goats and Thigpen to lay out dinner; it was past the dinner hour and they were in as fine a spot to dine as they could hope to find. In the center of Thigpen's bundle, it turned out, was a ham, cheese, and the Bordeaux. Plates, silver, and glasses appeared from his haversack and soon the two of them, Wentworth and Chandler, were enjoying a pleasant meal, which was shared equally with the sailors, who ate some distance away.

"This is quite the business you fellows are about, I dare say," Chandler said, turning his carving knife back on the ham. "It's been all the talk around the barracks, though the dear Lord knows those old women need something to talk about."

"What business do you mean?"

"Why, this business of arming your merchantman, putting all those guns on her. There's been quite a bit of speculation as to how much hard money is being laid out for all of that."

"Hard money? It was my understanding that the dockyard superintendent was helping of his own volition. That he was eager to help anyone who planned on doing violence to the French."

Chandler chuckled at that. "That seems damned unlikely to me. Dockyard superintendents are a corrupt lot, but this fellow here could teach a course at Oxford on how it's done. He can barely move himself to help His Majesty's ships if there's no gain in it for him, let alone a Yankee, beg your pardon."

Wentworth extended his pardon with a nod.

"No," Chandler continued, "your captain must have paid him well for all that *matériel*, and the help, to boot. I wish we could get *Warrior* attended to with that alacrity. Wallace—he commands *Warrior*—Wallace won't pay a sou to ease things along, and so we sit and ground out on our beef bones."

"Indeed," Wentworth said, taking a sip of the Bordeaux, which was better than Chandler had represented. *Did Biddlecomb bribe this dockyard cove?* he wondered. He probably would have no moral qualms about doing so, nor did Wentworth necessarily think he should. But did he have the ready money? Was it Oxnard's money?

Not Biddlecomb . . . Frost, he realized. Frost was the one who had arranged for the work at the dockyard, the guns, the additional crew.

"But tell me," Wentworth continued, feeling his way along, "surely you fellows are not adverse to our going out and tangling with these damned Frenchmen?"

"Never in life," Chandler said. "But . . . and I say this because I know you are a passenger, and thus none of this is your doing . . . but we think you're mad to try it."

"Mad? Why?"

"Well, because the French ships here, the privateers or whoever you might meet, they are heavily armed and well manned. This *L'Armançon* is a man-of-war, by God, and you are not. She will certainly be on the lookout for you. Sure, I can't say I hold the French navy in any high esteem . . . they're a damned sight better than they were a few years ago, but still they are a bloody floating circus . . . but that notwithstanding, they are still a navy ship, do you see? And you a merchantman."

"Certainly," Wentworth said, not sure if he should be feeling a wounded national pride, "but pray don't forget we beat them before."

"You escaped before. If you had beat them, they would be floating in the harbor down there with the Stars and Stripes wafting above the Tricolor. No, it was some damned fine seamanship from what I can see, and some excellent small arms fire . . ." Chandler raised his glass in salute and Wentworth raised his in return. "But if you stand up to them broadside to broadside, you'll certainly lose. *L'Armançon* does not mount six pounders, she mounts twelves, she has a crew twice as large as yours, even with these new hands you're getting. Her scantlings, that is, the thickness of the planks in her sides, and much greater than yours. Your six pounders will likely bounce right off."

"Oh," Wentworth said, and could think of nothing more. He did not know enough to counter Chandler's argument, nor did he necessarily think Chandler was wrong. During the course of their conversations Wentworth had learned that Chandler had been twelve years in the Royal Navy, had fought pirates in the Mediterranean and the West Indies, had fought the French in the Channel and throughout much of the Atlantic, had taken part in the Glorious First of June. Chandler understood naval affairs, and he had no cause to mislead Wentworth, at least none that Wentworth could see.

"So," Wentworth said at last, "what would you have us do? Surely we'd be in considerable danger venturing to sea without these new guns, and men to man them, what with the French eager for revenge."

Chandler considered the question for a moment. "Probably the best thing would have been to make right for Barbados, before *L'Armançon* had a chance to refit, before the story was out. Too late for that. I guess was I the master, that is, master of a merchantman in this situation, I would think it best to repair as quick as ever I could and get under way, not waste time with all this gunport nonsense. Speed and seamanship will save you, not those ridiculous six pounders."

"I see," Wentworth said, and they fell silent, enjoying the view, the heat of the sun, the rich smells of the land.

"I'll be honest with you, William," Chandler said at last. "I would wish you wouldn't sail with the ship when she leaves. No good will come of it, I fear. I would suggest you remain behind, but I know you are a man of honor, and staying behind is not a thing that a man of honor would do."

"No, it's not," Wentworth agreed. *But what*, he wondered, *what, in these circumstances,* would *a man of honor do?*

23

If William Wentworth was not certain what a man of honor would do, he knew perfectly well what such a man would not do. And that was ironic, given that he was about to do that exact thing.

It was something to which he had given considerable thought, several days of agonizing internal argument, analysis, justification. It had started as soon as his discussion with Chandler had ended, as soon as Chandler's words, delivered almost offhandedly, began to turn over and roll about in his head.

Ignorant as he was of such things, he had taken Frost's words, and Biddlecomb's, concerning how best to deal with the Frenchman as gospel truth, had assumed that their decisions were well considered. He had assumed that the only way out of their predicament was to fight their way out, because that was what Frost had said, and he assumed they had a good chance of winning. Why else would Frost and Biddlecomb have taken that course?

But of course they were merchantmen, not navy men. It was a distinction he had not really appreciated before meeting Chandler and his fellow officers. He saw now it was possible that Frost and Biddlecomb did not know one thing about a sea fight, their high talk be damned.

When *Abigail* was hove down, the men had moved ashore, rather than try to live aboard a ship that was nearly on her beam ends. The foremast hands were housed in one of the stone barracks built for ships' companies, and the officers and Frost and Wentworth took up residence in the same building that Chandler and the others lived. It might have actually been pleasant, living ashore on a tropical island with tolerably decent company, if Wentworth's mind was not so occupied with pondering what, exactly, was taking place.

He watched closely. Not the work on the ship so much. He was impressed with the process of heaving her down, but beyond that he did not really understand what was taking place, or particularly care. Being at sea was one thing. The storm was revitalizing like nothing he had ever experienced, the fight with the Frenchman was to dueling what the sun was to the moon, but this was just labor and it bored him.

Instead, he watched Biddlecomb and Frost closely, watched their interactions, made note of who was taking responsibility for what. He dined with them, kept quiet, observed and listened. When it came to the ship, there was no question that Biddlecomb was in command. He wore the mantle of authority easily, did not agonize over decisions but concluded quickly how things would be done, when and by whom. If the talk was on fishing the mizzen or sistering a frame or adding a dutchman to a strake or whatever indecipherable nonsense was under consideration, Biddlecomb simply informed Frost of how it would be, with the ease of real command.

Frost, in turn, deferred to Biddlecomb on these questions, because, as Wentworth at least could see, they did not really matter. Frost always appeared to acquiesce to Biddlecomb's orders; he was a master at that ruse. But in truth, Frost was the one making the decisions of any importance, and Biddlecomb did not seem to quite appreciate that fact.

For all his bombast, Frost was a subtle creature, Wentworth could see that. He did not make decisions. Rather, he steered Biddlecomb into making the decisions that he, Frost, wished him to make. Mounting the guns, taking on the additional crew, preparing the *Abigail* to fight her way to Barbados, Wentworth watched as Frost manipulated Biddlecomb into coming around to his way of thinking on all those matters. Wentworth listened and took note as Frost ever so carefully shifted the discussion from protecting the *Abigail* from French privateers to fighting *L'Armançon* once again, until Biddlecomb was talking as if that had been the plan all along.

Damn the fishing and the sistering, Wentworth thought, *doing battle with the Frenchman, that's the decision that matters, and it ain't Biddlecomb making it.*

Which led to the next plaguing question: Why was Frost doing this? Were these really Oxnard's orders? Or was Frost playing his own game? And in any case, what possible reason could either man have to bring the fight back to *L'Armançon*?

It was two days after his talk with Chandler that the idea for this dishonorable thing, this disgraceful act that violated everything Wentworth believed to be right, first germinated in his brain, and it was Frost who planted the seed.

Their rooms, Wentworth's and Frost's, faced one another across a hall on the second floor in the stone building, and so they would often meet there as they headed off for their breakfast or when they were retiring for the evening. "Ah, Mr. Wentworth!" Frost said one morning at just such a meeting. "If you have not heard, there is a ship outward bound in a few days, if the wind will serve, and we may get mail back to the States by her. So if you have any letters you wish to send home, I suggest you write them now."

Wentworth thanked him, though there was no one with whom he particularly wished to correspond. But Frost's suggestion did get his mind moving down yet another path. If Frost were taking this opportunity to write letters back to America, he might well be corresponding with Oxnard, might well be giving an explanation of their activities, particularly if whatever they were about was something he and Oxnard had hit upon together.

What that might be, he could not imagine. Oxnard was a Republican, an acolyte of Jefferson, proud of it, and vocal. Frost kept his political leanings to himself, but Wentworth had taken pains to disparage Jefferson, republicanism, and the French at every opportunity, just for the amusement of seeing Frost flare with anger and then struggle to hold it in check. He did not doubt that Frost shared Oxnard's inclinations. Why, then, would he wish to attack a man-of-war of their beloved Republic of France? And why would Oxnard risk losing his ship and cargo in a quixotic fight against a country he ostensibly supported?

"Oh, damn it all!" Wentworth said out loud, overtaken by frustration. It was entirely possible, likely, in fact, that sitting on Charles Frost's desk was a letter that would reveal everything. Wentworth had only to wait until the others were in the dockyard, which they were every day, then open the door, step in, read the letter, put it back, and leave enlightened, and Frost none the worse for it.

It was so simple. And so utterly wrong.

For two days he agonized over the question. This affair was none of his business. But—and this aspect both surprised and irritated him—he was coming to like Biddlecomb, in part because Biddlecomb was so unabashedly rude to him. No one had ever really been rude to him before. No one had dared. The power and influence his family wielded and his own prowess with sword and pistol had always meant people treated him with deference, feigned as it might be.

Biddlecomb, however, was not impressed and William found that amusing. And he did not care to see Biddlecomb led by the nose by the likes of Frost. But did that justify so base an intrusion into a man's privacy? And if he was found out, how could he tolerate the humiliation?

Then, at dinner, as he was indulging in his third or fourth glass of wine (he had quite lost track), Frost raised his glass and said, in that boisterous hail-fellow-well-met manner that annoyed Wentworth in the extreme, "Tomorrow the first of the guns goes back aboard and soon we shall be teaching Jean Crapeau a new tune to dance to!" Biddlecomb raised his glass as well, smiled, not nearly as broad a smile as Frost wore, and Wentworth, through the fog of wine, grit his teeth and thought, *Well, damn this fellow, let us see what you are writing, and to whom, shall we?*

The next morning his head had cleared but his resolve had not wavered, much. He breakfasted with the others as he usually did, wandered down to the quay as he usually did, then wandered back toward the barracks as he often did. He stepped through the door into the cool interior of the stone building, but his hands were slick with sweat and trembling slightly, his stomach churning, and he thought he might vomit.

I am bloody afraid . . . he thought, and the realization surprised him. Physical danger would not bring on this reaction, but now his honor was at stake.

Wentworth climbed the stairs and to his surprise met Lucas Harwar coming down, which made Wentworth start. The flush of guilt was already working on his nerves, but Harwar seemed not to notice. The mate nodded, said, "Good morrow, Mr. Wentworth. Forgot my knife, if you can believe it!" Unlike the lieutenants of the *Warrior*, the mates aboard *Abigail* took an active part in the labor of getting the ship ready for sea, yet another reason, Wentworth thought, that this naval service was such a civilized endeavor.

Wentworth returned Harwar's nod but did not trust himself to speak, and once Harwar was past he continued on up the stairs. He paused outside his own door, ready to reach for the handle in the most innocent manner if he heard anyone approach. But he did not. It was ten thirty in the morning and everyone was occupied elsewhere, or should have been at that time. He let his heartbeat and his breathing settle.

For a long time, ten minutes at least, he stood in the hallway and listened. The far-off sounds of men working, the creaking of a wagon, the occasional lowing of one of the dockyard's oxen, the call of a wild bird, all these things came in from the door below stairs, but not a sound of anyone approaching.

Wentworth crossed the hall and rapped on Frost's door, and realized as he did so that if Frost was there, he had concocted no reason for knocking. His mind raced for an excuse, his hands felt sweatier still, and just as he was coming up with some weak question about when the ship carrying the post might sail he realized that no one had responded to the knock.

He knocked again, a bit louder and bolder this time, but still there was no response. He wiped his palm on his breeches and grabbed the doorknob. He felt a momentary hope that it would be locked, that Frost's precaution might save him from this horrible conundrum. But it twisted easily and the door popped free of the jamb.

Wentworth pushed it halfway open, took a step in, and called softly, "Mr. Frost? Are you here?" No sound greeted him. He stepped all the way into the room. The door was still open, he could still leave. If he was caught he could still make some legitimate-sounding excuse about how he was simply seeking his fellow passenger. He looked over at the small table near the window. There was a quill standing in an ink pot and a paper lying in front of it, half written over. Wentworth closed the door and it shut with the click. Now he was committed.

He stepped quickly across the room and snatched up the paper. The window looked out on the dusty road below. Wentworth leaned forward and looked up and down the road to see if anyone was approaching, then realized that, standing where he was, he could clearly be seen by anyone on the street below, and if that anyone was Frost, he was done for. He stepped back into the shadow, cursing himself, and thought, *I am bloody bad at this underhanded sneaking about business . . .*

He held the letter at an angle to catch the light coming in from the window. *My Dear Oxnard,* it began and Wentworth felt a charge of excitement, a sense of satisfaction at having guessed so correctly.

Wentworth continued to read. *This letter, you will note, comes by way of Antigua, and though it was not our original intent to arrive at this place, and how we happened here I will relate, allow me to say firstly that our being here will greatly facilitate our plans, and indeed I suspect will ultimately render them an even more profound success.*

Wentworth's eyes moved quickly over the words, each sentence adding to his sense of revelation. His mouth was hanging open and he closed it. He finished the letter; it was no more than half written, and cryptic in the extreme, so that it could arguably be construed as completely innocent. But it was not, and for Wentworth, who was right in the middle of the affair, there was certainly enough to give him a decent understanding of what was acting, of the game that Frost and Oxnard were playing.

He started reading again from the beginning, reading more slowly, feeling more confident that he was safe from detection. He scoured the words for any deeper hidden meaning, any allusions or hints or double-talk. So intent was he on the words that he did not hear the footsteps on the wooden stairs until they were at least halfway up the flight to the second floor.

And then he heard them. A soft step, an odd creak. He felt a rush of panic and unreality. He looked wildly around but his mind seemed to have gone dark like a candle snuffed out. He looked at the letter in his hand, realized he had to be rid of that. He dropped it back on the desk. He looked wildly around the room for some place to hide.

No, no, stupid, stupid . . . out, get out!

He took two steps and crossed the room and flung open the door and realized that that was stupid as well. If it had been anyone but Frost they would have walked right past and never known he was in there.

Too late, too damned late . . . He stepped out into the hall, trying for all he was worth to appear entirely innocent, a man exactly where he should be, doing what he should be doing. He closed the door, turned, and found himself face-to-face with Thomas Chandler.

"Ah, William, there you are!" Chandler said.

"Yes . . . yes I was just returning a book . . . a book. Frost lent it to me."

"I understand," Chandler said in a tone that suggested he did not understand.

He doesn't know which damned room is Frost's and he doesn't care! Wentworth admonished himself. *Stupid, stupid . . .*

"Well now that you're done with your book, I was coming to enquire if you might be up for some shooting this afternoon?

"Shooting?"

"Yes, shooting. With guns, you recall."

"Ah, yes, yes. Yes, I should be grateful for any distraction," Wentworth said.

"I dare say," said Chandler. "Very good, then. Shall we meet at, say, three, when this beastly heat is on the ebb?"

"Certainly," Wentworth said. And it *was* hot, beastly hot. He could feel that his shirt was quite soaked, the sweat running down his forehead and back, but the odor was not entirely that of a heat-induced sweat. Wentworth could smell the fear on himself.

It was clear Chandler could see something was not entirely right, but gentleman that he was, he did not inquire, but rather left Wentworth in the hall with a pleasant nod and, "I'll see you at three, then."

Wentworth returned the nod and remained standing long after Chandler's footsteps had reached the bottom of the stairs and he heard them move across the stone surface of the bottom floor and out the door. The fear was gone, the nerves dissipated. He had done the deed, had not been caught. This dishonorable thing was his secret alone, and he could live with that. Because what he had learned could have implications far beyond the lives of just a few men.

At length he spoke out loud, to himself. "And now I'll . . . do what?" he asked. But he had no answer.

If Jack Biddlecomb was anything it was decisive. He made decisions quickly and he stuck with them and he did not second-guess himself. Sometimes his decisions were right and sometimes they were horribly, horribly wrong. But Jack did not waver in them. Until now.

Never in his life could Jack Biddlecomb recall a time when he was more

aggravated, confused, and irritated than he was in the Royal Navy dockyard in Antigua. He seemed to fly from rock-solid resolve to wavering uncertainty on a minute-by-minute basis. He had felt more sure of himself and
of the decision he was making on the day he had walked away from Amos
Waverly and the *City of Newport*, rejected his past, and turned his life 180 degrees, than he did just then. The heat was not helping, the damnable heat.
He had never done well in heat.

Abigail was on an even keel once more, floating alongside the quay, her
wounded strakes now well mended under his sharp scrutiny. That much
he felt good about, because there could be no question that repairs, and repairs well made, were the right course of action. But now he was engaged in
a discussion with the lead shipwright, who had suggested shifting the windlass aft a few feet to make for better clearance for the recoil of the forward-
most of the new six pounders, and that had set him off again in a frenzy of
self-doubt.

He listened with half an ear as the man had explained the benefits and
downsides of such a modification, but mostly Jack was thinking about the
decision to mount these additional guns in the first place, questioning the
wisdom of the whole thing. *The bottom is sound now, perfectly sound, and
clean as well,* he thought. *Mizzen's fished and near as strong as new . . . if we
were to just run for Barbados I'll warrant we could show our heels to any damned
Frenchman in our wake . . .*

And then, like a ghost in some Shakespearean drama, there was Frost's
voice, whispering about the dangers of sailing off so lightly armed, of
Oxnard's determination that *Abigail* not fall victim to any Frenchman, privateer or man-of-war.

But if he did stand and fight, could he win? Against a privateer, perhaps,
because a privateer would not be so big and would not have much stomach
for a hard fight. But *L'Armançon*? What if they encountered her once more?
He was very aware of how much their last encounter had been a close run
thing, even if Frost seemed to think it was a complete victory, and one they
could easily replicate. Would six more guns and two dozen more men make
that much of a difference? And what if he lost?

*Lord, this is my first command! Why does my first command have to be so
damned complicated?* It was a theme of self-pity he found himself returning

to often. Why could he not have been allowed to simply sail to Barbados, make a healthy profit there, load up, and make a healthy profit on the return voyage, the way the carrying trade was supposed to work? He did not think his career would be a grand success if his very first ship was taken by a French man-of-war while he was engaged in some idiotic attempt to play at naval hero.

They'll say, "Oh, he was just trying to emulate his father, you know . . . tired of living in the old man's shadow . . ." he thought, getting himself well bloodied in his emotional self-flagellation.

"Very well, then," Jack said to the shipwright, after half hearing the man's suggestion. "Shift the windlass, if you wish, but see it's mounted at least as secure as it is now. I won't have it tearing out of the deck once a load is put to it."

"Oh, never worry about that, sir, it'll be as good as it is now. Better, I'll warrant."

Jack moved aft, left the man to his work, considered the others who were busy cutting and finishing out the new gunports, getting eyebolts in place, narrowing the main hatch to allow for more room for the guns. He looked toward the gangplank in time to see Wentworth making his way aboard and thought, *Oh, my Lord, this day just gets better and better!*

He drifted farther aft, but it did no good. Wentworth drifted aft with him, and while Jack was trying to look as if he was not avoiding Wentworth, Wentworth was trying to look as if he was not seeking Jack out. But Jack could see that he was, and sure enough, it was not a minute later that Wentworth approached him where he stood by the newly rebuilt helm.

"Captain, how are you, sir?" Wentworth said with a forced casual air. "All's well, I trust?"

"Well enough," Jack said. "And you? You are surviving this heat, I hope."

"Ah, the heat . . . It's something, to be sure. Can't say I've ever experienced the like."

For a moment the two men were silent, looking forward at the work taking place near the bow, and Jack thought through various ways he might make his excuses and send Wentworth away. At certain times he might find Wentworth amusing, but this was not one of them. Wentworth, however, stopped him by saying, "Captain, I wonder if I might have a word with you?"

"Well, I'm quite occupied here, Mr. Wentworth . . ."

"Of course. And this won't take long. Or perhaps it will. In any event, I know this is really not my affair . . . but . . . it's about this business of arming the ship."

"Yes?" Jack said. He felt as if he had gone *en guarde*. Wentworth was broaching the very subject over which he had just been agonizing, and Jack did not care for it.

"Well, it's simply . . . I'm not entirely sure this is the right course of action. Are you certain that fighting this fellow is the best thing? The British officers, you know, they've represented to me that they think the whole thing is mad."

"Yes, well, I generally don't turn to British naval officers for advice," Jack said. "Mr. Frost and I have been over all of this, have thought it through. Surely he's explained to you our thinking here."

"Explained to me? No, why would he?" Wentworth asked.

"You're his assistant, aren't you? Aren't you assisting him on whatever business he's on in Barbados?"

Wentworth's expression was one of surprise, and that in turn surprised Jack. "No," Wentworth said, "I have no relationship with Mr. Frost. I'm bound to Barbados on family business. Actually, I think my father wanted to be shed of me for a bit, but that's neither here nor there. No, I first met Mr. Frost at the City back in Philadelphia when we were waiting to board. I certainly do not know him any more than you. Much less, I would imagine."

"Indeed?" Jack said. This took him very much by surprise, altered his entire understanding of the situation aboard his own ship. He had thought the two of them a pair, confidants. But apparently not.

"That's just the thing," Wentworth continued. "I don't know what Frost is about, but it all seems damned odd. I mean, at first he seemed only interested in defending against privateers, but to hear him now he seems damned eager to seek out and fight this *L'Armançon* again. Why, I wonder? And why did Oxnard set him aboard, almost as if he wanted Frost to be certain we tangled with the Frenchies?"

"Is that how it seems?" Jack asked. "Because it seems to me you know a bit more than you are letting on."

Wentworth appeared to flush at that, a slight reddening in the cheeks, but it might well have been the beastly heat. "I am only looking at the facts," he protested. "You seem like a perfectly competent mariner, but doesn't it strike you as odd that a fellow like Oxnard, who is a radical Republican to his very soul, would hire the son of a war hero who is so closely aligned with the Adams administration? One who is . . . what . . . but twenty years old?"

A perfectly competent mariner . . . Jack thought, but those were not the words that really struck him.

"I thought you said you didn't know who my father was." Jack could feel the irritation rising now, he felt those familiar danger signs. Concomitant with his decisiveness was a general inability to control impulses, and that failing applied to venting anger as much as it did to seeking pleasure. Both tendencies often saw him standing into danger.

"Strictly speaking, I expressed surprise that you had a father. But yes, of course I know who your father is. Here you are, a sailor from Rhode Island named Biddlecomb, it took no great leap of the imagination."

"Then you will not be surprised to know that I am quite determined to take this fight to the enemy. That should take no great leap of the imagination, either."

He could hardly believe those words had come from his lips. If anyone else had suggested he was eager for a sea fight because he was Isaac Biddlecomb's son he would have resented it bitterly, but here he had said it himself. But this discussion with Wentworth had served one purpose; Jack was now determined to fight and beat *L'Armançon*. Over the course of five minutes he had gone from maddening uncertainty to granite-hard resolve. Because that was how he was made.

"I understand that this sort of thing is in your blood," Wentworth said, starting to sound a bit annoyed himself, "but I think you would do well to consider what's going on here. The whole thing seems damned odd to me."

"See here, Wentworth, if you don't care to go into harm's way, you are certainly welcome to remain ashore. It should be no difficulty to secure some other sort of passage to Barbados."

Wentworth stood a little straighter, and with visible effort controlled his expression and tone. "What, pray, are you insinuating, sir?"

"I am insinuating nothing. I am saying, simply, that you need not sail with us . . ." Jack knew that he should stop there, keep his lips clamped shut, leave that suggestion hanging in the air, not take an ugly situation and push it over the edge. But he could not resist, because that was how he was made, so he added, ". . . if you are afraid."

With those four words Wentworth's entire demeanor changed. The conciliatory, hesitant quality was gone, and in its place was the full arrogance and pride of the Boston Wentworths.

"No one," he said, his voice icy, "not you, Captain, no one, will suggest that I am afraid. I will thank you for an apology, or I will thank you for satisfaction."

"I will certainly give you satisfaction, sir, but you will not thank me for it, depend upon it," Jack said, and though he had no qualms about fighting Wentworth, none at all, he did wonder if he might have handled that situation a whole lot better.

24

On the evening following his interview with Jonathan Ness, Ezra Rumstick called on his dear friend Isaac Biddlecomb. They did not have the opportunity to see one another as much as either man might have liked, but theirs was the sort of friendship that would not suffer because of it. They could sit by a fire, or by a bay window overlooking the street, drinks in hand, and their conversation would take up as if they had been apart only long enough for one of them to use the necessary.

"Well, Isaac," Ezra said, settling himself in a heavy upholstered chair in Isaac's parlor. Isaac sat in its mate, and between them stood the gaming table, which now held a decanter and glasses rather than cards or dice. "You are in the vortex of power now, how does it feel?"

"Ha!" said Isaac, filling the glasses. "Exhausting. Sessions, committees, salons, dear Lord it never ends. The bickering, I'd like to knock them all on their heads."

"Commanding a ship ain't the best way to learn to navigate these waters, I reckon," Ezra said. "Not a great deal of negotiating and, 'If you please, sir,' when you're on your own quarterdeck." He picked up a glass and took a sip.

"You've hit it right on the head," Isaac agreed. "A man gets used to ordering others to do this or that, gets used to the notion that there's no one of equal rank aboard, no one whose sensitivities must be considered. Even those fellows who served in the army, and there's quite a few of them in Congress, as you know, they are more accustomed to having superiors around, none of the autonomy of a ship's master. I think they have an easier time of it than me."

"I would imagine," Ezra agreed. They were silent for a minute, enjoying the drinks and the company.

"I tell you, Ezra, it was so wonderfully simple during the war. You knew who the enemy was, at least once he fired the first shot. Now, you have no notion of who the enemy is. Even after he slips the knife in your back."

"'Wonderfully simple during the war,' is it? Your memory is going in your old age."

Isaac smiled. "You're right. You're right."

More silence. More drinking. "Have you had any word from Jack, at all?" Ezra said at last, working his way around to the real reason for his visit, beyond a genuine desire to see an old friend and shipmate.

"No, no," Isaac said with something approaching a sigh. "It's rare that he writes when he's abroad. I suppose I could go around to Oxnard's, see if he has had word, but Oxnard's another one I'd like to knock on the head, and I hardly trust myself around the man."

"He's a rascal of the first order, to be sure," Ezra said. "So, no word if the voyage was uneventful? Nasty storm a few weeks ago, they likely felt that."

"No doubt. But whatever Jack lacks in judgment ashore he makes up for in seamanship when he's afloat, and then some. *Abigail*'s a good ship and Jack shipped a good crew, so I have no concerns on that front."

More silence. More drinking.

"Actually," Isaac said at last, "now that you mention Jack, it reminds me of a particularly odd letter I received . . . Lord . . . several weeks ago now. I was going to mention it to you, but I quite forgot the last time we were together. It was from Alexander Hamilton, of all people."

"Another rascal," Ezra said, "but at least he is a Federalist rascal."

"Just so. Did you ever meet him?"

"I've had the pleasure, if such it is," Ezra said. "A few times. I'm not certain he would remember me. Have you?"

"Oh, yes," Isaac said. "We've met several times, corresponded on and off. He's ostensibly in private practice, you know, but when it comes to politics he's like an octopus, has his tentacles wrapped around everything. Adams can't abide the man, but if one is in government, as I am, you can hardly avoid him."

"So . . . what was this letter about?" Ezra asked.

"It was about Jack, not what I expected. A warning that Oxnard was not to be trusted, that he shouldn't take command of Oxnard's ship. Said it might even be a danger to him, hinted at some intrigue. Damned odd. How he happened to know about Jack getting the *Abigail*, or why he would care, I can't imagine."

"Hamilton has people everywhere, and they make certain he knows what's acting. No doubt Hamilton keeps abreast of a political enemy such as Oxnard."

"No doubt," Isaac agreed. "But how Jack and the *Abigail* could play a part in any of that I can't imagine. I mean, I'm delighted that my son has his first command, and a good little ship she is, but she's still just an innocuous merchantman."

"True," Rumstick said, not entirely sure what innocuous meant. *Just a merchantman . . .* he thought, *but Oxnard saw to it she was a merchantman with guns.* He wondered if that might have some relevance.

"Anyway, I never did pass the warning to Jack," Isaac continued. "The letter arrived a few days after *Abigail* set sail."

The two men fell silent again, but Ezra's mind was racing. He considered telling Isaac about Bolingbroke and the duel, but saw no point. It was over, Isaac did not need the worry it would cause, and Ezra had every intention of finishing the business in whatever way it needed finishing.

"These fellows, the officers in Adams's administration, they are most of them holdovers from Washington, are they not?" Ezra asked, his thoughts setting a new course.

"They are," Isaac said.

"And so I would imagine Hamilton had a hand in their selection. He might still have some influence over them."

"Might? Surely does, I would think. Wolcott of the Treasury and McHenry in particular are acolytes of Hamilton. He may well control them like puppets, and you can be sure that won't be to President Adams's benefit."

"No . . ." Rumstick said, his mind continuing down this new line of thinking. But he was being rude, and he knew it. He was there to visit his friend, so he turned to Isaac and said, "Now, pray, give me all the gossip about progress with the navy." With that he could see in Isaac a renewed enthusiasm. He sat up a little straighter and launched into a subject of which he was genuinely knowledgeable, genuinely passionate.

And Ezra listened, nodded, even made the odd comment, but his mind was elsewhere, on Hamilton, Oxnard, a battery of six pounders.

Jack Biddlecomb was thinking about his father. It was early, dawn was still an hour away, and he was washing his face in the basin on the sideboard, pulling on his shirt and breeches, and thinking about his father. Any business that involved a sword made him think of Isaac. In his mind the connection was organic, swords and his father indivisible.

Jack's grandfather, John Biddlecomb, had been a soldier. Jack never met him. His father hardly knew him. John Biddlecomb died fighting with Wolfe in Quebec in '59. Isaac was eleven then. He had accompanied his father to Canada, had been beside him when he died.

In those earlier years of his father's childhood, on the little farm they owned in Bristol, Rhode Island, John had taught young Isaac the use of weapons, had labored to pass on skills he himself had gained through hard use. Isaac proved to have a modest ability with musket and pistol, and at best a moderate interest in them. But the sword was a different matter.

Young Isaac had felt an affinity for steel and shown a concomitant skill with a blade. John Biddlecomb recognized this, encouraged it, worked Isaac through various drills with swords carved from oak barrel staves. And when Isaac had skill enough that he could be trusted to wield a blade in practice without being a danger to himself or his instructor, John switched to short swords with the points dulled and corked. After a particularly prosperous year, Jack's grandfather had ordered a pair of the newly fashionable foils from London, their tips nail-headed and blunt, steel of such good quality that the weapons were still in use at *Chez* Biddlecomb.

All these things Jack remembered as he tucked his shirt into his breeches. He looked at his coat draped over the back of a chair and decided against putting it on. It was already warm, and he would only have to take it off again for the fight.

Instead, he picked up the sword and belt that lay on the bed and drew the weapon from the scabbard, let the light of the candle play off the lovely polished steel. The sword had been a gift from his father for his sixteenth birthday, though he had been nearly seventeen by the time he made it back from his various voyages to the family's home to be presented with it. He and his father had been fencing since Jack was five and old enough to hold his own oak-stave sword.

Jack held the sword straight out, felt the weight and balance in his hand, the excellent grip. Beautiful, beautiful. He thought back to those summer days fencing on the lawn at Stanton House, or in the big parlor with the furniture pushed aside. The past six or seven years had not been good between him and the old man. Jack set his own course, and his father did not approve. Jack was impetuous, often acted without thinking, and he knew it, and his father did not approve. Jack rejected all that he had grown up with: the money, the Biddlecomb name, the privilege that came with having a famous father, and Isaac did not approve.

But those early days had been good. Those days when Jack was young and his father had come home from sea to remain ashore and Jack could revel in the way other men looked at his father, the respect and even awe with which they regarded him. He had shown Jack the basics of fencing and the two of them had gone at it, wooden swords and then foils flashing, clattering, until they had collapsed with exhaustion or laughter or both. Jack had demonstrated all of Isaac's innate skill and then some.

Isaac had even hired a fencing master to visit their home and bring the instruction to a new level, and together, father and son, they had practiced the drills, the footwork, the blade work, under the sharp eye and lisping instruction of Sir William Wilde, Fencing Master to the Aristocracy. It was only years later that Jack came to understand that the "Sir" was as phony as the man's credentials, but for all that, he knew fencing and he knew how to instruct and he left the Biddlecombs much better off, swordplaywise, than he had found them.

His father had made that very point about Wilde's good influence on that June day, in Jack's eleventh year, when Jack for the first time had defeated his father's blade decisively, had struck Isaac in the chest with a flawless lunge that bent the steel in a lovely arc and left his father gasping and looking down at that perfect hit. Had it been a sword, uncorked, and not the foil, Isaac would have been dead already.

Jack stepped back and lowered the weapon, as surprised as Isaac had been. Isaac took two steps toward him, put his arm around Jack's shoulder, and squeezed. "Well done, son, well done!" he said. "You've bested the old man at last!"

Jack did not know what to say. He nodded in agreement.

"See," Isaac said, "I only had my father to instruct me, and only for a short time. I picked up what I could but never had the benefit of the regular instruction you've enjoyed. And that's as it should be, because the Biddlecombs have a different place in society now."

It was the same with the sailing. More so, because Isaac needed no outside instructor to help him teach his boy about the ways of wind and water, tides, currents, rudder, sails. The Biddlecombs seemed to accumulate watercraft so fast Jack's mother would joke about the boats breeding in the spring. Canoes, rowing boats, punts, bateaux, boats with sailing rigs, small sloops, they all seemed to find their way to the Biddlecomb dock, or upside down in the yard, or shoved into one of the outbuildings. There was never a dearth of boats to sail, and never a want of enthusiasm for sailing them.

If Jack loved fencing, he was mad about sailing. From his earliest days he and his father would be out on Narragansett Bay, tacking and jibing, running, reaching, sailing the rail under one or another of the boats. Indeed, Jack's earliest memory was of sitting in the bilge of some boat—he could not recall which—his bottom wet with the water sloshing around and looking up at his father, smiling, his eyes moving from the sail to the bow, to windward, to leeward. A sailor's eye, a weather eye. He had loved his father so profoundly at that moment.

Year by year, boat by boat, Jack learned the ways of wind and sea. By the age of nine he was taking his parents and siblings out on the water, insisting they were passengers, no more, insisting that every aspect of handling the boat was his alone. And he did it, did it well, brought them to where they were bound, whether it was a picnic on Hog Island or Prudence Island, or a run down to Newport. "Captain Jack," his mother called him, to his secret delight, or, "my sweet little sailor-boy," with which he was less thrilled.

The thrust-to-the-chest moment in Jack and Isaac's sailing life came when Jack was still ten. It came on an August day, a perfect day, if perhaps a bit lighter of wind than they might have wished. His father had acquired

two identical boats from whatever magic place boats seemed to material-
ize, twelve-foot jolly boats with lug rigs, and he and Jack had taken to racing them in Bristol Bay or out between Prudence Island and Pappasquash
Point. They had been at it for months, at least several times a week, and Jack
had loved every bit of it; it was companionship with his father and command of his own vessel, diminutive though it might be, all at once.

But when it came to racing, he did not win. For all his concentration, for
all the minute sail trim and delicate hand on the tiller, he could not coax
more speed out of his boat than his father could, regardless of the conditions, and Isaac would give a good-natured laugh as his boat glided over
whatever imaginary finish line they had agreed upon, a boat length or more
ahead of Jack. And Jack would try to tamp down his frustration.

It was different on that day in August. It did not start out different, not
in any way. They had crossed the starting line on starboard tack and perfectly even, but despite the light winds favoring Jack, who weighed half of
what his father did, Isaac was able to inch his boat to weather until he had
half a boat length on him. And then a full boat length, and drawing ahead
as they worked their nimble white craft to weather, tack on tack, like cav-
alrymen fighting on horseback, jockeying for position.

Jack had tacked around to larboard, hoping to creep up on his father, but
Isaac had tacked above him, covering him, giving him no room to pass. Isaac
handled his boat the way a master violinist handled his instrument, and he
sacrificed not an inch with every tack he made, and Jack could only try to
emulate that.

Jack's eyes were everywhere; to weather, to lee, on the sails, on his father's
boat, on his course. That was his father's training. And so Jack did not miss
the cat's paw of wind coming from the west, the telltale ruffle of water as the
small gust approached. He waited for his father to tack around, to pick up
the lift that would come with the breeze before Jack did. But he didn't.
Happy with his lead, Isaac maintained course and speed as Jack swung his
tiller in an arc, set the sail flapping through the wind.

He caught a glimpse of Isaac looking back in surprise as the cat's paw
enveloped his son's boat, heeled it over, set the water gurgling down its side.
Jack leaned to weather to hold the boat straighter and felt the little burst of
speed. A second or two later the cat's paw found Isaac's boat, but it was too

late. Jack had head reached on him, tacked to cover, and two minutes after that he crossed the line they had agreed upon, between Providence Point and the old battery, his father trailing astern.

Isaac luffed up beside him, his arm raised in congratulations. "Well done, Jack, well done!" he said, and there was genuine pride in his voice, and a touch of sadness as well. Jack was surprised by the sadness, because he imagined it was a sadness born of losing, and he had thought his father a bigger man than that. But when he related the story to his mother, she had put her arm around him and said, "Of course your father was sad. Not about losing. About what it means. Which is that you are growing up."

All this Jack thought about as he dressed, such reminiscing a rare indulgence for him, until he was interrupted by Oliver Tucker, who tapped lightly on the door and said, "We best be going, sir."

"Very good," Jack said. He buckled the sword belt around his waist, adjusted the way the weapon hung, then blew out the candle, and in the gathering light of dawn followed Tucker, his second, down the stairs and out onto the road.

They walked toward the quay, then Tucker led the way to a wide path that ran off in the other direction and Biddlecomb followed. "Tucker," Jack said after a few minutes of walking through the thick forest, "do you have any notion of where you are going?"

"Oh, yes, sir. I met with Mr. Wentworth's second and we agreed to this place."

"Very thorough, as usual," Jack said. If he was killed, Tucker would take command of *Abigail*. Jack wondered if he would be pleased with that, and guessed he probably would not. Tucker was a good mate, but Jack did not think he could find Barbados if there was a trail of breadcrumbs floating on the sea.

At last the forest opened out into a clearing, a wide-open area with short grass that ran down to a sandy beach and the ocean beyond. They were on the south side of the island and the heights to the west had the place still in deep shadows. But Jack was certain they were where they should be, because Wentworth was there with his second, and Lucas Harwar and John Burgess and Noah Maguire and most of the other Abigails, as well as most of the officers of the *Warrior* and several of the senior dockyard officials, entertainment being hard to come by on that island.

Jack took his place on the open ground thirty feet from Wentworth. Wentworth's second, he saw, was the British officer, Chandler, which was no surprise. The only Americans on the island were the Abigails, who certainly would not second a man who wished to run their captain through.

It was warm but not hot, and the light was growing with each passing minute. It was a perfect morning for a duel. And then the calm was ruined by the booming, familiar, unwelcome voice of Charles Frost, pushing his way through the crowd of onlookers.

"Gentlemen, gentlemen, pray, stop this madness," his said, his tone somewhere between a command and a plea. "Captain Biddlecomb, killing your passengers is not really the thing, you know. It will not do your career any good."

"Mr. Frost, please do not interfere in this," Jack said, his exasperation unchecked. Frost turned in the other direction.

"Mr. Wentworth, please see reason, if any harm comes to Captain Biddlecomb we will never reach Barbados!"

Before Wentworth could reply, Lieutenant Chandler broke away and crossed the ground to where Frost stood. He spoke low, Jack could not hear what he said, but there was no mistaking the forceful and unequivocal manner in which he addressed the big man. Frost listened, frowned, but then he turned and stamped back to join the others.

Jack unbuckled his sword belt, drew the blade and handed it to Tucker, who took it awkwardly. "Ah, and what am I to do with this, Captain?" Tucker asked. He did not have much experience with this sort of thing.

"Wentworth's second will meet you there," Jack nodded to a spot halfway between the men, "and he'll have Wentworth's sword and the two of you will see that there's no great difference in the weapons, length or anything like that."

"Oh, I see," Tucker said. He took the sword and walked away and Chandler met him in the middle of the space. They exchanged swords and looked them over, though Biddlecomb suspected Tucker had no idea of what he was looking for. Then both men turned and headed toward him.

"Good morrow, Captain Biddlecomb," Chandler said in his crisp British way.

"Good morning, Lieutenant," Biddlecomb said.

"Mr. Wentworth asks that I relate to you that he would consider honor to be satisfied if you were to make a private apology to him," Chandler said.

Biddlecomb thought about that. A private apology, not a public one. Wentworth was making it easy for him to get out of this fight if he wished, which would suggest that Wentworth wished to get out of the fight, which Jack took to mean that he was afraid. Ironically, just the supposition that had led to this whole brouhaha. "No, sir, I do not believe an apology is owed by me," Jack said.

"Very well," Chandler said. "That being the case, Mr. Wentworth asks if you will agree to make this fight to first blood."

First blood . . . Jack thought. Wentworth did not want to fight to the death, or until some great mischief was done. *He is a damned bloody coward.* But Jack considered himself a merciful man, so he said, "Very well, then, first blood."

Chandler returned to Wentworth's side. Jack stretched his arms and legs, took a few practice lunges. He would not have killed Wentworth in any case, he was not one of those who took pleasure in dispatching his fellow man. Dueling was as addictive as drink, he knew, and while he did on occasion wrestle with a fondness for drink, dueling still held no great fascination for him.

A few moments later he saw Wentworth stepping toward the center of the space, Chandler at his side, and he stepped forward as well. "Come along, Tucker," he prompted his first mate and Tucker hurried after him. The four men met in the middle of the clearing, surrounded by a half circle of spectators thirty feet inland. Wentworth stood about fifteen feet away, holding his sword easily at his side. A beautiful weapon, just as Jack suspected it would be. He could just make out various exotic inlays in the hand guard, could see the mirror finish of the steel.

But he was thinking about Wentworth, not his sword. Thinking about the first moment he had seen him, sitting so arrogantly at the table in the great cabin, assuming everything there was his for the taking. *This has been a long time coming*, Jack thought, and he was pleased that the moment had at last arrived.

"Gentlemen," Chandler said, nodding to each man. "This shall be a fight to first blood. At the sight of first blood the wounded man's second will raise his arm, the other second will cry out, "Strike up your swords!" and each combatant will disengage. They will remain in the *en guarde* position until such time as it is affirmed that first blood has been drawn. Is this acceptable?"

Jack nodded but he was not really listening. He was looking hard at Wentworth, because a big part of winning this sort of thing was finding a weakness one could exploit. He was looking for fear, looking for intimidation, hesitancy. But Wentworth was looking back at him, his face as expressionless as a bust of Caesar, and Jack had to admit he did not look afraid.

"Very well," Chandler said next. "Pray, each of you step back a few paces. Good." He held up a handkerchief. "*En guarde!*" Jack took the familiar position, his body folding into the stance with ease, perfectly natural. Wentworth went *en guarde* as well, and even that little movement was done with fluidity and grace.

Then Chandler dropped the cloth. It fluttered to the ground and its landing was the cue to begin. But neither man rushed into the fight, and indeed ten seconds after the handkerchief had settled they were still just inching toward one another, eyes focused on blades, and arms, and the eyes of their opponent.

Jack took two small advances, extended his sword arm just a bit, probing. He did not know what to expect from Wentworth, and now was the time to get the measure of his opposite, now was the time to poke about for weaknesses that could prove fatal. Metaphorically fatal.

Wentworth extended as well, and now their blades were overlapping. Jack pressed down on Wentworth's blade, just pushed it aside with the slightest pressure, and Wentworth did not offer any sort of resistance. Jack pressed a bit more, moving Wentworth's point out of the line of attack, leaving a straight shot in to Wentworth's chest. He tensed his back leg. Release Wentworth's blade, go straight in, and he could give Wentworth a nice, deep cut across the shoulder or arm and end this all.

He was poised to spring when Wentworth dropped his blade and the resistance holding Jack's in line was suddenly gone. His blade swung to the left as Wentworth's sword circled around and came darting in, snake-fast, and Jack, ready to move forward, now had to leap back and try for an awkward, backhand parry.

He connected, knocked Wentworth's blade aside, but Wentworth circled again, came in again and Jack stepped back and parried, a prettier move, Jack having recovered his wits a bit.

They both came *en guarde* once more, and Jack could see now that Wentworth was not afraid, he was not uncertain, and when it came to swordplay, he was very, very good.

25

Jack took a few steps back and lowered his sword. Not enough that he was undefended, or looked as if he was unready. He did not think he could fool Wentworth into making an attack by appearing unprepared. He just needed a moment to reassess, and he knew enough to marshal the strength in his arm. This might take longer than he thought, and if there was one thing he knew about swordplay, it was that it was damned exhausting.

Wentworth closed the distance, just a bit. His sword did not drop or waver, it was held in a textbook *en guarde* stance, like a copperplate from Angelo's *L'École des armes*. The point was steady at first, but as he neared it began to move a bit, up and down, side to side, in the way a snake might entrance its prey. But Jack was not entranced. He let Wentworth come on, and then swept his own sword up, beat the blade, made a lunge at Wentworth. It was not a lunge meant to strike, but rather to send Wentworth back, to throw his balance off for just that instant.

And it worked. Wentworth parried, stepped back, was still regaining his stance when Jack made up the distance, like a cat pouncing. He could see the surprise in Wentworth's face when he saw Jack coming, following up on the lunge with never a pause. Then it was Jack's turn to be surprised as Wentworth knocked Jack's thrust aside, stepped closer and swung at Jack's head with the hand guard of his sword.

Jack jerked his head back and felt the metal scrape along his cheek. He leapt back, touched the cheek with his left hand but his fingers came away clean, no blood. The swing had put Wentworth off balance, which Jack exploited, stepping in fast, thrusting, meeting Wentworth's blade, disengaging, thrusting. Wentworth stepped back once and he stepped back again, pushed along by the ferocity of Jack's offensive. He made no counterattack because Jack would not let him, and the most that he could do was back away and continue to turn Jack's blade aside.

Step for step they went, Wentworth backing away from Jack's flashing sword, working his own like it was the bow of a violin, the actions quick, precise, the angle perfectly gauged to keep the wicked point of Jack's weapon from getting past the arc of Wentworth's defense.

And then Jack saw what Wentworth was about. The man was fast, damned fast. He could do this all day, let Jack wear himself down with this brutal attack, keep turning his blade aside until Jack could no longer lift his arm. Already he could feel himself tiring. Any swordsman Jack had ever fought before would have been bleeding by now, but Wentworth seemed to just be working up a sweat.

So Jack stopped. He let his arm fall and turned his back on Wentworth and walked off to the spot where he had started the attack. His ears strained to hear any sound of movement behind. His eyes were locked on the faces of the men watching, because if Wentworth came at him Jack knew he would see it there. Five, six, seven paces and then he heard the light crunch of feet on gravel, saw the spectators clench as they braced for the sight of Wentworth running Jack through, and he spun on his heel and his sword came up and swept across his chest in a great arc.

He could see Wentworth was not trying to stab him in the back but rather smack him with the flat of his sword, get his attention. Still, Jack hit Wentworth's blade as it was coming at him, not a subtle parry but an ugly blow, wielding his weapon more like a cutlass than a fine sword. He knocked Wentworth's blade aside, turning Wentworth's fine forward momentum into a stumbling mess. Wentworth was too close for Jack to thrust with his sword and finish it, but Wentworth's face was there, right there, and Jack punched him with the handgrip of his weapon just as Wentworth had done to him.

Wentworth staggered again, straightened, stepped back quickly, weapon raised, ready for Jack to come at him, but Jack held his ground. Wentworth reached up with his hand and touched his face where Jack had punched him, the mirror image of Jack's motion, checked his fingertips for blood. But there was nothing. Jack's blow had not broken the skin. Honor was not satisfied.

Jack looked up at Wentworth, looked in his eyes, trying to guess at the man's next move. Wentworth met his gaze and did the one thing Jack would not have expected: he smiled.

It was not an angry grin or the manic smile of a man set on killing his opponent. It was a friendly smile, a "well done!" sort of smile, and Jack found it at once confusing and annoying. He had meant to draw first blood with an insubstantial scratch, but if Wentworth was going to continue in this insufferable way he might have to end the affair by delivering a more memorable wound.

Jack came *en guarde*, advanced with sword in the fourth position, ready to be done with this. He made a halfhearted lunge, let Wentworth parry, made a circle with his blade, and went in for the kill, one of his best moves, one that almost always found its target, but this time it found only air, as Wentworth stepped easily back.

Then it was Wentworth's turn. There was no smile on his face as he advanced, as his blade came straight, defeated Jack's parry, came again and again. Now it was Jack backing away, turning Wentworth's thrusts aside. He heard a murmur running through the spectators, was certain he heard one of the British officers say something about "five pounds on this Wentworth fellow . . ." but he heard no more and had no more time to think on it. Thrust, parry, repost, parry, lunge, they moved along the ground, the grass and the sod below their feet uneven and difficult to walk on, no fencing *salon* or the well-manicured lawn of Stanton House.

Jack's eyes flicked from Wentworth's sword to his face, just a glimpse, but he saw what he hoped to see; frustration, sweat. Jack's arm was starting to ache, his breath was coming harder, but he could feel that Wentworth's actions were slowing, his responses more dull. Wentworth thought he could end this with a decisive attack, but like Jack before he had succeeded only in tiring himself.

Now, now is my moment, Jack thought. Wentworth was not reacting with the *panache* of five minutes before, because five minutes of this sort of intense back-and-forth was enough to tire even a fit man. Jack let Wentworth come on, let his own defense slow, let Wentworth's blade get closer, let his own parries become more awkward. And then, as Wentworth parried in the fifth position, lunged for Jack's chest, Jack took the blade with his own, forced it from the line of attack, and pushed off hard with his left foot, right arm firing off like an arrow from a longbow, and he saw the point of his blade pierce the loose white sleeve of Wentworth's cotton shirt.

Chandler, standing just to the side, raised his arm, paused a moment, then called, "Strike up your swords!" because Tucker had completely forgotten what he was supposed to say. Jack let his sword drop to his side and Wentworth did as well and though they were both supposed to remain *en guarde* they were both far too winded to resist the chance to rest.

"Has Captain Biddlecomb drawn first blood?" Chandler asked. Biddlecomb's eyes were on the rent sleeve. He was looking for the telltale bloom of red on the white cloth but he did not see it.

"I believe not," Wentworth said. He handed his sword to Chandler and rolled the sleeve up to beyond the point where it was torn. He turned 180 degrees, demonstrating to all that his skin was untouched, blood had not been drawn.

"Very well," Chandler said. "There is no blood drawn, but will you gentlemen agree that honor has been satisfied?"

Jack and William said, "No" in virtually the same instant, but in neither case was the response overly forceful, as both men were still gasping for breath.

"Very well," Chandler said and Jack thought he heard a note of exasperation in his voice. "Pray, return to the center, here." He stepped back to the point where the duel had begun and Wentworth turned and followed and Jack followed him. Tucker followed as well on the inland side, unsure of what was going on. There was nothing energetic in Wentworth's stride, and he seemed to be limping a bit, and that would have made Jack happy if he himself was not dragging his anchors so.

Chandler called for them to come *en guarde* once more. They did, the handkerchief fell, and they came at one another, the athletic grace of the first few moments of the duel all but gone. Jack hacked at Wentworth's sword, hoping to disarm the man, or break the blade, or knock it aside just enough for him to make one little nick in the man's skin, but Wentworth parried in the first position, elbow up, blade down, and Jack felt the shudder through his sword and his arm as steel hit steel.

Then Wentworth brought his point up and Jack knocked it aside, thrust, had his blade knocked out of the line of attack. It was maddening, it was as if Wentworth was encased in a glass dome and every thrust, every perfectly placed attack, just bounced off. He could not get at the man. He danced back a few steps and wiped his brow. His eyes were stinging from the sweat running down into them. But he could see Wentworth's hair and shirt were soaked as if he had just been out for a swim. His mouth was open, his eyes wide, his strength draining fast.

They came at one another, slowly, weapons raised, and Jack was thinking that this was it, it had to end soon, because they could not go on, and he knew, just knew, that Wentworth was thinking the same. Their swords came together as each tried to take the other's blade. Jack thrust, Wentworth stepped awkwardly back, Wentworth thrust and Jack went back. And a heavy voice cut through the quiet, through the clash of steel, the only sound.

"Damn it all! That is enough!" It was Frost, and Jack could hear him puffing up, but he did not take his eyes from Wentworth, not for a fraction of a second, because that was all it would take, and Wentworth did not take his eyes from him.

"Stop this nonsense! Stop it at once, I say!" Frost roared, and the two men ignored him.

"Sir," Chandler said, "honor has yet to be satisfied," and the two men ignored him.

"Damn their honor!" Frost roared again and Jack and William went at one another in the same instant, swords clashing again, blade on blade. Jack thrust, though he was sure Wentworth would avoid the tip with the nimble, quick footwork he had so far displayed. But Wentworth did not jump back, because he apparently thought Jack would do the same and the two points reached out and each caught the loose cloth of their opponent's shirt and passed right through.

Jack saw his blade rip through Wentworth's sleeve right near the shoulder and he felt the blade tear across Wentworth's flesh. In the same instant he felt Wentworth's blade passing through the cloth of his own shirt, just at his stomach, felt the razor-sharp edge and the jagged nicks it had sustained that morning tearing the skin as it passed, lacerating his side but never piercing it.

The both of them, Jack and William, pulled their swords free, held them at their sides, point down. Blood gleamed on the steel of both. Chandler was shouting something. Frost was shouting something. There was a roaring in Biddlecomb's ears but he did not know what it was. Then he and Wentworth, simultaneously, sat down on the cool grass and closed their eyes.

Three leagues away to the east southeast and well to windward of English Harbour, Captain Jean-Paul Renaudin was also closing his eyes, and for the same reason; sheer exhaustion. His was not the exhaustion of ten minutes of extraordinary and intense effort. His was the exhaustion of a week and a half of driving men, overseeing every detail of their work, navigating a ship, planning, tamping down anxiety, and slowly stewing in fury and humiliation. It was the exhaustion of catching only a few hours' sleep here and there as he pushed the men, watch on watch, to set a battered ship to rights.

The fact that First Officer Pierre Barère had not been crushed to death by the falling boom was only one of a number of frustrations, and not even the worst. The fight with the American merchantman had been like nothing Renaudin had ever experienced, the shift of fortunes and emotions in those brief minutes unprecedented in his nearly two decades at sea.

They had stood into the fight confident. *L'Armançon* had the heels on the American, they could sail a circle around her. Their guns were bigger, their crew, even if they lacked the discipline Renaudin thought ideal, was experienced and numerous. Their adversary was a merchantman, for the love of God! Renaudin had not really considered the manner in which they would attack, he did not see the need, and perhaps that was where the problem was, because from that moment on, things had begun to go very, very wrong.

Renaudin stood on *L'Armançon*'s quarterdeck, leaning against the weather rail, his eyes closed, and played those moments out in his mind once more, and as he did so he drifted off into the edges of sleep. He swayed and began to fall forward and his eyes snapped open. To the east was the unbroken sea, the deep blue Atlantic. To the west the water faded into the lighter blue-greens of the Caribbean, and he could see on the horizon the green humps of Antigua and Barbuda, and to the southwest Guadeloupe. If those islands had been ships he would have said they were hull down, just their top-hamper showing.

He looked aloft. The mizzen topgallant yard was standing vertically, hanging from its yard rope, and even as he watched, it tipped over to the horizontal and the hands working up there scrambled to reeve off the lifts and see the clewlines and buntlines run fair to the deck. At the base of the mast, like a vicious dog that has chased a dozen squirrels up a tree, stood Second Officer René Dauville. Not a man aloft would dare come down until the mizzen rigging was squared away to Dauville's satisfaction.

Movement farther forward caught Renaudin's eye and he saw Barère emerging from the after scuttle and making his painful way toward the quarterdeck. His head was still bandaged and he squinted in the brilliant sun after coming up from the twilight of the 'tween decks, where he spent most of his time.

He struggled up the few steps to the quarterdeck and Renaudin made no move to help him. "*Citoyen* Barère, how are you doing today?" he asked when the first officer finally reached him where he stood aft.

"Better, *Citoyen*, better, I should think," Barère said. "My headaches are less frequent, a good sign, surely."

"Surely," Renaudin agreed. It would have been nice had Barère been killed outright, but still the vicious blow to the head had been helpful. He had spent a week below, under the incompetent care of *L'Armançon*'s incompetent surgeon. The amazing thing about the surgeon, as far as Renaudin could see, was that the man did not drink. Shipboard surgeons were generally useless because they were drunks, but the medical man aboard *L'Armançon* managed to be useless without the help of alcohol.

But in Barère's case Renaudin did not mind the surgeon's bungling. It allowed Dauville to assume the role of first officer and allowed the two of them to drive the men as if they were slaves on a West Indies plantation, not *citoyens* of the Republic of France and fellow revolutionaries. It allowed them to treat the men the way a ship's crew should be treated, so far below the status of the captain and first officer that they could barely see to those lofty heights from where they stood.

And that was important, because Renaudin was now a man possessed. He had been like a sleepwalker before, stumbling through the nightmare of his life, the destruction of his beloved navy of France, the exile of his family and his friends and fellow officers, the ceaseless propaganda from Paris. But now he was awake. The American's guns had shaken him from his slumber. Now he was awake and he would beat that arrogant merchantman into flotsam and there was not one other thing that mattered to him.

The fight had ended when *L'Armançon*'s mizzen had gone by the board. The men were running around like a herd of baboons but Renaudin kept his head, for all the fury he felt in his soul. He had ordered the launch away, with a crew of the better hands and Dauville once again in command. He ordered Dauville to follow the merchantman as far as he could, until she ran over the horizon, or until the boat was dangerously low on food or water, or until he knew where she was bound.

He returned five days later, having achieved the third possibility, or nearly so. He had followed her for several days, and though her lead stretched out quickly and continued to grow, he was still able to keep her topgallants in sight for some time. She must have sustained damage during the fight, he surmised, as she seemed to be nursing her mizzenmast and not driving as hard as she might. Otherwise, she should have been able to put the longboat over the horizon in no time.

Dauville followed long enough to be satisfied that she was bound for Antigua. If she were heading south she would not have kept the course she did, and most of the other islands she could be making for on that heading were French possessions, and she certainly was not bound for one of those. There were any number of harbors on Antigua where she could be putting in, but if she needed repairs, the best facilities would be found at English Harbour.

English Harbour, of course, was British, a naval dockyard. But even after a long and bloody war, and a victory made possible only through French intervention, the British and Americans seemed to be climbing into bed with one another, to the detriment of France. It was entirely possible that the Yankee would find a welcome there.

Renaudin was no fan of the *Directoire* and all that came before it, but he was a Frenchman to his very soul, and as such he could only resent the ingratitude of the Americans. Two governments born of revolution, and the Americans entirely beholden to French support for their unlikely victory, support that had nearly crippled France and led directly to the convulsions that nation had suffered. They should have stood together, but instead the Americans were cozying up to the historic enemy of both nations.

Renaudin would always fight for the pride of France, regardless of who was claiming political leadership, and in this instance he saw the duplicity of the United States as a slap to his country, not its revolutionary government.

While Dauville was away, Renaudin personally drove the crew, and he could see the shock and surprise they felt when their previously disinterested and disengaged captain was suddenly transformed into the most vicious and demanding of lunatics. They looked for Barère to restrain him, to remind him of their rights as *citoyens*, but Barère was not to be found, and no matter how often the surgeon bled him, he did not seem to improve overly fast.

The mizzenmast was hauled alongside and anything of use was stripped off it, including the yards, sails, the mizzen top, and much of the standing and running rigging. Sheer legs had been rigged to pull the stump of the old mast and then they had made their way to Basseterre where a suitable tree, a mostly suitable tree, had been felled, shaped, and stepped in the old mast's place. Standing rigging had been set up, the mizzen top got over, the rest of the top-hamper swayed aloft.

It had been done at sea, save for the cutting and shaping of the mast. It had been done pretty much on the same patch of ocean that *L'Armançon* now occupied, the most ideal spot to intercept any ship bound from Antigua to Barbados, the American's original destination, or só Barère had informed him. And Barère seemed to be right about these things.

The American was most certainly at English Harbour. Renaudin did not dare take his corvette within three leagues of Antigua for fear of tipping his hand, but he took the launch in close enough to intercept a fisherman, whom he paid to take him within sight of the place. From the deck of the filthy, stinking fishing sloop he once again laid eyes on that ship that was the focus of his waking hours and filled his dreams. And so he waited.

"Monsieur Dauville!" Renaudin called.

Dauville turned on his heel. "Sir?"

"Once the mizzen is squared away we will clear for action and exercise the great guns. Dumb show only, no powder. We shall remain cleared for action and the men may sleep at quarters."

"Aye, aye, sir," Dauville said crisply.

Barère took a step closer. "*Citoyen* Renaudin," he said, his voice raspy and noticeably weaker. "Allow me to remind you of the orders from the *Directoire*—"

"Masthead, there!" Renaudin shouted, ignoring Barère, mostly because he knew it drove Barère mad. "Do you see the fishing boat?"

After his look into English Harbour, Renaudin had decided to retain the fishing boat, assuring the owner and his small crew that he would pay for the boat's use, a promise that did little to mollify them, but Renaudin did not care. He kept the fishermen aboard *L'Armançon* as grudging guests and sent the smack off under the command of an *enseigne de vaisseau* to keep an eye on the vessels outward bound from Antigua. The *enseigne de vaisseau* was young but he was bright and competent, and there was no man aboard *L'Armançon* who would not recognize the American merchantman.

"Boat's still in sight, sir!" the masthead lookout shouted down. "No change! No signal!"

"*Citoyen!*" Barère said again, his tone more insistent, demanding to be heard. "Do not forget your orders, as I related to you, from the *Directoire*. You are to fight the American and you are to suffer some damage, but you are to take him without destroying him. Am I clear?"

"We tried that last time, *Citoyen* Barère, and it did not work out so well for us."

"Then I hope you learned a lesson. I hope you have devised some way to claim victory over a lightly armed merchant vessel, because I assure you,

Monsieur, the *Directoire* will not look kindly on yet another failure. Do you perceive my meaning?"

"Oh, yes," Renaudin said. In his mind he felt the snap and kick of the pistol, saw the back of Barère's head blow apart. "I perceive your meaning very well."

26

Among the spectators at Jack and William's duel was the surgeon from His Majesty's Ship *Warrior*, whom Chandler had asked be present, an unnecessary request given that, like his fellow officers, the surgeon would never have missed the fun of watching two Yankee Doodles go after one another with swords. He addressed the combatants' wounds, which were minor and required only bandaging. Chandler made the two exhausted men agree that honor had been satisfied. They shook hands, also on Chandler's insistence.

"Well fought, Captain," Wentworth said.

"And you, Mr. Wentworth," Biddlecomb said. They spoke in tones that were stilted, overly formal, what one might expect of two men who had spent the morning trying to run one another through.

They returned to English Harbour; the combatants, the seconds, the sizable crowd who had turned out for the affair. Jack went back to work on the *Abigail*. Wentworth, for lack of anything better to do, began to drink and to marinate in his various concerns. The officers of the *Warrior* continued to hope Captain Wallace would see his way to bribing the dockyard superintendent to speed up work on the seventy-four, and her crew continued to hope he would not.

Two days later, when *Abigail*'s hands began heaving the windlass to bring the anchor cable to short peak and prepare to weigh, the laceration on Jack's side was still sore and restricting his movements. He was standing on his quarterdeck in his favorite spot at the starboard rail, just forward of the helm. He looked down the length of the deck, and what he saw was very different from what he had seen from that same spot on the day they had put out from Philadelphia.

That sight had been odd enough, with six new guns run out through six fresh-cut gunports, but this was something new entirely. Rather than a cluster of guns aft there were now six guns per side, a dozen great guns evenly spaced fore and aft. Rather than a handful of merchant sailors he now had thirty or more men on the crew, twenty of whom were experienced men-of-war's men, hands from a sloop-of-war that had been condemned, stranding them in English Harbour. They were slated to be put on *Warrior*'s books, but somehow the dockyard superintendent had shipped them aboard *Abigail*, with the understanding that their passage back from Barbados would be paid for by Mr. Frost.

That must have set Frost back some considerable sum of ready money, Jack thought.

"Short peak!" Tucker cried from the foredeck.

"Hands aloft to loose sail!" Jack cried and the men swarmed up the shrouds, far more men than he was used to seeing on any vessel he had ever sailed aboard. They laid out on fore and main topgallant yard, topsail yards, lower yards, the mizzen as well, and after what seemed to Jack an extraordinarily brief time they were back on deck, the sails hanging in their gear.

Impressive . . . he thought. He could grow accustomed to these man-of-war-style crews, dozens of men to do a job that would be done by six aboard a merchantman. The sails were sheeted home, halyards hauled away. With many hands on the braces the foresails were braced aback, main and mizzen hauled around to cast the ship to larboard, with Israel Walcott the cook grumbling about the mouths to feed but happily ignoring his usual station at the foresheet.

The anchor tripped, *Abigail* fell off to larboard, the foresails were braced around, and the ship gathered way. The tide was ebbing and the sun was near her zenith as they stood out of English Harbour and met the Atlantic rollers coming in.

Ten knots of breeze was blowing from the east southeast as Biddle-comb put the ship on a larboard tack, full and by, plunging along and sending the occasional shower of warm spray aft. They had pretty well cleared the land by the time Jack felt he could stand it no longer, looked aloft, and shouted, "Masthead, there! What do you see?"

Lacey was on the main topgallant and Wentworth, Jack noticed, was in the maintop, but sitting with his back against the mast and looking aft, staring off at nothing in particular that Jack could see. Their interactions had been formal and stiff since the duel, and they had largely avoided one another. Or, more correctly, Wentworth had avoided Jack, because Jack did not have the time to give any thought to whom he might bump into or whom he wished to avoid.

There was a moment's pause as Lacey took one last scan of the horizon and called, "Looks like a fishing boat a half a league to weather, sir, nothing beyond that."

Jack was not sure if he was relieved or disappointed by this report. Certainly he had thought it very unlikely that the French corvette, or any armed French vessel, would be hovering around English Harbour. But Frost had disagreed, and said it was in fact quite likely indeed. Frost felt the master of *L'Armançon* would have been humiliated by his defeat and eager to make amends before the *Directoire* made amends for him with the help of a guillotine. And so far Frost had been right about such things.

"What ho, Captain?" Frost's big voice rang out from the leeward side. "No sign of Jean Crapeau?"

"No," Jack said as the big man approached. Frost was looking very much in his element, very pleased with the improvements to the *Abigail*. But there was a patina of anxiety there as well, as if he felt personally responsible for how things might work out. And well he might, given how much of their present circumstance was his doing.

"The man aloft said there was a fishing boat to weather, nothing more," Jack said. "Visibility is everything we might wish, so if the Frenchie was anywhere within three leagues we'd see him."

"Indeed?" Frost said, and the disappointment in his voice was unmistakable now. He looked aloft. *Abigail* had all plain sail set and topmast studdingsails on the weather side. "Mayhaps you should reduce canvas?" he suggested. "Not run clear of here so fast?"

Jack, who had been scanning the horizon to windward, turned and looked at him. This was an odd suggestion, bordering on the bizarre. Certainly Jack agreed with the plan to fight their way to Barbados if need be. He was enjoying the command of this ersatz man-of-war. He had come to appreciate the aesthetics of the neat row of guns, larboard and starboard, in their symmetrical perfection, the oversized crew that could perform tasks so fast, so efficient.

He secretly relished his role of naval commander, of being predator and not prey, and he was secretly embarrassed to be relishing it. Silently he assured himself that he was not his father, did not wish to be and would never be his father, while at the same time understanding at last why a man might want to stand on the quarterdeck of a man-of-war and think himself master of all before him, and of anything that might come up over the horizon.

But for all his embrace of things naval, Jack still preferred to run to Barbados unchallenged. He had been raised on stories of men-of-war and the bold men who sailed them, and he had learned a lot, even when he was not trying to. And so he knew that captains of men-of-war (which he reminded himself he was not) did not put their ships and men in harm's way without a good reason for doing so. And he was not sure what reason he might have to seek battle with *L'Armançon*.

"Mr. Frost," Jack asked, "you have said yourself many times that Mr. Oxnard wishes *Abigail* to reach Barbados unharmed, and not wind up a prize of the French. I would think if we could sneak past her in the night, leave her over the horizon by dawn, that would be preferable to fighting."

"Well, of course it would!" Frost said, all but spluttering. "Of course, only a fool would think otherwise. But I'm saying only we should proceed with caution, slow, you understand, like an Indian sneaking along through the woods, or some such. If Jean Crapeau is just over the horizon, say, and here we come blundering along, all the kites flying, and we run right under his guns as fast as ever we can, that would be a disaster. That's what I'm saying."

Jack nodded. "I see," he said, and thought, *what sort of fool do you reckon I am?* He glanced up at the maintop, and suddenly he was enveloped with the sickening thought that, possibly, contrary to all reason, Wentworth might actually have been right about Frost.

"Let me put some thought into that, Mr. Frost," Biddlecomb said, "but for the moment I am loath to not take full advantage of a fine topgallant breeze. No mariner could stand to lose such a main chance."

"Of course, Captain, of course, you would be negligent to do otherwise," Frost assured him. He retreated to the leeward side and Jack kept his station at the weather rail, kept his eyes moving from sails to the horizon, to the wake astern. Occasionally he would amble over to the binnacle and take a look at the compass. He felt the warm, comfortable, driving breeze flow over his face and judged from long experience any minute changes in strength or direction.

The glass was turned, the bells rang out, the sails were carefully adjusted until Jack was satisfied. But not an inch of canvas was taken in, and when he was not directly conning his ship, Jack's mind went over that odd conversation he and Frost had had. He was thinking on what it might mean, what might be at the back of Frost's enthusiasms, and his money. He was considering the unthinkable; asking Wentworth just what it was he suspected.

Abigail continued to plow her long, white furrow through the sea, heeling to leeward and pitching in a soft, pleasing, rocking sort of motion. Eight bells rang out and the watch changed, and then one bell in the afternoon watch. Jack was still thinking about whether he should shorten sail, if there was something that Frost knew but for some reason could not say, when the man at the masthead—it was Adams now—sang out, "Sail ho! Right to windward it is, sir, t'gan'sls is all I can see!"

Two hours, Jack thought. *Two hours and this fellow will be up with us, if he intends to come up with us. And if it's* L'Armançon *then it won't matter much what intrigues Frost or Wentworth or any of them are playing at.*

There was a spot on the second floor of the City Tavern where, if Rumstick squatted a bit, he could look down the stairs and see Ness seated at his familiar table by the fireplace. It was ten minutes before the hour they had appointed for their meeting, and both men were in place; Ness in his seat and Rumstick squatting down, ignoring the looks of the tavern girls and watching Ness wait.

He was not waiting calmly. He was nervous. Even though his back was mostly turned toward Rumstick (which is why Rumstick remained unseen) his agitation was clear. He was fiddling with the cloth on the table, fiddling with the pewter plate, darting glances around. It might have been a good idea to check the tavern to see if Ness had planted some of his compatriots around, but it was too late for that. And Rumstick had done what he wanted to do. He had taken the measure of the man, got a good sense for his state of mind, which was not pacific, not at all.

Rumstick went down the back staircase, out the door that led into the alley, around to the front of the tavern, and in through the front door. He looked around the room and did a credible job of appearing to see Ness for the first time, crossed the noisy, crowded space, and sat with care at Ness's table.

"Good day, sir," Rumstick said, pretending not to notice Ness's irritation. "Have you had a chance to make some inquiries?"

"I have, yes, I have," Ness said, speaking much softer than Rumstick had done, and in a more conspiratorial tone. He leaned forward, then back again as one of the serving girls brought two tankards. Rumstick thanked her and Ness shooed her away.

"Here's what I know," Ness continued, "and I'll warn you, it's not much. The truth of the matter is this: myself, some of my friends, we hoped to stop Oxnard's ship from sailing. The man is making money like a fiend, and he funnels it right to Bache and other enemies of the administration. Stop his money coming in, you stop it going to our enemies, you see?" Ness put just the slightest emphasis on the word *our*, no doubt to remind Rumstick that they were on the same side.

"In any event," Ness continued, "that was our thinking, and we acted on it. This Bolingbroke fellow was hired by an associate of mine. Not an associate, really, more a sort of glorified errand boy. He's the kind who knows his way about the waterfront, you understand. Knows, for instance, if you need someone for this or that sort of mischief, who to talk to."

"I know the sort," Rumstick said, and he did, very well. "But you're telling me, Ness, that Bolingbroke was hired to kill Jack Biddlecomb just to make a small dent in Oxnard's wealth?"

"Well, I never thought my man would try such a thing!" Ness protested. "I told him simply to find a way to stop the ship from sailing. I expected him to spread the word that no hands should sign aboard for the voyage, or keep the stevedores from off-loading the ship, something along those lines. I hardly expected him to find someone to challenge the master to a duel, which I dare say was the least effective means of keeping her tied to the dock."

Rumstick leaned back, took up his tankard, and took a long pull of the ale, but his eyes did not leave Ness's, and it made the man's discomfort visibly worse. At last he put the tankard back down on the table. He was sailing into shoal water now. It was time to cast the lead.

"That's interesting. Interesting," he said, and let it hang in the air. "But I'll tell you the truth, I had thought it ran deeper than that. And perhaps involved some more prominent people. Not that I don't think you're prominent, Ness, but I was thinking of men higher up than you."

"Such as who?"

"Well, Jack's father, my dear friend Isaac Biddlecomb, who you certainly know . . ." Ness nodded his agreement. ". . . he received a letter." Rumstick leaned closer and Ness leaned toward him. "A letter from Alexander Hamilton. Like you, Hamilton also thought Jack shouldn't sail, said it could be dangerous. Hinted at some intrigue. But here's the thing; he mentions your name."

"My name?" Ness said, surprise and a trace of fear in his voice.

"Yes," Rumstick continued. He had been tracking along the line of the truth, but now he started to veer off course. "Mostly he talked about McHenry, of course, but you as well, as McHenry's associate. He said something about you arranging to have some harm done to Jack, said if Isaac didn't prevent Jack from sailing, you and McHenry might have some intrigue cooked up to stop him. He wasn't clear about what, but there it is, in Hamilton's hand. You and McHenry."

For a long moment Ness was silent and Rumstick was silent as they looked at one another across the table, over the tankards. Then Ness said, "Why would Hamilton write such a thing? Why would he wish to expose McHenry? McHenry is his man, for all love!"

" 'Expose McHenry?' " Rumstick asked. "So, there was something to expose? Some intrigue?"

More silence. A long silence as Ness looked at the various implications of what Rumstick was asking. But rather than answer, he asked a question of his own. "If you do not get an answer that will satisfy you, Rumstick, what will you do?"

Rumstick shrugged as if he had given it no thought. "My only concern is to find the truth, and to see that no harm comes to Jack. I genuinely do not give a tinker's damn about Hamilton or McHenry or the rest. If harm comes to Oxnard or Bache I'll cheer. But if I don't find out what sort of danger my godson has been brought into, I'll give the letter Hamilton wrote to Isaac to the *Aurora* and let you all go to hell, even if we are supposed to be on the same side. I'll look to protect family over party every day."

There was another long silence. Rumstick was acutely aware of every small sound in the room, the murmured conversations, the clink of silver, the soft pad of footsteps on the worn pine board floor. Then Ness began to talk.

"This is very involved," he said with a note of resignation, "and it goes very high. But I will tell you, because I know you are a friend to the administration."

And because you think Hamilton has thrown you and McHenry to the wolves, Rumstick thought, but he did not speak.

"Hamilton has a man who's close to Bache," Ness continued. "Don't ask me who because I don't know. But this fellow informed Hamilton of a great plan cooked up by Bache and Oxnard. They've been at it for half a year. You know that these Republicans want nothing more than to show the world that Adams is eager for war with France, eager to help the British, which is nonsense, of course. War with France? Our entire navy consists of the half-built frigate lying at the dock half a mile from here."

"So Bache and Oxnard hit on some means of showing the world Adams wants war?" Rumstick said, steering Ness back on course.

"It was clever, I'll grant them that. What if an American ship, ostensibly a merchantman but well armed, were to attack a French man-of-war? What if the master of that ship were the son of a prominent Federalist, a former hero of the Continental Navy, a friend of President Adams? You could draw a straight line from that act of aggression to the administration, show the world that the Federalists are champing at the bit for war, turn the country against us."

Rumstick leaned back and shook his head. "Nonsense. It was Oxnard armed the ship, it would be easy enough to show that."

"Really? As I understand it, your Jack was the one who signed for all the guns, the powder, shot. It's likely he didn't even know what he was signing, but his name's on all of it. What's more, the young man is an intemperate hothead, everyone knows it. Forgive me."

"No, no," Rumstick said, "no forgiveness needed. No one knows the truth of that better than me. I've had to haul him out of many an ugly scrape. But that still don't explain how they knew Jack would get into this fight."

"Oxnard put an associate aboard, fellow named Chapman but he was going by the name Frost, put him aboard to goad Jack on. Apparently Bache has connections enough in France to see that a small man-of-war would be stationed where they needed it. He lived in France, you know, years ago, with his grandfather. In any event, they arranged to have this man-of-war on station. This Chapman, or Frost, convinces Jack to attack, they fight, the Frenchman sustains some damage but takes Jack's ship as a prize, and there's your international incident."

Rumstick shook his head again, slowly, trying to fathom the depth of this intrigue, but the man in the fore chains was calling *No bottom! No bottom, here!*

"It all hinged on Jack, do you see?" Ness said. "Son of Isaac Biddlecomb, young and impetuous enough to go after a man-of-war, with a little convincing. We thought if he could be wounded—not killed, mind you, just wounded enough that he could not sail, then the plan would fall apart."

"Why didn't you just inform Jack of this? Or Isaac? Convince him not to go?"

Ness said nothing. He looked at Rumstick, apparently waiting for Rumstick to figure it out on his own. "No, never mind. That was a foolish question." Which it was. Rumstick knew better than anyone that Jack would not listen, and that trying to warn him off would just make him want to do the thing even more. It was how he was made.

And it went beyond that. If Jack resigned from command of the *Abigail*, Oxnard would know something was acting, perhaps cotton to the fact that he had a spy in his midst. Hamilton would not allow that to happen. Hamilton was an intriguer, his plots more important than the life of one young sailor.

Rumstick was quiet again, but at length he spoke. "And what has happened? Has it played out as Oxnard hoped?"

"We don't know," Ness said. "There's been no word. We would have thought to have heard something by now, but there's been nothing. We fear the worst, and we are bracing for the news from the West Indies."

Rumstick considered that. There was one possibility that no one seemed to have considered. At the center of all this was Jack Biddlecomb, son of Isaac Biddlecomb. Did it occur to no one that in the fight with this Frenchman he just might win?

27

In the end it was not above an hour and ten minutes before Jack was certain that the distant vessel was indeed *L'Armançon*. She was right to windward and running down on them, and though the two ships were not heading directly at one another they were converging at a combined speed of probably eight knots, which meant that in the space of seventy minutes they had reduced the distance between them by ten miles or so, leaving only three miles to go.

Seventy minutes was as long as Jack could tolerate standing on the quarterdeck feigning disinterest. He shed his coat and hat, took up his glass, and climbed aloft. He did not know if Wentworth made a point of ignoring him because he made a point of ignoring Wentworth and so did not see if the man had even glanced his way as he came up over the edge of the maintop.

He settled on the topgallant yard beside Adams and focused the glass to weather. *Lovely ship,* he thought. And she really was. The steeve of her bowsprit, the sweep of her sheer, the degree of tumblehome, it all worked together to present an image of strength and grace, the famed work of the French naval architects, from the nation that had given the world Versailles and Notre Dame. And like those famed edifices, the French navy, as Jack understood, was looked on by the radicals as some leftover from the *Ancien Régime,* a suspect thing.

The corvette was running with a bone in her teeth, carrying much the same sail as Abigail, though, sailing with the wind betwixt two sheets, she had studdingsails set to weather and to lee. *Fight or flee?* Jack thought. Here was the question. Was it worth cracking on and making a run for it?

The only way they might succeed with that plan would be to keep the Frenchman astern until nightfall, and then do some clever thing to shake them. He looked to the west. The sun was at least six hours from setting. *L'Armançon* was at most an hour away from having *Abigail* under her guns.

"I guess that's settled, then," Jack said out loud.

"Pardon, sir?" Adams said.

"It's nothing. Keep an eye on her, Adams, let me know of any changes she makes, changes to sail or course, anything."

"Aye, aye, sir," Adams said as Biddlecomb swung down to the topgallant shrouds and began heading back to the deck, the shrouds sticky and warm under his hands, the tar and varnish mixture growing soft under the wicked sun. He climbed around the crosstrees and down the topmast shrouds. His feet were on the edge of the maintop and he still had not yet decided if he would do the mature thing, the thing he knew he should, but did not wish to do.

Oh, damn it all, he thought, then stopped and swung inboard. "Mr. Went-worth?" he said, trying for a conversational tone. Wentworth, still leaning against the mast, looked up, pretending to have not realized he was there.

"Captain?" he said. He climbed to his feet. Jack looked to see if there was any sign of soreness, any impediment to his movement in the wake of the wound he had delivered, but he could see none. Wentworth was standing easy, with the athletic grace he generally displayed. His sandy hair was bound back in a queue and he wore just a linen shirt and breeches, with wool socks and his now battered shoes. He looked more like a sailor than he did the macaroni who had come aboard. Jack had seen that sort of transforma-tion before. The sea had a way of doing it.

Jack hesitated because he had not decided what he would say, out of the various things he wished to say. He wanted to ask Wentworth what he knew about Frost's intentions, and how he knew it. He wanted to ask if he knew anything at all about who Frost was. He wanted to tell Wentworth he had probably been right all along, though that one was pretty low on the list of statements he wished to make.

He could not decide, and he could not stand there like an idiot any lon-ger, so he said, "That's *L'Armançon* to weather, as you may have guessed. I imagine we will engage her. If you would care to take your place in the maintop with your rifle again, I would be grateful. You did great execution the last time."

Wentworth nodded his head. "Thank you, Captain, for saying so." His voice was less rigid and formal than it had otherwise been since the duel. "I would be honored to help in whatever way I can."

They remained silent for a few seconds, neither man knowing what more to say, so Jack mumbled, "Very good . . . ," found the ratline on the futtock shroud with his foot, and continued on the deck.

Frost was aft, of course, though his presence was really starting to grate on Jack, just as Wentworth's had. "*L'Armançon*, I'll warrant!" he said, delight in his voice.

"*L'Armançon*, indeed," Jack said.

"Should we clear for action, Captain?" Frost said next, which Jack found supremely irritating. If he said yes he would be allowing Frost to take control. But if he said no he would just sound petulant, since they did need to clear for action, and he would have to give the order anyway, a minute or two after that.

"We'll clear for action when I give the order, Mr. Frost," he said and Frost took the hint, stepped back, removed the grin from his face, and said, "Of course, Captain, of course."

Jack managed to drag it out for another five minutes, examining the set of the sails, scrutinizing the corvette to weather through his glass, passing a word with Tucker. At last he said, "Mr. Tucker, let us clear for action and send the men to quarters." He said it softly and could not deny the thrill that he felt in saying those words, a burgoo of exhilaration, fear, uncertainty, and resolve.

Tucker turned, shouted down the length of the deck, "Clear for action! All hands, clear for action, there!" Jack wondered if Tucker had ever said those words before. He doubted it.

In the naval service, Jack understood, there would have been drums beating and boatswain's calls and all sorts of martial sounds, but aboard the merchantman they had only the strong voice of the mate.

But it was enough. The men, who had been anticipating the order, leapt to, casting off the gun tackles, laying out sponges, crows, handspikes, and rammers, getting fire buckets ready, spreading sand on the deck. The new men had sailed aboard *Abigail* for all of five hours but they showed the discipline and training for which the Royal Navy was so well known, and fell to their tasks with ease and familiarity. Jack had assigned them to the guns, mostly, because they knew far more about such things than did the Abigails, and the Abigails knew far more about sailing their ship than did the British jacks. To weather and lee they were heaving the guns in, drawing the tompions, casting off the lead skirts over the vents.

Meanwhile John Burgess saw chains rigged to the yards, and extra braces rove off. The Abigails hoisted the new launch up and over the side to tow astern, unwilling to make the dumb mistake of leaving it on deck this time. No hammocks were stacked in hammock nettings because there were no hammocks or hammock netting, nor was there netting to stretch above the deck to protect from falling debris, or a gunner to retire to the magazine or a carpenter to get plugs for shot holes, because *Abigail*, for all her fine armament, was still a merchantman.

A minute before, the deck had been the epitome of a merchant ship at sea in fine weather, the men moving about with a busy but unhurried quality. With one order all that changed as the men plunged into the job of getting the ship ready for a fight, of putting her in the proper state for battle, a battle for which they had been preparing since the day they arrived in Antigua. It was a wonder to Jack that not one of the original Abigails had pointed out that this was not at all what they had signed aboard for.

Too caught up with the drama of the thing, Jack thought, shaking his head at what blockheads such men could be. Irony was sometimes a foreign language to him.

"Cleared for action, the men are at quarters," Tucker said, his voice faltering as he was not sure if that was indeed what he should say, and likely feeling a bit silly using such naval parlance.

"Very good, Mr. Tucker," Jack said. He looked out to windward. *L'Armançon* was a mile and a half away, and the two ships were closing fast. He looked aloft. Wentworth was in the maintop, rifle in hand. He had not seen him go back up there. There were others as well, some of the new hands from English Harbur with muskets cradled in their arms.

Frost must have sent them up, Jack thought, but Frost was keeping his distance and Jack did not wish to call him over to ask. He turned back to

Tucker. "In ten minutes or so we'll clew up the courses and get stuns'ls in, leave the rest of the sails set. I want the guns on the starboard side depressed just a bit below the horizontal, if you follow me." He suspected there was some more technically proper way to express this, but what that might be he had no idea.

"Aye, sir, just a bit below horizontal," Tucker said, apparently understanding.

"We'll man the larboard battery, make it look as if we'll be engaging that side. Then, as we get close to *L'Armançon*, very close, we'll come about, just spin on our heel, and the men will cross quickly over to the starboard side as we're coming about, do you see, starboard guns will be run out and ready, and we'll give them that broadside as we pass. They'll be quite surprised, I should think."

Tucker was smiling. "Good plan, sir!" he said, and Jack found his approval a comfort, despite the fact that Tucker knew even less about such things than he did.

Twenty minutes later, looking through his glass, Jack could clearly make out individuals on the Frenchman's deck, the white shirts of the men, the blue coats of the officers. As he watched, the perfect smooth domes of the Frenchman's fore and mainsail collapsed and flogged and the clews rose up as those lower sailed were hauled up to the yards.

"Mr. Tucker," Jack said, "let us get the stuns'ls in and clew up the courses." He said it calmly, slowly, hoping to disguise the fact that he had completely forgotten about it until that moment. The speed dropped off and the *Abigail* stood more upright as the canvas was reduced. The men stood silent at their guns, the sail trimmers ready at the braces and bowlines. Frost was forward of the mizzenmast, supervising the three guns aft. A petty officer from the English Harbour men was in charge of the forward battery.

Jack no longer needed the glass to see the figures moving about *L'Armançon*'s deck. A minute or so more. All this effort, all this worry, leading up to this inevitable moment: two ships converging on the open sea.

"Stand ready . . ." Jack shouted. *L'Armançon*'s forward-most guns would bear, he wondered why they did not fire. A hundred yards separated the ship. Half a minute more.

The first time they had met *L'Armançon* Jack had been unable to give the order to engage but he felt no such hesitancy now. "Helm's a'lee!" he shouted and the helmsman turned the wheel and *Abigail* flew up into the wind. "Let go your headsail sheets! Mainsail haul! Gunners, shift sides, now!"

The headsails made a thundering sound as they flogged in the wind, the foresails came aback, pushing the bow around, and like a herd of spooked cattle the gunners abandoned the larboard battery and charged across the deck to take their places on the starboard side.

"Let go and haul!" Jack shouted as *Abigail* settled on the new course and *L'Armançon* came charging down on them, fifty feet off the starboard side.

"Fire as you bear!" he shouted and the foremost gun on the starboard side went off with a great roar, the jet of flame visible even in the brilliant sun, and a hole was punched right through *L'Armançon*'s bulwark, dead center between two gunports.

The next gun fired, the ball hitting the Frenchman's hull and lodging there. The next smashed two deadeyes on the main shrouds, and still the Frenchman did not respond. Then, in the instant before the fourth gun went off, Jack heard, clear as birdsong, an order shouted down the length of the Frenchman's deck and *L'Armançon* fired her entire broadside, six twelve-pounders fired from forty feet away, level at *Abigail*'s deck, and *Abigail*'s guns seemed like puny toys in comparison.

Jack had time enough to see the first jets of gray smoke and then a ball hit the bulwark just forward of where he stood and his world was knocked aside in a storm of shattered wood and splinters and smashed planks from the new-built sides. He was aware of putting his arm up, of being lifting off the deck, of the agony of coming down hard. He could hear shouts and high-pitched screams. His head spun and for an instant he thought, genuinely thought, that it was a dream, that it was all too unreal to be a waking moment.

He pushed himself up with his arms, felt a pain in his side. There was a splinter like a long knife sticking out, and without thinking he grabbed on to it and pulled and screamed in agony as the wood came free and the blood began to spread across his shirt.

The deck was a ruin. One of the guns had upended and the screaming was coming from the man, one of the British sailors, who was caught under it. His mates were working at the barrel with crowbars and handspikes.

Beyond him the bulwark had been beaten flat, the windlass, so recently moved, no more than debris. Ropes hung loose and swayed with the roll of the ship.

Jack realized that the motion was wrong, the ship did not feel right underfoot. He looked up. They were in irons, the bow pointing right into the wind, the sails aback. He spun around. There had been only one man at the helm, and he was down, knocked to the deck by splinters, alive or dead Jack could not tell. "Mr. Tucker! Get forward, get the sail trimmers to back the jibs! You there, Maguire," he called to the Irishman, who was captain of the aftermost gun but one, "get on the helm!"

He looked over at *L'Armançon*. She had sailed clean past and was rounding up behind *Abigail,* which meant they would be firing into the stern, a bad situation for a ship with a lower gun deck, but the merchantman did not have much below decks to hit. His cabin, Jack knew, would be destroyed, but if that was the worst of it he would be happy.

"Sail trimmers! Brace the foresails for a larboard tack! We'll cast to starboard!" He could see there were more dead and wounded than he had thought, great frantic patches of wet blood on the deck.

The fore yards swung around, the sails came aback, the bow began to fall off to starboard as *L'Armançon's* guns fired again, one after the other, destroying the great cabin windows below Jack's feet. He had a vision of the stern rail blowing apart the last time they were in this circumstance and every bit of him wanted to move forward, out of the way of any flying debris, but he fought that urge down, remained where he was, clasped his hands behind his back. He could feel the blood from his wound, warm and sticky and spreading over his side, just opposite the place where Wentworth had cut him.

Now I shall have matching scars, he thought and resisted the insane urge to giggle.

He looked down the deck. The man under the toppled gun had died and his mates had abandoned him and the other gun crews were busy loading and running out. *L'Armançon* had come up on a starboard tack and *Abigail* was casting off onto a larboard tack and the space between the two was opening up. For a wild moment Jack considered running for it, but there was no point; even poorly handled, the French corvette was faster than the

merchantman by a couple of knots, and it seemed to Jack that the Frenchman's ship handling and gunnery was much improved from the last time
they had crossed paths.

"Let go and haul!" Jack shouted and *Abigail* swung off the wind and
her sails filled and she gathered way once again. He turned to Maguire
on the helm. "Keep her coming around, we'll get the wind right aft." He
looked astern. *L'Armançon* was also turning, falling off, so soon the two
ships would be sailing side by side, right downwind and about fifty yards
apart.

That's no good, no good . . . Jack thought. That first broadside had showed
him the absolute folly of going up against a ship that mounted guns twice
as powerful as his own, with scantlings a third again as thick. He kept seeing the image of that six-pounder ball lodged in *L'Armançon's* side. It had
not even pierced her hull, while *L'Armançon's* twelves seemed to go through
Abigail as if she was made of wet paper.

And then the ships were broadside to broadside and *L'Armançon* started
in again, firing at *Abigail's* already crippled starboard side. Roundshot
screamed over the quarterdeck and like a magic trick the head of one of
the British sailors disappeared. One moment it was there, the next it was
gone, and his knees buckled and his headless body slumped to the deck and
Jack thought he might vomit.

Round after round slammed into *Abigail's* side. A ball struck amidships, just below the starboard gunwale, and Jack saw it burst from the
larboard side in a swarm of shattered planking, passing right through the
hull and plunging into the sea. The Abigails were firing back now, and
Jack could see some of the shot strike, saw a respectable hole shot through
the after side of the mainmast, but he could see no damage beyond that.

"Keep coming around, Maguire, keep coming around!" Jack shouted.
"Sail trimmers, starboard tack!" If he kept turning, then he would present
his ship's bow to the enemy, which at least would make for a smaller target.
Abigail was turning to starboard and Jack could see *L'Armançon* turning to
larboard so the two ships were coming bow to bow, fifty yards between
them, and Jack had another idea.

"Hold her there, Maguire!" he shouted. "Sail trimmers, stand by!" The
smoke was thick like a fog, or nearly so, a heavy morning mist, and the

guns belched more and more even as the breeze whipped the old smoke away.

"Fall off, Maguire, fall off! Sail trimmers, square up!" Maguire turned the helm the other way. *Abigail* stopped in her turn to starboard and began swinging back to larboard, downwind, turning to cross *L'Armançon*'s bow. The Frenchman checked in her turn as well, turned back to meet *Abigail*, but it was too late to stop the American from crossing ahead of her.

"Bear up now, just a point!" Biddlecomb shouted to Maguire and Maguire, good hand that he was when sober, turned the wheel. But he was a merchant sailor, not a man-of-war's man, so he felt he had the right to say, "Sir! We'll be aboard her!"

"Not full aboard her, Maguire!" Jack shouted, then thought, *Dear God I hope not!*

They were close, very close, *L'Armançon* coming down on *Abigail* as *Abigail* tried to duck under her bow. Jack saw the tip of the Frenchman's jibboom stretching up over his foredeck. The forward-most gun of *Abigail*'s starboard battery fired and he saw *L'Armançon* shudder and then the jibboom passed between the forestay and the foremast and fouled and the ships were locked together.

"Mr. Tucker! Hands up in those fore shrouds, cut that Frenchman's headstays!" Jack shouted, but some of the British sailors were ahead of him and already scrambling up the starboard fore shrouds, axes and cutlasses in hand, hacking away at the Frenchman's rigging. The second and third gun in the starboard battery fired and the two ships drifted together in their weird grappling dance.

L'Armançon's fore topgallant stay swung free, cut through by eager hands, and the guys that offered support to the jibboom were hanging limp. A figure in a blue coat appeared on the heel of the Frenchman's bowsprit and headed outboard, sword in hand, a gang of seamen behind him. He made it as far as the cap of the bowsprit before jerking backward as if suddenly coming to the end of his leash. His arms flailed out and he fell with an audible splash into the sea and the men behind him, discouraged by this, turned and raced inboard again.

Jack looked up into the maintop. The smoke was still wafting from the end of Wentworth's barrel as he slowly lowered the weapon to reload.

Another of the British sailors fired, but with his smoothbore musket it would be as much luck as skill if he managed to hit one of the fleeing Frenchmen.

Abigail was slowly drifting onto a starboard tack and the Frenchman was drifting to larboard and the result was an enormous pressure on *L'Armançon*'s jibboom and bowsprit, like a man wrenching a chicken leg apart. Jack could hear the popping and the cracking, the blessed cracking, of the Frenchman's head rig as it began to give way. He could see more boarders massing on the bow, ready to try once more to come up the bridge made by the bowsprit, but even as the officer leading this new rush stepped onto the bowsprit's heel the whole thing gave way. The jibboom snapped off like a twig. It fell onto *Abigail*'s deck, now so entangled there was no telling what was *Abigail*'s gear and what was *L'Armançon*'s.

With that release *Abigail* began to turn faster, dragging *L'Armançon* around. Jack could see the bowsprit pulled out of alignment by the force exerted by *Abigail*'s deadweight. He heard a louder cracking sound and saw the end of the bowsprit shivered, shards of wood sticking out like an ugly broken bone.

The first three guns in *Abigail*'s battery were run out, almost together, and they fired as one and the concussion dislodged *Abigail* from the Frenchman's head rig. *L'Armançon* was crippled now, her bowsprit shattered, and *Abigail* had only to pass her to windward and race away. The Frenchman could never follow because she could not hope to sail in any direction but right downwind, and even that would be chancy. Forward, someone gave a cheer and the cheer was taken up along *Abigail*'s deck, a wild, exuberant cheer, a release of all the fear and horror of the past hour.

But *L'Armançon* was turning, her stern swinging off the wind, and Jack could see they had hauled her spanker out to windward. They were turning her on purpose, and there was only one rational reason why they might do so with their bowsprit shot to bits.

The Frenchman's broadside went off, not all together but one gun at a time, slowly, and Jack thought they must have their best man moving from gun to gun, aiming each, no doubt because they knew that they had one last chance, and this was it.

The cheer died on the Abigails' lips as the first shot clanged off the muzzle of the third gun on the starboard battery. The gun reared like a mad

horse and men scattered and the ton and a half of iron crashed down to the
deck. The next shot struck the caboose and went right on through, taking
the upper half of the little building with it, leaving the oven and a smattering
of pots exposed to the afternoon sun. The third shot was high, no one saw
it strike, but the fourth passed right over the waist, the wind of its passing
knocking men to the deck, but, incredibly, it hit no one in its flight.

Then they heard the cracking sound, the rending of wood and a frantic
shouting from aloft. Eyes looked up as the next of the Frenchman's guns
went off, parting the forestay, but what the Abigails were watching was the
main topmast, shot through at the cap, leaning, leaning over, the sail flogging, the deadeyes exploding with the pressure, lanyards shredding, the
shrouds swinging free.

The topmast fell so slowly it was almost dreamlike. The terrible thunder
of the cannons did not stop, the Abigails having regained their senses and
turned to loading and firing the five remaining guns on the starboard side.

Then the topmast started gaining momentum in its fall. It paused, just
for a second, as the strain came on the main topmast and topgallant forestays,
and then those parted, too, or most of them, and the ones that did not
dragged the fore topgallant mast down as the entire thing fell in a thundering, wrenching crash, spewing cordage and shattered spars and torn sail-
cloth over the *Abigail*'s waist and quarterdeck.

Frost came huffing aft. He had a cut on his cheek and his face was
streaked with blood and his shirt and coat had a rent that showed white
flesh below. "Captain! Captain! We're done for now! Dear God, you must
strike! You've done all a man could do!"

It was all so unreal Jack was having a hard time thinking, but the
thought did occur to him that this was the second time Frost had insisted
he surrender, which seemed an odd thing for someone who played the fire-
eater as he did. He looked over the hundred yards of water between him
and *L'Armançon*. The French ship was still turning. They had brailed the
spanker up to try and keep the ship from spinning like a weathervane up
into the wind but that was not working. What they needed to do was sheet
the jibs flat, but there were no jibs left because there was no bowsprit to
speak of. They might back the foresails, but Jack could see how the master
might not care to do that, with so much rigging torn up.

L'Armançon slowly turned to weather and in the odd quiet Jack could hear the Frenchmen shouting fore and aft and he could see men scrambling to do something, what, he could not imagine. The Frenchman's stern turned past them and two of *Abigail*'s guns fired into it. Then the French ship came up into the wind, pointing right into the wind, turning out of control. The steady trades caught the foresails and laid them aback, normally not a problem, but now there was no head rigging to keep them from falling backward.

The Abigails were silent, fore and aft, watching with disbelief as *L'Armançon*'s fore topmast and fore topgallant mast, and all the rigging and gear, tilted aft, tilted as slowly as *Abigail*'s had, then picked up momentum in its fall because it did not have the intact rigging to slow it down. It looked like a felled tree as it came down and the mainsail jerked and the main topgallant was ripped from its place high aloft and the whole thing collapsed, half on the deck and half over the side. *L'Armançon* came to a stop, now two hundred yards away, spinning slowly on that patch of ocean. Two ships, crippled, drifting apart, a battle tabled until one or the other could get under way.

Jack was the first of the Abigails to return to his senses. "Clear this wreckage away! That topsail yard is kindling, get it overboard. Someone cut those lanyards free!"

The men leaped on the wreckage, because the tactical situation was clear; whoever could make sail first was the winner, and the other, helpless, could do nothing but strike or be beaten to death. So they swarmed over the wreckage, axes rising and falling, sheath knives working at spun yarn.

They were at it for twenty minutes before Jack remembered his great cabin. "Mr. Tucker," he called to the mate, "carry on here. I am going below and see what's left of my cabin."

"Aye, sir," Tucker said. He had a bandage on his hand and blood on his face that had been imperfectly wiped away.

Jack climbed down into the 'tween decks. It was better lit than usual, with the gaping holes larboard and starboard where the ball had passed clean through the hull. He made his way past Wentworth's and Frost's cabins, which he could see had taken a number of hits, and forced the door to his own cabin open.

The stern windows, just replaced at Antigua, were gone again. His hanging bunk, which he used at sea, was shot clean through, both ends still hanging from their hooks, the midsection on the floor. His sea chest and its contents, or what remained of them, were scattered about.

He saw his barometer, his beautiful barometer, lying facedown on the deck. He picked it up with a knot of sadness at its loss, but when he turned it over he saw to his surprise that it was intact. Indeed, it looked as if it had not suffered a scratch. Jack smiled in delight, one little bit of happy news in all of this destruction. And then he looked at the mercury, and then looked again. He had checked it only a few hours ago. He was not sure he had ever seen it fall so fast.

28

J ack carefully wrapped the barometer in layers of bedding he pulled from his shattered hanging cot and wedged the instrument into the corner of his fixed bunk. He took one last look around and then climbed back on deck. The work had not slowed in his absence; if anything, the momentum had built as wreckage was cleared away, torn sail cut free and pulled clear, allowing more hands to get at the job.

John Burgess, with the frugality of boatswains the world over, was overseeing a gang of men flaking down the much torn main topsail, the topgallant waiting its turn in a heap on the larboard side. The sails represented a considerable quantity of canvas, as did the piles of broken cordage waiting to be coiled. Jack was not terribly concerned with saving Robert Oxnard's property just then, but he did not wish to offend Burgess's sensibilities, so he said nothing.

The starboard end of the shattered topsail yard was free of its gear and a dozen men grabbed it up, walked it to the leeward side, and heaved it into the sea. It struck with a great splash, bobbed, and settled.

The deck was swarming with men. If Jack was ever grateful for the extra hands Frost had brought aboard, it was now. He had no notion of how many men had been killed or wounded in that exchange, but guessed ten at least were out of action. Some of the men-of-war's men had pulled the casualties toward the bow, the most out-of-the-way spot on deck.

Even with his expanded company, he suspected his crew was a third the size of *L'Armançon*'s. But at least he now had a chance of getting his ship under way before the Frenchman. Without the British jacks, there would be no chance at all.

He saw Wentworth straddling the main topgallant yard, lying half across the bulwark, half across the main hatch, which it had stove in when it fell. He was wielding a knife, a sailor's knife, cutting away the robands to free the topgallant sail from the yard. Jack guessed that Tucker or someone had told him what to do, what to cut. Wentworth certainly could not name any one of the lines he was so aggressively attacking with his blade.

Jack looked out to windward. In the short time he had been below, the trade winds had blown away the lingering cloud of powder smoke and Jack was suddenly aware of just how obscured his vision had been. It was like fog. You often did not realize how little you could see until the visibility was back to what it should be. Now he could clearly see *L'Armançon*, every detail visible over the half mile separating them. Like *Abigail*, she was lying ahull, her remaining sails clewed up. The wind and current had slowly turned her, and now Jack was looking at her bow and he could see the swarms of men there and on the bowsprit as well, could see the glint of axes rising and falling as the rigging and shattered wood was cut away.

The bowsprit would be their focus, their alpha and omega. Without it they might be able to sail, but they would never be able to maneuver in any meaningful way. Without that heavy spar forward, the support it would give to the foremast and the leverage exerted by the jibs that flew there, they would never have control enough to outsail *Abigail*, or to avoid having her hang on their quarter and pound them to death when the duel resumed.

Jack's eyes tracked farther off to the east, and there he saw what he had missed in the smoke of the battle and the distraction of having a French man-of-war trying to batter his ship to shivers. An ugly dark line was building on the horizon, and above it great billowing anvil head clouds. This was not the usual late afternoon rain squall of the Caribbean Sea, this was something more profound and menacing. This was the sort of weather that made the mercury in the barometer fall at an alarming rate, bad in any instance, but much worse with *Abigail*'s hull and rig so frighteningly compromised.

Tucker hurried over to him. He was stripped down to shirtsleeves and sweating heavily. "Two of them guns were upended, sir, carriages smashed. I had thought I might—"

Jack cut him off. "Use the boat falls to drop them overboard, just be rid of them. The carriages as well."

"Aye, sir," Tucker said and turned to go but Jack called him back.

"See here, Oliver," he said, low, so no one else would hear. "There's some very nasty weather coming in from the east . . ."

Tucker turned and looked, running his eyes along the horizon, let out a low whistle, then turned back to Jack. "I should say nasty, sir."

"No need to bring it to the men's attention, they're working as hard as they can right now," Jack said, "and they'll notice it soon enough. But once this wreckage is cleared away I want the fore topgallant mast and yard sent down, and the mizzen as well. If we have time we might strike the fore topmast. The French were kind enough to take care of the main for us."

"Aye, sir."

"Get the boat aboard and double-griped. Lifelines fore and aft. And for all love let's see the guns double-lashed, inspect the eyebolts, and set some of the more godly hands to praying that none of them come adrift this time."

"Aye, sir," Tucker said, paused a second to see if more was coming, and when he realized Jack was done he turned and hurried forward, calling out orders.

Jack looked to the west, a direction he had not looked in a while as there had not been much there to command his attention, but now there was. They had run to the southeast during their fight, and the wind and current had been drifting them around some distance since the engagement ended. Jack had not been paying much attention to where on the watery globe they were, but he knew now, and he did not have to use a sextant, a chip log, or any other navigational tool to figure it out.

They were right to windward of Guadeloupe. Jack could see the high, dull green mountains at the center of the island looming above the horizon. They were a hundred nautical miles or more from actually running up on the island's sandy beaches, but that was not that far as measured at sea, particularly not with the wind and current setting them down on shore and them with no way to sail clear, not at least before the considerably damaged rig was set to rights.

And that was no simple job. It was not just a matter of clearing the wreckage away. When the main topmast and the topgallant came down they tore out great quantities of running rigging in their plunge to the deck; braces, bowlines, lifts, clewlines; not to mention the shrouds, backstays, and forestays that had been pulled out or shot through, without which the masts would not bear the pressure of the sails. It all had to be knotted, spliced, or replaced before *Abigail* could sail, fight, or beat clear of a lee shore. Incredibly, *L'Armançon* had suddenly dropped to number three on Jack's list of most immediate threats to his life and the lives of his men.

Barère was dead. That at least was a good thing. Renaudin had had the supreme satisfaction of seeing it, close up. But he had been wounded in the process, and Barère did not die by his hand, and that tempered his pleasure.

It had happened near the end of the fight, a fight that had been going just as Renaudin hoped, though to be sure the Americans were better prepared for battle than he had expected them to be. If ever one needed evidence of the perfidious nature of the Americans and the British, here it was. The Americans had sailed to Antiqua, which meant they had turned to the British navy for help. The British navy. The same navy that France had fought in those very waters to defend the United States, the navy that had made Renaudin a prisoner while he fought for American freedom, and the British had not only repaired their ship but also doubled the armament and crew. Incredible.

Renaudin did not like to think that Barère and the *Directoire* could be right about anything, but he could not argue with this clear example of American treachery.

In the end, however, it did not matter, because Renaudin did not see this as an issue of international relations, or republicanism versus monarchy, or the world's attitude toward the new French Republic or the *Ancien Régime*. For him, this was personal. For nearly a decade his professional pride had been smothered under a blizzard of orders, propaganda, and useless revolutionary officers sent out from Paris. His honor had been slumbering, and this impudent American had woken it up, and now he was focused entirely on crushing him, to the exclusion of all else.

He and Dauville had driven the bastards on the lower deck hard, watch on watch, pushing them through gun drills and sail-handling drills. They had met protests and grumbling with fists and belaying pins. And the drills paid off. The first broadside, fired point-blank range into the American, who once again thought himself so clever in his quick ship handling, had been devastating. One gun upended, the thin strakes of the merchantman punched clean through. They had come under the American's stern and fired again, right through the transom, the most satisfying volley of round-shot Renaudin had ever fired, his guns twice as powerful as those the American mounted.

The American had flown up into irons, rocked by the onslaught, and Renaudin had worn around to come back and end it, the *coup de grâce*, as the American flatted in his headsails and cast onto a starboard tack. That was when it happened. Barère was shouting something, Renaudin managing to ignore him, until Barère took a grip on his forearm and turned him so they were face-to-face, Renaudin with his back to the American ship.

"See here, *Citoyen* Renaudin!" Barère said, his finger raised as if admonishing a child, but Renaudin was still too stunned by the fact that the man had had the audacity to actually grab him by the arm and spin him around that he could not speak.

"You have your orders, straight from the *Directoire*, by way of me, who speaks for the *Directoire*," Barère spluttered. "You are *not* to destroy this ship, you are to capture it." It was apparently clear even to Barère what Renaudin had in mind. "You will call for them to strike before you fire another shot, is that understood?"

Renaudin's shock dissipated but he still did not speak. Instead he reached for the pistol in his coat pocket, thinking that the weapon could express his feelings better than any words. But just as his hand found the walnut grip of the gun, he felt a burning on the top of his ear, heard a loud buzz like a swarm of bees, and a round hole appeared in Barère's forehead. His mouth flew open and the back of his head exploded in a spray of blood. It was just as Renaudin had always envisioned it.

Barère's blood sprayed over the helmsman, who flinched at the sight, and Barère was flung backward. He crashed against the barrel of the helm, hung there for a moment, and then slumped to the deck.

At that moment the burning in Renaudin's ear became a pain like a knife thrust. He reached up and felt warm, wet blood on his fingers. He turned and looked across the water at the American. *The rifleman*, he thought. The damned rifleman who had shot down his helmsmen and the *enseigne de vaisseau* the last time they had tangled. This time he nearly took down the captain and the first officer in a single shot. Instead the bullet had clipped Renaudin's ear on its way to taking off the back of Barère's head.

Renaudin looked back at Barère's immobile form. His eyes were open and crossed, giving him an expression that might have been comical if not for the gore and great quantities of blood soaking his uniform and the deck below him. Renaudin felt the rage building. All of this, all the humiliation, the death, the insanity, Barère had brought it all.

Straight from the Directoire, *by way of me, who speaks for the* Directoire . . .

"Bastard!" Renaudin shouted. He stepped across the deck and kicked Barère's body hard, then kicked him again, but the dead man only slumped over in a most unsatisfying way. Renaudin grabbed him by the collar of his coat and hefted him up, surprised at how light the man was. He half carried and half dragged him over to the taffrail, hoisted him up, and flung him over, watching with satisfaction as the man spun through the air, slowly twisting as he fell the fifteen feet to the sea, then hit with a splash that hid him from view for a moment before he bobbed up and settled, face up, still wearing that expression of surprise. Renaudin hoped he might see a shark set into that despised corpse.

"Sir!" It was the helmsman and there was an urgent tone in his voice. Renaudin spun around. The American, who had been bearing up as if to pass astern of *L'Armançon*, was now falling off again, apparently looking to pass ahead, and in doing so threatening to take *L'Armançon*'s head rig clean off.

"*Merde,*" Renaudin said. "Bear up, bear up!" He saw *L'Armançon*'s bow swing to larboard but already it was too late. The end of the jibboom was reaching out over the American's foredeck and the corvette was driving closer still. Renaudin felt a gentle thump as the two ships locked together and *L'Armançon*'s way was checked.

René Dauville came racing aft, his face streaked with soot, a tear in his blue coat. "Sir, where is Barère?" he shouted.

"Dead," Renaudin shouted back. "Get a boarding party, right up that bowsprit and see if you can't get aboard that whoreson!" Renaudin could see the American sailors hacking at *L'Armançon*'s rigging, could see the jibboom twisting dangerously under the pressure being exerted by the American ship.

"Aye, sir!" Dauville shouted, but before he could turn, Renaudin stepped closer and said in a lower tone. "Do not lead the boarders yourself. Send an *enseigne de vaisseau* to lead it."

"Sir, I must protest . . ." Dauville began, but Renaudin was thinking about the rifleman. He could not afford to lose his second officer. First officer, now.

"That is an order, Lieutenant Dauville, a direct order, understand?"

"Aye, sir," Dauville said, not mollified, and ran forward. And five minutes later, Renaudin was vindicated in his decision when the damned rifleman dropped the *enseigne de vaisseau* into the sea, and the rest of the boarders, cowards to a man, turned and fled.

Then the American ship, twisting in the breeze, snapped *L'Armançon*'s jibboom and wrenched the bowsprit sideways until it was hanging like a broken wing. Renaudin ordered the spanker backed, and as *L'Armançon* turned under the pressure of that sail they gave the arrogant, cheering bastards a broadside they would remember. He ordered Dauville to personally aim each gun for Dauville had brought down the American's main topmast. But without the headsails they had been unable to check *L'Armançon*'s swing. The corvette turned up into the wind and the fore topmast came down around their ears.

And here they lay, crippled, frantically trying to sort things out, to get steerageway at least, as a half mile away the Americans tried to do the same. Because the American master knew, as Renaudin did, that the first ship to get under way was the ship that would bring the other in as a prize of war.

They worked like madmen, the newly disciplined crew, and Renaudin and Dauville drove them in the manner to which they were becoming accustomed. At such times, a mariner's world closed down to the space between the bulwarks and straight up into the rigging, as if nothing existed beyond the gunwales or above the trucks of the mast. At first Renaudin would glance over at the American now and again, to see the state of their readiness, but he soon realized they were making no more progress than he was, and he stopped looking.

And so it was several hours after the battle that he happened to look out to the east. He was actually looking at the bowsprit to see what progress was being made there, and it happened that the bow, which had been swinging all over the compass, was pointing east at that moment. Looking past the bow, Renaudin saw for the first time the long black line creeping up over the horizon, the great heaps of clouds building above it, the sign, well known to a man who had spent as much time in the West Indies as he, of a quick-moving and brutal storm.

He looked over the wreckage strewn around *L'Armançon*'s deck, the rigging hanging in shreds above his head. *"Merde,"* he said for the second time that day.

By the time the sun was near to setting, the ugly black clouds, which earlier had been confined to the eastern horizon, were spread overhead, with the leading edge of the storm off to the west of them, making for a weird red-and-yellow sunset that bathed Guadeloupe, closer now by thirty miles, in its unearthly light. The Abigails were exhausted but their efforts had barely slacked because every man aboard could now see what they were in for. They needed no encouragement from Biddlecomb or Tucker to step it up. The black sky and the dull gray water, the breaking waves flashing dull in the fading light, the first stirrings of a cold wind like a spirit wafting by, these were enough to provide all the motivation needed.

"Adams, Fowler, take a turn there!" Jack shouted to two of his seamen tending the fore topgallant heel rope. The hands had turned their attention to getting the remaining topgallant masts and yards down on the deck, reducing the weight and windage aloft in preparation for the storm, but those two were getting sloppy in their exhaustion. If the line got away from them, the mast would come crashing down. "We don't need it to come down that damned fast," Jack added, as Fowler took a turn of the line around a belaying pin.

The debris had been cleared, the rigging knotted and spliced. Frost seemed to have disappeared after Jack broke off the fight with *L'Armançon*, but soon he was back on deck, fussing about the cannons, seeing they were double-lashed, then checking them and checking again. The topgallant yards were down and Tucker was seeing the mizzen topmast down to deck, and Jack was seeing to the fore topgallant. The fore topsail was triple-reefed, a narrow strip of canvas quickly being lost from sight in the gloom. The mainsail was also reefed, though Jack did not imagine they would hold on to that for long.

Abigail had way on at last, driving along under the reefed topsail, mainsail, fore staysail, and the spanker with a balance reef. She was plunging into the chop, pitching and throwing up spray as the wind built and the seas came on, steep and breaking, and getting steeper still.

"Deck there!" a voice called from the mizzen top, one of the British hands. "Lost her, sir!"

Jack had sent him up there to keep an eye on *L'Armançon*. For all their worry about the storm, she was still a threat as well, she had to be considered. If her captain felt particularly ambitious he might fire a ball into *Abigail* as they were struggling to claw away from Guadeloupe. It would not take much damage to the rigging to put the merchantman in serious jeopardy.

But it did not appear that that would be a problem. The Frenchmen were still struggling to get sail on, and they were being set downwind much faster than *Abigail*. It was not necessarily a matter of seamanship. The loss of the bowsprit and fore topmast was much more significant than the damage *Abigail* had suffered. Now *Abigail*, with sail set and making way, was nearly holding her own, fighting to windward to keep off Guadeloupe's lee shore. The corvette was fighting the same fight and losing. The lookout had kept an eye on her for as long as he could, calling down occasional reports, but now he had lost sight of her.

"Very well!" Jack shouted up, " "You may lay back to deck!" A gang of men came staggering aft. Walking was becoming markedly more difficult with the wild motion of the ship and the stumbling exhaustion that all hands were feeling. The men had a lee cloth in their hands and they began to lash it up into the mizzen rigging, a luxury Jack had not expected but one for which he knew he would be grateful. And he knew he had Tucker to thank for it.

Another figure came aft, barely seen, and Jack realized it was nearly full dark. *Abigail*'s bow rose up, hung there, plunged down, and the water ran inches deep along the deck, rushing like a receding tide to the leeward side. William Wentworth pulled himself to the quarterdeck by the lifeline.

"Captain!" he shouted, the word more like a greeting.

"Mr. Wentworth!" Jack called back. Wentworth had his oilskin coat on, but half of it seemed to be hanging in tatters. "Your coat has suffered some injury, I see!"

"Ah, the Frenchies, damn their revolutionary eyes! Put a ball right through my sea chest. This coat got off easy compared to some of it!"

"I'm sorry to hear that!" Jack shouted.

Wentworth shrugged, the gesture barely visible. "Casualty of war!" he said, then added, "It would seem we're in for yet another nasty night!"

"May be worse than the last!" Jack shouted back. "But shorter!" Along with the deteriorating visibility, Jack saw that it was becoming more difficult to speak. There was water in the air, some rain, some spray.

"How do you know that?" Wentworth asked.

"The barometer! Recall, I told you about it, second night of the voyage! When it drops fast, it means the blow will be short but strong!"

Wentworth nodded. He was silent for a moment. "Captain, I wanted to say, I'm sorry about that incident back at Antigua! I have a notoriously short temper, and maybe have become a bit prickly on the matter of honor. Or I've come to like dueling too much, that can happen, you know!"

"Never think on it, Mr. Wentworth!" Jack shouted. "In all decency I should say you were probably right all along!"

Both men fell silent once again thoroughly embarrassed. "Is this normal, all this dirty weather we've managed to find?" Wentworth shouted at last, certainly to break the silence as much as anything.

"We are at sea, Mr. Wentworth! There is no such thing as 'normal' at sea!" They were silent again, and then Jack added, "But we do seem to have had our share of foul weather! And this business about being shot up by a French man-of-war, that is not what I would call normal, in my experience!"

Wentworth nodded. Jack reached up and grabbed on to one of the mizzen shrouds, an ingrained gesture, and Wentworth steadied himself on the lifeline. And then the note in the rigging rose an octave, the *Abigail* heeled far to leeward, then farther still, and the brunt of the storm rolled over them.

29

Wentworth remained where he was and Jack remained where he was but neither tried to speak, because the effort required was too great. *Abigail* rolled hard to leeward, held there, shipping green water over the lee rail like a dipper in a scuttlebutt, tons of water. Then she stood again, slowly, the groaning and popping audible even over the shrieking wind. The water cascaded across the deck as the ship righted herself. It hit the fife rails and masts and combings and the legs of the men clinging to the lifelines like surf on a rocky shore, jetting high and foaming white around the obstacles.

The water gushed from the scuppers and through the gunports, partially blocked by the big guns thrust out and lashed in place. It rolled back across the deck and out the gunports on the other side. *Abigail* seemed to Wentworth like a man struggling over a rough road with a heavy load on his back.

The bow rose up again as the sea passed under, plunged down in a welter of spray, water jetting up on either side. She rolled and scooped another sea and once again the tidal surge crashed across the deck. Wentworth looked at Jack, a dark shape by the mizzen shrouds. Lightning flashed and in the same instant thunder cracked like the cannon blasts of their fight with *L'Armançon*, but much louder, much sharper, more frightening.

Jack was looking aloft; in the flash of lightning William saw him, contemplating the sails. Here was the calm he had seen during that first awful storm, so far beyond anything Wentworth had ever experienced. Then, as now, Jack looked as if he might be considering a painting hanging on a gallery wall.

Wentworth had seen storms of course, several worse than this one, but

always from the solid foundation of his Beacon Hill home. Save for the few
occasions when he had been caught in the rain, a storm had never caused
him any real discomfort. It certainly had never caused him to think he might
be dead within a few hours.

That was what made this unique. The storm was tossing them, rolling
them, making the ship pitch wildly. They were part of the storm—the
wind, the seas, the lightning, the ship, they were all part of this mad world.
The storm was not an academic consideration, and Wentworth, for once,
not a disinterested observer. This storm could kill him, could take the *Abigail* to the bottom or pile her up on the shore of Guadeloupe, and that made
Wentworth as interested as a man could be. The same had been true of the
fight with *L'Armançon* and Wentworth wondered if it was also the reason
for his growing addiction to dueling. He was like a man waking up.

Jack let go of the shroud, grabbed the lifeline, and stumbled forward, the
water breaking around his legs. In the odd flashes Wentworth could see
someone, he thought it was John Burgess, going from gun to gun, taking
hold of the many, many ropes that bound them to the sides, and pulling to
check they were still taut. Jack waited for the ship to stand more upright,
then leapt across to the midships gun, and grabbed hold as the ship rolled
off to leeward.

With every burst of lightning Wentworth could see Jack frozen in a
different pose; arm pointed toward the sails, arm pointed to the bow, both
hands grabbing on the breech rope of the gun to keep himself from being
swept away. And then he was heading back to the quarterdeck and the lightning showed Burgess and a gang of men at the pin rails, the men on the
leeward side sometimes waist deep in the boarding seas as they cast certain
lines off the belaying pins and grabbed hold, swaying with the rolling of
the ship.

They are clewing up the mainsail! William thought. He had been watching the men at work long enough now that he understood these basic opera-
tions, and he was secretly proud of that. Jack had paused on his way aft and
was taking one of the thicker ropes off . . . not a belaying pin . . . Wentworth
struggled for the word. *A kevel!* he recalled, and then realized he could be
of help here, and not just a passenger standing dumb and useless on the
quarterdeck.

He shuffled forward, knee deep in water, then made the leap to the weather rail, grabbing hold of the ring behind where Jack stood. "I can tend the . . . main sheet!" he shouted, the name of the rope coming miraculously to mind just as he needed to speak it.

Jack turned and looked at him, water streaming down and filtering through the stubble on his unshaved face. William could see the indecision, the internal debate as to whether the useless passenger could be trusted with this task. "Very well!" he shouted at last. "Pay it out as they clew up! Don't let it get away from you, but don't hold it fast and make those poor bastards work too hard!"

Wentworth nodded. He almost said "Aye, aye," but he could not summon the nerve, so he said, "I understand, Captain!" and took the line from Jack's hand.

Jack made a lunge for the lifeline and almost missed as the ship took an unexpected roll and hit him with a rush of water that knocked him sideways. But he hung on, and soon he was moving aft and Wentworth turned to his assigned task.

He understood in principle what he had to do; as the hands at the starboard clewgarnet hauled that line, which would pull the starboard corner of the sail up, he had to ease the main sheet, which held the corner of the sail down. Presumably he had an opposite number on the larboard side. The main sheet was still wrapped in a figure eight around the top of the kevel. He had to unwrap it enough that he could let it slip free as the sail went up, but not so much that he could not hold it and keep the sail under control. It was the sort of thing that seemed very simple when he watched others do it, but appeared much more nuanced now that he had to do it himself.

Carefully he removed a turn from one of the kevel's horns and felt no added pressure. But the men of the clewgarnet were hauling, pulling, swaying, stumbling, and Wentworth knew he was keeping them from hauling the sail up. He took another turn off. The rope was hard to hold now, he could feel the enormous tension both from the clewline and from the shrieking wind. But his hands were tougher now than they had ever been. After having his palms flayed in the last storm while trying to hold back the sliding gun, the skin had grown back nearly as calloused as a sailor's hands would be.

He considered the pleasure of running his hands over a young lady's smooth skin and wondered how much that sensation would now be diminished. Quite a bit, he concluded, but nonetheless, like his growing understanding of the workings of a sailing ship, he took certain delight in his tough hands.

Foot by foot the line snaked through his hands and around the kevel and the men at the clewgarnets hauled it up. They fought with the line, pulling against the force of the wind, struggling to keep their balance as the boarding seas bashed against them again and again. Then the sail was up: in the seconds of illumination Wentworth could see it hanging below the yard and beating angrily, as if it was infuriated at having been brought in.

The men at the lines made them off to the belaying pins and Wentworth looped the sheet around the top of the kevel. Then the hands forward began to stumble and pull their way across the deck to the main shrouds on the weather side. The first of them stepped up on a gun carriage, swung outboard, took hold of the shrouds, and began the long struggle aloft to stow the sail. They moved like men off to be sacrificed, but Wentworth knew it was just the difficulty of climbing with so wild a motion of the ship, and not any shyness about going aloft, that made them move that way.

There seemed to Wentworth to be quite a few men, and then he recalled that they had the British hands aboard, more than doubling the crew, which would make the work of stowing the sail blessedly simpler. That fact aside, Wentworth was determined that this time he would join them. He could not stand to think he was backward in his courage, and he did not think he was, but his memory of declining to go aloft nagged at him. He headed forward now, determined to kill that ghost.

"Mr. Wentworth!" he heard the voice roll down the deck even over the wind. He turned and could just make out the figure of Captain Biddlecomb, waving him aft. He reversed direction and fought his way back to the quarterdeck, up to Biddlecomb's side.

"Well done with the sheet!" Biddlecomb shouted. "But going aloft in this weather is not for landsmen! Best keep your feet on the deck! If you can!"

Various reactions hit William like a boarding sea. Relief was one of them, he could not deny it. It was no decision of his, but a direct order from the master that kept him relatively safe on deck. But there was also disappointment, and anger. Was Biddlecomb implying a want of aptitude on his part? A want of courage? His thoughts turned, as they always did in such situations, to whether he should demand satisfaction.

Don't be an idiot! he thought. There was not the least implication of anything in Biddlecomb's voice. And what's more, Biddlecomb was right. Proud as he might be of his gained knowledge, Wentworth had to admit he was still a landsman and would only be in the way up aloft.

"Very well, Captain!" he cried. He reached for the lifeline but Biddlecomb put a hand on his arm.

"If you wish to remain on the quarterdeck, I suggest you get behind the lee cloth here!" he shouted. The lee cloth, tied up in the mizzen shrouds, offered a modicum of relief from the rain and spray. Wentworth nodded his thanks, stepped up to the weather rail, and sheltered himself as best as he could.

It was immediately obvious, even to Wentworth, that the ship was behaving much better with the mainsail stowed. She still rolled heavily, still took boarding seas, but the water did not run so deep along her deck, and her motion had less of the laboring, desperate motion of earlier.

Wentworth remained on deck for an hour more, watching the ship plunging along, utterly unable to determine if she was making headway, sternway, or staying in one spot. She did seem to have a sort of equilibrium; the amount of sail set was enough to drive her, not enough to overwhelm her, and the seas rolled in steep and breaking but with a certain regularity to which he became accustomed. The deck was snugged down, the watch seeking what shelter they could because, for the moment, there was nothing they needed to do but wait it out.

Jack kept looking astern. Wentworth could not help but notice it, and once he himself stole a look aft but could see nothing but blackness and the occasional flash of a breaking wave, and, when the lightning came, the huge and unruly seas lit up with that strange yellow light and deep shadow.

"What are you looking at?" Wentworth finally asked, as Jack did it again. He still had to shout to be heard, even from a few feet away.

"Guadeloupe!" Jack shouted. "Or *L'Armançon*! Or both!"

Wentworth nodded. Jack paused, then added, "If it were not for those, I'd likely turn and run before this! But we have no sea room! If we hit either the island or the Frenchie we're done for!"

William nodded again and turned and looked astern once more. He could not help himself. And again there was nothing to see, and half an hour later, when the helmsmen were relieved, there was still nothing to see, and William was soaked through and chilled, despite the relatively warm West Indian night. He thought about leaving the deck, but his pride suggested if Biddlecomb was going to remain there all night, he should, too, even though he served no function whatsoever. Finally good sense asserted itself and he bade good night to Biddlecomb and fought his way below. A storm lantern was hanging from a hook, which gave him light enough to find what remained of his cabin and he lay down, fully dressed, in his bunk and slept.

He woke some hours later with the sense that it was daylight and that something was taking place on deck. He lay still and listened. The motion of the ship was not as bad now, the shudder of the hull in the water, the sound of the wind in the rig all diminished a bit. There were feet running topside and muffled shouts, heard through the planks of the deck. And not just topside. He could hear activity in the 'tween decks and down in the hold, the entire ship's company at some urgent task.

William swung his legs over the edge of the bed and stood. His clothing was no longer wet, but it was far from dry. It was damp, clammy, and considerably uncomfortable, but he imagined that once he had been moving around a bit it would not be so bad. Or so he told himself.

He forced his way out of the cabin and down the alleyway. The cover was off the main hatch and the cool, fresh air that was filling the narrow space smelled good and clean. A gang of men were working at something, and at first glance William thought they were doing battle with some great monster of legend, but then he saw they were hauling the end of one of the massive ropes out of the hold.

He climbed the ladder to the deck above, stepped from the scuttle, and looked forward. The dawn was an hour past and the world topside was gray and wild. The seas were leaden and still immense, waves ten feet high rolling down on *Abigail*, making her lift and plunge. The sky was nearly the same color, a variegated gray and white and near black. The wind was whistling through the rigging, but the pitch was lower, the strength not what it had been; thirty or thirty-five knots, perhaps.

He looked aft and sucked in his breath. The high mountains of Guadeloupe, gray-green in that light, were practically looming over them, so close Wentworth could not take in the whole island in in a single glance. He stepped to the rail and leaned over and looked astern. He was no great judge of distance, but there seemed to be five or six miles from where they were to where they would run aground, and that seemed like a significant distance to him, enough that they were in no immediate danger, but he knew he was no judge of those things, either.

A gang of men were aft and they seemed excited about something and William guessed it was the proximity of the island. Then Tucker appeared and shooed them forward, and reluctantly they turned from the taffrail and headed amidships, throwing glances back as they did. Wentworth passed them, heading aft to where Biddlecomb and Tucker were standing at the rail. He was not sure if the general order to get the hell off the quarterdeck applied to him as well, but he was curious enough that he was willing to risk the embarrassment if it did.

"Captain, what ho?" he asked as he stepped up to the rail. "Are we in danger of running ashore on this island, which I take to be Guadeloupe?"

"No, we have room enough, and enough way on if we don't suffer any damage aloft. It's this fellow that could well be done for."

Wentworth followed Biddlecomb's pointed finger. At first he saw only the succession of waves. Then the seas lifted *L'Armançon* up from the trough, water streaming through her gunports, a great tangle of wreckage on her decks. She was rolling hard, and there was nothing beyond the stump of a mainmast left standing. The rest of her rig was either gone, or lying across the deck and pounding the ship to bits. Wind and sea were driving her to the west, and even Wentworth could see that she had an hour, perhaps an hour and a half, before she foundered on what was undoubtedly an inhospitable shore.

The longest nights, Jack had long ago discovered, were the ones that were spent waiting for dawn to come. Such was the case with this last night, just coming to its end. The storm had been bad, certainly, but for all the damage she suffered in the fight with *L'Armançon*, *Abigail* was in good shape, standing rigging repaired, running gear set to rights, and once they had the main stowed she drove along nicely under the triple-reefed fore topsail and the fore and aft canvas. Jack would have been perfectly content if he had not had the island and the French corvette somewhere under his lee.

Wentworth had been on deck for a bit, had even tended the main sheet, which was a genuine help since it meant he did not have to do it. To Jack's great surprise, he no longer seemed to mind having Wentworth around. Command was the most lonely of positions on shipboard, but Jack was not by nature a solitary person. A close friendship with any of his subordinates would have been inappropriate. But Wentworth was a passenger, and while Jack did not think of him as a friend, and in fact thought of him as someone he could barely tolerate, it was oddly pleasant to have his company on the quarterdeck. What's more, unlike Frost, he did not have to worry about Wentworth second-guessing his decisions, because Wentworth did not know a damned thing about anything that was going on.

Jack had kept the deck through the dark hours, though he allowed the off watch to go below, no need for all hands on deck. The first inkling of light outlined the threatening, hulking presence of Guadeloupe right under their lee and about two leagues off. Close enough to be worrisome, but not enough to be frightening. Unless the rig failed.

But what of *L'Armançon*? He did not think she was much of a threat now, but he did need to know where she was. He pulled his best glass from the binnacle and swept the horizon astern. She had been to leeward of *Abigail* when the sun went down and he seriously doubted that she had worked her way to weather during the night.

He saw no sign of her as he looked along the raggedy edge of the horizon. He was starting to wonder if perhaps she had foundered when some object, low and dark, caught his eye. He shifted the glass. There she was, about two miles to leeward. Her masts had gone by the board, no doubt rolled clean out of her. She was riding bow on to the seas, which surprised him, as he would have thought she would turn broadside to the waves, and that would have been an end to her. As it was, they were only postponing their doom.

The wind and seas were driving her right on shore, and in those conditions it would be no more than an hour or two before she was aground. She would strike bottom some ways from the island, hang up, roll hard on her side. The next wave would lift her and drop her and probably stove her in like an egg. And if it did not, the next one would, or the one after that. Some of her company might live, clinging to wreckage, washed into shore, but for most, their bloated corpses would be flung on the beach, their pockets would be picked by the islanders come down to scavenge the wreck, and their bodies would become a meal for crabs and gulls and sharks.

Tucker came up next to him. "Any sight of *L'Armançon*, sir?" he asked. Biddlecomb pointed and Tucker gave a low whistle. He handed Tucker the glass and the mate looked and whistled again. "Done for, ain't she, sir?" he said.

"Yes," Jack said. *All those men . . .* He harbored them no ill will, which was somewhat surprising, given that they had tried to kill him, and he was not a terribly forgiving sort. But, enemies though they might be, they were fellow mariners as well, and he felt a kinship with men of the sea, particularly those in such grave peril, a kinship that went beyond the animosities of war.

Wasn't personal, Jack thought. *The officers were no doubt following orders, and the dumb sods on the lower deck had no say.*

"Yes," Jack said again. "They are done for. Unless . . ."

30

Word that the disabled corvette was in sight astern spread through the crew in that indescribable, telepathic way of ships' companies. The men came aft to stare out over the water at the pathetic sight. Jack gave them two minutes to look and blather their sundry opinions before he told Tucker to set them to rousting the two-inch hawser out of the cable tier and flaking it out, ready for running, on the 'tween decks.

Wentworth appeared and Jack showed him the source of all the excitement. "Their case is hopeless, is it not?" Wentworth asked, his eyes fixed on the distant hulk of the corvette. "It would seem with no masts or sails they have no way to avoid being driven ashore. Can they anchor?"

"By the time they are in water shallow enough to anchor in, they'll be pounding on the beach," Jack explained. "Frankly, I do not think they can save themselves."

"So they are . . ." Wentworth began and stopped. He pulled his eyes from the battered ship and looked at Jack. "You are going to save them?"

"I am going to try. We'll see if there is any way to pass a hawser to them and tow them clear."

"Really?" Wentworth said, not as if he thought it was a bad idea, but as if he was not sure what he thought.

"Do you think this a mistake, Mr. Wentworth?" Jack asked. He certainly was not looking for any advice from the man, but he was curious to see what Wentworth would say.

"I'm not sure," Wentworth said. "I'm no great fan of Frenchmen, and even less of Frenchmen who shoot at me. But I guess there's that brother-hood of tarpaulins, and all that."

"There is, indeed," Jack said. "And who knows, if we succeed in this mad-ness we may strike a great blow for international relations, undo some of the damage that Mr. Jay and his treaty with England has done."

Before Wentworth could answer, their conversation was interrupted by loud footsteps on the deck and the call of, "Captain Biddlecomb!" as a red-faced Charles Frost came huffing up. "I hear the Frenchie is dismasted, be-ing driven ashore."

"He is there, Mr. Frost," Jack said, pointing, and he could hear the clipped tone in his own voice. In the dark hours of the night, alone on the quarter-deck, he had been thinking a great deal about the subtle influence that Frost had been exerting over the affairs of his ship, and he did not like the real-izations that had come to him.

"Why are the men getting out that cable?" Frost demanded.

"It is no affair of yours, Mr. Frost, but out of courtesy I will tell you that I mean to drop to leeward and see if I can pass a cable to the Frenchmen, see if we can tow them off this lee shore."

"Are you mad?" Frost demanded. "Have you lost all your senses? These are the fellows who were trying to kill you not twelve hours ago!"

"That was war, or some such," Jack said. "In truth, I don't know what it was. But this is a matter of the sea."

"Damn the sea, and damn these Frenchmen! You will not tow them off, do you hear me, you will not!"

Jack clenched his teeth together and took a few seconds before he trusted himself to speak. "You forget yourself, sir," he said at last. "Mr. Oxnard may have given you leave to assist with these damned guns, but you have no authority aboard this ship. You most certainly do not have any authority in matters of seamanship."

"I do not think Oxnard would agree with you, sir."

"If you see Mr. Oxnard you may ask him," Jack said, "but until then, I am in command."

"Are you?" Frost asked, his voice a growl, all of the bonhomie quite gone. He was furious in a way Jack had never seen him before, in a way

Jack would not have imagined he could become. "We shall see about that, *Captain*."

After having commanded *Abigail* through two violent storms and the same number of sea fights, Jack would have thought that having someone address him as "Captain" in an ironic tone would no longer have made him furious. But apparently not. In that instant his smoldering anger flashed into a white-hot rage.

His hand shot out and grabbed Frost's right arm and jerked it toward him, which spun Frost right around, a thing that might not have been so easy if the big man had not been so surprised. Then Jack wound up and kicked him hard in the rear end, kicked him hard enough to send him stumbling forward a few feet. Despite his fury, Jack was aware enough to see the suppressed grins on the faces of the men around him, but that had no calming effect.

"Get below, Mr. Frost, get below and stay below and stay the hell out of my affairs, or by God, sir, I will give you worse than that!"

Frost turned, slowly. His face was red, and the anger seemed etched upon it. His eyebrows and lips came together, and he looked as if he might speak. No one on the quarterdeck moved. Then Frost turned in a flurry of coattails, stomped off forward, and disappeared down the scuttle.

Jack turned to Tucker. "Is that two-inch hawser rousted out yet?" he snapped.

Biddlecomb seemed to think that Mr. Charles Frost was on his way below to remain there and not interfere until this business was done, but Wentworth was not so sure. From what he had observed, Frost was not one to be easily dissuaded, and his silent retreat from the quarterdeck seemed more a change of plan than a capitulation.

Wentworth headed for the scuttle as well. No one on the quarterdeck seemed to notice his leaving, being engrossed as they were in a discussion of hawsers and drogues and drift and messengers and any number of tarpaulin issues he did not understand. He climbed down to the 'tween decks and headed aft.

Frost was in his cabin. Wentworth could hear him thumping around in there, though he was not sure what the man was about. Then he heard the familiar rattle of a steel rammer clicking against the barrel of a pistol and Wentworth knew that his worst fear was indeed the case. He knocked on the cabin door.

"Be gone, damn you!" Frost shouted from behind the thin, white painted wood.

"Mr. Frost, a word, sir, if you will," Wentworth called.

"I will not! Begone!"

Wentworth turned the handle and opened the door. Frost was standing at the far end of the cabin, and once again Wentworth considered the size of the place, twice that of his own cabin, and thought, *Damn your eyes, Biddlecomb, you vengeful little bastard . . .*

But he was there on other business, and he turned to face Mr. Frost. The butt of one pistol was jutting out of Frost's coat pocket and he was tamping down the wadding and shot in the second.

"I said 'Begone,' and still you let yourself in like you are the damned admiral of the fleet!"

"Mr. Frost, whatever you are planning, sir, it has no hope of success. Will you shoot Biddlecomb and Tucker? And then what?"

"This is none of your affair!" Frost thundered. "You arrogant, spoiled, cocksure little whelp! This business is more important than you could even imagine! The very life of our nation, sir!"

Wentworth had not been certain until that point what he would do, but being called an arrogant, spoiled, cocksure little whelp had settled the issue for him. But he was still curious.

"Oh, but I *can* imagine, Mr. Frost," he said. "I know more of this than you might think. I know that it was your intention all along to steer Biddlecomb into fighting the Frenchman. Son of the Federalist leader Isaac Biddlecomb attacking a vessel of the French navy, initiating war. The bellicose designs of the Adams administration on display for all the world to see." Frost had not written that last part in his letter to Oxnard, of course, but Wentworth guessed it was the reason. He could think of no other.

Frost looked as if he had been struck with a buggy whip. "Damn your eyes, how do you know that?" he demanded, confirming Wentworth's hypothesis.

"I am kept informed, sir, well informed. But, pray, how did you arrange it so you yourself would not be killed in the fight? And how would you be let go from the prison to which we were all bound?"

"If you know so damned much, you should know that as well," Frost said. "And if you do not, then by God you'll not hear it from me."

Wentworth nodded. He was only going to get so much, and no more, but he continued to prod.

"When the Frenchman failed to take this ship, you had the idea that Biddlecomb might actually beat them in a second fight, is that correct? If you saw to her being better armed and manned? You thought that would be an even greater show of Federalist aggression."

Still Frost remained silent, but the flush in his cheeks was like a signal lantern that Wentworth was correct.

"Then tell me this," Wentworth said, "why do you not wish for Biddle-comb to rescue *L'Armançon*? They are doomed if he doesn't tow them off, and you are a great friend to the French, are you not?"

Frost slipped the pistol's rammer back into its slot under the barrel of the gun. He seemed to be regaining some equilibrium. "This is bigger than a single ship, or the lives of the men who sail her. This pup Biddlecomb wants to play the grand naval hero, and Adams will crow to the world about what a friend he is to all nations, the son of his man Isaac Biddlecomb saving the very ship that attacked him." With that Frost smiled, actually smiled. "After all of our careful planning, the irony of such an outcome would be more than I could bear."

Wentworth nodded again. "I understand. But before you do anything rash, there is something I think you should see."

"What?"

"Something Captain Biddlecomb has secreted in his cabin. I saw it only by accident. But I think it might change your perception of this entire matter."

Frost cocked his head, then cocked his pistol. "Very well, Wentworth, you lead the way."

Wentworth stepped out of the big cabin and moved aft. The great cabin door was jammed and he had to put his shoulder to it to swing it open. When he did, he was stunned at what he saw. The aft windows, that elegant wall of glass, were blown out, and only a line of jagged frame and sundry shards around the periphery were left. The hanging cot was shot in two, the sideboard was in several pieces and tossed around the room, great holes in the walls provided an unobstructed view of the sea beyond. Everything was wet, and half an inch of water rolled back and forth on the deck.

He stepped further in and Frost came in behind him. Frost held the gun low but it was unambiguously pointed at Wentworth. "What is it, then?" Frost demanded.

Wentworth crossed the cabin to the settee below the aft windows and removed the plank that made up the seat, revealing the storage space beneath. "There," he said.

"What?" Frost said.

"There. Come have a look."

"Lift it up," Frost said.

"I can't lift it, it's nailed in place," Wentworth said. Frost crossed the great cabin to Wentworth's side. He peered down into the settee. In the storage space sat a wooden box of what was once a decent set of china before the Frenchman had put a ball through it and turned into potsherds.

"What is it?" Frost asked and Wentworth grabbed his wrist, pushed the pistol aside, grabbed a handful of Frost's breeches with the other hand and flung him out the stern window.

Or at least he tried. Frost's leg hit the edge of the settee and he fell, coming down on a jagged bit of window frame. He screamed in agony, twisted his head, looked right at Wentworth, swung the pistol around, and fired.

Wentworth jerked his head to the side as he saw the gun coming his way. The shot made a huge sound in the confined space and Wentworth heard the buzz of the ball as it tore past his ear, inches or less away. He grabbed Frost's boots and hefted them up, tilting Frost aft. Frost made a strangled sound. He seemed to be caught up on the broken window frame. Then, whatever was holding him let go and he tumbled out of the window and hit the water astern.

He was gone in the white wake, gone for some time. Wentworth wondered if he could swim. A moment later he saw an arm waving madly, much farther off, an arm, no more, and then that went under and he saw no other sign of Charles Frost.

No, I guess he can't, Wentworth thought. He listened for sounds from the deck above, some shout of, "Man overboard!" or some such, but he heard nothing. They were too engrossed in their noble effort to save French lives.

Jack was trying to get a feel for how *Abigail* would handle in the steep seas as they worked their way downwind when the gun went off. He was standing by the helm, gauging the motion of the ship as she rode the waves. He waited until the bow came down in a trough, the sails shivering as the seas blocked the wind, and then rose up again. The bow began to mount the next wave, the tip of the jibboom spearing the oncoming roller, pulling free and shedding a trail of salt water like a dagger pulled from a victim, dripping blood.

"Now, Maguire, fall off!" Jack said.

Maguire spun the wheel. *Abigail's* bow turned gracefully off the crest of the wave, and then, just as the ship might have gone broadside to the seas, Jack said, "Come up! Meet her!" Maguire spun the wheel back and *Abigail* turned back, bow into the sea, ready to meet the next roller. In the process she had dropped farther to leeward, closer to the wallowing corvette astern.

"That went well," Jack said.

"Aye, sir," Maguire said but he did not sound as sanguine as Jack did. The question of course was whether that evolution would get them down to *L'Armançon* before *L'Armançon* piled up on Guadeloupe, and if they did get down to her, could they pass her a line? Was her company still intact enough to take their part in her rescue?

And then a gun went off, right under Jack's feet, a pistol by the sound, and it made him jump. "What in all hell was that?" he demanded but everyone on the deck was staring around with dumb looks on their faces. "Mr. Burgess," he said to the boatswain, "get below and see what that was about!"

"Aye, sir," Burgess said and headed forward. *Abigail* was coming up on the next wave and Maguire fell off again as the bow reached the crest, hardened up as the ship plunged down into the trough. They were meeting the next wave when Burgess reappeared, Wentworth following behind, a grim look on his face.

"Well, what was that?" Biddlecomb demanded, but Burgess just turned to Wentworth for an answer.

"Mr. Wentworth?" Jack asked.

"Mr. Frost's dead, I fear," Wentworth said, and he sounded genuinely troubled.

"Dead? Dear God!" Jack said. "What . . . ?"

"Killed himself. I went below, looking for him. He wasn't in his cabin, but I saw the door to your cabin was open so, forgive me, I looked in. He was there by the window, just sitting on the settee. He had a pistol. I pleaded with him not to do it, but . . ."

"Dear God!" Jack said. "Was it . . . was it my . . . discourteousness?" He was horrified to think that he might have been the cause of this, him and his temper.

"No, no!" Wentworth said. "Never think that! He looked me right in the eyes and he said, 'Wentworth, I failed. I had a task, an important task, and I failed.' I asked him what he meant, but he put the gun in his mouth and pulled the trigger. The shot knocked him right back, out the window."

There was stunned silence on the quarterdeck. *Abigail* rose and fell on the next wave and Jack never even thought to turn her to leeward on the crest. Wentworth spoke again. "There were things acting, Captain Biddlecomb, things Frost was about, that we'll likely never understand. He was playing at some game, I fear, and we were his pawns."

Again there was silence. The seconds ticked by. And then Lacey came aft and reported the hawser flaked out on the 'tween decks and the morbid spell was broken, because there was, at sea, only so much time that could be spent dwelling on the dead.

For the next hour Jack continued to turn the *Abigail* to leeward, just a bit, at the crest of each wave. The seas were too big, the ship's rig too compromised, to actually turn and sail downwind. If they tried, there was every chance *Abigail* would also lose her masts and then she and the corvette would go ashore side by side, die like lovers in a suicide pact. Jack did not care for that possibility, so instead he dropped his ship down to *L'Armançon,* wave by wave, yard by yard.

They were just above a cable length away when Jack realized why

L'Armançon was not drifting as fast toward Guadeloupe and her destruction as it seemed she should. He and Tucker saw it at the same time, a churning in the water like a submerged ledge, one hundred yards ahead of the corvette. Jack felt a flash of panic when he saw the white water boiling and rolling just below the surface, and Tucker cried, "What's that? A reef?"

Jack put his glass to his eye. He could see some dark mass in the water, and as it rose on a wave a line rose up from the sea, running just above the surface, right back to *L'Armançon*'s bow. "It's a sea anchor of some sort," Jack reported. "No wonder they're not yet on the beach." He studied it a bit more, waiting see what the lifting seas would reveal. It was the mainmast, the ship's mainmast, her main yard and sail still attached, or so it seemed. When the mast had gone by the board they had managed to bend a heavy line to it and let it drift away, with the other end of the line made fast to the bitts in the corvette's bow. The drag of the mast and gear had kept *L'Armançon*'s bow pointed into the wind and sea and slowed her rate of drift.

"Good work, for Frenchies," Tucker said. "Might have saved their hides."

"Maybe," Jack said. "Maybe not." The sea anchor might have kept the French ship off the beach, but it would stop *Abigail* from getting close enough to pass them a line. Jack could not risk the possibility of smashing his rudder into that massive trunk of wood as he tried to get down to the stricken ship. He could not risk having the shattered mainmast rear up and punch a hole clean through *Abigail*'s bottom.

"We'll get a bit closer," Jack said at last, "and see if there's a way around this damned wreckage. But if there's a risk to this ship, I'm afraid *Monsieur* is on his own."

The men of *L'Armançon* had done well, Renaudin had to admit as much. They had worked like mad to clear the wreckage. They had made what repairs they could to the standing rigging, set the running rigging to rights, so that the sails they set could be controlled to some degree. They had plugged the few shot holes and secured the great guns with double lashings. But it had not been enough.

In preparing for sea, one never knows what is or is not lashed properly until that first big wave rolls the ship hard. Likewise, in preparing for foul weather, one is never sure how adequate the preparations are until the first punch of the storm staggers the ship, and then she stands up or she does not. In the case of *L'Armançon*, she stood up. But not for long.

The bowsprit had been bowsed down as tight as it could be, and a new forestay set up, but that had not been enough. The seas struck the wounded bowsprit again and again, glancing blows that shifted it and loosened the lashings. They were making little if any headway, and Renaudin was painfully aware of Guadeloupe, just to leeward of them.

The corvette was on a starboard tack, trying to claw her way out to sea, to get away from the looming threat of the island. It occurred to Renaudin that if he could tack, get the seas striking the bowsprit on the larboard side, it might knock that spar back into place before it was torn loose and took the rest of the rig with it.

It was an enormously risky move. Tacking with an undamaged rig in those conditions was no mean feat, and *L'Armançon* was far from undamaged. They could wear ship, but Renaudin knew he could not afford to lose all that distance to leeward. They put their helm alee as the ship came up on the crest of a wave, and for most of the evolution it seemed as if all would be well, their improvised fore staysail bringing the bow around.

But then as Renaudin called, "Let go and haul!" the main topsail yard snapped like a twig. Rot, perhaps, or an unseen injury, it didn't matter. The result was the same. The spar folded like a jackknife, the bow spun off the wind, out of control. *L'Armançon* ended up broadside to the seas, in the trough to the waves, and rolling so violently that the main shrouds tore from the channels and what remained of the rig came down around their heads.

And when that happened, Renaudin was done. The bad luck, the misery of the Revolution, the destruction of his beloved navy, the destruction of his beloved *L'Armançon*, it was all too much. His ship was dead, and he saw no reason that he should outlive it. He walked aft to the stern rail, leaned against it, folded his arms, and waited for his life to end on the reefs beyond Guadeloupe's sandy shores.

René Dauville, however, did not share Renaudin's wish to let it all come to an end. Once again he drove the crew beyond what any rational man would think possible. They hacked the standing rigging away, tossed topmast and topgallant overboard. They rousted out a cable from the cable tier, bent it to the mainmast and yard, and with blocks, tackles, handspikes, and the power of desperate and frightened men they sent the whole thing over the side, let it stream to windward. They could feel the tension come on the line as *L'Armançon*'s bow swung up into the wind and the seas, and her motion went from the gut-churning, deathly wallow of a ship broadside to the sea to the more reasonable motion of a ship riding bow to.

Dauville came aft to report their success, but Renaudin showed little interest, and said even less. No man aboard thought their efforts would do anything but delay what was going to happen, but unlike the others, Renaudin did not wish for even those few extra minutes. *Let us be done with this* . . . he thought.

Dawn came and the island was still three or four miles under their lee, the seas still steep, the wind still strong, but lessening. The American, the damned, damned American, was to windward, her rig still as it had been at nightfall, the main topmast shot away, fore topgallant sent down. She was making way under a close reefed fore topsail, staysails, and spanker. Renaudin glared at her. The only thing that would make his death any easier was the thought that he might take her with him. But he saw no chance of that. She was under way and would sail clear of the island, and the Americans would watch as *L'Armançon* was shattered on Guadeloupe's shore.

Then Dauville was aft again and Renaudin wondered why the man didn't just leave him alone. "Sir, the Americans, they're coming down to us," he said, "they seem to be working their way to leeward."

Renaudin looked past the bow, heaving, rolling, and dipping. He could see the American ship rise on the crest of a wave, dip to leeward, and then as her hull was lost from sight behind the rise of the sea he could see her straighten in her course again. Dauville was right. They were dropping downwind, yard by yard.

"What do you think they intend?" Renaudin asked. "Do they wish to rejoin the fight?"

"I can't imagine that, sir. Safer for them to simply let us go up on the lee shore," Dauville said. "My thought was . . ." He hesitated, sounded unsure. ". . . that they wish to tow us free."

Renaudin's eyebrows came together as he tried to understand this. "Tow . . . us?"

"Yes, sir. They are making tolerably decent way. The seas and wind are going down. My guess is they wish to pass us a hawser."

"How could they? In these seas, how could they get a line to us?"

"They don't have to, sir," Dauville said, and Renaudin was shocked to see that his first officer actually seemed pleased with this prospect. "We're streaming that wreckage as a sea anchor, recall? If they can get the bitter end of that rope aboard, there's the tow line, set!"

Renaudin saw it all play out in his mind. They would drift a boat aft, bend a messenger to the hawser Dauville had run out, haul it aboard. They would make it fast, perhaps to the base of the mainmast. They'd set more sail, claw off the lee shore with the wallowing and helpless *L'Armançon* towing astern. They'd tow his ship to English Harbour, American flag flying over the Tricolor. He'd be a prisoner again, but worse, he would be utterly humiliated. His pride was all but ground into dust now, what would be left when the American dragged him like a helpless baby into the arms of the British, at the end of his own hawser, no less?

He pushed himself off the rail and stepped around Dauville and headed forward. The boatswain was there to ask a question but Renaudin pushed him out of the way. He could hear Dauville following behind, but they were amidships before his first officer asked, "Sir? Is there something I can do, sir?"

"You've done enough, Lieutenant," Renaudin said, his eyes fixed forward, his pace increasing. By the foremast he found an ax, discarded after the long night's struggle. He snatched it up and stepped up to the bitts where the heavy line running out to the sea anchor was made off. He raised the ax over his head.

"Sir!" Dauville shouted, with an urgency that could not be ignored. Renaudin paused, looked over at the lieutenant. He was sorry to waste the man's life, but there was nothing for it now, and Dauville would hardly be the first promising officer to die young.

"I'm sorry, Dauville," Renaudin said.

"As am I," Dauville said, and Renaudin saw that he had a belaying pin in his hand. He saw the oiled wood come around in a wide arc, and before he could react in any way, he saw a burst of light and then he was enveloped by blackness.

Epilogue

Lieutenant René Dauville was a knowledgeable and competent mariner, as was Jack Biddlecomb, so it was little surprise that Jack's rescue of *L'Armançon* played out pretty much as Dauville had envisioned it.

Jack worked *Abigail* to leeward, as close as he dared get to the drifting wreckage. The launch Frost had procured in English Harbour was still towing astern, they had not bothered to get it on deck as it was the least of their worries. It was hauled up on the leeward side and a crew of the most skilled of the Abigails, led by Oliver Tucker, went aboard, making the tricky leap from the rolling, heaving ship into the wildly bucking boat alongside.

None of the British sailors joined them. They would not take part in the rescue of men it was their life's work to kill, which Biddlecomb could understand. But that was fine, as the Abigails' seamanship was at least a match for theirs, and in many cases more than a match.

The boat was drifted down with a messenger made fast to a thwart, a stout one-inch line that would be used to get the Frenchman's hawser aboard. They bent it to the heavy line and cut the wreckage free. The shattered mast and yard swirled away downwind and the launch was hauled back alongside and a strain taken on the messenger, lifting the Frenchman's hawser from the sea.

With the windlass being *hors de combat* they used a series of heavy blocks and tackle to get the messenger and then the hawser aboard. They secured the bitter end to the base of the mainmast and then trimmed the sails to get the most drive they might from them.

For a long time, nothing seemed to happen. *Abigail*'s sails were set and drawing, the tow rope lifted dripping from the sea, the tremendous tension squeezing the water out of it. But they appeared to make no headway. They seemed fixed to that spot of ocean, certainly not going forward, possibly being knocked back with each successive sea. Jack wondered how long he would hang on before giving the order to cut the tow away, to leave the Frenchmen to their fate.

"Let us get the foresail set, with a single reef," he said at last. The wind was still strong, he was pushing his luck, but the only other choice was to cut *L'Armançon* free. The men moved quickly and soon the big sail dropped from the yard. Hands tailed into the weather tack and the lee sheet, hauled them out, and with a snap the sail was set and drawing.

And that made the difference. The tow line rose again from the sea and stayed suspended this time, and every hand aboard could feel the motion, like the ship was waking up, like Lazarus coming out of the tomb. The wake began to flow astern in a broader and more defined way, streaming white, like a road leading from Guadeloupe, and they were walking down that road, leaving the island and its deadly lee shore behind.

They towed all through the day, and by sundown the storm that Jack had predicted would be of short duration had blown itself out. The seas settled down, the trade winds dropped to their usual, sensible strength, and *L'Armançon* towed easily astern. Once the seas were such that a boat might pass between the ships with little peril, Jack knew there were negotiations to be carried out and he knew, as master, it was his job to do it.

The only man aboard *Abigail* who spoke fluent French was William Wentworth, which came as no surprise to Jack. As the sun began its descent in the west, Jack donned his best suit, or those parts of it that were not destroyed by water or cannon fire, and Wentworth did the same. They looked odd indeed, with fine breeches above torn wool socks, once-elegant coats with tears left in the wake of passing roundshot, hats crumpled and pushed back into place. But it was the best they could muster, and they climbed down into the boat and the boat crew rowed them across the long swells to the battered corvette in their wake.

A French officer stood at the gangway as Jack and William came up the side. *"Bonjour, Monsieur,"* he said, bowing. He said more, but *Bonjour* had exhausted Jack's store of French, so he stood back as William listened to the man speak, and then made some reply that Jack hoped was only courtesy, and not a promise of any sort.

"He says his captain was hit on the head by a falling block and is indisposed," Wentworth explained. "He is the first officer, Lieutenant René Dauville, and he says he is most grateful for the rescue and will consider himself your prisoner. He says he will happily relinquish his sword if you feel it appropriate."

"His sword?" Jack asked. He had not really thought of that, had never considered *L'Armançon* to be a prize of any sort. "Tell him I do not believe a state of war exists between the Republic of France and the United States," Jack said. "Ask him if he has heard differently."

Wentworth translated. Dauville made reply and Wentworth turned to Jack. "He says, though there has been violence done by the privateers to American shipping, he does not believe a state of war exists. He seems to have anticipated your next question and says he does not know what orders his captain was following in attacking us."

"I see," Jack said, though he really didn't. "Very well, I can hardly call this ship a prize if there's no war. Nor am I much inclined to start taking prizes. This is a French naval vessel. By God, we could start a war by claiming it as a prize! No, tell him we'll tow them to someplace we might agree on, and if he pleases, I would be most grateful to be able to sail to Barbados unmolested."

In the end it was decided they would tow *L'Armançon* to Saint-Louis on Marie-Galante, which had a tolerably good anchorage. Guadeloupe was in French hands but had suffered a revolt by former slaves, and Dauville was not sure how things stood there. Besides, Jack could not stand the irony of making for Guadeloupe after having suffered so much anxiety trying to keep away from the place.

With the clear weather and flattening seas it was no great task to reach the harbor, *L'Armançon* towing easily astern. *Abigail* came to anchor in the clear, aquamarine water, within a cable length of the long white sand beach, shaded by palm trees that waved in the trade winds. If any locals thought it odd an American coming to anchor there, they did not say anything, and Dauville made it clear she was there under the protection of *L'Armançon* and the navy of France.

The British sailors did not join them. Dauville's assurance that they would not be molested was not enough to convince them to willingly sail into a French port. So Jack gave them *Abigail*'s launch and Dauville gave them *L'Armançon*'s longboat, and enough food and water for the short sail back to English Harbour and they were off, and apparently quite enthusiastic for their yachting holiday.

Abigail lay in the roadstead at Saint-Louis for several days, during which Dauville saw they were provided with what they needed: cordage, iron-work, blocks, deadeyes, a new main topmast and yard. The Abigails sent it all up, crossed yards, bent sail, rove off running gear, and missed the abundance of experienced hands they had enjoyed before the British jacks had left them.

They set sail for Barbados a few days later, the hovering French privateers still a threat, but they saw only one sail on the passage, and it turned and fled while still hull down, so if it was a privateer, it was not a particularly bold one. They were only two days under way, a quick passage, but quicker still was word of their bold rescue of *L'Armançon*. From Marie-Galante and from the British sailors at Antigua word spread of the master who ignored the fact that he had been attacked without provocation, with no state of war existing, and had plucked the disabled ship from the clutches of certain death.

The first inkling of their newfound fame arrived with the pilot, who met them as they stood into Carlisle Bay at Bridgetown. He scrambled up the ladder and pumped Jack's hand, exclaiming that all of Barbados, all of the West Indies, was talking about his bold and selfless act. *Abigail* was brought directly to one of the most convenient berths along the busy waterfront, with men sent aboard by Oxnard's agent to handle lines, so that the crew of the *Abigail* could stand back and enjoy their well-earned leisure.

Business was conducted amid a series of dinners and various celebrations. No one on Barbados was particularly interested in saving the lives of Frenchmen, but as an island colony they were all intimately bound to the sea, and so were quick to recognize the heroism of one mariner saving another. And when a mariner saved another who, the day before, had tried to kill him, it made the act all that more selfless.

Captain Biddlecomb's health was drunk all over town, and Captain Biddlecomb was often called to join in, so it was no surprise that he woke one morning in his bunk feeling not so very healthy at all, head pounding, eyes declining to open. He managed to get one lid up, slowly, and found himself staring at the same reddish-brown homespun stockings, the same set of beefy calves, the same cuffs of brown breeches he had seen on his first morning in that cabin.

"Ah, Captain Biddlecomb," the familiar voice said. "You are awake."

Jack sat up and swung his legs over the edge of the bunk. The great cabin was nearly set to rights, and only those places where the patched woodwork had yet to be painted and the furniture that was not so perfectly repaired indicated that any violence had been done to the place.

"Good morning," Jack said, scratching and looking around through the one eye he'd managed to open. "I don't believe I ever caught your name."

"Tillinghast," the man said. "Jeremiah Tillinghast."

"Is it an odd quirk of fate that you should happen to be here?"

"No," Tillinghast said. "Captain Rumstick sent me. I come out in that lovely Bermuda sloop of his, the *Town of Bristol*, do you know it?"

Jack nodded. Tillinghast continued. "We finally smoked what was going on, why that Bolingbroke cove tried to kill you."

"Because he hates me," Jack offered.

"There's that," Tillinghast agreed. "But more. He was well paid, you know." Tillinghast went on, telling Jack a story that he had in part guessed at himself, and in part been told to him by Wentworth, and in part did not know and wished he had not found out.

It had, in the end, been all about his father. The command of *Abigail*, the way he had been manipulated into fighting *L'Armançon*, it had all happened because he was the son of the great Isaac Biddlecomb. Jack could hardly stand the irony.

"How did you manage to find me?" Jack asked.

"This is where you were supposed to be," Tillinghast said. "But in truth, everywhere we called they knew the story. You're a famous man, in the West Indies, at least."

"Uncle Ezra sent you out to protect me?"

"To warn you. But I'm too late for that, it seems. So now I have another task."

"To protect me?"

"No," Tillinghast said. "Don't seem you need much protecting, but if you can stay out of any tavern brawls, it would be best all around. Tide turns in an hour and I mean to be under way then."

"So soon? Where are you bound to in such a great rush?"

Tillinghast did not answer at first. "Do you know Captain John Derby, of Salem?"

"Certainly," Jack said. Derby was a venerable old seaman, part of the Derby clan of merchants and mariners.

"Well, right after the fighting at Lexington and Concord, just days after, Dr. Joseph Warren sent him to England in a fast schooner. Derby carried eyewitness reports, and a letter from the good doctor to the people of England. You see, Warren understood that the most important part of getting your story told the way you wish it to be told is getting your story to market first. So what I need from you, young Master Biddlecomb, is your story. Tell it all to me, the fighting, towing the Frenchman off, every detail."

Jack sighed. He had told this story many times already in the week or so since those incidents had taken place. But he told it again, and Tillinghast asked questions as he did, questions that spoke to his intimate understanding of the affair. He probed in a way that the others to whom Jack told the tale would have considered impolite. And when Jack had finished to Tillinghast's satisfaction, Tillinghast stood and extended a hand.

"Thank you, Captain Biddlecomb," he said, shaking Jack's hand. "You did an admirable job, and everyone who hears the story will agree. At least those parts of the story we want them to hear. So, now I know I can report to Captain Rumstick that any hurt done you was done by your own hand, and with that I will bid you good day, Captain."

Tillinghast clapped his hat on his head, and then he was gone.

Jack was another week securing a cargo for *Abigail*'s return voyage, setting the ship to rights, and playing the honored guest in various households, it becoming a mark of one's place in Bridgetown society to entertain Captain Jack Biddlecomb. It was a great relief when he finally ordered *Abigail* warped away from the dock and set the fore topsail to the steady breeze.

They were three weeks in returning to Philadelphia, greeted by light and baffling winds as they made northing past the Turks and Caicos. It was midsummer when they made that familiar landfall at Cape Henlopen. The shores of the Delaware Bay and the Delaware River were a rich green, the forest filled out with leaves, and fields showing substantial growth at last. They anchored in the stream and were assured that a berth would be ready for them on the turn of the tide. No waiting for Captain Jack Biddlecomb, whose fame had preceded him by weeks, and whose return was so greatly anticipated.

Mail was sent out, and a flurry of invitations, and copies of the latest papers. Jack begged off the invitations, claiming too much work to do in preparation for coming alongside the dock, but in truth he was giving himself the gift of one last night of peace before the maelstrom that he knew was coming his way.

The headlines said it all: *True Account of the Rescue of a French Man-of-War by Son of Naval Hero Isaac Biddlecomb.*

Captain Jeremiah Tillinghast Reports News of Jack Biddlecomb, Son of Captain Isaac Biddlecomb, Late of the Continental Navy.

Apple Does Not Fall Far from the Tree.

Jack sighed, tossed the papers on the scarred table in the great cabin, and drained his glass.

"Oh, come now, what honestly did you expect?" William Wentworth asked, refilling the glass. "You're not the only one living in the shadows of the old man, you know."

"I know. But I suspect it will be hard to remember that, these coming days."

"Honored, toasted, given lavish meals. The young ladies of Philadelphia swooning over you, their fathers lauding you as a great hero. It will be a hellish time, Jack, hellish indeed."

Jack smiled and picked up his new-filled glass and drained it again. The barometer was falling fast, the storm would be on him soon, the next day, as soon as his foot hit the dock. It would blow hard but it would blow itself out and then there would be calm.

And then soon enough the barometer would fall again. At sea, there was no such thing as normal.

Glossary

ABLE-BODIED a rating applied to a sailor that indicates he is entirely proficient in all the sailor's arts, in particular working on a ship's rigging.

AFT toward the back end of a ship, the opposite of *fore*.

ATHWARTSHIPS from one side of a ship to the other.

BACKSTAY a heavy rope running from the top of one of the masts aft to a place near the deck where it is secured. The backstay prevents the mast from falling forward.

BEFORE THE MAST refers to a member of a ship's crew, as opposed to an officer. The term in an allusion to sailors living in the forecastle, forward of the foremast.

BELAYING PIN a wooden pin resembling a long billy club and mounted through a hole in a pin rail. The lines of the rigging are hitched to the belaying pins to secure them.

BEND to attach one thing to another. A sailor bends a sail to a yard.

BINNACLE BOX cabinet mounted to the deck just forward of the helm that houses the compass and other navigational equipment.

BLOCK pulley.

BOATSWAIN sailor in charge of maintaining a ship's rigging and other maintenance duties, overseeing the work of the crew, and often enforcing discipline.

BOOM a heavy spar running fore and aft that secures the bottom edge of a sail.

BOW the front end of a ship.

BOW CHASER cannon mounted in the bow of a ship at such an angle as to allow it to fire as directly forward as possible.

BOWLINE   a line attached to the edge of a square sail and used to prevent the sail from curling over when the ship is sailing close hauled. Thus when a ship is sailing on a taut bowline, she is sailing close hauled.

BOWSPRIT   a type of mast extending at an angle up from a ship's bow to which the stays for the foremast are attached.

BREECHING   a heavy rope running between the sides of a ship and the back end of a cannon to limit the distance a cannon can recoil when fired.

BULWARK   the low wall around the outer edge of a ship's deck.

BUNTLINE   line attached to the lower edge of a square sail and used to haul the sail up prior to furling.

CABLE   a nautical unit of distance, about two hundred yards.

CAPSTAN   a vertical manual winch turned by the use of horizontal bars inserted like spokes into the capstan's upper part. Used for very heavy lifting.

CAST   to turn a vessel's head away from the wind when getting under way.

CEILING   planking on the inside of a ship.

CLEWGARNET   line used to pull the lower corner, or clew, of a course sail, the lowest square sail on a mast, up to the yard above.

CLEWLINE   line used to pull the lower corner, of clew, of any sail above the course up to the yard above.

CLOSE HAULED   point of sail in which a ship is sailing as directly into the wind as she is able. A square-rigged ship could sail at best about forty-five degrees toward the wind, a fore-and-aft-rigged ship somewhat better.

COURSE   the lowest square sail on a mast.

CROSSJACK YARD   the lowest yard on a ship's mizzenmast. Pronounced *cro' jik*.

CROSSTREES   short, horizontal timbers running side to side at the base of an upper mast which spread the base of the shrouds supporting that mast and used as a place for a man aloft to stand.

END FOR END   to run a piece of rope in the direction opposite of how it has been run to more equally distribute the wear.

FIFE RAIL   a three-sided, freestanding pin rail at the base of a mast where running rigging from that mast is belayed.

FORE   in or toward the forward part of the ship.

FORE AND AFT   running along the centerline of a ship, the opposite of athwartships. Also used to denote the entire expanse of the ship.

FORECASTLE   the compartment in the bow of the ship. In merchant vessels it was traditionally where the sailors lived. Pronounced *fo'c'sle*.

FOREMAST JACK   colloquial term for a common sailor.

FREEBOARD   the part of a ship or boat's hull from the waterline to the edge of the deck.

FURL   the act of pulling a sail up to a yard and tying it in place.

FUTTOCK SHROUDS   short ropes extending from the edge of the top to the mast below. These secure the upper shrouds and are used by sailors to climb around the edge of the top.

GAFF   a spar that supports the upper edge of a trapezoidal sail such as a spanker.

GIRTLINE   a line extending from the deck to the top of a mast and back to the deck, used for hoisting aloft whatever needs hoisting. Also called a gantline.

GREAT CABIN   the captain's cabin at the very after end of the ship. It generally runs the full width of the ship and features windows in the after wall looking astern.

GRIPE   special line used to secure a ship's boat to the deck. Also, the process of setting up gripes.

GUNNEL   corruption of gunwale. The upper edge of a ship's side, where the bulwark and deck meet.

HALYARD   line used to raise a sail. The halyard is attached to a yard in the case of a square sail, or to the sail itself in the case of a jib or staysail. The line on which flags are raised is also called a halyard.

HANDING   stowing a sail by means of pulling the sail up in bunches by hand and securing it. The same as furling.

HANDSPIKE   a wooden bar used as a lever to turn a windlass or to lever a cannon from side to side.

HANGING KNEE   a heavy, right-angle bracket that reinforces the junction of a ship's frame and the deck beam above.

HAWSE   the situation of a ship's anchor cables when she is moored by two anchors. Thus a ship riding correctly at anchor might be said to have a clear hawse. Also denotes the distance from the ship's bow to where the anchors are set.

HAWSER   a large rope used for various purposes such as warping.

HEADSAIL   any of the fore and aft sails set on stays forward of the foremast.

HEADSTAY   a heavy rope, or stay, running from some point of the foremast down to the deck, bowsprit, or jibboom to support the foremast.

HEAVE TO   to adjust the helm and sails of a ship in such a way that she will remain stopped in the water, making no headway or sternway.

HELM   the machinery by which a ship is steered, including the wheel, tiller, and rudder.

IN IRONS   when a ship is caught pointing directly into the wind and is unable to make way.

JACK   colloquial term for a sailor.

JIBBOOM   an extension to the bowsprit.

KEELSON   a timber sitting on top of the keel on the inside of a ship and running the full length of the ship, a sort of inner keel.

KEVEL   a large cleat, generally in a V shape, used for tying off large ropes.

LARBOARD   archaic term for the port or left side of a ship when looking forward.

LEAGUE   a distance of three miles.

LEECH   the vertical edges of a square sail.

LEEWARD   downwind.

LIGHTERING   to take cargo or supplies on or off a vessel by means of placing it in another vessel, called a lighter, which moves between the ship and shore.

LINSTOCK   a wooden staff on which is carried a smoldering match used for igniting a cannon's priming powder to fire the gun.

LOWERS   shorthand term for lower masts, the lowest part of a ship's mast extending from the keelson up to the junction with the topmast.

MAINMAST   the largest mast on any ship. On a three-masted, square-rigged vessel it is the mast in the center.

MAINSAIL   the lowest and largest sail on a ship's mainmast.

MAINTOP   a platform on the mainmast located at the junction of the main lower and main topmast. The same platform on the foremast is the fore-top and on the mizzen the mizzentop.

MAIN-WALE   plank on a ship's side that is thicker than the rest and serves as a sort of fender. A ship might have more than one wale, the main-wale being the most prominent.

MIZZENMAST   the smallest, aftermost mast on a three-masted ship.

ORDINARY   the intermediate rating a sailor might achieve, between boy and able-bodied.

PIN RAIL   a shelflike structure mounted on the inside of a ship's bulwarks and pierced with holes into which belaying pins are set.

QUARTER   the aft corners of the ship.

RAMMER   a wooden pole with a wooden head used to push the gunpow-der cartridge, ball, and wadding down a cannon's barrel.

RATLINE   thin lines tied horizontally to the shrouds to form a rope ladder used by sailors to climb aloft.

RELIEVING TACKLE   block and tackle hooked to the tiller in heavy weather to take pressure off the wheel and to steer the ship in case the wheel suffers damage.

ROLLING TACKLE   block and tackle used to steady the yards when the ship is rolling in heavy seas.

SCANTLINGS   the thickness of a given piece of timber, in particular those that make up a ship's sides.

SCUD   to run before a gale with little or no sail set.

SCUTTLE   any hole cut in a ship's deck, such as a hatchway.

SCUTTLEBUTT   a cask with a hole cut in it, kept on deck and filled with water for general use. The equivalent of a modern watercooler, hence "scuttlebutt" meaning casual talk.

SHEER   the curve fore and aft of the upper edge of a ship's side as seen from a broadside view.

SHROUD   heavy, tarred ropes running from the head of a mast at an angle athwartships to keep the mast from falling over. Lower masts, topmasts, and topgallant masts each have their own sets of shrouds.

SLUSH   fat skimmed off the surface of water after meat is boiled. It was used for various purposes such as lubricating the masts so the yards would travel up and down more easily. Cooks would often sell slush to the crew as a butter substitute, hence the term "slush fund."

SLUSHING DOWN to rub slush on the masts to allow the yards to slide more easily. Not a pleasant job.

SNOW a type of two-masted, square-rigged vessel.

SOUNDINGS water shallow enough that the depth might be measured.

SPANKER a fore and aft trapezoidal sail, attached to a gaff on the upper edge and often to a boom on the lower, that is set behind the mizzenmast.

SPAR general term for all masts, booms, yards, any of the poles in a ship's rig.

SPRITSAIL a small square sail carried under a ship's bowsprit.

STAY 1. A line running from a mast forward to prevent the mast from falling back. The foremast is supported by a forestay, the mainmast by a mainstay, etc. 2. To turn a ship's bow through the wind in order to change direction. The same as tacking.

STAY TACKLE a heavy block and tackle hanging under the mainstay used for lifting objects in and out of the hold.

STEP to put a mast in place. Also, the slot into which the base of a mast fits.

STRETCHER a pole lashed to the lower end of a set of shrouds.

STROP a piece of rope spliced around a block to hold it together and to attach it to something.

STUDDINGSAIL pronounced *stuns'l*. Light sails set on the edges of a ship's square sails ton increase sail area in light wind.

SWAB a wooden pole with sheepskin or the like wrapped around the end. It was dipped in water and run down a cannon's barrel to extinguish any sparks left over from firing.

SWORD MATS a type of mat woven from old rope and secured in certain places to prevent chafing.

TAFFRAIL a rail around a ship's stern.

T'GAN'SLS standard pronunciation of *topgallant sails*.

TILLER a horizontally mounted bar, attached to the head of the rudder, by which a ship is steered. A tiller is either turned directly by the helmsman or is attached to the ship's wheel by means of ropes.

TOMPION a plug to stopper the mouth of a cannon, chiefly to keep water out.

TOP a platform at the junction of a lower mast and a topmast.

TOPGALLANT SAIL the sails above the topsail. Used in light to moderate wind. Pronounced *t'gan'sls*.

TOP-HAMPER general term for all the masts, spars, sails, rigging, and other gear that comprise a ship's rig.

TOPMAST the second highest mast, mounted on top of a lower mast, in a mast made up of multiple parts.

TOPSAIL the second sail up from the deck of a square-rigged ship, just above the course. By the eighteenth century the topsails were the primary sails used to propel a ship.

'TWEEN DECKS corruption of "between decks": the space between any two decks of a ship.

WARP to move a vessel by means of running a hawser to a fixed point and hauling the ship up to it. Also the line used in warping.

WARPING POST a piling some ways from a dock to which a vessel is warped.

WEAR to alter a ship's course by turning her stern through the wind.

WEATHER 1. To windward of something. 2. To pass to windward of something.

WORM a corkscrew-type device set on a long pole and used to pull wadding or cartridges from a cannon's barrel.

YARD horizontal spars from which square sails are suspended.

YARDARM the outer ends of a yard.